Lady Flora . . . . . . . . . . . . . om a far corner he was following her progress as she descended the stairs. Their gazes locked. That look he was giving her! Full of . . . Was it pity? Accusation? Admiration? All three? She heartily wished she knew. For the first time, she realized she valued his opinion. Lord Lynd was not just some nonentity lurking in Richard's shadow. He was a man to be reckoned with.

*Through Lord Lynd's eyes, I must indeed look like a fool.*

Before, she had been positive she'd done the right thing. But now, for the first time since she'd consented to marry, she questioned her decision.

*What have I done?*

# Lady Flora's Fantasy

Shirley Kennedy

A SIGNET BOOK

SIGNET
Published by New American Library, a division of
Penguin Putnam Inc., 375 Hudson Street,
New York, New York 10014, U.S.A.
Penguin Books Ltd, 80 Strand,
London WC2R ORL, England
Penguin Books Australia Ltd, Ringwood,
Victoria, Australia
Penguin Books Canada Ltd, 10 Alcorn Avenue,
Toronto, Ontario, Canada M4V 3B2
Penguin Books (N.Z.) Ltd, 182–190 Wairau Road,
Auckland 10, New Zealand

Penguin Books Ltd, Registered Offices:
Harmondsworth, Middlesex, England

First published by Signet, an imprint of New American Library,
a division of Penguin Putnam Inc.

First Printing, November 2001
10  9  8  7  6  5  4  3  2  1

Copyright © Shirley Kennedy, 2001
All rights reserved

① REGISTERED TRADEMARK—MARCA REGISTRADA

Printed in the United States of America

PUBLISHER'S NOTE
This is a work of fiction. Names, characters, places, and incidents either are
the product of the author's imagination or are used fictitiously, and any
resemblance to actual persons, living or dead, business establishments, events,
or locales is entirely coincidental.

# Chapter 1

"We shall all be drowned," declared Lady Rensley, wife of George Winton, Earl of Rensley. She dug in her heels and pressed her palms to the wooden sides of the bathing machine.

"No, we shall not, Mama," answered Lady Flora Winton, Lady Rensley's older daughter. As usual, Flora exercised great patience in her reply, having long since learned to curb her exasperation with her supremely cautious mother.

Flora's younger sister Amy declared, "If Flora says it is safe then it is safe, Mama." Her firm voice echoed her sister's confidence, although she, too, looked a trifle unnerved as the bathing machine, which resembled nothing more than a tiny, steep-roofed house set atop a wagon, jolted toward the sea, pulled by a swaybacked horse that had seen better days.

"Quite safe," Flora murmured, only half listening. *The ocean at last.* Eagerly, she peered through the small opening at the front of the wagon. For as long as she could remember, her family had taken their summer holiday at the seashore, yet never had she stuck so much as a toe directly into the surf. Not that she hadn't begged countless times to be allowed to bathe in the ocean, but her mother had always refused, citing vague tales of unsuspecting bathers swept out to sea by precipitous tidal waves, or eaten whole by nameless monsters suddenly arising from the deep. And the immodesty! The very idea of a lady exposing her delicate complexion to the dangerous rays of the sun, to say nothing of the intrusive intimacy of the coarse, salty waves, was too shocking even to contemplate.

Flora had pleaded in vain, until this summer, when her deliverance finally arrived in the form of her mother's dearest friend, that pillar of society, Lady Constance Boles.

Advised by her doctor to seek the sea's curative effects for her lumbago, the ebullient Lady Boles immediately embraced the sea by announcing her intention to bathe daily in the ocean. Sea air and sea bathing together were nearly infallible, she stoutly declared, insisting that one or the other was a cure for every disorder of the stomach, blood, and lungs known to mankind. No one could catch cold by the sea. No one could possibly suffer from want of appetite or lack of spirit.

Under this barrage of enthusiasm, Flora's mother, who held all Lady Boles's opinions in high esteem, quickly relented. "If Lady Boles says it is so, then it is so," she said, adding under her breath, "I do not have to like it, though."

Whether her mother liked it or not, Flora was most grateful. She had lived the twenty-two years of her life under her parents' strict rules. When her mother relented, it was like a gift from heaven, even though Flora was forced to endure once again her mother's favorite lament.

"Well, Flora, you've gotten your way again, haven't you? I trust you're grateful for my change of heart. Perhaps you should return the favor and in future be more amenable to finding a husband."

"I am simply awaiting the right one," Flora declared, not for the first time. "If I'm not madly in love with him, he won't do."

"But what if you don't find him?" Here came her mother's meaningful, eyebrows-raised look that Flora knew so well. "Daughter, I fear you will end up a bitter old ape leader."

"I do not give a fig."

"And this latest—do you really intend to skip the next London Season?"

"I'm sick of the marriage mart. Never again shall I be paraded about as if I were someone's prize cow."

"But what on this earth could be more exciting than the London Season?"

Flora tossed her head. "To me it's just three months of utter boredom. I cannot stand another moment of those vain London dandies comparing my skin to peaches, the color of my eyes to violets, the softness of my hair to baby's breath. Am I naught but a botanist's delight?"

"Flora!"

"Well, I just can't stand the stupefying artificiality of it all. I can think of nothing more delightful, more gratifying, than *not* having to travel to London this spring."

"So what will you do?" asked her mother.

"I shall stay home at Sweffham Park for at least a year. How I shall adore the peace and solitude, instead of the awful noise and stifling air of London. I shall take lovely, quiet strolls, write poetry, study history, and"—she scowled at her mother—"I would ride if only you'd let me have a decent horse."

"You know how I feel. Much too dangerous." Lady Rensley set her thin, near colorless lips into a prim, nonnegotiable line.

"But I'd be ever so careful," Flora protested in frustration. Years ago, one of her cousins had gotten thrown off her horse and killed. Since then, her mother had decreed that both Flora and Amy could only ride old Buttercup, an ancient nag who couldn't get herself into a gallop if she tried.

Lady Rensley regarded her sharply. "Really, Flora, how many times have we been over this before?"

"Too many."

"All you want to do is daydream," her mother accused, highly annoyed. "So you might as well stay home. I declare, you'd rather dream of a handsome husband than actually find one."

Flora didn't answer. In truth, she knew she daydreamed too much. Why she did, she wasn't sure, except that daydreams helped her escape the chains of her circumscribed life. How else but through a fantasy could she soar beyond the farthest limits of her existence to wherever she wished to go?

Her mother finished her diatribe with her usual warning: "Mark my words, there will come a day when you'll listen to your parents. You will see we were right in all things. That's when you'll marry, settle down, and start caring for a husband and children, which is why God put you on earth in the first place."

Flora had long since arrived at the point where she deigned not to answer. What was the use? She had explained again and again that she was not going to marry just anybody, so her mother had best not even try to foist some arranged marriage upon her.

In return, Lady Rensley sighed but said no more. Despite her rigid rules, she dearly loved her daughters. In truth, Flora was a delightful companion, witty and wise, and although Lady Rensley lamented her lack of grandchildren (Lady Boles already had seven), at least she had good-natured Amy, who, at eighteen, showed every sign of wanting to marry soon. The problem was, Amy was so plain she hadn't attracted many beaus, whereas Flora, who turned up her nose at marriage, had more suitors than she knew what to do with and didn't care.

The bathing machine swayed as Mrs. Duffy, a gruff old woman of large and rather intimidating proportions, guided the horse and wagon to the water's edge. Amy squealed. Lady Rensley, wide-eyed with alarm, fervently declared, "These contraptions should be outlawed."

Flora answered, "Mama, just because *you* don't like the bathing machines, does not mean other people don't like them. They're a great attraction."

Lady Rensley did not appear in the least placated. "There had better not be any men lurking about." She glanced back toward the shore. "Lady Boles says some of the Corinthians bring telescopes to Brighton so they can ogle the lady bathers. The very idea!"

Flora suppressed a smile. "Let them look. Who cares?"

Mrs. Duffy turned on her wooden seat at the front of the wagon. "Rest assured, m'lady, they're warned to stay away. No man 'ud dare lurk around 'ere." Her firm jaw jutted determinedly. "They'ud have to deal with me, mum. I've got my rules, and I stick to 'em."

"I am still uneasy." Lady Rensley glanced at the bathing costumes into which her daughters had just changed from the bathing dresses they'd worn to the wagon. "Bathing in the ocean—the whole idea of it is scandalous. And those skimpy costumes!"

*Skimpy?* Flora wanted to laugh aloud. Not only did her bathing costume cover her from neck to ankle, she wore ruffled pantaloons underneath. "I'm wearing so much clothing now that when I get over my head I shall doubtless sink like a rock."

"Don't be flippant, Flora. This is no laughing matter."

*Why not, Mama?* Flora wanted to ask. Why was nothing a laughing matter with her sobersided mother? Her father, too. Although she loved him dearly, she found him much too somber, too guided by society's onerous rules. Worse, his daily life was much taken up with dosing himself with various medicines, since he fancied he had every affliction known to mankind.

All four wheels of the bathing machine were now in the water. "Here's where you go in," announced Mrs. Duffy, letting down the green hood at the front of the wagon. She hooked a ladder into position. "Go down slowly. When you're in the water you must walk a little and constantly move around." She scowled at her charges. "But do not go jigging and prancing about. Young females who do so defeat the whole purpose of bathing."

Flora's mother peered over the edge and nodded in agreement. "Do as Mrs. Duffy says, girls, and mind you don't stay in too long. Lady Boles says saline immersion should not be prolonged, lest depression and languor set in."

Flora only half listened. Eagerly, she started down the ladder. When her feet touched the shockingly cold water, she did not hesitate but immediately waded out to where the water was deeper. "Here I go," she cried. Arms spread, she dropped into the gently moving waves, gasped, and called, "The deuce, but it's cold!"

"Flora, your language is most unseemly," admonished her mother.

Flora ignored her. Gasping, she started moving her arms, and in a few seconds she grew accustomed to the tingling cold of the seawater and the surge of the waves lapping past her. She hoped she wasn't over her head. Carefully, she extended her feet downward and was relieved to find they could be firmly planted on the bottom. Perfect. Mrs. Duffy was called the Queen of Dippers with good reason. She had indeed found just the right spot.

At first Flora's eyes were dazzled by the brilliant shimmer of the sun on the sea, but as her vision cleared and her body grew accustomed to the chill temperature of the water, her spirits lifted. Smelling the tangy salt air, she lifted her face to the warm sunlight and saw gulls gracefully flying to and fro against a background of bright blue sky. A sudden joy spread through her as the satiny water lifted her slender body in its rhythmic flow. "Oh, it's lovely!" she called. Never before had she been totally immersed in water. What a buoyant feeling! "Hurry and get in, Amy!"

Her sister still clung hesitantly to the ladder, but hearing Flora she stepped into the water. After a cry of shock from the cold, she, too, smiled, waded in deeper, and, despite Mrs. Duffy's warning, began splashing about. "Oh, it's grand," she called to her mother. "You should come in, too."

"Never!" their prudent mother called back from the bathing machine. "I'm only here to chaperon."

Flora held her tongue. As if she and Amy needed a chaperon when the Queen of Dippers was watching their every move!

They spent the next few minutes paddling about, never too far from the bathing machine. Flora was enjoying every moment. As an undulating wave lifted her gently, she mused how glorious it was that here, buoyed by velvet water, she could drift and dream to her heart's content. She could be . . . yes, a princess! In a ship that was just sunk by pirates and she was struggling in the water . . .

*"Look there, sir. There's a woman in the water," cries the sailor as a ship with skull-and-crossbones pulls alongside. The pirates! Terror fills her heart as she bobs up and down in the waves.*

*"Fish her out," says a tall, dark, swarthy man, who, she can tell by the arrogance in his voice, must be the captain.*

*"No, let me drown!" she calls, but they pay her no heed and soon she is lying on the deck of the pirate ship, dripping wet and glaring up defiantly at the tall, powerfully built captain grinning down at her.*

*"What have we here?" he asks.*

*As he bends over her, she is intensely aware of the muscles rippling under his white shirt, of his ruggedly handsome face, and the menacing cutlass hanging at his waist. "Throw me back," she boldly declares. "I would rather drown than have anything to do with bloody pirates."*

*He gives her an easy smile as his eyes rake her boldly. "I have no intention of throwing you back to the fish, my beau-*

*tiful princess. Don't worry. I won't ravish you, much as I . . ."*

"You're drifting out too far, Lady Flora!"

*Mrs. Duffy.* The swarthy pirate and his ship disappeared fast as vapors. As Flora dutifully paddled closer to the bathing machine, a vague thread of discontented yearning began to run beneath her pleasure. At first she didn't know why, but she'd just discovered the ocean was a fine place to meditate as one paddled about in the lovely sunshine, and she soon had an answer. Why, she wondered, did it take twenty-two years before she had this lovely experience? Despite her cumbersome bathing costume, despite her mother and old Mrs. Duffy watching every move she made, she felt a new freedom of movement that, in her tight little world, she had never felt before. *Why?*

*God's blood, but I live a boring existence!*

Rules, rules, rules. In her mundane world, every moment of her waking day was planned and organized. Breakfast at nine, half-hour stroll at ten, embroidery at eleven, a light lunch at noon, then calling on friends in the afternoon, no visit to exceed precisely fifteen minutes, dinner at eight, to bed at ten. Next morning start all over again. And so her life went, day in, day out. She would marry someday, but only if she found a man she could truly love, which so far, she had not. Would she ever? Perhaps not, and that being so, the frightful possibility nagged that until the day she died, she would continue doing the same old boring things, relieved only by her dear friends and her love of poetry and books.

*All so dull, when what I really want . . .*

She pondered a moment, and then she knew. What she wanted was to find her own place in the world. Not with her parents, much as she loved them, but to strike out on her own, do whatever she wanted to do. Impossible, of course. Young ladies should never even think of such things. Only in her dreams could she ever escape, but dreams were silly. Pirate, indeed! How could she waste her time on such nonsense? Surely, no one else did. How people would laugh if they knew she dreamed of being ravished by a pirate.

*What is wrong with me?*

Lady Boles was right about too much saline immersion. Depression and languor truly had set in. *I'm such a fool.* Flora laughed aloud at herself.

"What did you say?" called Amy, who floated languidly nearby.

"I said . . ." Flora's humor returned. Nothing should spoil this beautiful day. Feeling the weight of her unwieldy bathing costume, she answered, "I was thinking how silly this bathing costume is and how I'd like to strip off my clothes and drift naked in this lovely water."

Amy feigned a look of shock. "Better not let Mama hear you say that, or this will be your first and last bath." An ebbing wave lifted Flora and caused her to float away. "Watch out, sister," Amy called playfully, "or you'll be swept out to sea."

"Indeed, she might, miss," a male voice boomed from the shore. "You had best attach a rope to her, Mrs. Duffy."

# Chapter 2

Startled, Flora swirled around in the water and looked toward shore. There stood two men in bathing costumes. One she hardly noticed. But the other! He was tall, with hair the color of burnished gold. He had broad, square shoulders, a slender waist, and powerful legs. At least from a distance he was quite the most handsome man she had ever seen.

But this was the ladies' section of the beach. The two men were most definitely in forbidden territory.

Frowning, Mrs. Duffy peered around the corner of the wagon. When she saw who it was, her sour mouth lifted in a smile. "Why, Lord Dashwood, what are you doing here? Should 'a known 'twould be you. You know the rules, you naughty boy."

With a laugh that revealed dazzling white teeth, the golden-haired man bent in an exaggerated bow. "How lovely to see you again, Mrs. Duffy. Rules are meant to be broken, do you not agree?" He glanced toward Flora and Amy. "And who are these beautiful young ladies?"

"You're much too bold, sir," Mrs. Duffy playfully replied. "My ladies are interested in their bath, not you, so you and your friend had best leave." She gazed at the other man, who was tall, dark, and also well built. "Lord Lynd, I am surprised at you."

If the dark-haired man gave a reply, Flora didn't hear. Her eyes were fixed upon Lord Dashwood. From the distance, she couldn't judge the fine points of his features, or tell whether his eyes were brown or blue. Still, she admired the confident way he was standing, bare feet dug into the sand, legs apart, hands on hips, powerful chest thrust out, chin tilted at a teasing angle. She also liked the rather daring attire he was wearing. In town she was accustomed to seeing men completely clothed in their London tailoring, nothing like the simple shirt and bathing pants that Dashwood wore. She could tell he'd recently been bathing, and the ocean wetness had given his clothes a daring look.

*Oh, my!*

Surely from this distance he could not see the direction of her gaze, but she quickly raised her eyes, noting how, despite the coldness of the water, she had felt a definite twinge of interest running through her.

"Oh, come now, Mrs. Duffy," Lord Dashwood called again, "I must have the names of these lovely sea goddesses."

"And why is that, sir?" called Flora. She was never shy.

"So that I might carry one of you off to Neptune's pearly chambers," came Dashwood's reply. He spread his arms wide and recited, *"I sing of beautiful Aphrodite of Cyprus and the sea, where the force of Zephyr's breath carried her along on waves of the resounding sea and soft foam."*

Flora lifted her hands above her head to applaud. "Bravo, sir! You are paraphrasing the Second Homeric Hymn from the seventh century BC, are you not?"

Dashwood replied with a grin and another exaggerated bow.

Flora was about to speak again when suddenly the surf receded, unbalancing both Amy and herself. They had been standing in water up to their necks; now it swirled around their knees.

"Ah, my two golden mermaids have emerged from the depths," Lord Dashwood remarked with delight. His companion said something Flora couldn't hear and started away. "Oh, all right, Lynd," Dashwood called after his friend. He looked back to the girls. "My friend says I'm making an ass of myself, but how could I resist such a charming sight?"

Lady Rensley called, "Flora, Amy, get back to the bathing machine this instant!"

Mrs. Duffy declared, "Time to get out of the water, ladies."

Flora protested, as did Amy, but the old woman was adamant. "Twenty minutes is more than enough for your first time."

As Flora and Amy climbed back up the ladder, Mrs.

Duffy's gaze swung to Lord Dashwood, who still stood watching on the beach. "Off with you now! If you want to meet the young ladies, you had best attend the ball tonight."

"Indeed, I shall," he called, flashing his charming smile before he turned and started away, hastening to catch up to his friend.

Back inside the bathing machine, as Mrs. Duffy toweled them both with vigor, Flora asked, "What ball is that, Mrs. Duffy?"

"The ball that everyone who is anyone attends," the old woman replied. "Especially whatever nobility 'appens to be in town, such as Lord Dashwood and his friend, Lord Lynd."

"I cannot understand why you were so nice to them, Mrs. Duffy." Lady Rensley looked down her nose at the Queen of Dippers with disdain. "They were rude and not dressed properly. I am flabbergasted you'd even speak to them."

Mrs. Duffy appeared unfazed. "Rude or not, 'e's Richard Prescott, Viscount Dashwood. 'E don't have money of his own, but 'e's heir presumptive to the estate of Charles Fraser, the Earl of Dinsmore. Only a distant cousin, I believe, but his lordship has no sons."

Lady Rensley look impressed. "You mean Lord Dinsmore, the Hero of Seedaseer?"

"The very same," answered Mrs. Duffy. "So Lord Dashwood ain't only handsome and titled; someday soon 'e's going to be filthy rich besides. So, m'lady, if I was you, I wouldn't be too picky about a fine catch like 'im bein' on the wrong section of the beach."

"Well!" Lady Rensley's mouth dropped open, but she quickly closed it and looked thoughtful. "So he'll be at the ball tonight . . . You are planning to go, aren't you, Amy?"

"I suppose," Amy answered in her hesitant way. "Though I know I shall sit in a corner all evening and no one will ask me to dance."

"Nonsense, Amy." Lady Rensley looked toward her older daughter. "You, too, of course, although I note your enthusiasm for balls seems to have waned of late."

How true, thought Flora.

As the wagon jolted back toward shore, Flora awkwardly changed from her bathing costume to her purple bathing dress trimmed with green, and her purple and green slippers that matched the dress. "I must say, Lord Dashwood is quite handsome," she murmured softly.

"Do you hear that, Mama?" said Amy. "Flora's actually interested in a man."

"Humph!" answered Lady Rensley. "I shall believe it when I see it. I have yet to see her even begin to lose her heart to a suitor."

*But there is always a first time, Mama.* Flora drifted into her princess-in-the-sea fantasy again, only this time the arrogant pirate with the cutlass at his waist had hair the color of burnished gold, dazzling white teeth, and a smile so captivating she didn't know how she could ever resist.

Back on shore, as they began their drive to their summer home, the Brighton Comet from London came rumbling past with a great jangling. Flora watched in awe and waved to the coachman who sat atop, whip held high over the four-horse team, bedecked in a white beaver hat and a box-cloth coat with a posy in his buttonhole. "Wo-ho! So-ho!" he called as he passed by.

Flora watched in awe. Ah, to be a coachman on a high-flier! Nothing in the world could be more exciting . . .

*Whip in hand, she sits at ease atop the crack flying machine as it rattles through the ill-paved streets and approaches the inn. The bugle plays a lively air as she turns into the courtyard. Slowing, with easy skill she undoes the buckle that keeps the ribbons together. The second the coach stops, she throws off the ribbons with a flourish. "Bravo!" calls Lord Dashwood, who happens to be standing in the courtyard. "You're as good as any man!" Oblivious to the applause and the admiring stares of the crowd, she climbs down, keenly aware of one set of admiring eyes upon her. . . .*

Oops. Flora caught herself, inwardly amused that she'd gone from princess-in-the-sea to dashing coachman in but a twinkling.

Imagination was a wonderful thing. Not very practical though, she thought glumly. Thank heavens no one could read her mind.

"Wait up, Sidney," Richard called as he hastened across the rocks and sand to where Sidney Bruxton, Lord Lynd, was fast retreating from the beach with purposeful strides. "Are you angry?" he asked as he drew parallel.

Sidney turned his head and drilled Richard with a look that was long, dark, and silent.

"But see here," Richard continued. "I was only flirting a bit, which is something you might try, instead of being so damnably serious most of the time."

Sidney remained silent.

"Oh, very well, then. Since it appears I've upset you, I promise I shan't disturb the ladies while they're bathing. God forbid I should break one of society's silly rules."

Sidney gave a snort. "Do you honestly think I give a groat about the rules? I left because I didn't care to be a part of your fawning performance. It was painful, seeing you preen like a conceited rooster before two young ladies who could not have cared less."

"Not care?" Feigning puzzlement, Richard touched one well-manicured finger to a golden eyebrow, shook his head, and grinned. "You know what a catch I am, Sidney. Despite my social faux pas, I'd wager both those chits will be at the ball tonight, dying to be introduced."

Sidney stopped and turned to face his friend, thick brows over wide-set brown eyes drawn together in disgust. "You have such conceit, Richard. I cannot imagine why I put up with you."

"Because we've been friends since childhood," Richard answered as they started walking again, his mouth curving into that charming, irresistible grin that Sidney knew so well. "And because I'm witty, entertaining, delightful to be with, and aside from all that, I saved your life."

Sidney rolled his eyes skyward. "Must I forever be reminded?"

"How quickly we forget!"

*Of course I have not forgotten*, Sidney thought glumly. The events of that long-ago winter day were etched forever in his memory. He and Richard had been eight when it happened. They had foolishly been crossing the thin ice of a pond in the woods when Sidney plunged into the freezing water. Young though he was, Richard had not gone screaming for help. He realized time was precious, so instead, with great presence of mind for a lad so young, he found a branch and crawled across the ice, shoving the branch

ahead of him. Disregarding the great risk to his own life,
he pushed the branch close enough so that Sidney could
grab hold. At the very last moment, when he was numb
from the cold and about to lose consciousness and go down
for the final time, Sidney was pulled to safety. "Do you
need to be thanked again, Richard?" Sidney asked with
feigned disgust.

"Don't be absurd," Richard answered cheerfully. "What
did you think of them?"

"Think of who?"

"The girls of course—the sea nymphs. The shorter one
appeared a bit drab, I thought, and a bit on the chubby
side. But the other—the tall one with all that auburn hair—
was quite pretty, don't you agree?"

"I didn't notice."

"Didn't notice!" Richard's azure blue eyes went wide
with surprise. "You mean to say you didn't see the sweet
curve of her hips, so deliciously revealed, I might add, by
that clinging, wet bathing costume she wore?"

"I said I didn't notice, Richard," Sidney cut in irritably.
A lie, of course. Indeed, he had noticed. Not the shorter,
who was unremarkable, but the taller one. She had immediately caught his attention. In fact, he could not remember
the last time the sight of a woman had caused that jolt in
the pit of his stomach that had not struck him since he was
a randy teen. At the age of twenty-eight, he considered
himself old and jaded; still, the sight of that long-limbed,
auburn-haired beauty rising like Aphrodite from the sea,
her gown wet and clinging to the luscious curves of her
long, lithe body . . .

Sidney realized what he was thinking and chuckled to
himself. Amazing, how the powerful allure of a beautiful
woman's body could manifest itself at the most inopportune
moments to unsettle a man. Ironic, too. Chances were, his
Aphrodite was a bubblehead, full of giggles, with nothing
more weighty on her mind than finding a suitable husband.

"What would you wager we'll see them at the ball tonight?" asked Richard.

Sidney sighed patiently. "My dear old friend, when I
agreed to accompany you on your holiday, did I not make
it clear I had no desire to participate in any social events?
I am here to enjoy the sea. Simply put, I want nothing

more than to stroll along the shore, as we are doing now, and occasionally sit upon a rock and gaze upon the vast waters of the Atlantic while I contemplate . . . shall we say, the meaning of life."

"How dull, and really, Sidney, not why I wanted you to come at all. You went through hell at Waterloo, what with your wound and all. I invited you because of the parties, the fun, the women—not so you could sit on a rock and brood."

"Perhaps I'm not in the mood to converse with some empty-headed, husband-hunting young chits at a ball."

"I suppose, but I thought I could talk you into it," Richard answered brightly. " 'Pon my soul, you've been a widower for . . . how long? Going on three years now. Enough of mourning! You're turning yourself into a hermit at the rate you're going, and a cynical one at that."

"Thanks."

"Well, I hate to see you isolating yourself. What happened? You were in the thick of the polite world before your marriage. Why can't you go back? I mean, really, Sidney, what is more important than your standing in society?"

Sidney shrugged. "Take me as I am, or else. I've long passed the stage where I think my life depends on how I tie my cravat."

"Not that you ever really cared." Puzzled, Richard shook his head. "I don't understand you. You'd do well with the ladies if you'd give it try. You're not all that bad looking."

"Ha!" Sidney retorted, thinking of his craggy face with its not-quite-straight nose and too-prominent chin.

"Well, looks aren't everything," Richard conceded. "Besides, if you so much as wiggled your little finger, the ladies would flock to you in an instant. Forget looks. You're titled. You're wealthy—much richer than I, though that will soon change, what with Dinsmore's poor health, and look how well I do with the ladies."

Sidney grimaced. "Do you have any idea how shallow that sounds?" He decided not to continue. What was the use? His friend would never understand. Coming here was a mistake, he thought glumly. "I should be home, looking after my estate."

"Hogwash! You have a perfectly fine overseer," Richard answered indignantly, "so there's no possible excuse for hiding yourself deep in the countryside, as you've been doing ever since . . . Well, I feel you've grieved enough, and besides, you know very well—"

"I suggest you not finish that sentence." Sidney knew exactly what his friend was going to say. His problem was not that he had grieved enough, but that he had grieved more than enough for a woman he had never loved in the first place. His parents had arranged the marriage with Hortense, and he, being the dutiful son at the time, had allowed himself to marry a woman who wasn't a bad sort, but they'd had nothing in common. When Hortense died, childless, of typhoid, he'd been genuinely sorry to see her go. But when his parents, both now gone, started hinting he should find a new wife, he put his foot down. He firmly informed them marriage didn't suit him. Perhaps it never would, although he could not say for sure. Unlike many men, he felt no driving need to beget sons. When he died, his estate could go to his uncles or his uncles' kin. Meantime, he kept busy managing his estate with the help of Louisa, his older, widowed sister. When he wanted to relax, he traveled to London for a visit to Tattersall's, where he could view horses to his heart's content. He enjoyed hunting and fishing. He was an active and enthusiastic member of the Four-in-Hand Club, where he spent countless enjoyable hours with Richard and other friends. Also, the occasional mistress came and went. Unlike some of his more foolish friends, he had never fallen in love with one of his cyprians. Instead, long after the flames of passion had cooled to dying embers, he maintained a friendship with each and every one.

". . . So you must come to the ball tonight," Richard was saying.

"I would rather stay home and read a book."

Undaunted, Richard went on. "Stop being so bullheaded. Did it ever occur to you that you could be wrong? Why don't you see for yourself whether or not the tall one has a brain? Perhaps she's not so empty-headed as you might think." He brightened as an afterthought struck him. "She knew who Homer was, did she not?"

Richard had a point. Besides, Sidney suddenly realized he would like to see her again, if only to assure himself he was right the first time. "Very well, if you insist. I shall go to the ball."

"Splendid!" Richard was all smiles. "You might be pleasantly surprised."

"I doubt it."

"I'll even leave you the tall one and take the short. I guarantee, I'll soon have her eating out of my hand."

"But why, Richard?" Sidney asked, genuinely puzzled. "You have no intention of marrying anytime soon."

"It's all a game, isn't it?" Richard answered, chuckling. "Played for the trophy. For some men, the trophies are the heads of savage beasts mounted upon their walls. For others, it's elaborate collections of snuffboxes."

"And what trophies do you collect, Richard?" asked Sidney, already knowing the answer. This was the thing about Richard he detested. This was why Richard, contrary to what he assumed, could never be Sidney's best friend. As the years went by, he grew more debauched, more selfish, and though he didn't know it, at times he came dangerously close to becoming an ex-friend.

"I collect broken hearts," said Richard, laughing.

*How loathsome,* thought Sidney, but he kept quiet, not caring to admonish the man who had once saved his life.

Flora's own eagerness surprised her as she and Amy, chaperoned by their mother and Lady Constance Boles, mounted the steps of the Brighton Assembly. The thrill of attending balls had long since faded, but tonight was different. The weariness, the disillusion, were gone. With Lord Dashwood much on her mind, she felt as if she were about to attend her very first ball. With the help of Baker, her caustic lady's maid, she had enjoyed donning her prettiest ball gown. Of white satin, it came direct from Paris and featured lovely clusters of pink roses and bands of white lace around the hem. Even Baker had admired it and outdid herself sweeping Flora's auburn curls into a Grecian coiffure, pinned with a comb of feathers and pearls.

All the while Flora was getting ready, the image of that handsome face she'd seen on the beach kept popping into her head. A little tingle of excitement coursed through her as she thought of the conquest ahead.

What was he like?

Would she be disappointed?

She reminded herself she had been attracted to many a man before, only to discover that when she got to know him, she found he possessed some major fault. One was too self-centered, another just plain dull, another mean-spirited, while another had a roving eye. No doubt Lord Dashwood was in some way flawed. What man was perfect? Still, wouldn't it be wonderful if he were? Once again she pictured him as he stood upon the beach, hair golden in the sunshine, his powerful, well-muscled body so completely revealed she felt a wicked shiver of excitement just thinking about it.

*But what if he doesn't ask me to dance?*

What a horrible thought! And a most unlikely one, too. She had always been popular, in great demand as a dance partner, so of course he would ask. Since when could she not attract a man with just the crook of her little finger?

Flora stepped into the ballroom and surreptitiously looked around. No Lord Dashwood. She had no time to dwell on her disappointment, though, for soon she was asked to dance, and from then on she never sat down. She danced to a polonaise, then a set of country dances, all the while trying to prevent her gaze from wandering to the front entrance, but to no avail. At last, when she had just about decided Dashwood wasn't coming, she spied his handsome figure at the entrance, accompanied by his friend—what was his name? She could not recall.

Had Dashwood remembered? Would he notice her? She closed her eyes for a moment, her mind drifting. . . .

*His gaze sweeps the room, as if he is looking for someone. Finally he finds her. Even across the ballroom she can see his body stiffen, for only a fleeting moment, but long enough for her to know she was the object of his search. His gaze is fastened upon her as he crosses the room. He greets Lady Constance Boles, then asks, "Would you introduce me to this young lady?" She dips a cool curtsy as introductions are made. "Will you dance with me?" he asks. She nods and gracefully extends her hand. Soon they are whirling in a waltz around the floor, his azure blue eyes gazing long-ingly into hers. Finally, shaking his head in wonderment, he says, "What have you done to me? I have not stopped think-ing of you a moment since I first saw you on the beach this morning. . . ."*

"Flora?"

Her mother. Flora exited her fantasy posthaste. "Yes, Mama?"

"I do believe those two gentlemen we saw on the beach this morning have arrived."

Flora raised an indifferent eyebrow. "Do tell."

Lady Rensley, her thin self encased in black, snapped her fan shut disapprovingly. "Lord Dashwood is a fine catch, Flora, if ever there was one. Pray he will ask you to dance."

Amy clasped her arm. "Oh, look, they're coming this way."

It was all Flora could do to maintain her outward calm. Lord Dashwood really *had* found her. He really was going to ask her to dance!

Soon Lord Dashwood stood before them, resplendent in a black, double-breasted wool frock coat with claw-hammer tails, breeches, gloves, a waistcoat, and a white shirt with a beautifully tied cravat. With graceful gallantry, he presented himself to Lady Constance Boles and asked for introductions, just as Flora had imagined. "Delighted to meet you, Lady Flora, Lady Amy," he said with his charming smile and bent in an exquisite little bow. She was positive his next words to her would be, *Would you care to dance?* So positive, in fact, she half lifted her arm to his, so that he could lead her to the dance floor.

But what was this?

Instead of asking her to dance, Lord Dashwood turned to Amy and flashed the same charming smile. "What a pleasure to meet you, Lady Amy. Might I have this dance?"

Feeling herself blush with embarrassment, Flora quickly lowered her arm and watched as the handsome viscount led Amy to the dance floor and spun her away to the lively melody of a waltz. Crushing disappointment overwhelmed her. She had been so certain! Then her common sense took hold. She saw how vain she was to assume he'd choose her first, over every young lady present in the dance hall. Obviously not every man in the ballroom was dying to dance with her, and that, she informed herself, should be a good lesson in humility. Still, she was hurt, much more than she should have been, given the circumstances. Good

grief, she and Lord Dashwood had just been introduced,
yet she felt like a lovesick schoolgirl.

"May I have this dance?" came a man's voice beside her.

Flora turned and through a kind of daze saw it was Lord
Dashwood's friend, the one who had been at the beach that
morning. Gratefully she nodded a yes. At this point she
would dance with the devil himself rather than be obliged
to stand, humiliated, on the sidelines. The orchestra struck
up another waltz. "It appears we shall be waltzing,
Lord . . . er . . ."

"Lynd," he said flatly and led her to the floor.

"So you are a friend of Lord Dashwood," she remarked
as they started dancing, hardly aware of what she was saying. With a conscious effort, she forced herself to keep her
eyes on her partner, although her mind was elsewhere.

"Lord Dashwood is a cousin of my neighbor, Lord Dinsmore. Also his heir presumptive since Dinsmore has no
sons. Dashwood visited often when he was a boy. We're
the same age and used to play together. I know him well."
Lynd cocked an eyebrow and inquired, "And where do you
reside, Lady Flora, that is, when you're not arising like—
how did Dashwood put it?—Aphrodite from the sea, if
memory serves."

She supposed he had intended the remark humorously,
but she could not muster so much as a faint smile. "My
family has a country home in Sussex. Also a town house
in London."

"Ah, so you'll soon be enjoying another Season, I'd
wager."

She bristled immediately. "I'm not planning on another
Season. I have better things to do."

"And what *do* you do, Lady Flora?" His intense gaze
drilled into hers.

The way he asked was rude, she thought. She wished she
didn't have to dance with this man. Too late now, but at
least she could make sure he would not ask again. "Well,
I shall tell you what I don't do," she replied bluntly. "I
have no talent for art, so I don't paint. I don't sing, either,
because my voice is so abominable that when I sing, our
dog runs and hides. Nor do I play the piano, because I
hated it and rebelled after one lesson. As for needlework,
I embroidered a sampler once. It was so terrible, my

mother threw it away and never mentioned the subject again." There, that should show him. She gave him a smug smile. "And what do *you* do, Lord Lynd?"

He gave her a smug smile right back. "The proper answer to that is nothing, since we of the *ton* are all aware that ladies and gentlemen would not be caught dead doing actual work."

"So you do nothing, sir?" she inquired, none too politely.

Not hesitating, deadpan serious, he replied, "I, too, cannot sing or play the piano. As to what became of my sampler, its fate is too terrible to relate."

In her cranky mood, she didn't immediately perceive he wasn't serious. Then the humor of it struck her and she could not help but laugh, especially when he managed to keep a straight face the whole time. She felt better, knowing laughter had somewhat assuaged her disappointment. For the first time, she regarded Lord Lynd with genuine curiosity. He was tall, with powerful shoulders, just like Lord Dashwood, but his face could not compare with the enchanting perfection of the viscount's sharply chiseled features. In fact, this man looked like some sort of brigand, with those heavy brows over dark, brooding eyes, slightly crooked nose, and that prominent, set chin that suggested a stubborn streak. Nor did he possess a charming smile. In fact, he hardly smiled at all, but instead kept looking at her in a quizzical fashion. She realized she'd been rude and hastened to answer the question he'd asked in the first place. "The things I do are not too terribly interesting, I'm afraid. When in London I practically live at Hatchards because I read a lot, various things like military history and—"

"The classics," he ventured.

"How did you know?"

"Your reference to Homer."

"I've never seen you in London," she lightly remarked. "Surely you go for the Season?"

"I go to London for two reasons—an occasional visit to Tattersall's, but mainly for the Four-in-Hand Club."

Her interest peaked immediately. "You belong?"

He nodded.

She knew she shouldn't ask, but curiosity spurred her on. "Does Lord Dashwood belong?"

The shadow of a frown crossed his face before he answered, "Dashwood, too." For the first time, he actually smiled. "When we were boys we had a pact that when we grew up we would both be coachmen on the Brighton Road."

She opened her mouth to say, *Oh, I, too* . . . but thought better of it. Perish the thought that a well-brought-up young lady would dream of being a coachman. But then, why shouldn't she speak her mind? Lord Lynd was most certainly not a suitor, so there was hardly a need to impress him with her feminine charms. "Don't laugh, but I would love to try four-in-hand, myself, sometime." She waited for his derisive laughter. The few men in whom she'd confided always laughed at the thought that a woman wanted to drive four-in-hand.

He didn't laugh but replied, "Then you *should* try. I've always thought it absurd—this notion that our women must be treated like delicate flowers. Such hypocrisy! And what's truly outrageous is that our concern for the so-called 'gentler sex' extends only to those in the *ton*. Among the so-called 'lower classes,' women toil as hard as their men, but that's acceptable." He looked her up and down, but not in a licentious way. "You're young and strong. I've no doubt you could handle driving four-in-hand. Have you ever tried?"

"Never. I can just see my mother if she caught me attempting such a thing. She won't even let me on a horse, except for an old nag we own."

"Of course," he answered with a rueful shrug. "Naturally it would be considered most unseemly."

"But still, I would like to try it sometime. I can't think of a more exciting sight than a coach just ready to start from the courtyard of an inn."

"Ah, yes, and the coach itself, all gleaming," Lord Lynd agreed, "and the harness, so skillfully arranged—"

"—And the beautiful horses, impatient to be off. The inside of the coach full and the outside covered with men, women, and children and—"

"—Boxes, bags, and bundles," Lord Lynd enthusiastically continued. "And then there's the coachman himself, master of all he surveys, taking his reins in one hand, whip in the other. He gives the signal with his foot and away they go—"

"—With the coachman calling, 'All right! Wo-ho! So-ho then!' " Flora spiritedly supplied. "Imagine, soon they're going a whole ten miles an hour!"

"Astonishing." Lord Lynd paused a moment, as if to savor their mutual delight at coaching. "You have it exactly right." A faint light twinkled in the depths of his brown eyes. "I hope your wish comes true someday. I've no doubt you could drive a coach-and-four with the best of them." He gazed down at her with a thoughtful look in his eyes. "You are not what I thought you were, Lady Flora."

"And just what did you think I was?" she asked. If he answered, she didn't hear, because just then, out of the corner of her eye, she caught a glimpse of yellow floating by. It was Amy in her yellow silk ball dress trimmed with yellow satin bows. She was still dancing with Lord Dash-wood, who, judging from that dazzling smile he was flashing at her, was enjoying the dance immensely.

A stab of envy filled Flora's heart. How strange, for she was never jealous of her sister. They had always gotten along just fine, perhaps because they were completely un-alike and their interests differed. Come to think of it, she had never been jealous of anybody. But when it came to Lord Dashwood, perhaps her's and Amy's interests had converged. If that was true, she wouldn't dream of standing in Amy's way.

The music stopped. She heard, "I shall return you to your chaperon, Lady Flora," and suddenly remembered with whom she was dancing.

"That will be fine," she said with scarce attention as Lord Lynd led her from the dance floor. By rote she added, "I enjoyed the dance."

His eyebrows raised inquiringly. "Did you?" he asked, and before she could answer he gave her a slight bow and moved away.

She knew she'd been rude, but she couldn't bring herself to care. Lord Lynd was nice enough, she supposed, but Lord Dashwood—so dashing, so spirited, so handsome!— had stirred a fire within her, and she could think of nothing else. Eagerly her gaze swept the throng of dancers. Where were they? she wondered. She must find out if Amy was attracted to the handsome viscount. Pray God, she was not.

When Flora found Amy alone for a moment, she asked, "What did you think of Lord Dashwood?"

Amy shrugged and answered, "Oh, he's all right, I suppose. Awfully handsome, isn't he? And charming, too. But still . . . he's not for me."

Flora's heart was gladdened, but only briefly. Lord Dashwood still hadn't asked her to dance. As the evening wore on, she invented all sorts of reasons why he was ignoring her. He had not had the chance, she told herself, what with eager mothers pressing their daughters upon him. Or perhaps he was saving her until last. Yes, that was it! Once he got his obligations out of the way, he would appear before her, that wicked little gleam in his eye. . . .

*"Come dance with me, Lady Flora. It's you I have wanted to dance with all evening."*

*"Really? I am surprised. You have shown no indication of it."*

*"Please, give me a chance. Don't you understand? It was only out of courtesy that I was forced to dance with all those other young ladies. . . ."*

But he never asked. As the evening drew to a close, she convinced herself he wasn't going to. *How can he not ask! How can he possibly ignore the belle of the ball?*

She caught herself, and inwardly laughed at her own arrogance and stupidity. *Let that be a lesson to you, Miss Fancy Flora. You can't catch every man with the crook of your little finger, after all.* And why should she care? Not only had she danced every dance, she'd been showered with compliments and attention—things she ordinarily didn't care about. But tonight the attention was a boon to her wounded pride. *Blast you, Lord Dashwood, you insignificant coxcomb.*

At the beginning of the last dance, Lord Dashwood finally appeared before her and flashed his dazzling smile.

"Lady Flora, I must have a dance before it's over."

The anguish of the evening disappeared, although she was not about to let him know how her heart had suddenly filled with joy. "I would be honored, sir," she answered none too warmly. "Luckily you found me without a partner."

"I know," he said as they started dancing. "You've been the belle of the ball tonight."

She cocked her head and tartly asked, "Really? How would you know?"

"I am aware of every man you danced with, starting with that milksop, Lord Farley. Then Lieutenant Kenniston, followed by that major, then the milksop again—I saw him step on your toes, followed by—"

"Stop!" she said, finally laughing, her doubts replaced by a gush of pure joy. She smiled back at him coquettishly. "You could have asked me sooner."

"Ah, but I saved the best until last."

They danced mostly in silence with Flora noticing how quick, how graceful he was. At the end, he stepped back and said, "You're a marvelous waltzer, Lady Flora. I vow, you waltz as quick, if not quicker, than Madame Lieven, herself."

What a marvelous compliment! Her heart swelled with delight to think he was comparing her with one of the esteemed patronesses of Almack's.

When he led her back to the sidelines, her mother spoke up. "My dear Lord Dashwood, you must come visit us tomorrow." She added as an afterthought, "And your friend, Lord Lynd, of course."

At any other time, Flora would have been embarrassed over her mother's blatant invitation, but now she held her breath, waiting for his answer.

A broad smile spread over Dashwood's face. "We'd be delighted. The house on the hill, is it not? Don't worry, we'll find our way. Tomorrow then." He bowed to Flora, a definite gleam of interest in his eyes.

# Chapter 3

The moon barely shone through the heavy ocean mist as Richard flicked his whip over the bays pulling their curricle back to the house on the Marine Parade he'd leased for the summer. He glanced sideways at Sidney, who sat silently beside him. "You did not enjoy the ball."

Sidney took a long time answering. "All things considered, no." He wished his friend were not so damnably observant.

Richard nudged his companion's arm. "I note that you and that old reprobate, Lord Marshall, sat in a corner most of the evening. No doubt exchanging your tedious war stories."

"As a matter of fact, we were. I found my conversation with Marshall to be far more interesting than dancing with a passel of giddy young debutantes."

"But you hardly danced, except the once with Lady Flora."

"Had you nothing better to do all evening than observe me?"

"That's absurd. You very well know I devoted myself to the ladies tonight." Richard's voice lightened as he continued. "But of course, I kept an eye on you. You are my guest. I wanted to see you had a good time."

Sidney felt a twinge of guilt. In this life, a man could count on but a handful of friends who truly cared about his well-being. Despite his many faults, Richard was one of those. "Sorry. As for Lady Flora, yes, I danced with her once and wished I hadn't."

"But she was the most beautiful girl there tonight, and by far the most popular."

"Then why did you dance only one dance with her, yourself, and the last one at that?"

"Ah, so you noticed," Richard replied, his voice suffused with self-satisfaction. "But you see, that's my strategy. I know women well enough to know they want what they cannot have. If you want a woman, the worst thing you can do is chase after her like some puppy dog, especially one with as many suitors as Lady Flora. How old is she? Twenty-two or -three? Been out since she was eighteen? So she's had several years of men begging for favors, throwing themselves at her feet. She's utterly spoiled, and that's what she expects now. But by God, she won't find me fawning over her. *Au contrair!*" Chuckling, Richard snapped the reins, bringing the bays to a swift, trotting pace.

Sidney cast his friend a look of disgust, even though he knew Richard couldn't possibly see it in the dark. "So just what is your strategy?"

"Indifference, that's the key. Amazing, how well it works. When I see a woman I want, I ignore her, though not entirely, of course. I give her a sample of that old Dashwood charm, just enough to rouse her interest. Soon she's dying for my attention. It's not long before she's dying for more." Even in the darkness, Sidney sensed Richard's triumphant little smile. "Works every time."

"Richard, you are absolute scum."

His friend met the insult with a hearty laugh. "Scum, perhaps, but I assure you my strategy works. Did you notice Lady Flora tonight? She could not keep her eyes off me. At the end of the evening when I danced with her, or, to put it another way, when I finally threw her a crumb, she was not only exceedingly grateful, she was ecstatic with relief that at last I had deigned to notice her."

*So that's why she ignored me.* Sidney gritted his teeth, surprised at his own irritation. After his unsatisfactory dance with Lady Flora, he had vowed not to dance again, telling himself he'd be an idiot if ever he attended another ball. He asked, "Why do you do this? What's to be gained?"

"Am I not free to pursue my pleasures?"

"That's not the point."

"Since when are you such a prude?" Richard asked with mild exasperation. "Am I not doing what most men do?"

"I can't argue." Sidney would say no more. Far be it from him to preach and moralize. Besides, in a society like the *ton*, prudish on the surface, but rife with corruption underneath, how could he possibly explain how, in recent years, he increasingly found the loose morals abhorrent? "So go pursue your pleasures," he said with a sigh.

Richard thought a moment. "So far, it's been a game—the chase, the conquest. But lately . . . You know how Cousin Charles has been after me to marry. I have resisted, of course. Why should I give up this delightful life I lead?"

"Why should you, indeed?" Sidney cynically observed. "Women, drinking, gambling, more women . . . The word *decadent* comes to mind."

"Exactly." If Richard was the least insulted, he gave no indication. "But on the other hand, I am sick to death of my cousin plaguing me, so lately I've been thinking, why not marry? Then I shall do what most men do—take a wife, get her with child, then go about my 'decadent' life just as before."

"Not every woman would have you on those terms."

"My dear boy, what woman would not have me? Aren't I titled and soon-to-be rich? My dear cousin grows more feeble by the day." He hastened to add, "Not that I want him to go, mind you, but facts are facts."

"The fact is, you can hardly wait for your cousin's demise." Sidney did not bother to hide his annoyance.

"Well, it's true, isn't it?" Richard breezily inquired. "I could marry any woman I choose, but where's the fun in that? I enjoy the challenge—the chase. So I shall choose a woman with spirit, like Lady Flora, who's not only beautiful and charming, but has a munificent father who will doubtless provide an obscenely generous dowry. I'll have my fun with her, marry her, get her with child, which will thrill Cousin Charles no end and stop him plaguing me. Then I shall be free to resume my carefree life while my obedient wife stays home and produces a pack of little Dashwoods to carry on the family name." Laughing aloud, Richard slapped his friend on the back. "A fine scheme, don't you think?"

"You are despicable."

"Now there's a true friend," Richard answered warmly. "One of the things I like best about you, Sidney, is you always say what you think."

*True enough,* thought Sidney. *But that's not all I'm think-*

*ing*. Despite the Four-in-Hand Club in which they both took an active part, despite the history of their friendship that extended back to before he could remember, there were times he could barely tolerate his wayward friend. Richard had been a sweet child, obedient, pleasant, never whining, but when he reached his teens, he began to change into the arrogant, uncaring man he was today. Sidney suspected the death of Richard's parents in a carriage accident when he was twelve was much to blame. Richard had come to live with Lord Dinsmore. A military man, highly respected if not revered, the earl tried to instill in his late cousin's son the importance of a high moral character. That is, when he was around. The trouble was, Dinsmore was away much of the time, fighting one war or another, leaving Richard to be raised by servants and a doting Lady Dinsmore who, having never had children of her own, caved in to his every whim.

Now Lady Dinsmore was dead and his guardian, Lord Dinsmore, back at Pemberly Manor to stay. Dinsmore had returned a hero, battered and scarred from the ardors of battle, but too late for any favorable influence on his ward. Richard's unsavory character had already formed, set in a mold of self-indulgence, arrogance, and greed. *Which I have ignored up to now,* Sidney mused. *But no longer can I countenance such behavior.* Richard would always be a friend, but surely not his best friend, and it would be better, as time went by, that they drift apart. Not easy, though, considering that Vernon Hill, Sidney's own estate, lay adjacent to Pemberly Manor, which someday would belong to Richard. It was inevitable their paths would cross from time to time. If they did, fine. Considering Richard had once saved his life, Sidney could never completely turn his back on the man, no matter how unprincipled he became.

Richard inquired, "So what did you think of Lady Flora?"

"Attractive . . . Personable enough," was Sidney's careful answer. That would suffice. He would not mention that earlier that morning on the beach something intense had flared deep within him the moment he had first seen Lady Flora Winton standing in the surf, a sea breeze stirring her wealth of auburn hair, the wet folds of her bathing costume clinging like a second skin to her alluring curves.

My God, but it had been a while since he'd felt that overpowering urge for a woman. In fact, he could not recall ever receiving such a jolt. And so out of the blue! He had not exactly lived the life of a monk since Hortense died, but never anything serious. Up to now, he simply had not been interested.

Having seen Lady Flora only at a distance, he was surprised at the number of times throughout the day that thoughts of her kept popping into his head. Each time they did, he tried to convince himself that up close she would doubtless look quite ordinary.

But not so. Up to now, he'd found the task of beginning a dance with a young lady about as exciting as pulling on his boots. Tonight, though, he'd had a rather interesting reaction when Lady Flora Winton floated into his arms, smelling of lilac, her face perfection, with its delicately pointed chin, full, rosy mouth so temptingly curved, soft cheeks of rose and pearl, straight, uptilted little nose, and dark violet eyes, fringed with long, dark lashes. There was intelligence in those eyes, as well as humor. They were bright with energy and life. He had begun the dance with a first-time-ever heightened awareness that he held a desirable woman in his arms, and he'd felt her beguiling presence right down to his fingertips. From there, it got better—or worse, depending how he looked at it—when he discovered he might as well be guiding a piece of dandelion fluff; she was so light, truly a marvelous dancer. Most disturbing, though, was that in a room full of low-cut gowns exposing soft white flesh, which he had long since learned to ignore, when they began the dance, he found the close-up view of her bosom disturbing in a way he'd never known before. He was keenly aware of her in every way!

And she'd ignored him. Sidney could almost laugh at the irony. Richard wasn't the only bachelor considered a good catch. Since Hortense died, more than one aggressive mother had thrust her daughter at him, visions of a fine marriage to a wealthy and titled widower on her mind. He had avoided them all like the plague.

As for Lady Flora—enough! From this moment on he would entertain no more thoughts of her. He had more pleasant things to think about.

Richard interrupted his thoughts. "Lady Rensley mentioned they're having an at-home tomorrow afternoon."

"Are you suggesting we call?"

"Of course, old boy. Want to come along? I fancy I'd like to see the beautiful Lady Flora again."

"You mean, throw her another crumb?"

"You needn't be sarcastic," Richard answered congenially. "You should come. I know you detest the very thought of matchmaking, but perhaps the sister? A bit on the plump side, I suppose, and rather plain, but, still, her dowry is quite attractive."

Sidney's first impulse was to give Richard a polite but firm no. He caught himself as an image of Flora's face filled his head. What would it hurt to see her one more time? Just once, then never again. Besides, if he got to know her better, he might find some major flaw that would surely cure him of this irrational obsession.

"I'll come along, Richard, if you insist," Sidney answered with scant enthusiasm. With any luck, he would find Lady Flora prone to silly gossip, or perhaps she talked too much, or was a braggart, or at the very least, slurped her tea.

Flora loved the comfortable home her family leased each summer. Sitting atop a gently rolling hill, the rambling old house afforded a fine view of green fields surrounded by a forest of trees. In addition, one could find a magnificent view of the sea from both the terrace and the low French windows of the drawing room. On an ordinary day, Flora was eager to arise the moment she awoke. She would dress and go downstairs where, on days warm enough, the family would take breakfast on the terrace, enjoying the always breathtaking view.

Not this morning, though. Instead of springing from her bed, Flora snuggled deeper into her covers and thought of last night and Lord Dashwood. How crushed she had been when he hadn't danced with her! How overjoyed she was when he'd claimed the final dance. "I saved the best until last," he'd said, thus sending a vast wave of relief coursing through her. Was she falling in love? She had been attracted to one man or another from time to time, but no

man had caused the feelings Lord Dashwood had stirred
within her last night.

Amy, still in her nightgown, entered and perched herself
on the side of Flora's bed. "Wasn't it lovely last night?"
she asked, her gray eyes clear and bright. "Now, tell the
truth—are you interested in Lord Dashwood? I saw you
looking at him all evening."

Flora returned a noncommittal "Hmm." Amy might be
naive, but she didn't miss much.

"And then I saw he danced the last dance with you,"
Amy babbled on, "and he was looking at you as if he was
*most* interested." She clasped her hands in front of her.
"Oh, how exciting! He is *such* a catch. What did he say?
Did he—?"

"He is absolutely mad for me and begged me to marry
him. We are eloping to Gretna Greene tonight."

Amy looked startled, then giggled. "Oh, you are not!
Just the same, wouldn't it be lovely if you married Lord
Dashwood?"

"That's not likely to occur," Flora answered. "Since I
shan't be attending the Season this year, I doubt I'll see
him after we return home."

Amy looked thoughtful. "Then perhaps you should
reconsider."

"About another Season? You know when I make up my
mind, I mean it."

"Must you always be so stubborn?" Amy sighed, then
brightened. "At least you'll see Lord Dashwood when he
attends our at-home this afternoon."

Despite herself, Flora felt her heart give a little leap.
Offhandedly she remarked, "Oh, yes. I do recall now.
Mama invited him."

"As well as that friend of his—that rather rude man who
looked so aloof and hardly danced."

Flora only half listened. Already her mind had drifted.
Lord Dashwood must come! She desperately wanted to see
him again. As for his friend, she hardly remembered . . .
What was his name? Ah, well, no matter.

When she finally arose, the morning proceeded in its
usual tedious fashion. After breakfast, at exactly nine
o'clock, she took her usual short walk with her mother and
Amy—down to the first oak tree and back, the same every

day. At precisely eleven, her mother and Amy took up their petit point and Flora, because of her shortcomings in needlework, was allowed to read.

Because of the at-home, their usual afternoon schedule of either receiving visitors or paying visits was changed. The relaxed pace of the day disappeared. Instead, there was an extra fuss as they changed for the afternoon, Flora donning a white muslin tea gown with a double row of flounces around the hem, trimmed with pink satin. Under their mother's fidgety direction, Flora, Amy, and the parlor maid scurried about the drawing room, plumping out cushions that Lady Rensley imagined hollowed, straightening slightly rumpled seat covers, shifting a footstool that for some unfathomable reason had been moved an inch from its appointed place.

"Everything looks fine," Flora assured her nervous mother, as she smoothed a slightly disturbed small hearth rug.

Amy whispered, "I wish she wouldn't have these at-homes. She near kills herself with worry."

Flora heartily agreed. Lady Rensley reveled in her at-homes, and she never failed to hold them, whether at their London town house, their country home in Sweffham Park, or here in Brighton. But she never relaxed and enjoyed herself. Instead, she worried that the silver would not be polished to its highest possible glow, or that the lemon wedges would not be cut exactly straight, or one of her fine china cups might contain some infinitesimal crack. *Will that be me someday?* Flora often wondered. When and if she married, would she end up like her mother, worried about every little thing? *I do not want to be like my mother,* she thought dismally. *Never!*

Lady Constance Boles was the first to arrive, followed by an elegantly dressed collection of Lady Rensley's lady friends. They were deep in a predictable and utterly boring discussion of furniture, china, and ormolu when there was a stir, and every female eye in the room turned to the door. Flora could almost hear the swift intake of breath. It was as if a shining god had dropped from the heavens as Lord Dashwood appeared, resplendent in top hat, serge spencer jacket over a waistcoat, drill trousers, and a magnificently tied cravat over the high starched points of his collar. He carried a heavy walking stick and wore kid gloves and leather Hessian boots with a tassel. He also wore a devastatingly charming smile.

Amid tittering admiration he strode into the room and bent with courtly deference over Lady Rensley's hand. "My dear Lady Rensley," he said in his mellow, deep voice, "how utterly kind of you to invite me." His gaze swept the room. "Ah, a room full of lovely ladies. I must meet each and every one." He noticed Flora as she rose to greet him. "Ah, Lady Flora!" Bending low again, he kissed her hand. "How delightful to see you." For a fraction of a moment, his gaze swept over her, soft as a caress. His eyes met hers, insolent, compelling. She felt a tingle down her spine. His eyes were sending a message that clearly said, *I'm interested in you. I want to see you again.*

Her senses leaped to life as she became acutely aware of the charm he projected. He was so compelling she felt an urge to reach out and run her fingers through those glorious golden curls, which he wore romantically long, just like a poet. *No time to think about it now.* Fighting to control her breath, she cleared her throat, pretending not to be affected. She must greet the friend who stood behind him. *His name,* she thought frantically. *Whatever is his name? Ah, I remember. It's Lord Lynd.* He, too, was fashionably dressed but looked not nearly as splendid. He did not bend to kiss her hand, nor did his eyes send any kind of signal except *I am extremely bored.*

Flora sat through Lords Dashwood and Lynd's mandatory fifteen-minute stay hardly hearing the desultory conversation around her. She had always suspected a strong passion lurked within her, as yet unleashed, but now, as if she were in some sort of daze, she slowly came to realize she was falling in love with Richard, Lord Dashwood. *I must have him,* she thought as she decorously poured tea. "Sugar, Lady Boles?"

"One spoonful, my dear, and you must tell me about your bathing excursion yesterday. Of course, you know how much I heartily approve. I feel both health and pleasure must be equally consulted in these salutary ablutions. An occasional dip in the purifying surge of the ocean can restore . . ."

Did Lord Dashwood find her attractive? Flora wondered as her mind slipped its bonds and returned to the shore. . . .

*In the pitch blackness of the night they are alone on the beach. . . . Never mind how they got there or why she is unchaperoned. . . . Her back is pressed tight against the sand, her arms spread wide, wrists pinned securely by Lord Dashwood as he bends over her, breath coming hard, trembling with passion.*

*"Lord Dashwood, we must not be alone like this!"*

*"I had to get you alone, my darling, don't you understand?"*

*"Understand what, sir?"*

*"That I am mad for you. That I cannot sleep for thinking of you. That if you don't agree to marry me, I shall take you here, right on the beach. Then you'll be ruined and you'll have to marry me. . . ."*

"Are you listening, Flora?" Her mother was looking at her quizzically.

"Of course I'm listening." What was happening? Flora felt as if she were returning from the moon.

"Then answer the question and stop daydreaming."

"I found the saline immersion to be most invigorating, Lady Boles. Most . . . uh, energizing and most edifying, and . . . and . . . ."

"And we most certainly extol the pleasures of bathing," declared Amy, jumping in. Waving her arm dramatically, she continued. "To plunge into refreshing waves and be wrapped around with liquid element is indeed . . . uh . . ."

"Gratifying!" said Flora, signaling her sister a silent thank-you. This wouldn't be the first time Amy had saved her from her fantasy.

When the two lords announced they were leaving, Amy and Flora accompanied them to the door.

"I am so glad you could come," Flora said, making sure her face was arranged into the mask of the polite hostess.

Lord Dashwood bent toward her, his smile as intimate as a kiss. "A pity you're not coming for the Season, Lady Flora. I would like to see you again."

"Oh, but I am coming for the Season. Did I not tell you? Certain circumstances have caused me to change my mind."

She was astounded at herself. The words had flown out

of her mouth through no conscious effort on her part—strictly on their own. Beside her, she sensed her sister's start of surprise. At least Amy had the sense not to say a word.

"That's marvelous news," Lord Dashwood exclaimed. He bestowed his charming smile upon her. "I shall see you in London, then."

Her whole being felt uplifted. They might have to anchor her to the ground! But she must remain calm. Out of strict politeness she looked at Dashwood's friend and casually inquired, "And you, Lord Lynd, will you be coming for the Season, too?"

"I have an estate to manage, so I shall skip the so-called delights of the Season," he replied.

Lord Lynd had spoken lightly, yet Flora noticed no amusement in his eyes, but rather . . . How strange, but could that be concern?

Lord Dashwood laughed. "I fear the social life of London holds no interest for my friend. He would rather be on his horse, clomping around in his fields in the hot sun, than set foot in London, except for Tattersall's and the Four-in-Hand Club."

"Time to go, Dashwood," said Lord Lynd. There was a certain weariness in his voice that Flora did not understand.

Later, after all the guests had gone, Lady Rensley expressed her delight that Flora was coming to London for the Season. "What made you change your mind?"

"I'm not sure," Flora abruptly replied. Not for the world would she reveal her infatuation with Lord Dashwood.

"Well, whatever the reason, I am very glad, not only for your sake, but Amy's." A shadow of concern crossed her face. "Your sister doesn't attract suitors the way you do. If only she weren't such a little mouse."

"She's not a mouse," said Flora, hotly defending her sister. "When she's around us, she's not a mouse in the least. It's only when she's out in public she turns shy."

"True." In a rare instance of perception Lady Rensley added, "It must be difficult, having an older sister who's the belle of the ball. Doubtless Amy feels inferior because she's so plain."

"Exactly!" Flora heartily agreed. "Amy feels she's passed over. No wonder, the way everyone puts such a high value on shallow beauty. Why can't men see how witty she is? Why will they not notice the glorious poetry she writes? How kind and patient she is?" Flora grimaced. "Much more so than I."

Her mother sniffed, quickly returning to her usual insensitive self. "Well, she needs to be a little less dull and a bit more slender."

Flora heaved an inward sigh. "Don't worry. I shall keep an eye on her. She'll be fine." Flora knew her reassurance was oversimplified. The only possible way Amy could blossom would be if she, Flora, were married and out of the picture. A week ago, she would not have thought such a solution was possible. Now, thinking of Lord Dashwood, she wasn't so sure.

# Chapter 4

**London**

"Amy, you look"—Flora struggled to keep a straight face—"very nice."

"I do?" Amy, who was trying on her court presentation costume, turned, regarded herself in the mirror, and burst into laughter. She playfully tweaked one of the nine huge purple plumes of her elaborate headdress that Baker, their lady's maid, had just placed upon her head. "Oh, my stars, I look ridiculous."

"You look marvelous, and most appropriate," said the ever-sober-faced Baker, a stringent follower of all society's rules.

Flora silently agreed Amy looked ridiculous, although she would never say so. When she herself was presented at court, she railed at the costume she was forced to wear: the huge, high-waisted hoop skirt, of waxed calico over whalebone, three layers of skirts, and over them a skirt of pink satin so elaborately decorated there was hardly a spot that wasn't covered by lace, garlands of flowers, little tassels, or lavish embroidery. Worse was the headdress that had to be constructed according to the many strict requirements made by a court protocol that had to be absolutely obeyed. Since a minimum of seven plumes was required, her mother had insisted upon eight, just to be on the safe side. "Elaborate" was the key. Aside from the plumes, the headdress consisted of a garland of white roses upon a ringlet of pearls, a diamond comb, diamond buckles, and white silk tassels. Absolutely the worst of garish taste! To make matters worse, Flora, who adored the empire-waisted styles of the Regency, which were simplicity personified, was required to adorn herself with every piece of jewelry for which she could find a place. The result was an absurdity.

Flora hated wearing such ornate trappings atop her head, but at least, being tall, she could carry it off. Not so, short, chubby Amy, who now looked totally overwhelmed beneath the same headdress, subtly changed so that the plumes were pink instead of purple, and there were nine this time, so that their mother could be doubly reassured she had not broken any rule. "How can I even walk with these hoops and headdress?" asked Amy. "I fear I shall do my curtsy to the queen, lose my balance, topple over on my hoops, and roll out the door."

"Disgraced!" Flora laughingly replied. "Ruined forever! Poor Lady Amy Winton, banished to the countryside, never to show her face in society again, and all because of bad curtsying."

Amid peals of laughter, Lady Rensley entered the room and exchanged disapproving glances with Baker. "Girls, whatever are you talking about?" she asked, her forehead creased with concern. "Being presented at court is no laughing matter. You should be grateful you are given the privilege—"

"Yes, Mama, we know," both her daughters chimed. Flora, knowing how her mother worshiped protocol and was naturally upset by her daughters' flippant attitudes, hastily added, "It is indeed an honor. Amy looks fine and she'll do well."

Lady Rensley still appeared uneasy. "Just think of all the girls in England who would *die* for the chance to be presented at court but never will be." She left the room muttering, "I vow, I do not know how I could have raised two such ungrateful daughters."

When their mother had gone, Amy laughed again. "Court protocol or no, this headdress and high waist and hoops really are overdone." She pulled off the garish headdress and handed it to Baker. "Take it out of my sight, will you, please?"

She turned serious. "Despite this foolishness, the court presentation is well worth it." Her face wreathed in a smile. "I'm coming *out*, Flora! I'm a woman now, and not a little girl, at long last!" Her face fell as, standing in her soft batiste chemise, she examined herself in the mirror again. "But look at how fat and ugly I am. What's the use? No man would have me."

"That's not so," Flora instantly protested, most sincerely. "You've got lovely, soft gray eyes. Your skin is smooth as a petal, and you have hair that's a lovely shade of brown. So don't you dare say you're ugly."

"But I am." Amy ran her hands over her waist and down her hips. "Look at how short and squat I am. Why wasn't I tall and willowy like you? You have a bosom, whereas I am flat. Your waist curves in like an hourglass, whereas mine"—she punched her fingers at her waistline—"I've the shape of a tree stump."

Unfortunately, her sister was mostly right, Flora thought as she searched for something positive to say. Amy's figure did leave a lot to be desired, and her face, although certainly not ugly, was a bit pudgy, a circumstance brought on by Amy's unfortunate extra weight. But beauty wasn't everything. "Amy, you're as pretty as the next. Besides, you're lively, and witty, and you have a sparkling personality. I'd wager you will draw suitors in droves."

Amy sighed. "I shall find a husband, all right. But it won't be because of my beauty. I shall have suitors, but for only one reason."

"Your dowry." Flora sank thoughtfully to Amy's bed. "Papa is most generous. I can't dispute the drawing power of a dowry, but still, I would hope you'll marry a man you love, who loves you in return." She smiled gently. "Surely you'll find him." She felt a sudden ache in her heart for her sister, who was so beautiful in so many ways, with her generous nature, loyalty, and bright humor. But most men, being what they were, would not look beyond surface beauty to see such things. Flora sent up a silent prayer that some worthy man would see in Amy all her virtues and fall madly in love with her. She smiled brightly. "Just stop worrying about it and simply enjoy the Season. We shall attend every ball, every concert, every soiree. We shall have a marvelous time."

"And what of you?" asked Amy. Aware she alone knew Flora's secret, she lowered her voice. "What will you do if Lord Dashwood doesn't come to London?"

"He will come." Flora lifted her chin with confidence. "I

know something very special passed between us that day he and Lord . . . whatever-his-name-was came to call."

"Do you suppose he'll be at Almack's Wednesday night?"

"Surely he'll have a voucher."

Flora had spoken with a confidence she didn't feel. She had confided some of her feelings to Amy, but even her sister was unaware of the turmoil that churned within her whenever her thoughts focused on Lord Dashwood, an event that occurred more times than she cared to admit, even to herself. Day and night she thought of him, fixating on his handsome face, with its teasing little smile, his commanding presence, those London-tailored clothes that fit to perfection over his broad shoulders, slender waist, and long, muscular legs. She'd even tried to picture Pemberly Manor, where he lived when not in London. She'd never seen it, but she had heard it was known far and wide for its size and beauty. The estate wasn't Dashwood's yet—his cousin was still alive—but he would inherit someday. Often she tried to picture what Lord Dashwood's life at Pemberly Manor was like—his horse, even his dog. Or did he even have a dog? What was his bedchamber like? She tingled at the thought of it. Oh, yes, surely he had a bedchamber, and a bed. . . .

*He is lying beside her, looking down at her as she lies in her diaphanous gown beneath him. "Darling, how beautiful you look with your gorgeous hair spread across your pillow." He raises a thick strand of her hair, presses it to his lips, and with a shaking voice whispers, "My dear wife— how I must get used to saying it! I'm the luckiest man in the world, and I promise you I shall always be faithful."*

*"You mean you'll never have a mistress?"*

*"How could I, when I'm madly in love with you, my darling, and will be until the day I die?"*

*She gasps with pleasure as he runs his hand slowly along her thigh and bends to kiss her full on the lips. . . .*

"Flora, are you listening?"

Flora quickly removed herself from Lord Dashwood's bed. "Of course I'm listening. Almack's. Next Wednesday night. I'd wager my best ball gown he'll be there."

Lord Dashwood did not appear at the first ball at Almack's, nor did he appear anywhere at all.

A week went by, then two, then three. Committed to another Season, Flora went around with a gay smile on her face, pretending she was having a wonderful time at all the events she and Amy attended. But her only true enjoyment came from seeing Amy's awed reaction as she plunged into the glittering excitement of her first Season. Just as Amy predicted, the dandies did not swarm around, not in droves anyway, yet neither was she a wallflower, although Flora suspected more than one of her sister's suitors was attracted more to her dowry than her charm and beauty.

Flora kept smiling on the surface, but underneath she ached with an increasing inner pain. She hadn't realized how much she'd pinned her hopes on Lord Dashwood's coming to London. In truth, the thought that he wouldn't come had never crossed her mind. But as the third week of the Season came to an end, she faced the fact that she might not ever see him again. For a while she had made excuses. Perhaps duties on his cousin's estate had kept him away, or perhaps he was ill, or perhaps . . . But why fool herself? If he'd wanted to see her badly enough, he would have come to London, no matter what. Since he had not, doubtless he had met someone else. Her heart twisted at the thought. She hated being brutally frank with herself, but that might well be the case.

So here she was, *stuck* for another Season, going through the motions, not enjoying herself at all, except through the excitement of Amy's first Season.

At the beginning of the fourth week, Flora was standing on the sidelines at Lady Hemple's ball, thoroughly bored, when a strong male voice beside her said, "So we meet again, Lady Flora."

She turned. "Why, Lord . . . Lord—?"

"Lynd," he said, smiling easily down at her.

"Oh, yes, of course. Lord Lynd," she replied, hardly aware of what she was saying. Her pulse raced. Here was Dashwood's good friend who lived on the neighboring estate. They had been in Brighton together. Had they come to London together, too? Thank heaven, she was wearing her prettiest ball gown tonight. Oh, she must know, and quickly.

"So are you enjoying the Season thus far?" he asked.

It was the most mundane of questions, yet when she

looked into his inquiring brown eyes, she caught a genuine interest, as if he really cared whether she was enjoying the Season or not. Even beyond that, there was something about the way he looked at her that was sharp and assessing, as if there was much more he wanted to ask her than her opinion of the Season.

"I am having a lovely time, Lord Lynd, and you? Have you been in London long?"

"Just arrived."

His answer flooded her mind with questions. If he'd just arrived, had Lord Dashwood just arrived, too? Was he at the ball tonight? How could she ask without giving herself away? She wanted desperately to shift her gaze from Lord Lynd so she could scan the room, but that would be the height of impoliteness. She searched for something of interest to say. Forcing herself to keep her gaze directed into his eyes, she recalled his enthusiasm for four-in-hand. "Well, Lord Lynd, judging from our previous conversation, I am compelled to ask, did you drive your own coach to London, or did you allow your coachman his task?"

He lifted an eyebrow. "Ah, so you remembered my passion for four-in-hand, if not my name." She started to apologize, but he equitably continued. "I did, indeed, drive up from Kent by myself. Left my coachman at home."

"Do tell." He had caught her interest with his mention of four-in-hand. "Even in this foul weather?"

"It could be worse," he lightly replied. "I assure you, I'm not as bad as some. Did you know there are certain members of the *ton* who revel in being amateur coachmen? They drive the public stagecoaches with unflinching regularity, in all weathers. They delight in the opportunity to associate with professional coachmen, no matter what the sacrifice."

"I know just how they feel," she enthusiastically replied. "I would be mounting the box, handling the ribbons, bowling along the highroad, too, if it weren't for my . . . uh, gender." She had almost slipped and said that forbidden word—*sex*. She had the feeling he wouldn't have minded, though. He appeared unshockable. She liked that in a man. *Lord Lynd,* she repeated to herself, setting the name indelibly in her memory. She would not forget it again.

"There is no good reason why a woman could not drive a

coach-and-four," he was saying, "provided she had the
strength and was in good health." He smiled, as if he'd just
pictured something. "Although I can hardly picture you
touching your hat to the passengers, just as your regular
coachmen do, or even . . ." Lord Lynd looked briefly around
the room. "I see a young man or two in this very room who
would not even disdain the tip of a shilling or half crown."

He had sparked her interest, although lately her mind
had been on other things and she hadn't thought much
about four-in-hand. "You intrigue me, Lord Lynd. I understand perfectly. If ever I come back in another life, I should
like to be a coachman."

He nodded in agreement. "I, too. Although I doubt I
would go as far as one of our Four-in-Hand Club members,
Mr. Akers."

"Pray, what did he do?"

"The fellow was so determined to be looked upon as a
regular coachman he had his two front teeth filed."

"But why?" she asked. She stopped looking for Lord
Dashwood out of the corner of her eye. Lord Lynd had
her full attention.

"It's a matter of spittle," Lynd said, mischief in his eyes.
"I shall not go further. Far be it from me to offend your
delicate sensibilities."

She glanced around to make sure none of the chaperons
overheard before she firmly declared, "*Blast* my delicate
sensibilities. Rest assured, I shan't faint over spittle."

"Akers had his teeth filed so he could expel his spittle
between them, in the true fashion of our most distinguished
stagecoach drivers."

She burst into laughter, her first of the night. "Much as
I'd love driving four-in-hand, I'm not sure I would go to
that extreme."

An easy smile played at the corners of his mouth. "Perhaps you shouldn't. As enchanting as I find you, I might
be a tad put off if I saw you spitting between your filed
front teeth."

"Then, alas, I fear I must forgo the filing," she replied
with a light laugh. Lord Lynd really was amusing. She'd
hardly noticed him before, but now . . . She looked up into
his craggy face with the crooked nose—well, only slightly

crooked—and decided he wasn't bad looking by half, and most interesting, too, with a wicked sense of humor.

"Good evening, Lady Flora."

Lord Dashwood suddenly appeared before her. Her knees went wobbly. She had to catch her breath. She snapped open her fan and inhaled a big gulp of air, anything to disguise the dizzying constriction of her heart at the sight of him. "Why, Lord Dashwood," she managed, "how delightful to see you again."

He held out his arms to her. "Shall we dance?"

"I would love to." On a cloud of bliss, without a backward glance, she floated into his arms. The orchestra struck up a waltz as they started around the dance floor. As they danced, he gazed into her eyes, as if she were the only girl in the world. "I've thought of you many times," he murmured. "Would have come to London sooner, but certain matters delayed me."

"Oh, have you not been here?" she inquired, all innocence. " 'Pon my soul, I have been so wrapped up with the Season, I didn't notice."

"Then it appears I have my work cut out for me." He bent scandalously close. "Take notice, Lady Flora. From now on my chief goal will be to make you notice me." He squeezed her hand and looked deep into her eyes. "Surely you have not forgotten Brighton."

Flora was so stunned with delight her facade of indifference instantly fell away. For a moment she could not speak over the lump of excitement that formed in her throat. Finally, willing her voice not to shake, she managed, "Of course I haven't."

He pressed closer still. Surely by now the chaperons would be noticing this flagrant breach of propriety, but she carefully didn't look their way to find out.

"My sweet Aphrodite," he whispered in her ear. "My powerful enchantress, I remember every moment of Brighton."

In her flummoxed state, feeling his body close against her, she could only think to say, "Oh, really?"

Completely composed, he answered, "In Euripides' *Medea* the chorus sings, 'May you never launch at me, Lady of Cyprus, your passion-poisoned arrows, which no man

can avoid.' " He pulled back and gave her a smile so oozing
with warmth and charm she thought she might swoon on
the spot. "You see what you've done to me?"

She started to answer, but he pressed a gentle finger to
her lips. "No, not a word more tonight, my sea goddess. I
cannot bear such loveliness. I must leave."

The music stopped. His face became impassive as he pulled
away, led her back to Lady Rensley, bowed, and departed.

She wanted to cry after him, "But aren't we going to dance
again?" but contained herself and managed to remain silent
as she watched his massively broad shoulders disappear.

There was a stir in the crowd. Flora watched curiously
as a beautiful woman, dressed to the nines, more or less
floated into the ballroom, escorted by two of London's
leading dandies. "Who is she?" Flora asked.

"She's Countess Marie-Elizabeth de Clairmont," Lady
Constance Boles volunteered. "From France, although I
hardly need tell you that." From behind her raised fan,
Lady Boles continued. "Her mother was a mistress to the
king before she married Duke Clairmont. After, too. And
then"—she lowered her voice to a hissing whisper—"she
was guillotined in 1793. The Revolution, you know."

Flora refrained from an annoyed, "Of course I know,"
as Lady Boles warmed to her task. "Can you imagine?
Such a dreadful thing! So was her husband, the duke. Both
of them, off with their heads!"

"That is most unfortunate," Flora remarked, ignoring the
obvious relish in Lady Boles's voice. "Then how . . . ?"

"Their daughter was smuggled into England as a small
child. The poor thing is penniless, of course, although I
hear there's a fortune waiting for her—left by her father,
the duke—if she can ever get her hands on it."

"She certainly doesn't look penniless," Flora observed as
the countess conspicuously waved her oversized white
plumed fan and gayly tossed her head, causing gold tassels
to dance as they dangled from her gold and white crepe
turban. Clusters of diamonds dripped from her ears and
circled her neck. Her sheer yellow gown was a masterpiece
of undress, with an exceedingly wide V neckline that displayed a vast area between her ample, well-rounded breasts
and a good part of each breast itself.

"She may be penniless, but she does have certain resources, which she puts to good use," Lady Boles snidely remarked.

Amy giggled. "The countess had best not lean over too far, or her resources will fall out of her gown."

"I admire her audacity." Flora suppressed a smile and glanced down at her own bodice, cut low but modest compared to that of the countess. "If she's looking for a rich husband, I'm sure she'll do well."

Flora spent the rest of the evening in a daze, thrilled beyond belief, yet totally confused. Once, she saw Lord Dashwood approaching the countess. She felt a stab of jealousy but reminded herself that the dandies had been swarming around the Countess de Clairmont all evening. Some were even richer than Lord Dashwood would be someday, so it stood to reason if the countess was fortune hunting, Dashwood would not be at the top of her list. It was nothing to be concerned about, Flora told herself. Still, she wondered what they were talking about.

Countess Marie-Elizabeth de Clairmont's eyes lit upon Lord Dashwood, who had just approached and begged her current companion for an introduction. The plumed fan waved even faster as she tilted her head to one side, fluttered her long eyelashes, and gave him a dazzling smile. "*Mon Dieux!* I have just met zee most handsome man in London."

Dashwood bowed in his usual gallant fashion and kissed the countess's hand. "I am honored that one of the most beautiful women in London has chosen to flatter me."

"Only 'one of?' " The countess pouted. "Ah, well, I am but a poor refugee and should be grateful for the smallest of favors, *n'est pas?*"

"*Au contraire, mam'selle.* A woman like you could never be a 'poor refugee.' " Richard gave her a dazzling smile of his own. "You are looking positively radiant tonight. Shall we dance?"

Flora felt a tug of despair when she saw the countess melt into Dashwood's arms. They danced the next dance, too, and the next.

He never came back.

After the ball, when they were home again, and she was chatting with Amy about the events of the evening, Flora said

with a frown, "How could he call me his 'powerful enchantress' and then simply walk away and not dance with me
again?"

"It's a puzzlement," Amy agreed. "But I am inclined to
think . . . No, I shouldn't say anything."

Instantly alert, Flora demanded, "Speak up. Say what's
on your mind."

Still hesitant, Amy answered slowly, "We know Lord
Dashwood is as handsome as they come, and ever so
charming, but don't you think he's a bit . . . Well, the word
*effuse* comes to mind."

How could Amy think such a thing! Rarely did Flora
ever feel like snapping at her sister, but now was one of
those times. "I have no idea what you mean by effuse,"
she responded coldly.

Amy appeared to take a deep breath, as if she were
preparing to jump off a cliff. "What I mean is, all his fancy
words and quoting of poetry out of the blue I equate to
insincerity."

Flora quelled a sudden surge of anger. How dare Amy!
Could she not see that Lord Dashwood was near perfect in
every way? Still, she took a moment to consider, reminding
herself that over the years, Amy's perceptive remarks on
human nature had always been quite keen for one so
young, and her opinion should be respectfully considered.
But no! Her sister's opinion of Lord Dashwood was *wrong,
wrong, wrong!*

"I appreciate your concern, Amy, but in this case you
are mistaken."

Amy answered, "Forgive me for saying this, but I fear
you have a blind spot when it comes to Lord Dashwood.
Quite frankly, I think he's a bit of a wastrel."

Flora drew herself up. "Lord Dashwood is a well-
mannered gentleman who is a great credit to the English
nobility." Resentment welled within her. In a gust of emotion she could not control, she continued. "He is honorable,
creditable, altogether delightful, and"—the words burst
out—"how could you even imply he's not sincere? I would
stake my life that he is. If he only danced with me the
once, then he had good reason. Perhaps he was tired, or
not feeling well, or did not wish to monopolize my time."

Amy thoughtfully bit her lip. "Flora, forgive me for saying so, but I'm worried about you. You've always been so sharp-witted, and in most matters so temperate. It rather surprises me that when it comes to Lord Dashwood, you're not listening to reason."

Flora's anger deepened, but she had never argued with her sister, not since they were children, and would certainly not start now. "You have your opinion and I have mine. I have nothing more to say on the subject, so shall we talk of something else?"

Amy, always the tactful one, nodded in agreement. "Forgive me. That was just my humble opinion, and of course we'll change the subject."

"You're forgiven." Amy's words didn't really hurt because Flora knew she was wrong. But what caused that strange look that had flashed for the briefest of moments through Amy's eyes? Surely not concern, mixed with pity. Surely not that.

"I saw you talking to Lord Lynd tonight," Amy said.

*Lord Lynd.* Flora gasped and clapped her hand to her mouth. "Oh, no, I hadn't thought till now! I left him without saying a thank-you or good-bye—just walked off with Lord Dashwood and started dancing. How rude of me."

Amy shrugged. "A trifle rude, but I doubt you'll be banished from the *ton* because of it."

"I feel bad. Mama taught me better than that. It's not like me to forget my manners in such a fashion."

Amy smiled. "Could it be you were distracted by a certain enchanting gentleman whom we're not going to discuss?"

"Perhaps Lord Lynd didn't notice," Flora replied, ignoring Amy's comment. "After all, why would he care? Even if he had noticed, he's surely forgotten my slight social faux pas by now."

When Flora finally crawled into bed that night, she knew she'd have a hard time getting to sleep. Lord Dashwood liked her! She knew he did . . . Or did he? She would spend a restless tossing, turning night trying to figure him out. As for Lord Lynd, she really should apologize next time she saw him. And she certainly would, *if* she remembered.

In his London lodgings, Sidney yanked off his Hessian boots and dropped them with resounding thuds upon his

plush Axminster carpet. His valet had built a fire before
Sidney sent him to bed. Now he stretched his long legs
before it and remarked to his guest, "Well, Richard, it appears you were the darling of the ladies tonight, yet again."

Richard, equally at ease in front of the fire, smugly replied, "I was, wasn't I?" Looking exceedingly pleased with
himself, he took a leisurely sip from his brandy glass before
remarking, "Did you see me with Lady Flora?"

"I did, indeed." All of a sudden, Sidney realized he
gripped the stem of his glass so tightly it might break. He
forced himself to loosen his grip. "So how is your campaign
to marry the beautiful Lady Flora proceeding? Do you still
plan to capture the lady's heart?"

"My campaign is coming along quite well, thank you."
Richard's smile of satisfaction set Sidney's teeth on edge.

Richard set his glass on the gilt-wood side table and
clasped his hands dramatically to his heart. "Ah, my
dearest Aphrodite," he mockingly recited. "Ah, my powerful enchantress!"

"Don't tell me she believed such garbage."

"She's ready to fall at my feet, dear boy. I even quoted
Euripides—that always impresses them." He waved his
hand theatrically through the air. " 'May you never launch
at me, Lady of Cyprus, your passion-poisoned arrows,
which no man can avoid.' A nice touch, don't you agree?"

"If she believes your drivel, she's not as smart as I
thought she was. You're an ass, Richard."

Richard gave an elaborate shrug. "Am I really so terrible?
After all, I plan to marry the chit, unless something better
comes along. Not likely, though. Rumor has it her dowry is
more than plentiful." He leveled a keenly curious gaze at his
host. "You wouldn't happen to know, would you?"

Inordinately annoyed, Sidney snapped, "I have no idea
what Lady Flora's dowry is worth."

Richard looked genuinely puzzled. "See here, Sidney . . .
You don't have feelings for the young lady yourself, do
you? Because if you do—"

"Nonsense." Again, Sidney got a grip on his emotions.
"Are you sure you know what you want, Richard? Tonight
I saw you dancing with Countess de Clairmont, enjoying
yourself immensely, if I'm any judge."

"Ah, the countess!" Richard broke into a delighted

smile. "What a woman! That dress!" He kissed his fingers and flung the imaginary kiss into the air.

"Isn't she more your style?"

"Of course she is. I find her beautiful, delightful, enticing—all that, but, alas, the lady is penniless. Therefore, voilá! Lady Flora is more my style, that is"—he leveled a quizzical gaze at his friend—"are you sure you don't want her, Sidney?"

Sidney sighed wearily. "She's all yours, if you can catch her. I could not care less." *And I'm speaking the truth,* he assured himself. He had already recovered from the sharp disappointment he'd felt tonight when Lady Flora waltzed blithely away with Richard without so much as a word. Actually, what he was feeling was not disappointment so much as a natural reaction to her rudeness, which, if it had been some other young lady, he would have felt exactly the same. Of course, what made matters worse was that Lady Flora and he had been getting along famously, or so he had thought, talking about their mutual interest in four-in-hand, enjoying a laugh or two. All that before Richard appeared, of course.

The chit was besotted with Dashwood, that was obvious. *And I don't give a groat.*

Why should he, a titled landowner, rich, passably good-looking, give a thought to a young woman who was fast becoming enamored of his supposed best friend, and whose manners were atrocious?

Well, he shouldn't, he didn't, and he wouldn't.

A pox on Lady Flora Winton. He had more important things to think about than a completely hopeless cause. In fact, he'd only come to London in order to see the latest offerings at Tattersall's, and would not have dreamed of attending the ball had not Richard talked him into it. His attendance had nothing to do with Lady Flora.

*Sidney, you're a liar,* came a voice within, a voice he stilled immediately. He had too much pride to even think of entertaining lascivious thoughts about a rude young woman who didn't know his name and walked away from him. He might worry about her, though. Yes, he would permit himself to feel concern for that poor, weak girl who, because of her stubbornness and bad sense, was falling in love with one of the most devious rakes in all England.

# Chapter 5

Halfway through the Season, Flora sat in the drawing room of the family's London town house, taking tea with her parents and sister. It was one of the rare afternoons they were not receiving visitors or gone calling themselves.

"You seem quite cheerful of late, Flora," her mother said. "Don't you agree, George?"

"Quite," responded Lord Rensley. He eyed his older daughter over the top of his spectacles. "You've been seeing a lot of that Dashwood chap, haven't you? At least the fellow comes from an excellent bloodline. I suppose you know he's the heir presumptive of Charles Fraser, the Earl of Dinsmore?"

As usual, Flora's heart executed a flutter of excitement at the sound of Lord Dashwood's name. She chose to ignore the way her father said, "at least," although she wondered what he meant. "I have yet to meet Lord Dinsmore, but I have certainly heard enough about him. He's one of England's greatest heros."

"Indeed, the man's a legend." Her father harrumphed and signaled the butler. "Time for my pill, Trent, the 'Dr. Warens,' if you please. Bring it here." He returned his attention to Flora. "I could spend the day relating Dinsmore's exploits on the field of battle. Egypt . . . India . . . What a grand soldier he was. Most courageous!"

"And quite a dashing figure," added Lady Rensley.

"Now, alas"—Lord Rensley took the pill Trent proffered and washed it down with a swallow of tea—"poor health notwithstanding, I am better off than Dinsmore." As an afterthought, he muttered, "If you could believe such a thing."

"He's sick now, Papa?" Flora asked politely. She wasn't

too concerned over her father's health because her whole life she'd heard him complaining of various ailments that never seemed to materialize.

"Dinsmore's not sick," her father went on. "Last I heard, he was still in possession of his health. That is, he's not suffering from any disease. It's the injuries that keep him at his country estate most of the time." He shook his head and clucked with sympathy. "The man's a wreck. Lost an eye in Egypt. Got thrown from his steed at some battle or other in India and banged up his leg. Now he walks with a limp. At Seedaseer his face was slashed with a saber. He never looked right after that. I suspect that's what keeps him practically a hermit."

"Such a pity," chimed Lady Rensley. "I knew him before the scar and all those other dreadful wounds. Such a handsome man he was, and quite the swashbuckler. But now . . ." She shrugged and made a little moue. "The ladies used to swoon over him. Now they turn away in horror, what with that dreadful scar on his face. These days they swoon over his heir." She glanced fondly at Flora. "Popular though Lord Dashwood is, it appears our daughter has a definite edge."

To Flora's surprise, her father did not express his delight but instead issued an unresponsive, "Hmm."

She had to know. "You don't appear enthused in the slightest, Papa. May I ask why?" A touch of trepidation ran through her. Did her father find Dashwood less than perfect? If so, how could that possibly be? Didn't he realize how lucky she was that as the Season progressed, Dashwood was paying more attention to her? Such sweet torture she'd gone through at the beginning, after Lady Hemple's ball, when Dashwood kept her in a constant dither. One moment he appeared to adore her, the next she wasn't sure he even knew her name. She recalled the dreadful night at Almack's when he'd totally ignored her—not asked for one single dance! She had been so crushed, she spent much of the next day fighting the lump in her throat that wouldn't go away. But the next day he sent her a bouquet of roses, and that night at King's Theater, he appeared at the family's box, all charm and attentiveness. Invited to join them, he sat next to Flora, surreptitiously took her hand, and whispered such sweet compliments in her ear that when the great Catalani sang *Semiramide* she never heard a single note.

One day Amy remarked, "Flora, this isn't like you. I detest seeing you in this lovesick state."

"I am *not* lovesick," she protested, not willing to admit that when she thought of Lord Dashwood, which was most of the time, she, the fiercely independent Lady Flora Winton, grew weak-kneed with desire, sometimes to the point where she had to plead a headache and go lie limply upon her bed, giving herself up to fantasies of Lord Dashwood.

Her father said she needed a good physic.

Her mother blamed the dreadful London air.

Flora knew exactly what she needed. The question of whether or not she could capture the dapper Lord Dashwood was driving her mad.

Amy had continued. "Well, it seems to me he is just toying with you—attentive one minute, ignoring you the next. Like a cat with a mouse."

"I don't own him," Flora indignantly protested. "Not yet, anyway. I'm sure he'll come around."

Slowly he had. Lately, Flora's happiness had soared as Lord Dashwood appeared more often, obviously paying court. "Well, Papa?" she asked again, determined to find the cause for her father's long silence.

"Lord Dinsmore is of sterling character, no question," replied Flora's father, "but I'm not sure about his cousin."

"Whatever do you mean?" demanded Lady Rensley. "What are you not sure of? Really! He's titled, soon-to-be rich, and all that. What more could we ask for?"

"Of late, he's been most attentive," Flora contributed, her worry burgeoning. "I could very well marry him, Papa, so please, tell us why you sound so unsure."

Lord Rensley bluntly replied, "The man's a gambler."

"So are many in London."

"Not like Dashwood. *On-dit* has it he's not only deep in debt, he's a welcher."

Lord Dashwood? Flora was shocked and refused to believe such a thing. "That can't be true, Papa. I've never even heard him mention gambling."

"Of course he wouldn't, but I have it firsthand from the Duke of Bedford. Dashwood's been banned from the racecourse for defaulting on his bets."

"A misunderstanding, I'm sure," Lady Rensley protested.

"Is it?" Lord Rensley regarded his older daughter with concern. "I hope it's just a misunderstanding, Flora. Believe me, it would give me great pleasure to link our name with that of Lord Dinsmore. On the other hand, I've no wish to see you marry a decadent profligate who's only after you for your dowry, which is considerable, as you well know."

"He is not just after my dowry!" Flora set down her teacup with a clatter, sprang to her feet, and glared at her father. "Lord Dashwood possesses the most sterling integrity! What must I do to show you how honorable he is, how trustworthy, how much he genuinely cares for me?"

"You needn't do a thing, my child. Calm yourself. Sit down." With a wise smile, Lord Rensley continued. "I sincerely hope you're right. If you're not, time eventually sheds its light on matters of the heart."

"Then I know you'll soon see Lord Dashwood for what he's really like," answered Flora, sinking to her seat again, taking up her teacup, vastly relieved. She knew in her heart any misunderstandings there were could be easily cleared up.

Lady Rensley shifted to a more pleasant subject. "Meantime, George, Lord Dashwood has most kindly invited Flora to Vauxhall Gardens tomorrow night."

"Properly chaperoned, I trust?"

Flora's high spirits were quickly restored. "Mama and Amy are attending, too, so don't worry." She glanced playfully at her mother. "I'm sure Mama will track my every step. Tomorrow is a gala night at Vauxhall. They're paying tribute to military heroes. Lord Dashwood mentioned that Lord Dinsmore might join us."

"Dinsmore at Vauxhall?" Lord Rensley's face wreathed in a smile. "Splendid! I'll join you. Simply to meet the man is a great honor."

Lady Rensley interjected, "But be careful, Flora, that you don't flinch when you first see his face."

"Of course," Flora answered only half listening. She added as an afterthought, "Lord Dashwood said Lord Lynd should be there, too. So you can see, I shall be in good company."

"Lord Lynd," her father repeated. "Now, there's a man

of high moral character, if ever there was one. Widower . . . wealthy . . . titled . . . Why couldn't you show an interest in a fellow like Lynd?"

"Let us not even speculate." Lady Rensley regarded her daughters fondly. "What more could I want for my daughters than a love match for each, to a man highly suitable?"

*And that's just what you'll have, Mama.* Already, Flora had set aside her father's negative remarks concerning Lord Dashwood. No way could they be true. A tiny thrill ran through her. She had been to Vauxhall before, and had heard many a story about how easily a young couple could "accidentally" wander away from a chaperon and get lost in one of the many small, dark paths. Although she wasn't supposed to know, she'd heard of the most notorious of the walks, Lovers' Walk, which was dark and very narrow, where scandalous events, the nature of which she had a fairly good idea, took place. She wondered if she and Lord Dashwood . . .

*"Alone at last," Richard whispers, pulling her into his eager arms.*

*"Lord Dashwood, we mustn't—"*

*"The deuce we mustn't. I am desperate for you, Flora."*

*He pulls her close. He bends to kiss the pulsing hollow of her throat. Suddenly his lips are crushed against hers, and she revels in the feel of his kiss singing through her veins . . .*

"Watch out, Flora, you are about to spill your tea."

Flora quickly removed herself from Lovers' Walk, in time to see her cup was at a precarious angle. "Sorry, Mama. I was thinking about . . . what I was going to wear to Vauxhall's."

"May I ask why you've returned to London so soon, Sidney?" After a leisurely dinner at Watier's, Richard pushed his plate back and looked quizzically across the table at his friend. "You were at Tatt's less than a month ago, so I doubt you need another horse." His eyebrow raised suggestively. "My guess is, you've finally grown weary of the utterly boring countryside. You crave a bit of excitement, eh? Well, I say tonight we stay here and gamble. Later, we shall take ourselves over to Regent Street to see what we can find." He raised a lascivious eyebrow. "You know what I mean."

Sidney sighed wearily. "When will you learn? I did not come to London to fritter away my time with ladybirds."

"Do tell! Then why did you come?"

A good question, Sidney reflected. He had come to London because . . .

Richard was right. He had no need to visit Tatt's so soon again. In fact, he had no need to come to London at all. So why had he come? He hated to admit it, but Lady Flora was the reason. This past month since he'd been home, she had constantly been on his mind. Whether he was dining with a neighbor, or galloping across a meadow atop one of his thoroughbreds, or discussing the harvesting of the wheat crop with one of his tenants, thoughts of her crept, totally uninvited, into his head. Not smart, and most impractical. How very unwise to have such an interest in a woman who obviously cared for someone else. Or did she? Richard had not mentioned her once throughout dinner. Perhaps the relationship had cooled. Perhaps . . . ?

"So, Richard, how is your courtship of Lady Flora proceeding?"

A slow grin spread over his friend's face. "Even better than I expected. The poor girl is so enamored of me I've taken pity on her. I'm spending more time with her than I'd intended."

"How noble of you."

If Richard detected his subtle sarcasm he gave no indication. "Besides, I've got to marry soon. Confound it, I'm nearly rolled up."

"How fortunate Lady Flora's ample dowry will bail you out."

This time Sidney made no effort to conceal his contempt, but Richard seemed not to hear the sarcasm in his voice and glanced slyly around before he bent closer and confided, "Mark my words. By the time I finish, that dowry will be larger than it is already."

"How is that possible?"

"I've got Lady Flora so desirous of my . . . er, company, that if I reject her dowry, she'll have dear Papa selling off his land, if necessary, to up the ante so she can get what she wants. Just wait until I start the marriage negotiations. It'll be through Lord Dinsmore and his solicitor, of course, but I'll be in the background to help matters along. By the time we finish, her dowry will be fit for a queen, and her jointure, pin money—all that frippery women ask for—will be minimal, if nonexistent."

Richard sat back, wearing such a smug expression Sidney wanted to smack him. "Lord Rensley's a tough old bird. He would never agree to such an affront."

"He loves his daughters. He'll agree soon enough when he's witness to Flora's despair should she lose me."

Sidney could hardly control the combination of shock and outrage that welled within him. "That's despicable. Have you no shame?"

"Desperate measures for desperate times, my boy. Besides, where's the harm? I shall give her exactly what she wants, thus making her exceedingly happy and myself, as well. After all, not only shall I then have the wherewithal to pay my debts, I shall have the additional pleasure of bedding a woman who's not bad looking by half and quite lively. Should be fun, especially since she's madly in love with me." His lips curved into an infuriating grin. "What's wrong with that? By the way, did I tell you my esteemed cousin is in London? He's come mainly for the sales at Tatt's and the gala at Vauxhall's tomorrow night, where he said he'd join us. Fortuitous timing, don't you agree? He'll be here to help negotiate the dowry."

"Why didn't you tell me?" Sidney asked, delighted. Next to his own father, who had died two years before, he admired the Earl of Dinsmore more than any man in the world. "He's staying with you, of course."

Richard frowned. "He's at the Clarendon." At Sidney's quizzical glance, he reluctantly admitted, "He won't stay with me. I . . . have not been in his favor of late."

"Perhaps if you stopped wallowing in your unrestrained pursuit of pleasure, he might regain his respect for you."

Richard bristled. "Restraint is for fools. Rest assured, despite our differences, Dinsmore is more than pleased I'm planning to wed. He's anxious to meet Lady Flora. It appears he thinks marriage will bring some, what he calls 'stability' to my life." He laughed and continued. "He's so old-fashioned I doubt he ever once cheated on his wife. What a fool. Look what he missed."

Sidney threw down his napkin and rose from the table. "I cannot stomach this. Good night, Richard."

"Cool off, Sidney," Richard, jovial as ever, called after him as he left. "Come with me to Vauxhall Gardens tomorrow night. I shall need your help. I want to get the lady alone long enough to propose."

"Rot in hell!" Sidney flung over his shoulder as he strode out, his anger turning to scalding fury as he thought of Richard's loathsome plan to capture Lady Flora. He quickly regained control. By the time he reached his lodgings, he had not only calmed himself, he was searching his innermost self as to why he'd had such a violent reaction to Richard's revelation of his devious scheme. Rarely, if ever, did Sidney lose his temper. That he had done so tonight was a cause not only of puzzlement but great concern. He was *not* in love with Lady Flora, even though he had to admit he found her deucedly attractive. Still, why he should react to Richard's plan with such vehemence was beyond him, other than that he, being an honorable gentleman, would doubtless react the same upon hearing of any lady treated so abominably.

Honor carried a heavy price, though, he mused. For one thing, it decreed he could never reveal the confidences of a friend. But even if he did choose to reveal the truth about Richard to Lady Flora, he had been in the world long enough to realize that in her love-besotted state, she, stubborn wench that she was, would never listen to reason.

Still, he *would* go to Vauxhall with Richard, if for no other reason than to see his idol, Lord Dinsmore, once again. As for the feckless Lady Flora, she would doubtless ignore him. Ha! He would consider himself fortunate if she remembered his name.

Regardless, if he could help in any way, he would do so. Beyond that ... Yes, he was loathe to admit it, but he looked forward to seeing her again. He felt a stir of yearning deep within himself just thinking about—curse Richard for giving her such a ridiculous appellation!—but, yes, beautiful Aphrodite rising from the sea in that clinging wet bathing costume.

That evening, as Flora strolled along The Grand Walk in Vauxhall Gardens, she felt giddy with delight, almost beyond all reason. But then, she wondered, why shouldn't she be giddy? On this glorious warm evening it seemed nearly every member of the polite world had come to Vauxhall. All were dressed to the nines in their jewelry and fancy clothes. All, it seemed, were staring in her direction, some boldly, some surreptitiously, but staring all the same. Without doubt, she was the center of attention, and all because Lord Dashwood hovered close beside her, bending toward her attentively, gazing at her adoringly. How the *on dit* would fly tomorrow! That one of England's most eligible bachelors was openly courting her, there could be no doubt. *He loves me!* Her heart raced with excitement. *He might even propose tonight.*

"Aren't the gardens lovely tonight?" Lady Rensley called from where she, Lord Rensley, and Amy were strolling close behind.

"Indeed, Mama," Flora answered exuberantly. She had attended the gardens several times, thoroughly enjoying the fairyland spectacle of walkways lined with tall trees, incredible numbers of globe lamps casting a myriad of lights, glorious music, the Chinese Pavilion, fountains, dancing, entertainment, fireworks, and patrons beautifully dressed. But tonight held a special magic. Never had she felt more thrilled as she strolled past the statue of Handel, toward the amphitheater in the middle of the garden, her hand lightly resting on Lord Dashwood's arm. Never had she felt so happy, so gloriously alive.

"You look beautiful," Lord Dashwood whispered in her ear, bending intimately close.

"And you look marvelously handsome, sir," she lightly replied, giving a silent thanks to Baker, who had spent diligent hours dressing her in a pale green crepe gown, worn over white satin. It had long sleeves of white crape, and was ornamented around the bottom with an appliqué of white satin decorated with crescents of flowers. Baker had arranged her hair in a simple but elegant style, curled in ringlets around her face, and in back, very full curls confined with a pearl comb. Pearl earrings, white kid gloves, and white satin shoes with gold rosettes completed her outfit. Flora knew she looked her best.

Lord Dashwood spoke again. "I've a feeling this will be a special night." He took her gloved hand and lightly ran his finger across the back, causing a wild current of desire to run through her veins. "Very special. I warn you, my beautiful Lady Flora, I plan to get you alone."

She felt such joy she could hardly contain herself, but managed to whisper back, "But you know such conduct is not appropriate."

He squeezed her hand. "Who cares what's appropriate when one is in love?"

He loved her! He had said so. Throughout the early evening, as Flora, her parents, sister, and Lord Dashwood dined in one of the small booths in the middle of the garden, Flora was so excited she lost her usually healthy appetite.

"Are you not feeling well?" inquired Lady Rensley, pointing to Flora's untouched plate of thinly sliced ham, assorted biscuits, fruits, sweetmeats, and cheese cake.

"Perhaps it's the excitement, Mama."

"And no wonder," helpful Amy exclaimed. "Just think, an orchestra with over a hundred musicians! All that music, dancing, fireworks"—she slanted a knowing glance at her sister—"almost too much to bear, isn't it, Flora?"

"Oh, indeed, I . . ." There was a stir in the crowd. Flora saw that everyone was looking toward the entrance.

Lady Rensley remarked, "Someone important must be coming. Prinny, do you suppose? Or . . . Oh, look!"

"It's my cousin and Lord Lynd," said Lord Dashwood. He rose from the table as they all did. "High time you met the old gentleman. Be prepared for . . . Well, you'll see."

# Chapter 6

Looking toward the entryway, Flora recognized Lord Lynd, who was following an older man resplendently attired in a uniform consisting of white breeches, red jacket abundantly decorated with gold braid, plumed hat, and a sword at his side. A swelling murmur arose from the crowd, then swelling applause and warmly shouted greetings as the Hero of Seedaseer acknowledged the crowd with a modest wave and small nod. He paused, and with the utmost equanimity took his time to gaze about the amphitheater. Not until he spotted Dashwood and started toward their booth did Flora perceive he walked with a decided limp and leaned heavily on a cane. She noted, though, that despite his affliction, he had a regal bearing about him, a spring of confidence in his step. Lord Dashwood was wrong. His appellation of "old gentleman" simply did not fit. Unlike her father, this man was not baldheaded, nor all soft and out of shape. Rather, he was lean and sinewy. Not only that, even though he was sixty at least, there was an alertness about him, and a toughness she could sense from clear across the garden.

Her mother nudged her. "Don't flinch when you meet the man. He's not a pretty sight."

As Lord Dinsmore drew closer, Flora saw that a black eyepatch covered his left eye. There was something about his face . . . How awful! Flora fought to hide her revulsion, but it was hard not to react to the first startling sight of the hideous scar that cut a jagged, puckered path from the corner of Dinsmore's good eye, down his cheek, to the bottom of his chin. It was the ugliest scar she had ever seen. To make matters worse, his deeply tanned face was a weatherworn map of deep wrinkles, no doubt a permanent

reminder of his arduous life in the military. *So grotesque!*
She was truly taken aback, but because of all the warnings,
she managed to keep her own face a mask. When Lord
Dashwood greeted his illustrious cousin and began the introductions, she put on her most pleasant smile.

"I am so delighted to meet you, sir," she recited with
great aplomb. She bobbed her best curtsy, proud she hadn't
flinched at the sight of the man's disfigurement or shown
her horrified reaction in the slightest way. "I have heard
so many wonderful things about you."

"Have you now?" Lord Dinsmore asked in a deep, reso-
nant voice that was polite enough, yet contained an acerbic
edge. He did not smile in return. The piercing gaze from
his one good eye drilled into her, sending a message that
clearly read, *Beware. I do not tolerate pity.*

She suddenly felt gauche, as if he knew exactly what she
was thinking. "Indeed I have, sir," she answered, not quite
as confident as before. She plunged ahead. "Who has not
heard of your heroic feats in India at the battles of Seedaseer and . . . uh, Argaum."

"I did not fight at Argaum," Lord Dinsmore stated, regarding her with a granite-eyed stare. "That was
Wellington."

"Oh, of course not. It was . . ." Her mind went blank.
Panic swept through her. Frantically she searched her memory for the correct name of the battle. "Uh  . . ." Damnation! *What* was it?

"Assaye," supplied Lord Dinsmore, his one eye examining her as if she were utterly witless and had just crawled
out from under a rock.

"Oh, yes, Assaye," she answered, feeling the complete
fool. She had wanted Lord Dashwood's cousin to like her,
but, alas, she'd gotten off to a terrible start.

As introductions were made all around, Flora caught
Lord Lynd's eyes upon her. Such kind eyes! She was glad
he was there. She dropped a curtsy and murmured, "Lord
Lynd, how delightful to see you again."

An expression of surprise, mixed with amusement,
crossed his face. She had no idea why. He bowed and said
with a wry smile, "And I you, Lady Flora. How delightful
you remembered my name."

For an instant his smile intrigued her, but her attention quickly returned to her gaffe with Lord Dinsmore. "I hope I didn't offend him," she whispered to Lord Lynd.

"The man has been through the horrors of war countless times," Lynd whispered back. "It's not likely he would fly into a pet over a young lady's momentary lapse of memory."

"Er, hrmph!" began her father as he addressed Lord Dinsmore. "We are honored, sir, to be in the presence of one of England's greatest heros. Such gallantry as yours—"

"My days of glory are long gone, Rensley." Dinsmore had broken in so brusquely, Lord Rensley was visibly taken aback. With a cynical laugh, Dinsmore continued. "Take a good look. Do you see a bloody hero standing before you or do you see a crippled, half-blind old man?"

" 'Pon my word, I see a hero," exclaimed Lord Rensley in a reverent, ringing tone that made Flora proud. Her father wasn't perfect, but he never allowed himself to be intimidated and always stood up for what he thought was right. "All England owes you its gratitude," her father went on. "Once a hero, always a hero, sir. Nothing will change that."

Dinsmore appeared to concede, or at least not argue, and awarded her father a mocking bow. "Then I accept your accolade, sir, and offer my apologies. My public appearances are few these days, and my social skills rusty."

"Lord Dinsmore was never one for public gatherings," contributed Lord Dashwood, who had not lost his composure in the slightest, despite his cousin's brusque behavior.

Lady Rensley, looking definitely uncomfortable, said to her husband, "Shall we take a stroll?"

"Of course, my dear. We shall go directly," said Lord Rensley.

"We shall accompany you," Lord Dashwood said.

Good, thought Flora. She would love to take a stroll with Lord Dashwood and in the process get away from his abrasive cousin. War hero or no, Lord Dinsmore was making her feel horribly uncomfortable.

To her astonishment, Lord Dashwood turned to Amy.

"May I escort you, Lady Amy?" He flicked a glance at Flora. "We shall give Lord Dinsmore and Lady Flora a chance to become better acquainted."

Flora was assailed by a rush of mixed feelings as her sister nodded a yes. How wonderful that Lord Dashwood wanted her to become better acquainted with the man who had practically raised him! That could mean only one thing. Still, she watched, dismayed, as everyone left. Even Lord Lynd moved away, leaving her alone with this singular man, one of England's greatest heros, to whom, at the moment she could think of nothing to say.

She stood nonplussed before she remembered her manners. "Won't you sit down, Lord Dinsmore? We have finished eating, but I'm sure the warder can bring—"

"Not necessary. I wanted to have a word with you. It shouldn't take long." Dinsmore slid his cane under the table, sat down, and motioned for her to sit.

As she did so, she decided that first she would further apologize. "I regret I forgot the name of the battle. Call it a momentary slip. I know that battle very well."

"Do you, now?" Lord Dinsmore raised a skeptical eyebrow. "I would have thought well-brought-up young ladies confined themselves to the study of watercolors, music, and the like, not bloody battlefields."

"I am the despair of my mother," she replied with a smile, making light of it, and proceeded to describe the Battle of Assaye in some detail, ending with, "You led your battalion through the thick black jungles of the Coorga Country, into the jaws of battle. Eighteen thousand of the Tippoo sultan's best troops opposed you, led by the sultan himself. But did you retreat? No! You bravely stayed the course and won the battle, and then . . ."

By the time she finished, Dinsmore's face had lost its skepticism. He looked impressed. "Is that the only battle you are familiar with?"

She had not meant to show off her considerable knowledge of England's greatest battles, but being a student of history would surely not hurt her at this point. When she mentioned Waterloo, they engaged in a lively discussion concerning the tactics of Napoleon. Minutes went by in which she enjoyed herself thoroughly, almost forgetting the importance of making a good impression on the esteemed cousin of the man she adored.

He said finally, "I admire your knowledge of military history, Lady Flora. It is indeed a pleasant surprise to meet a London belle who has something on her mind besides herself."

"I grow tired of being considered a flighty London belle, sir," she said, none too kindly. "I do have a mind."

"It is obvious you do, and a keen one," he answered with sincerity. "Now, since time is short, we must get down to business, but I trust that someday soon we shall talk history again." His one good eye assessed her boldly. "As you may know, I have acted as guardian and mentor to Lord Dashwood since his parents died. I feel more like a father to him than a cousin, and thus am always concerned for his welfare. He has expressed an interest in you. Tell me frankly, what do you think of him?"

Where were his manners? His directness was making her distinctly uncomfortable. Still, he was Lord Dashwood's distinguished cousin, obviously concerned, and she would grow to love him and always be exceedingly polite. "I love Lord Dashwood, sir, with all my heart."

He looked skeptical. "No man is perfect, including Richard. So tell me, what do you love about him?" Dinsmore signaled a waiter. "Bring me a brandy. Something for you, my dear?" She shook her head. "I'm waiting." He sat back expectantly.

Certain she was on sure ground, she plunged ahead with great enthusiasm. "I love him for his sunny disposition, his noble demeanor, his impeccable manners, the way he dresses—always so well tailored, his cravat perfectly tied, and . . . and . . ." As she talked, she'd noticed Dinsmore's mouth slowly curve into a faint, disbelieving smile. "You don't believe me?"

"You seem to be an intelligent young woman," Dinsmore replied, "and yet . . . well tailored? Impeccable manners? Are those your measurements of a man? I find it strange that those frivolous traits are the ones you appear to deem most important."

She immediately saw where she had erred most grievously. "Oh, but there are other things, too! Lord Dashwood is honorable, trustworthy, dependable, truthful . . ." As she searched for more metaphors, he regarded her oddly. She glanced down. Oh, dear! In her zeal, she had clutched his arm and still gripped it tightly, her white-gloved fingers resting in stark contrast to the scarlet of his sleeve. What was she thinking of? she wondered, quite horrified that she had possessed the temerity to touch the aloof, untouchable Hero of Seedaseer. Yet another faux pas. She withdrew her hand, as fast as if she'd touched a hot coal. "My apologies. I didn't mean—"

"Don't apologize." After a silence, he said in an odd but gentle tone, "It's not often a beautiful young woman touches me without flinching."

For a moment his poignant words left her speechless. What was she supposed to say?

"You needn't say anything," he replied as if he'd read her mind. "I am more aware of my disfigurement than you. I know how horrified you must be, sitting there, having to act polite when all the time you wish you could avert your eyes."

"But . . ." She paused to get her words right, knowing she must be scrupulously honest. This man was much too perceptive for any kind of flattery, fancy words, or half truths. "I cannot deny you have a disfigurement, but as I sat here talking to you, it faded in importance. I truly mean that."

Lord Dinsmore was silent for a moment. When he spoke again, his mocking tone had vanished. "I can see you're sincere."

"Of course I'm sincere." How could he think she was not? But before she could ask, her family returned, along with Lord Dashwood. The music began and he asked her to dance.

No sooner was she in his arms, away from the booth, when he inquired, "So what do you think of Lord Dinsmore?"

"He's rather strange, but I like him."

Lord Dashwood smiled. "That's good, considering . . ." He glanced around. They were on the opposite side of the dance floor, out of sight of her family. He stopped dancing but kept hold of her hand. "Quick. Come, we are going for a stroll."

Words of protest rose to her lips. She shouldn't. Such behavior was not appropriate. Her mother would not approve. She said nothing, though, as, her heart beginning to pound, he led her quickly off the dance floor.

Soon she was on a path that was growing progressively

darker, Lord Dashwood close beside her, dance music wafting in her ears. An occasional couple drifted by, laughing in the darkness. She whispered, "I have never done this before."

"Time you should." His arm slid around her shoulder as they progressed down the path. His fingers rested on her upper arm, not moving at first, then gently caressing. "Your skin, so soft, like a rose petal," he whispered in her ear.

*Not appropriate!* Her mother's voice rang loud in her ears, but when they came to a stop and Dashwood's arms crept around her, she was helpless to resist. He kissed her forehead, sending a shock wave through her entire body. With tantalizing persuasion, he feather touched his way down to her lips, then roughly seized her to him as his mouth hungrily covered hers. Almost of their own volition, her arms crept around his neck. She returned his kiss eagerly, forgetting what her mother had said, forgetting everything except the strong hardness of his lips and the masculine feel of his body, so intimately close—she had never been this close to a man before!

He finally lifted his lips from hers, long enough to murmur in a breathless voice, "My darling, how beautiful you are."

"We shouldn't be doing this," she managed, making no effort to break from his embrace.

"Ah, but we should! You *are* going to marry me, aren't you?"

A soft gasp escaped her. She could hardly keep from laughing aloud with joy. "This is a proposal?"

"What else would you call it?" He nuzzled her ear with his nose. "Would you prefer I beg you on bended knee in your stuffy drawing room, or here, where I can . . ." He seized her again and kissed her soundly. Her emotions whirled and skidded as his hands caressed the soft lines of her back, her waist, her hips, then started up again. She felt transported on a soft, wispy cloud until, in a moment of truth and clear introspection, she realized what she was doing and with a gigantic effort seized his wrists and pushed him away.

"Stop," she whispered. "We cannot."

"It's only that I love you so much I cannot stop myself." He started to embrace her again, but she held him back.

"No! Oh, much as I would like to, this is wrong and I cannot."

He appeared to consider a moment, his breathing coming fast. "Of course you cannot. Forgive me. It's just . . . Your beauty has swept me away. I shall speak to your father tomorrow. I don't think he likes me. Do you suppose he'll have me?" He uttered a small, wry laugh that wrenched her heart.

"Of course he'll have you!" she replied with heartfelt meaning. "I shall inform him that should I lose you, my heart would break and I would pine away." She had to touch him. With great forbearance, she allowed her fingers to rest lightly on his arm. "I love you, Lord Dashwood—"

"Call me Richard."

"I love you, Richard," she said, savoring the sweet words she had never said to a man before. Such a wonderful moment! "I shall love you until the day I die."

"Then it's settled." His voice had lost the hoarse shakiness of passion and returned to normal. He took her arm, and they started back along the path. "If your father allows—"

"Of course he will." A small doubt nagged her, but she could not believe her father would stand in the way of her happiness.

"Then we shall begin the dowry negotiations immediately. Shouldn't take long. Just think, in but a few weeks we'll be man and wife."

"Promise, not a word until we receive Papa's blessing."

"Of course not."

Flora's mind was full as they returned to her family. They hadn't been gone long. She didn't think they'd been missed until her mother drew her aside.

"Well, Flora?" Lady Rensley eagerly inquired.

Nothing escaped her mother. She shouldn't have been surprised. "Oh, Mama, he asked! You mustn't tell though, not until Lord Dashwood comes calling tomorrow and formally asks for my hand."

Lady Rensley clasped her hands in front of her. She looked as if she could burst with joy. "We've caught an heir presumptive! Titled! Soon-to-be rich!"

"And handsome, besides," Flora added with satisfaction. "And altogether wonderful." Just one small shadow marred her bliss. "Sometimes I get the feeling Papa isn't overly fond of Lord Dashwood. I do hope he'll give his consent."

"I've no doubt but that he will." Lady Rensley caught sight of her dear friend, Lady Constance Boles and started fanning herself vigorously with her small daisy fan. "I am *dying* to tell. How can I keep quiet until tomorrow?"

"You must, but only until tomorrow. When Papa gives his blessing, we shall tell the world."

Flora spent the rest of her evening at Vauxhall in a blissful haze. In the arms of Dashwood, she danced every dance. She was so happy she didn't mind a bit when the flamboyant Countess de Clairmont, wearing a gown even more daring than the yellow sheer, made her usual grand entrance, a dandy on each arm.

"Go dance with her if you like," Flora told Dashwood after the countess cast a long, flirtatious gaze at Flora's newly betrothed. "I shall never be one of those jealous wives."

Her beloved looked down at her, eyes brimming with tenderness. "It's you I love, now and forever. I shall never give you the slightest cause for jealousy."

How sweet life was! She could hardly wait until tomorrow when she could tell the world.


Next morning, Flora awoke in a wonderful mood. At breakfast, in a frenzy of anticipation, she made her mother and sister promise not to say a word to her father concerning Dashwood's intentions.

"It's best Papa be properly surprised," she said, "so he has no time to mull. He is nothing if not polite. I cannot imagine that when Lord Dashwood personally asks for my hand, he could summon the audacity to refuse."

"But what if he does?" Amy asked.

She replied with firmness, "We shall cross that bridge when we come to it."

Society's rules forbade Dashwood arriving for his visit in the morning, but by one o'clock, the hour when a visitor could properly call, Flora could not keep herself from peeking out the town house window that faced the street. By two o'clock, she was pacing the drawing room, her nerves in shreds. By three, she declared, "I vow, I shall sink into a decline if I must wait a moment longer."

"Then let's go for a walk in the park," Amy said. "After all, you don't have to be here. Lord Dashwood is coming to see Papa, not you."

Lady Rensley frowned. "But it's only three o'clock. And if Lord Dashwood is asking for your hand, shouldn't you be here? Oh, dear, I do not know if it's suitable—"

"Amy and I are going," Flora declared, grateful for her sister's suggestion. "Mama, you stay, but I must get out of here before I lose my mind."

"You were smart to get away," said Amy as she and Flora strolled toward the park, Baker close behind. "We shall go for a long, long walk. Just think, by the time we return, Lord Dashwood will have talked to Papa."

"It's the most important thing in the world to me," said Flora. "I love him so much. If anything goes wrong—"

"Stop worrying. Think ahead. Imagine what it will be like when he takes his cousin's title. Just think, you'll be Lady Flora Dinsmore, esteemed wife of Richard, Lord Dinsmore, mother to his . . . How many children would you like to have?"

"Umm, five, I think. The heir first, of course, then a girl, and so on."

"You'll live at Pemberly Manor. What's it like, do you suppose?"

Flora knew her sister was only trying to distract her, but her thoughts easily drifted to the grand estate in Kent where someday she would be mistress. "Lord Dashwood has told me it's many acres of trees and rolling hills. The house itself is said to be quite magnificent, so many rooms he never counted, he once said. I picture high-ceilinged rooms with Italian painted murals, scrolled moldings, and elegant crystal chandeliers."

"There must be tons of lovely china, crystal, and silver-ware. Do you suppose Lord Dinsmore uses it much?"

"I doubt he entertains much. He's been a widower for years." An image of Dinsmore's face flashed through her mind. "No doubt everything's put away, ready for the day a new mistress will put it to use. Just think Amy, that will be me!" Her words set her to thinking. . . .

*"The guests are arriving, m'lady."*

*"Thank you, Jeffers." Dressed to perfection and beautifully coiffed, she awaits her guests serenely in the marbled, vaulted entryway, her five beautiful, blond, blue-eyed children standing obediently by her side.*

*"This will be another glorious night, m'lady!" There is a gleam of excitement and pride in the butler's eyes. "After all these years, you have brought Pemberly Manor to life again. Never have I seen such a marvelous hostess as you. Your fetes are the talk of the countryside, if not all England."*

*"Jeffers is right," Lord Dashwood calls as he descends the wide, gracefully curving staircase, its mahogany railing polished to a high gleam. He slides a loving arm around her waist. "How I bless the day we met, my darling. I cannot thank you enough for giving me five intelligent, beautiful, well-behaved children! I love you more each day. What would I do without you . . . ?"*

"Watch it, Flora!" Amy pulled her back from the street to the curb as a dray came hurtling by. "Do you want to get squashed flat?" she asked crossly. "I vow, your day-dreaming will get you killed someday."

Flora hardly noticed. "Dreams do come true, Amy. They really do."

They were gone two hours. Flora couldn't wait to get home. Lord Dashwood would have been there by now, talked to her father. At this very moment, without question, she was officially betrothed.

The town house was silent as they stepped inside. "Where is her ladyship?" Flora asked the butler.

"She has a headache, m'lady, and has gone upstairs to rest."

How strange. Her mother never had a headache. "His lordship?"

"In his study."

Just then the doors to the study flew open. "Flora!" Her father wore a broad smile.

"He's been here?" she asked.

"Indeed, he has."

"And did you give your permission?" There could be only one answer, but still, she held her breath.

"Of course I gave permission. How could I not?"

"Oh, Papa!" Flora threw her arms around her father and gave him a hug.

"You see?" Amy joyously exclaimed. "All that worry for nothing."

A cry of relief broke from Flora's lips. "How could I have been so foolish as to have harbored even a scintilla of doubt! Oh, Papa, you must know how deeply I love Lord Dashwood."

"Lord Dashwood?" Her father frowned, his eyes troubled under drawn brows.

"Of course, Lord Dashwood."

"It was not Lord Dashwood who came here today."

With a sense of impending doom, she asked, "What do you mean?"

"I don't understand." Lord Rensley looked deeply perplexed. "The decision is yours, of course, but I just gave my permission for you to marry Lord Dinsmore, the Hero of Seedaseer."

# Chapter 7

Through the west windows of Sidney's London lodgings, specks of dust danced in rays cast by the late-afternoon sunshine. Seated in his drawing room, Sidney was deep into reading a tome on ancient history, a most welcome distraction from the unsettling events of the night before at Vauxhall Gardens. The doorbell rang. He was curious. Nobody called at this unfashionable hour. Moments later, Carlton, his valet, appeared, followed by Richard.

Sidney closed his book and rose to greet his guest. "What a surprise. It isn't like you to call at this hour." He noted his friend's unsmiling face. "Is something wrong?"

Richard slung himself into Sidney's Louis XV gilt-wood chair. "I warn you right now, you had better refrain from your usual snide remarks. I am not in the mood." He looked toward the valet. "Bring me a brandy, Carlton." Slumping his long body further in his seat, he stretched his legs straight in front of him with a heavy bang of his heels. "Quickly. Drat, what a mess!"

Sidney sat down again. "Last I saw you, you were in fine fettle, about to propose to the beautiful Lady Flora. Don't tell me she refused."

"Oh, God, if only she had," Richard said with a groan, momentarily covering his face with his hands. "Of course she accepted."

"So you're betrothed." Sidney was struck by a sick feeling in the pit of his stomach, which he hastened to conceal.

"Yes and no. Well, no."

Damnation! Where was this leading? Carlton reappeared. Sidney waited while his agitated friend took a healthy slug of brandy. "So tell me what's occurred. I am all ears. I cannot imagine—"

"I am not to be blamed for any of this," Richard vehemently declared.

"Will you kindly tell me what's occurred?" Sidney was losing patience fast.

"It was the countess's fault, not mine."

"The countess," Sidney repeated, squeezing his eyes shut in exasperation. "For pity's sake, get on with it. Start from the beginning."

"As you know, I proposed to Lady Flora."

"And she gave you a definite yes?"

"Of course she said yes." Richard regarded him as if he were a candidate for Bedlam. "You know she's madly in love with me. She was thrilled, I can assure you."

Sidney chose to ignore the arrogance. This was Richard, after all. "So what happened next?"

"As you are aware, I have always been fond of the Countess de Clairmont. I find her a most desirable woman."

"You and half the men in London."

Richard bristled. "The Countess de Clairmont is a respectable woman. Granted, a bit flamboyant, but with her lineage and title, she's *accepted,* Sidney. You *know* how the *ton* idolizes all things French. Makes all the difference in the world."

"True enough." *Get on with it.*

"For years the countess has been in desperate straits financially, albeit she has always held out hope for recovering at least part of her father's estate."

"Stolen during the Revolution after the duke lost his head."

"Exactly. Poor sod was filthy rich. Not only did he own a large estate near Dijon, he possessed a vast fortune in artwork of all descriptions, jewels, antiques, and the like, as well as cash." Richard's eyes sparked. "A huge fortune, Sidney!"

"So?"

"So last night, after Lady Flora and her family left Vauxhall Gardens, I stayed on for a while. How could I not? The countess had been giving me a come-hither look all evening. You know what I mean. Naturally, I asked her to dance. It was then she told me her astounding news. Through faithful friends she has recovered much of her father's wealth! Not the estate near Dijon, of course. During the troubles, it was confiscated. But the rest! Jewels, artwork, gold coins, all hidden away. Faithful followers of the duke finally tracked them down. The fortune has just been shipped to England. So, *voila!* The Countess de Clairmont is suddenly very wealthy, indeed."

"Fine. I'm happy for the countess, but how does that pertain to you?"

Richard straightened out of his slump, his confidence restored. "She adores me. Always has. She knew I'd never marry her without a dowry, but last night she could hardly wait to inform me of the favorable changes in her fortune. She made it abundantly clear she would be delighted if I proposed and would accept in an instant. Practically threw herself at my feet. I would have proposed on the spot, if I had not . . . er, apparently indicated earlier to Lady Flora I wanted to marry her."

"Indicated!" Now Sidney sat straight. "What do you mean, indicated? Did you propose to Lady Flora or did you not?"

Richard rolled his eyes to the ceiling and back. "Er . . . The thing is, there's a delicate difference here. I cannot deny that I did propose, but we were not yet betrothed."

"And why not?"

"Because I had not yet spoken to her father. Don't you see? If Lord Rensley had not yet given permission, then how could we be officially betrothed?"

"Talk about splitting hairs!"

Richard sprang from his chair and started pacing. "Curse the timing! What wretched luck. If only I had waited one more day. You've got to understand, Lady Flora's dowry is a drop in the bucket compared to the countess's fortune. You know how deep in debt I am. I would be a fool to turn it down."

"Damn it, Richard, I . . ." About to chastise his friend, Sidney took a moment to collect himself. Perhaps it wasn't too late. Perhaps reason could still prevail. He spoke softly. "Do you realize what you're doing? A gentleman *never* reneges on his proposal. It simply isn't done, Richard. You know as well as I, you will absolutely ruin your reputation if you do. Mark my words, you'll receive the cut direct from everyone you think counts in this world. You'll be ostracized."

"Perhaps, perhaps not. I'll take that chance."

"And what of Lady Flora?" Sidney thought of the radiant young woman he had seen the night before. "Is she not brokenhearted?"

"Uh . . . I don't know."

"What? You haven't told her?"

"I sent Cousin Charles to break the news."

"You sent Lord Dinsmore? I am appalled!"

"Well, he wasn't very happy about it. Mad as blazes, actually." A worried frown creased Richard's forehead. "When he was calm enough, he talked much the same way you just did—all that drivel about how I'd be booted from the *ton,* exiled to France or a far corner of Siberia, all that rot."

"I take it you didn't listen."

"Certainly not. At that point, he wasn't about to be appeased, no matter what I did. He even said he'd marry the woman himself rather than see the family name disgraced."

As a dull, growing ache of foreboding swept through him, Sidney said, "Surely Dinsmore didn't mean it."

Richard shrugged. "Who knows? Have I ever understood the man? I do know he was quite taken with Lady Flora. Said so last night, before all this happened. But what if he did mean it?" He laughed, genuinely amused. "Lady Flora is lively, witty, beautiful—everything a London belle ought to be. Too bad if I've broken her heart, but be honest, Sidney, how long do you think it will take to mend? Probably one night, perhaps two at the most."

"Don't judge others by yourself," Sidney commented, resisting a sudden urge to grab Richard by the throat and shake him as he well deserved.

"Nonsense. She'll be back to flirting with all her beaus in no time. In a week she'll have forgotten my name. As for my cousin, I hate to sound unkind, but do you really think she'd be interested in a scar-faced, one-eyed, old wreck? Ha! Highly unlikely."

Sidney did not immediately answer. For a time he sat silently, absorbing the shock, suddenly realizing . . .

*Do I care too much for Lady Flora?*

Despite her insane obsession with Richard, she had been on Sidney's mind constantly since that day on the beach in Brighton. Just now, when Richard revealed his latest perfidy, Sidney found he had met the news with mixed emotions. He was appalled, of course, as who wouldn't be over such callous treachery. And yet, an unexpected surge of joy had welled within him. Despite himself, he had relished the moment immensely, keenly aware that now Lady Flora would forget Richard, and perhaps . . . ? *What do I feel for her? What exactly do I want?*

Sidney wasn't sure. Marriage was the farthest thing from his mind. He only knew he wanted her. He only knew his idiot friend was wrong when he insisted Flora's heart would be broken for only a day or two.

*She must be devastated.*

Sidney felt a twist of commiserate pain, just picturing her anguish. If only there were something he could do to help her! He felt sick at heart. So sick, in fact, that a troubling question popped into his head. If a man felt that deeply over a woman, might it not be love?

But love or not, he thought of a way in which he might help her.


"Flora?" Lady Rensley, Amy behind, tentatively poked her head through the doorway of Flora's darkened bedchamber. "You have a visitor, dear."

Flora lay prone on the bed, eyes closed, hardly able to move. Was it only a few hours ago her world had come to an end? She had to summon up the strength to ask them both to enter.

They came to her bed and hovered around it, deeply concerned. Lady Rensley asked, "Are you all right?"

Flora opened her eyes. "Fine," she whispered back, knowing she would never be fine again. She had only the vaguest memory of crying, "No!" to her astonished father, running up the stairs to her bedchamber, flinging herself upon the bed. No tears as yet. They were sure to come, but for the moment she felt nothing except a gnawing numbness.

Her mother sat on the side of the bed and patted her shoulder. "That cad. I am so incensed! At least I refrained from telling anyone." She paused. Her brow furrowed. "Well, almost anyone."

Flora groaned. "Whom did you tell?"

"Only Lady Constance Boles, and you know how discreet she is."

"Mama, she's not discreet in the slightest," Flora declared in near panic. "There's nothing she loves more than a juicy bit of *on-dit*."

"I *swore* her to secrecy," Lady Rensley vehemently reassured her.

"Let's hope you're right."

Lady Rensley clenched her fists. "That beastly man! What Lord Dashwood did was just . . . just unspeakable. If word leaks out, he must be punished. I shall make sure he receives the cut direct from everyone."

"Let it go," Flora wearily replied. "What good would it do, except to call attention to the fact I've been jilted?" *Jilted*. Even the sound of the word struck anguish in her heart.

Amy said, "I cannot believe Lord Dashwood would do this to you."

"But he did, didn't he?" Flora managed a faint, bitter smile. "I cannot fathom why he asked me in the first place if he was so quick to change his mind."

"Lord Dinsmore was quite vague on the subject," declared Lady Rensley. "Hinted about 'unforseen circumstances.' "

"Such rot!" Amy said. "I'd wager the Countess de Clairmont has something to do with this. Did you notice how she was ogling him at Vauxhall Gardens?"

"What difference does it make now?" asked Flora, knowing the facts could hardly lift the bleakness from her heart. "You say Lord Dinsmore has asked for my hand? I find that incredible. I only met the man last night." She sat up, swung her legs over the side of the bed, and went to her full-length looking glass, where she examined her crumpled image. "I am *such* a mess. Amy, will you get Baker? Lord Dinsmore mustn't see me like this."

"Lord Dinsmore hasn't arrived as yet," her mother answered. "Your visitor is Lord Lynd."

Flora entered the study knowing that on this, the worst day of her life, she looked the very best she could possibly look. She had chosen a gown of rose-colored calico, the brightest and most cheerful she owned. Baker had swept her hair up into soft curls atop her head, festooned with a jeweled comb.

Not that she cared what she wore, since she felt nothing

but numbness inside. But she must put up a brave front and not let anyone, including Lord Lynd, know she was in a state of despair. *Oh, Richard, I loved you so much! How could you change so suddenly?*

Lord Lynd stood as she entered and gave her a greeting accompanied by a formal bow.

"How delightful to see you, Lord Lynd," she said, closing the double doors behind her. "To what do I owe—?"

"Don't say you're delighted when you're not," Lynd bluntly replied. "You don't have to pretend with me. I am well aware of Dashwood's latest . . . shall we say, lapse. May I say, I am appalled."

Her first response was a rush of gratitude for Lynd's words of sympathy. She concealed it, though, as her pride took hold and with dignity she tilted her chin. "Lapse is hardly the word, sir. I appreciate your sympathy, although I assure you, I shall be fine."

"Will you?" Tenderness glowed in his warm brown eyes, as well as a touch of skepticism. "Come, I have something to say to you." He reached for her hand and led her to the green-striped settee, where they both sat down.

"What do you want to say?" she asked, extremely puzzled.

"I've come to ask for your hand."

For a moment she sat frozen with astonishment. "Am I hearing correctly?" she asked.

"You are, indeed."

"But . . . why?"

He easily replied, "You're an extremely desirable woman, Lady Flora. In the months since Brighton, I've grown quite fond of you."

"But that's not why you're here," she cried, shifting away from him. "You're here because you know Lord Dashwood jilted me." She regarded him with horror. "You feel sorry for me!"

"It's not that," he began, then thought a moment. "True, I'm shocked at Dashwood's actions and can only imagine the scandal that's sure to follow. You don't deserve such a fate."

"So you're here to save me?" she asked, her resentment rising.

"Yes," he replied bluntly. "Agree to marry me and there

will be no scandal. It'll be obvious the gossip came from a misunderstanding. No one will be the wiser."

"I cannot accept," she answered with a proud lift of her chin. "For one thing, I don't love you. For another, there will be no gossip. Only a few people know of Lord Dashwood's . . . change of heart, and they're not going to tell."

"I see." He stood and looked down at her, his face a mask. "Well, then, it appears the matter is in hand."

She stood to face him, realizing as she did so that much as she disdained it, his offer was made out of kindness and she shouldn't be resentful. "Lord Lynd, I truly appreciate—"

"Say not another word," he declared, raising his hand.

He had reached the door when she realized how rude she'd been, how hurtful. "Lord Lynd! Please don't think that I . . . I mean, when I said I didn't love you, that doesn't mean I'm not fond of you. And I'm truly grateful—"

"Further words are not necessary," he replied in a frosty voice. "Rest assured, I was not motivated by love but rather a fondness for you, as well as a desire to mitigate some of the heartache my friend has caused."

Here came her resentment again. "I can handle my heartache quite nicely, thank you."

"Fine." He opened the door. "My offer stands, in case you change your mind."

"I won't!" she flung at him in a burst of pride.

She waited for Lynd's answer, but after casting a long, compassionate look in her direction, he said nothing more and left.


Not long after Flora reached her bedchamber, her mother entered, wringing her hands. "Oh, dear. Oh, dear."

"Mama, what's wrong?"

"I just remembered. I fear I told one other person besides Lady Boles."

"Who?" Flora asked, bracing herself for the worst.

"Mrs. Millicent Edwards."

"Oh, no!" Mrs. Millicent Edwards was notorious for her love of *on dit* and her poisonous tongue.

"I'm so sorry, dear. If only I had known!"

The damage was done. Realizing nothing was to be
gained by reproaching her mother, Flora managed a shrug.
"Nothing for it now but to wait for the gossips to spread
the word."

Looking contrite, Lady Rensley continued. "Now Lord
Dinsmore has arrived. He's in the library awaiting your
answer, which of course must be no."

Flora nodded. "Of course."

"The nerve of the man!" Lady Rensley continued. "And
why should you be bothered? I do believe I shall go downstairs and tell him myself."

"No, I shall come down." Flora glanced in the mirror
and smoothed the skirt of her rose-colored gown. "I must
talk to Lord Dinsmore."

Her mother's eyes widened with horror. "You're not
thinking . . . ? You wouldn't marry that horrid old wreck
of man, would you?"

Flora managed a feeble smile. "He may be an old wreck
of a man, as you say, but isn't the rich and titled Hero of
Seedaseer the ultimate 'catch'? Wouldn't you want me to
marry him, especially now we know the whole story of Lord
Dashwood's proposal is out?" She laughed harshly. "The
perfect way to quiet people's tongues."

"Absolutely not." Lady Rensley took her daughter's
hand. "More than anything, I want you to be happy. I know
there have been times when I've pushed you too hard, hoping for a good match, not caring what was in your heart. I
was trying to be a good mother, but underneath all my
maneuvering, a tiny, secret part of me has always wanted
you never to marry." Lady Rensley put her arms around
her daughter and hugged her tight. "I so enjoy your companionship—your wit, your bright smile. I should not complain if you never left home."

"Well, it's nice to know my mother loves me." Flora
had tried to sound flippant, but her mother's unexpected
kindness suddenly brought a huge lump to her throat and
she couldn't talk. She clung to her mother and cried, "My
heart is broken, Mama. I thought he loved me. I
thought . . ." She could not hold back the sobs.

For a time her mother silently held her until her sobs
subsided and she dried her eyes. "I am not going to cry
any more," she stated firmly, knowing full well she would.

"I'm glad. He's not worth a broken heart," her mother replied.

"Trust me, my heart is not broken." But it was. For her mother's sake, she would have to pretend, but she felt hollow inside and doubted she could ever care about anything in life again.

Her mother remarked, "As I said, you don't have to see Lord Dinsmore. I can go down and talk to him, or your father can. After all, how long does it take to tell him no?"

Flora drew back her shoulders. "I shall do it myself. After all, he is a hero. I owe him the courtesy of seeing him in person before I give him my refusal."

Darkness had fallen. The weak rays from one small lamp provided the only light in the study. In the semidarkness, she perceived Lord Dinsmore standing by the desk, hands behind his back, waiting to greet her. She dipped a quick curtsy. "Good evening, Lord Dinsmore. Excuse me while I summon a servant to bring us more light."

Dressed in somber black, Lord Dinsmore returned a courtly bow. "Good evening, Lady Flora. Shall we leave the light as it is?" He added dryly, "Darkness is my friend these days, for obvious reasons."

She could think of no appropriate answer, so she gestured toward two Roman gilt-wood chairs placed on either side of the fireplace. "Please, sit down, sir." She was grateful for the semidarkness. Despite warning herself to be tolerant, she hated the thought of once again having to look upon his grotesque face.

When they were seated, he wasted no time in saying, "You know I have asked for your hand?"

She had to bite her lip to stop the rush of anguished words. *What happened to Richard? Why did he jilt me? Why are you trying to take his place?* But she must refrain from honestly expressing herself. It was one of her mother's lectures: *one must maintain one's decorum at all costs.* She took a deep, careful breath and replied, "I am aware you've spoken to my father." Although holding herself in tight reign, she allowed herself to fling out her hands and inquire, "Why on earth do you wish to marry me?"

"Many reasons."

Anger welled within her. How dare he smugly ask for her hand when her heart was broken and her whole world had just fallen apart? "If you're trying to save me from the embarrassment of being jilted by your heir, you're too late. The word is out. There will be a storm of humiliating gossip, I've no doubt. Rest assured, though. I am strong." She managed a wry smile at the pun she was about to make. "I shall weather the storm." Thus far, she'd managed to keep the bitterness from her voice, but she finally succumbed. "At least the banns weren't posted. Think what a lucky girl I am! What a—"

Entirely beyond her volition, she choked and her voice broke into a sob. Oh, and she hadn't wanted to cry in front of the Hero of Seedaseer! At least she'd brought a handkerchief along. She dabbed her eyes and said in a tear-smothered voice, "My apologies. Give me a moment and I shall be fine."

He bent forward earnestly, his one good eye intense upon her. "My dear young lady, I am mortified at what my young cousin has done. You must believe me. He was not raised to behave in such a dishonorable fashion. It is beyond me to fathom . . ." At a loss, he slowly shook his head, seeming genuinely concerned. "Richard spent much of his childhood at Pemberly Manor. He was almost like a son to me. Despite his shortcomings, I held every hope that when he grew to manhood . . ." Dinsmore's expression held a note of mockery. "How could he have become such a selfish, vainglorious fop?"

"No," she cried, her heart swelling with resentment. "You must not say those terrible things about him."

"What's this?" Lord Dinsmore looked at her askance. "You still defend him? After what he's done to you?"

She, herself, was astonished at her outburst. "I . . . I hardly know, but I surely don't hate Lord Dashwood or wish him ill. I cannot fathom why he reneged on his proposal. Perhaps he had good reason."

"If you call the Countess de Clairmont and her newly found fortune a good reason," came Dinsmore's sharp reply. He leaned forward. "It pains me deeply to say this, but my cousin is a money-grubbing scoundrel. You must forget about him."

"And marry you?" she asked, unable to keep an edge of scorn and disbelief from her voice.

"Yes," he said simply.

"And why should I do that?" She raised her chin proudly. "I am hardly an object of pity, Lord Dinsmore, so if you think you must make up for Lord Dashwood's disgraceful behavior by marrying me, I assure you, your sacrifice is not necessary. I shall do very nicely, thank you."

He ignored her scornful reply. "There are several reasons why I think marriage would be good for both of us. Will you do me the courtesy of hearing me out?"

She shrugged. How futile this all was! "Why not? Do go on. I have all the time in the world."

He thoughtfully began. "When I met you last night at Vauxhall Gardens I was most impressed. Not only did I find you charming, your knowledge of military history amazed me."

"Oh, I'm sure of it," she cuttingly replied, "coming from a mere woman."

"Frankly, yes. And our short meeting made me realize how lonely I have been these past few years."

"Have you been a widower long?"

"Ten years, now. My wife died young, only forty-nine."

"How tragic."

"She was a good woman. I loved her dearly."

"But weren't you away in the army, fighting battles most of the time?"

"You must understand, I've been a military man all my life, unaccustomed to drawing-room manners. Matter of fact, I cannot abide the idle chatter our society values so highly."

"Neither can I," she said, smiling ruefully.

"You said last night you were tired of being considered a—I believe the words you used were 'flighty London belle.' "

"That's true."

"Then don't be one. You like horses, don't you?"

"They are my passion, although"—she hated to confess it—"I am not allowed to ride, except on old nags. Too dangerous, my mother says."

"Then I suspect you would blossom at Pemberly Manor.

Since my retirement, I've been raising thoroughbreds. That means you could ride anytime you liked—have your own horse, naturally. If you wished to entertain, we are equipped to do so with the finest china, silver, crystal—that sort of thing. You could be the most celebrated hostess in all England, if you so desired. Or, if you prefer a simple, quiet life, you could have that, too. Just think, you could ride when you pleased—stay in the saddle all day if you liked. Did you know a good-sized river winds through my estate? It is bordered by many acres of deep woods, by the way, full of riding trails.  Peace . . quiet . . no gossiping tongues, none of the endless backbiting and social climbing one finds in London.''

*Gossiping tongues.* She hated the thought of how they were soon going to wag with the delicious news of the high-and-mighty Lady Flora's downfall. How wonderful it would be to get away from all those members of the *ton* who would soon be ripping her to shreds, crying false tears of pity for her plight.

"Doesn't being your own mistress appeal to you?" Lord Dinsmore continued on. A little smile played on his lips, as if to say, *I know I'm tempting you.* "Or would you prefer to live under your parents' thumb the rest of your life? Or at least until you marry." He shrugged. "But then, who knows? You might succumb to one of those perfumed London dandies, after all.''

"Highly unlikely," she retorted. "If I married anybody—" *It would be Lord Lynd,* she'd almost said. Thank heaven, she'd stopped herself in time. Lynd had made it perfectly clear he didn't love her and had proposed only out of pity. Pride alone would prevent her from ever admitting to Lynd she'd made a mistake.

"Well, then . . . ?" Lord Dinsmore sat comfortably at ease, awaiting her answer.

She remembered the countless whispered stories she had heard about cruel husbands. "I don't know you well, sir. How do I know you're not some sort of tyrant?"

He appeared to smother a smile. "In the heat of battle, I have killed or maimed more men than I care to think about, but I have never raised my hand to a woman and never shall.''

*Why am I asking all these questions?* she wondered. It

was almost as if she were considering the man's proposal. It dawned on her that perhaps she was. Lord Dinsmore had made his proposal most tempting, all the more so because she was beginning to see how vital was her need to escape London's wagging tongues. How wonderful it would be to find the peace and solitude she yearned for on a remote estate where she could spend her days riding her very own horse through the woods, by a river. But on the other hand . . .

A horrible thought struck her. Despite her abysmal ignorance concerning certain facets of married life, she knew enough to realize she'd be sharing the same bed with this disfigured man and doing what married people did. No, she couldn't! The very thought was repulsive.

Dinsmore said offhandedly, "By the way, to be perfectly fair, I must warn you we would *not* be having children."

"What do you mean?" she asked warily.

"I mean exactly what I said. We won't be having any."

Had he read her mind? She felt the start of a blush. There was only one way she knew of that she could *not* have children and that was—

"I am aware what I look like," he said with a patient smile. "We shall be beauty and the beast. Only be assured, this beast will never force himself upon you. We shall occupy separate bedchambers."

There was only one thing he could mean. She felt herself turn crimson. She knew very little of what she and Amy furtively referred to as "*that* part of a marriage." Their parents had maintained a stony silence on the subject. What paltry information they had gleaned came mostly from whispered hints from their married friends. Also, though she would never admit it, she had put two and two together from watching animals, like horses, in the fields. Although how human beings could possibly . . . Oh! She had an urge to avert her eyes and duck her head, but vowed she would not. To cover her embarrassment, she said, "You do understand, I do not love you and never shall."

He laughed. "I never for a moment thought you would."

"More than that. I"—she searched for words that wouldn't wound him—"I do not find you handsome in the least."

Now he laughed uproariously. "Not handsome? What a polite way to put it, my dear. I am ugly. My face is grotesque. Last night when we met I felt fortunate you didn't swoon from the shock."

She found herself laughing with him, as if they were old friends. Suddenly, he rose from his chair, took her hands, and pulled her to her feet so that they stood facing each other, she, startled, gazing up wide-eyed, only inches away. "Marry me, Flora. You shall be the mistress of Pemberly Manor, which is, as you know, one of the greatest estates in all England. You will have clothes, jewels, all the servants you could ever want."

"My father is rich, sir. I have those things now."

"You will have freedom—"

"Ha! Women are never free!"

"Let me show you." His rough hands clasped her shoulders. "You needn't love me. I don't care about that. But inside this old man's body there's a man who would very much enjoy making you happy. I don't fit your dream of a romantic young lover, but I promise for the rest of my days, I shall try to make you happy. I shall never hurt you. You will never want for anything."

*Except Richard* her heart cried. But what was the use? It really didn't matter. Nothing mattered. All she wanted was to get away, start a new life somewhere far from here. As for love . . . All she could feel was bitter irony. Love was but a dream, her futile fantasy. "If I married you, sir, would we be staying in London?"

"Whatever you like. We can stay, or we can leave for Pemberly Manor immediately."

She frowned, her thoughts in great confusion. "I must be honest—I mean, I do not want you to think—"

"For God's sake, just say yes," he said, not impatiently but with a great depth of feeling. "You'll not regret it."

Somehow, despite his advanced age and his ugliness, she believed him. She believed, too, that anything would be better than staying in London, subject of cruel gossip, hiding a broken heart, abjectly miserable.

"Yes, then."

"Are you sure?"

She gathered her words and for a split second examined them. She was about to change her life—plunge into the unknown. But she didn't care. Nothing really mattered. "I am sure, Lord Dinsmore. Yes, I'll marry you."

# Chapter 8

"Such a happy occasion," bubbled Lady Constance Boles to Flora as they stood chatting with guests at her wedding breakfast. Her gaze swept Flora up and down. "Your wedding gown is exquisite, my dear. Silver lamé on net, is it not?"

"Over a silver tissue slip," interjected Flora's mother. Beaming, she indicated the hem. "See all those little shells and flowers embroidered in silver lamé at the bottom? Well, you cannot imagine the difficulties involved with a gown as intricate as this. Poor Mademoiselle Guiteau and her seamstresses literally stitched their fingers to the bone day and night to finish it. The results are magnificent, are they not?"

Lady Boles awarded them a beneficent smile. "The perfect gown, the perfect bride."

"We are so thrilled for our Flora," Lady Rensley airily continued on. "Of course, I had always hoped that Flora would marry well, but Lord Dinsmore, himself? Beyond my wildest dreams! How fortunate we are." She slanted a sharp gaze at Flora. It lasted only a fleeting moment but was quite long enough to remind Flora yet again of her mother's displeasure and intense disapproval. One would never know it, though. Smiling brightly, Lady Rensley presented the ideal picture of a proud mother, exultant that her daughter had made such a brilliant match.

*Mama should have been an actress,* Flora reflected, recalling her mother's near swoon when she heard the ghastly news. "Flora, how could you marry a man who looks like a monster?" she had wailed.

"Hero of Seedaseer," Flora succinctly reminded her.

"I would not give a fig if he were Wellington himself! Lord Dinsmore may be a hero, but he's old, lame, one-eyed, and scarred. You'll *not* be happy with him. Oh, why couldn't you have said yes to Lord Lynd? Change your mind! Lord Lynd would be a much better choice than—"

"I do not want to hear it," Flora interrupted. "I have given Lord Dinsmore my promise. Surely you want your daughter to do the honorable thing."

Flora had retained her stubborn attitude, even when her father also expressed his dismay. "I know I gave Dinsmore permission to offer for your hand, but only because I was loath to insult the man. Never did I dream you would actually accept! You are not obliged to marry Dinsmore. Obviously you weren't thinking clearly. I shall go to him and explain—get you off the hook."

She adamantly refused to change her mind and felt a certain relief when, that morning at ten o'clock, she set the matter to permanent rest by marrying Charles Fraser, Lord Dinsmore, in a small ceremony at St. George's Church in Hanover Square.

A larger, most convivial crowd gathered for the *déjeuner* that immediately followed at their town house.

Were it not for the fact that her heart was broken and her life ruined, Flora might have enjoyed herself.

As it was, standing and smiling next to her dignified, elderly husband, she knew at least she looked the part of the happy bride, dressed in her silver lamé gown so elegantly trimmed with point Brussels lace, a pretty wreath of rosebuds crowning her flowing hair. This wasn't real. She felt numb inside. In her head a little voice kept calling, *You should be married to Richard, not this pitiful old man.* She regarded the crowd through a sort of haze. What would they think if they knew her heart was breaking, these merry guests who brimmed with congratulations and well wishes, who heartily partook of the full-course meal, drank champagne, devoured her bride's cake to the last crumb?

Lord Dashwood was not present. Dinsmore had assured her he'd made it clear to his prodigal cousin that he was not welcome at the wedding. Even so, she was vastly relieved when it became apparent Lord Dashwood had the decency not to show his face. Not so, his good friend, Lord Lynd. Not only was Lynd present at both the ceremony and the wedding breakfast, he was groomsman for Lord Dinsmore.

"I've known Lynd all his life," Dinsmore explained. "He was like a second son to me when he was growing up. Now he's a true friend."

Today there was something about Lord Lynd that kept drawing her attention. For some reason, she found her gaze following him. Perhaps her attention was drawn by his fine, broad shoulders that so stood out above the crowd, shown to perfection in his finely tailored cutaway coat. Then, too, there was the easy, confident manner in which he carried himself while doing an admirable job as groomsman: circling among the guests, paying particular attention to the shy ones who sat in a corner and the elderly whom everyone else ignored. His toast to the bride and groom was both witty and heartfelt, causing the guests to plunge from hearty laughter to sentimental tears in a matter of moments.

Now, as Flora stood chatting, desperately striving to play the part of the world's happiest bride, she could feel Lord Lynd's eyes upon her, just as she had felt his gaze earlier at the church. Such a strange look—or rather, looks, plural. At times his eyes appeared to be dark and unfathomable, at other times, full of sympathy, at others, anger. Once, they even appeared to be full of pain, although she had no idea why.

In a quiet corner, she finally had the chance to speak to him alone. At first, words failed her as she suddenly realized here was a man she could not deceive. He knew of Richard's defection. No doubt he'd guessed that her real reason for marrying Lord Dinsmore was to contain the gossip that was about to spread. How humiliating! She would die if he said anything. Looking up into his craggy face, she managed, "I trust you have enjoyed the wedding, Lord Lynd?" She knew, before the words left her mouth, how utterly inane that sounded, but too late now.

"I always enjoy a good wedding, Lady Dinsmore," he replied with an enigmatic smile. "May I extend my best wishes for your future happiness?"

She wanted to say, *Stop that nonsense and tell me what you're really thinking,* but, of course, she did not. "Lady Dinsmore," she repeated, running the words slowly across her tongue. "It will take a while before I am accustomed to my new name."

"Just as you must become accustomed to many new things," he replied.

Oh! What exactly did he mean by that? Did he mean the marriage bed? She felt a blush creep over her cheeks. For some unfathomable reason, she was seized with a compelling urge to inform Lord Lynd her marriage would not be . . . what he was implying, and that Lord Dinsmore had clearly stated they would occupy separate bedchambers and would not be doing *that*. "I understand we shall be neighbors, Lord Lynd," she said, happy she'd found a safer, more acceptable topic.

"Indeed," he answered pleasantly. "I look forward to your meeting my sister, Louisa, who lives with me at Vernon Hill. It's less than two miles from Pemberly Manor, by the way. When we were boys, Lord Dashwood and I . . . played together frequently."

Noticing his obvious pause, she hastened to salvage her pride. "It's quite all right, Lord Lynd. You needn't hesitate to mention the name of the man who jilted me." She raised her chin. "I'm quite past that now."

"No, you're not."

How did he know? Startled, she declared, "You are mistaken. I'll have you know this is the happiest day of my life."

"Balderdash." He bent forward, eyes sharp and assessing. "You tried to force an impossible fantasy into reality. It didn't work. I hope you learned something."

She was disturbed to think he somehow knew of the secret dreams she harbored but managed to ask lightly, "What should I have learned, sir?"

"Dream all you like. Everyone entertains impossible fantasies from time to time. Just don't expect them to come true, because they won't. Life's not like that."

"My love for Lord Dashwood was *not* impossible," she snapped. "It was simply the circumstances—"

"Circumstances be damned," he said in a tone that was affable enough, yet she noticed a certain hardening around his eyes.

She replied, "I would prefer you not say anything derogatory about Lord Dashwood. After all, he's not here to defend himself. As for circumstances, we don't know them all, do we? He might have had good reason for doing what he did."

Lynd's expression clouded with anger. "Foolish woman. Can't you see Dashwood is a liar and a cheat?" He appeared agitated—something she'd never seen in him before—and fighting for control. "Do you realize you have just thrown your life away with both hands? How ironic, when you and I could have . . ." He bit his lip, looked away, and said abruptly, "Never mind."

"What's wrong?" she asked, confused. At least, angry though he was, he'd spoken softly. Still, she peered around to make sure no one overheard. "Why are you so angry?" she said in a near whisper. "Do you think I didn't realize you had proposed to me out of pity? And how could you say such things about your dearest friend?"

"Damn it. He's not my dearest friend. He—" Lynd caught himself, and after a long moment, forced a smile. "What am I doing, arguing with you on your wedding day? Lord Dinsmore is one of the best men who ever lived. Who better than I should know?" He shook his head regretfully, seeming to bring a curtain down on his emotions as he backed a step away. "Forgive me, Lady Dinsmore. I have said too much. Don't forget we'll soon be neighbors. If ever you need help, or if even you just need someone to talk to, I'll be there. Always remember that. Always remember—"

"Flora?"

Lady Constance Boles appeared. "Come tell us where you're going on your honeymoon, my dear."

Flora dipped a quick curtsy to Lord Lynd and excused herself. She would have loved to continue the conversation, but now was not the time. "We are not going on a honeymoon as such, Lady Boles, but later today will travel directly to Lord Dinsmore's estate in Kent. . . ."

After talking to Lady Boles, Flora was dismayed to see her sister across the room talking in animated fashion to the Duke of Armond. Flora didn't care for the duke, a cold passionless man, now a widower. He was much sought after by mothers attempting to secure an outstanding match for their daughters, despite dark rumors concerning certain of the duke's personal preferences and the oft-reported deep unhappiness of his now-deceased wife.

Later, in her bedchamber, Flora, dressed for travel, found herself alone with her mother. "One thing before I go, Mama. Surely Amy isn't interested in the Duke of Armond?"

"He's the catch of the Season," said Lady Rensley. "Surely you wouldn't mind if your sister married a duke?"

There was no time to discuss the matter further, Flora decided as she watched two footmen carry the last of her trunks out the door. "It's time to go."

Her mother gave her an unexpected hug. Her eyes dampened as she said, "More than anything else, I want you to be happy, Flora. If I have been too harsh, too judgmental, please forgive me."

Flora warmly returned the hug. "It's all right, Mama. You mustn't worry about me. I know Lord Dinsmore will treat me with the greatest consideration and respect."

"Of course! I never meant to imply he wouldn't." Her mother smiled through her tears. "I shall never say another derogatory word. In fact, I shall rejoice at your marriage and eagerly await the day when you make me a grandmama."

"Oh, dear." Flora smiled ruefully. "I guess I should have told you there will be no babies."

Lady Rensley's eyelids flew wide with surprise. "Just what do you mean?"

"I mean . . ." Flora searched for the proper words, beginning to feel uncomfortable as the conversation strayed into delicate territory. Such matters were never discussed in their family. "Lord Dinsmore and I will be occupying separate bedchambers."

"I find that hard to believe."

"It's true, though. Lord Dinsmore assured me he had no interest in . . . you know."

To Flora's amazement, her mother started to laugh. "No interest? They *all* have interest."

"He's a gentleman of his word."

Her mother laughed all the harder. "Of all men, gentlemen are the worst, hiding behind all their pretty words." She grew serious. "My dear girl, I'm afraid you're in for a rude awakening. Take my word, be they saints, devils, or anything in between, men will all, and I mean every last

one of them, plot, lie, cheat, and scheme to lure you into
their beds.''

"Mama!" Flora was quite shocked, not only at her
mother speaking so frankly, but the import of what she
said. "That may be true of other men, but not Lord Dinsmore.''

Baker entered. "Are you ready, m'lady? His lordship
awaits below.''

Flora gave her thanks to Baker and assured her mother,
"Don't worry. I know what I'm doing.''

Lady Rensley sighed. "We should have had this talk a
little earlier.''

*Yes, we should have.* "I had best get downstairs.''

As Flora headed for the door, her mother called, "Don't
forget, Flora. We're expecting you to become the greatest
hostess in all England. With a mansion such as Pemberly
Manor, how could you not?''

Mumbling, "Perhaps, Mama," Flora left her bedchamber.
With all eyes upon her from below, she descended the staircase, as regally as she could manage. Ordinarily she would
have been pleased, knowing she looked very smart, indeed,
in her new brown redingote with multiple capelets and
matching bonnet, carrying a large fox muff. Now she didn't
care what she wore and was hardly aware of it. Her new
husband awaited her at the bottom, the glittering candlelight from the chandelier casting an uneven glow on the
terrible scar.

*What has happened to me?* she wondered, her thoughts
increasingly in a turmoil. How could it be that in the space
of a few short weeks she'd lost the only man she could
ever love for reasons she knew not why; then, to compound
her misfortune, she had turned right around and married a
crippled old man. Was her mother right? Would Lord Dinsmore demand his marriage rights? She had believed him
when he'd assured her he would never force himself upon
her, but according to her mother she had been exceedingly naive.

She caught sight of Lord Lynd. From a far corner he was
following her progress as she descended the stairs. Their
gazes locked. That look he was giving her! Full of . . . Was
it pity? Accusation? Admiration? All three? She heartily

wished she knew. For the first time, she realized she valued
his opinion. Lord Lynd was not just some nonentity lurking
in Richard's shadow. He was a man to be reckoned with.

*Through Lord Lynd's eyes, I must, indeed, look like a
fool.*

Before, she had been positive she'd done the right thing,
but now, for the first time since she'd consented to marry
Dinsmore, she questioned her decision.

*What have I done? I should never have married a man I
don't love! Now it's too late and my life is ruined.*

Although Lord Lynd had many friends, since early childhood he had never minded being alone, unlike his friend,
Lord Dashwood, who could not abide solitude and demanded lively companionship at all times. When he wasn't
managing his estate, Lynd enjoyed his solitude in many
ways: reading, studying history, writing letters, or simply
strolling around his gardens, contemplating life's mysteries
and the role he was intended to play in the world. He was
not a dull, studious scholar, though, and on a more active
note, enjoyed nothing more than riding, oftentimes accompanied by his sister, their horses hell-bent along a verdant
path through the woods, or cantering along the splendid
trail that followed the river that flowed through his estate
and Dinsmore's.

Lynd was fortunate in that he had received from his parents the gifts of tolerance and acceptance, not only of the
foibles of others, but of his own. Not that he had many
foibles. Those he did have, he accepted, content he was not
perfect, maintaining the utmost confidence in himself.
When he was alone, he found himself in good company.

The night of Flora's marriage, Lynd preferred not to be
alone. Thus, he dined at White's with Lord Sefton and Sir
John Lade, two of his Four-in-Hand cronies. After, he
agreed to play a few hands of whist. He didn't care much
for cards and could not have explained why he craved companionship that particular night except that a heavy cloud
of gloom had seemed to follow him around all day, pressing
him down. After some thought, he suspected Lady Flora
might well be the reason. No. He must remember, Lady
Dinsmore now. Although why he should be the least con-

cerned about that stubborn, wrong-headed woman was beyond him. He knew she was a dreamer. He could tell by the occasional faraway look in her eyes that her thoughts had drifted to a far-off land of fluffy, skittish clouds, where Richard was not a scoundrel, where Dinsmore's countenance was not the ultimate horror to look upon.

He'd wager when she and Dinsmore made love it would be in the dark. That way, she wouldn't have to look at him. . . .

*What am I thinking?*

Good God! Lynd nearly let his cards drop, shocked at where his mind had wandered. He had idolized Lord Dinsmore since before he could remember. That he could so much as entertain one single thought concerning the private life of England's hero was unthinkable. The intimate portion of Flora's marriage was entirely her own affair and her husband's, most certainly not his.

And yet . . .

*Candles snuffed, pitch-black dark. She and the old man lie entwined in bed together. He runs a hand through her soft hair, spread enticingly on the pillow. She wraps her arms around his neck and whispers, "I love you, Charles. I'm yours, completely. I do not care that you're disfigured, I only know that you're a hero. . . ."*

"Your play, Lynd. Lynd?"

"Yes, sorry, Sefton." As Sidney discarded a deuce, a deep, unaccustomed torment gnawed deep within him. He felt so bereft and desolate that when he finished the hand he announced he was leaving. "Good night, gentlemen. Must arise early tomorrow. Sir Thomas can take my place."

On the way out, he was shaking his head in disbelief at himself, when who should walk into White's but the last man on earth he wanted to see.

"Sidney!" Richard loudly exclaimed. Too loud. Hair disarrayed, cravat crooked, he was obviously in his cups, although the hour was not all that late.

"Hello, Richard. I was just on my way home."

Sidney tried to pass by, but Richard grabbed his arm. "No you don't, old man. I am in a frenzy to hear about the wedding. Did they—?"

"They did. Lady Flora is now Lady Dinsmore."

"That so? Well . . ." To Lynd's surprise, Richard's face

fell and his lip protruded in a pout. "Cousin Charles could at least have invited me to his wedding."

Lynd groaned inwardly. "Is your mind so jumbled you don't have an inkling why he did not?"

Ignoring the question, Richard grew thoughtful. "So the chit actually married the old boy."

"What did you expect?"

"She might have waited."

"What does *that* mean?"

"Can't you see? If she hadn't rushed into that stupid marriage with Dinsmore so precipitously, I might have come around and married her, after all."

Amazing, thought Sidney, how Richard could outdo himself and reach new depths of the absurd. "Last I heard, you were about to propose to the countess. Don't tell me—"

"Women are a devilish, conniving lot, Sidney." Richard looked much put-upon. "The countess led me on. Oh, indeed, she put on a fine show of being madly in love with me, but when the tidings of her newly found fortune traveled far, wide, and fast, *poof!* The romance was over. Our dear countess immediately received offers far more tempting than mine. By the time I proposed, she practically laughed in my face. How ironic that I, who could have practically any woman I choose, was done in by a French featherbrain who allowed herself to fall into the clutches of greedy fortune hunters."

*And you are not one?* Sidney thought to ask, but why bother? Talking sense to Richard was wasting one's breath.

In a sulky voice, Richard continued. "As if that weren't enough, the high-and-mighty Lady Flora deigned not to wait for me."

Sidney wondered if he heard correctly. "But you spurned the poor girl."

"So what? If she truly loved me, she would have waited, in hopes I would change my mind." Richard scowled. "I really had a fondness for her, you know. I don't like it that she married my cousin."

"God's blood!" Sidney had to restrain himself.

"Now don't get into a snit," Richard went on. "The mistake is hers, not mine. Mark my words, our proud Flora will soon regret her hasty marriage, if she hasn't already. And when she does regret it"—a smug grin crept over his face—"I see now, I shall be visiting Pemberly Manor more often than before. After all, the new Lady Dinsmore might soon be looking for a shoulder to cry on, and who could better provide it than the man she adores?"

How Sidney longed to plant a fist in the middle of that unbearably smug face. "Her love belongs to someone else now."

"Does it?"

"You had best be careful. If you're thinking to cuckold Lord Dinsmore, you're playing a dangerous game."

"I would never dream of such a thing." Richard broke into one of his wide, charming smiles. "You've known me all my life, Sidney. Do I not brim with family loyalty? Do I not possess the most sterling of characters?"

"Yes, Richard, I *have* known you all your life," Sidney replied, his words charged with a vibrant intensity. "That's why I'm warning you. If I see the slightest impropriety in your dealings with Lady Flora, you'll have me to reckon with. Do you understand?"

Richard looked abashed. "Where's your sense of humor? It was just a little joke."

"No, it wasn't," Sidney said with feeling, and he forced himself to walk away.

# Chapter 9

*Pemberly Manor. Richard's home.*

As the exquisite gardens and rolling green lawns of Lord Dinsmore's country estate came into view, Flora poked her head out the window of the heavy oak coach to get a better view. "How lovely," she exclaimed.

"Like it?" asked Lord Dinsmore. He had been asleep. Now he sat up straight and stretched on the seat beside her.

Flora had always believed no estate in all England could be more beautiful than Sweffham Park, her family's country home, but as the coach rolled through graceful wrought-iron gates and up a winding driveway shaded by poplars, she was struck by the perfection of huge Pemberly Manor with its well-proportioned exteriors of gray stone and rosy brick and enchanting sequence of bays and gables. "I am most impressed."

Dinsmore looked pleased. "It's been in the family since Tudor times." He slid across the seat until he leaned against her back and arm as she gazed out the window. Resting one hand on her shoulder, he pointed out the window with the other. "See the stables? And there, on the other side and up the hill is the greenhouse."

"Oh, yes, I see," she responded automatically, more aware of his sudden close proximity than the beauty of the vast estate unfolding before her. He did not appear to be taking liberties, though. Logic told her he was only trying to point out the superlative features of his estate. Still, a feeling of aversion stole over her as she felt his warm breath behind her ear. A deep-seated repugnance stirred within her, giving her an impulse to flinch away.

*Tonight is our wedding night. What am I going to do?*

All the way from London, she had wrestled with the growing realization of what might happen that very night.

Would her new husband claim his marital rights? He had clearly stated he would not, but her mother had laughed at such a ridiculous notion and just as clearly stated he would. *Mama is usually right,* Flora mused, although she hated to admit it. But how horrible! The very thought of this one-eyed, scarred old man crawling into bed with her, his mottled hands undressing her—perhaps ripping off her nightgown to reach the most intimate parts of her body . . .

Oh, no! She nearly shuddered. She had heard men did that sort of thing, especially a husband, who was well within his rights to do what he pleased with his wife. *Oh, dear God.* Despite her admonitions to herself to remain stoic no matter what, she stiffened and pressed herself away from him, against the squabs.

Dinsmore immediately slid away, back to his own side of the seat. Had he sensed her revulsion? She hoped not. So far, he had been nothing but kind, and she certainly did not want to hurt him in any way. *But how can I endure it if he comes to my bed tonight?*

As the coach rolled to a stop in front of the marbled portico, Flora saw a group of servants waiting, including Baker, her sharp-nosed lady's maid, who had traveled ahead in a separate coach loaded with Flora's clothes, jewels, and furbelows. Flora immediately noticed there was something different about the servants. Not Baker, of course, who stood on the steps with the others, unsmiling as usual, her face unreadable as a stone. But the rest of the servants presented a far different picture from that which Flora was accustomed to. They were not lined up in rigid order as they would be at Sweffham Park. Instead, they seemed to be milling about in no order at all. Most were smiling, appearing quite at ease. And their uniforms! Flora reflected how horrified her mother would be if she saw what this straggly group of servants was wearing. At least the housekeeper looked like a housekeeper, with her dull brown dress and dangling set of keys, but the rest? Where was the butler? Not one man there was dressed in formal attire. Were those the maids, dressed in an assortment of caps, gowns, and aprons, not one of which matched? Were those the footmen who, like the maids, seemed to wear what they pleased instead of matching, elaborate livery?

As she stepped from the coach, a tall, dignified white-haired man, dressed in simple attire, stepped forward to assist. "Welcome to Pemberly Manor, Lady Dinsmore. I am Gillis, the butler." His deep gray eyes warm and welcoming, he handed her from the coach with gracious ease. Flora liked him at once, even though he was not dressed properly.

The thin, angular woman who Flora had guessed was the housekeeper also stepped forward. "I am Mrs. Wendt, your ladyship, the housekeeper." In contrast to the butler, there was a cold look in her eye that was definitely not warm and welcoming.

Smiling, Lord Dinsmore stepped from the carriage. "Well, Gillis, are you surprised?"

The butler, who appeared to be around the same age as Lord Dinsmore, nodded pleasantly. "Very much surprised, sir, as well as delighted, and may I say what a pleasure it is to see you smiling again?"

"High time, eh, Gillis?" Dinsmore took Flora's arm and faced the group of servants. "Introductions are in order here. Let me begin with our cook, Mrs. Bannister. . . ."

To Flora's amazement her new husband introduced all the servants by name, down to the youngest stable boy and scullery maid. So different from home, where the lower servants would not even have been acknowledged, let alone mentioned by name. Come to think of it, she doubted her parents even knew the names of all their servants, whereas Lord Dinsmore seemed familiar with each and every one.

"Shall we go inside?" Lord Dinsmore asked when the introductions were done.

"Of course," Flora answered politely. As she turned and viewed the grand entrance to Pemberly Manor, a sudden panic welled in her throat, but she would die before she let it show. This was the beginning of her new life, and she *would* endure it. She would! Head high, taking her husband's arm, she followed him through the marble arched front entrance.

Inside, Lord Dinsmore paused in the vast entry hall. "I should imagine you're tired, as well as hungry. Gillis will take you to your room, where you can refresh yourself, and then we'll eat."

"I suppose we're too late for tea," Flora ventured.

"Tea?" Dinsmore appeared momentarily perplexed. "Er . . . You're quite right. Teatime is past."

"Then I shall see you at dinner," Flora said. Following a footman laden with luggage, she started up the stairs, noticing immediately that something appeared to be agitating her lady's maid beside her. Baker's back was rigid as a board. One of her nostrils twitched. "What's wrong?" Flora whispered.

The somber, ever-proper lady's maid cast her an enraged glare. "Wait until you see your bedchamber," she hissed.

After her maid's dire warning, Flora had no idea what to expect when they stepped into her bedchamber, but to her relief she found the room airy and bright, furnished with an empire cherry-wood bed, elegant marble and walnut tables and commode. The walls were covered with a delicate mauve wallpaper. The fabric of the drapes and spread was of a lovely violet pattern.

"Baker, what on earth is wrong?" Flora asked when the footman left. Her lady's maid now appeared visibly upset. "Is this not a lovely room?"

Baker sniffed and marched to one of the marble side tables. "This is unbelievable!" With a grand sweep, she ran an index finger across the marble top and held it up. "Do you see?" she cried triumphantly. "Do you see this?" She waved her finger practically under Flora's nose.

"See what?" asked Gillis, who had just entered.

"And what, pray, sir, is this?" the indignant woman asked, holding out her finger toward the butler.

Gillis carefully examined her fingertip. "I do believe that is dust," he replied with grave solemnity, yet Flora detected a slight gleam of amusement in his eye.

"Dust!" Baker exclaimed, her whole body quivering with indignation. "This room is in a ruinous state of disorder and I am appalled. Just look, m'lady." She circled the room, pointing at various objects. "Dust everywhere, and that's not all. Regard the dullness of that mahogany table. Have they no wax?" She pointed to a slight lump under the bedcover. "Is that a way to make a bed? It's disgracefully sloppy." She eyed Gillis. "Are you not in charge of the staff, sir? How could you allow this"—Baker sputtered, searching for the proper words—"*deplorable devastation* to take place?"

Flora listened with mixed feelings. To her, the room looked perfectly fine, charming, really, and quite cozy. Even so, she must remain loyal to her lady's maid. Despite her lack of humor and constant carping, Baker always had her mistress's best interests at heart. Diplomacy was essential here. "Do you think, Gillis, it would be better if we took up the matter with Mrs. Wendt?" She gave the butler her most charming smile. "Considering I just arrived, I most certainly do not want to cause any trouble. What small . . . uh, adjustments need to be made, I am sure we can discuss with the housekeeper."

Gillis nodded agreeably. "Indeed, your ladyship, the matter should be taken up with Mrs. Wendt." Before he continued, his butler's mask of indifference was replaced by an irreverent, highly amused expression that raced like lightning across his face and fast disappeared. "I am sure Mrs. Wendt will be delighted to hear of any improvements you might wish to suggest."

Although she didn't fully trust Gillis's last statement, Flora made a note to herself to have a chat with the housekeeper as soon as possible.

*New husband, new home, new servants, new life.*

Finally alone in her bedchamber, Flora's trepidation grew as the time for dinner approached. She longed for her sister, who always managed to put a humorous slant to things. She even longed for her parents. They had so constricted her life in the past, yet with them she had always felt loved and protected. How she wanted to return to the security of her well-ordered life, boring though it might have been! At least she'd known what to expect each day—each night!— whereas now . . .

Underlying all her fears was her ceaseless, inner question: would her new husband come to her bed that night? What would she do if he did?

*Nothing.* She suppressed a choked, desperate laugh. Nothing she could do but accept her dismal fate. Terrible regrets assailed her. Yes, her heart had broken when Richard jilted her, but why had she acted so precipitously? She hadn't thought things through, and now . . .

*Oh, Richard,* she silently cried, *why did you leave me when I loved you so much?*

What if he still loved her? She'd been so certain that he did. What if he realized he'd made a terrible mistake? And what if . . . ?

*A soft knock sounds on the door. She opens it. Richard! Her heart starts to pound as she asks, "What are you doing here?"*

*He raises his finger to his lips. "Shh!" He swiftly steps in and shuts the door. "Gather your things. We must be quick!"*

*"But what . . . ?"*

*"I have made a terrible mistake. I love you with all my heart. I realize that now. I shall explain everything later, but now I want you to come away with me."*

*"But I can't. I just married your cousin."*

*"Is the marriage consummated?"*

*"No, but—"*

*"That's all I needed to know. I want you, Flora, Lord Dinsmore be damned. The world be damned! Your marriage must be annulled. When it is, you and I shall run off to Gretna Green, marry, and live happily together the rest of our lives."*

*"Oh, Richard, I love you so! I—"*

"What do you wish to wear for dinner, your ladyship?" asked Baker, who had just reentered the room.

"What? Oh." Flora's vision of the man she loved vanished as she brought herself back to cold reality. "Dinner. What to wear. Hmm, nothing fancy, I should think. The gray muslin will do."

She had been right to choose a simple gown, Flora reflected at the dinner table that night. In fact, the meal was so informal that she wondered when, if ever, she had dined in such an unceremonious fashion. At home, dinner was a formal affair without fail. At the very least, the meal consisted of six courses and was attended by the butler and a cadre of maids and manservants. Not so at Pemberly Manor. Some sort of simple cotton cloth covered only one end of the long, dining room table. Eating utensils were of pewter, glasses were ordinary, and the dishes were of plain pottery, one of them chipped. True, it was a small chip, but one that would have aggrieved her mother no end had she spied such a major blemish upon her finely laid table. The meal itself was a single course, consisting of roast beef, boiled potatoes, and vegetables, and was served by a plainly dressed footman who quickly withdrew. Gillis poured the wine, wished them a good meal, and withdrew also, leaving the two alone.

Lord Dinsmore picked up his glass of wine and held it high. "Here's to you, my dear, on the occasion of our wedding supper." With his one good eye he regarded her with affection. "May we have many more."

"Many more," Flora answered flatly, raising her glass without enthusiasm. Wedding supper? Practically a peasant's meal! Flora tried not to show her dismay as she took a small bit of roast beef upon her fork. Before the fork had traveled halfway to her lips, she stopped and regarded it with distaste, suddenly aware her normally healthy appetite had disappeared.

"Is it not to your liking?" asked Lord Dinsmore.

Flora looked across the table at her new husband. In the dim light cast by flickering candles, she could not clearly distinguish his face, but her imagination conjured the scar, the eyepatch . . . Oh, indeed, she knew exactly what was there. "I seem to have lost my appetite. All the excitement—I trust you understand."

He nodded gravely. "You have much to get accustomed to here at Pemberly Manor."

"Yes." So very much!

"If you like, we shall go riding in the morning. I'll invite Lynd if he's back from London. His sister, Louisa, too. You'll like her. She's a fine figure of a woman. Loves horses." He spoke with enthusiasm, as if he could detect Flora's reluctance and was attempting to assuage it. "You may have your choice of horses. If nothing in my stables suits you, then we shall see about buying you whatever horse you choose."

Ordinarily, the thought of finally having her own horse would have excited her no end, but now she could not bring herself to care. "That will be nice," she answered stiffly. *He's the Hero of Seedaseer,* she reminded herself bleakly. All England revered this fine, honorable man, and she should feel greatly honored to be in his very presence. Instead, it was all she could do to stay at the table, not to leap to her feet and flee.

For a time they ate in silence, he seeming to give his full attention to his meal, she, forcing down a few bites. "You will forgive the simple fare," he said at last. "The first Lady Dinsmore was adamant we dine formally every night. Naturally, I went along with her wishes, although . . ." He gave a little laugh and continued. "At heart I'm a military man, accustomed to living at times under the most primitive conditions. Alas, I have fallen back into my old bachelor ways since Edith . . . Ah, well. There's a fine set of French Haviland china packed away somewhere. Also silver, crystal, and the like. Mrs. Wendt would know. Gillis also. I should imagine you'll be eager to, shall we say, resurrect our fine dining things, so in the morning, feel free to talk to Mrs. Wendt."

He was trying to be kind, Flora knew, but she was in such a state of inner tumult she could hardly answer, let alone make herself appear enthused. "I shall if you wish me to," she said, knowing how deadly flat her voice sounded.

"I see." Finishing his meal, Lord Dinsmore laid his knife and fork carefully on his plate, all the while appearing to be in deep thought. "You must be very tired."

"Oh, yes, very tired," she eagerly replied, knowing she was grasping at straws. But if she could just put off the inevitable for one night—just one night—she would offer up a prayer of thanks.

Lord Dinsmore stood and regarded her thoughtfully. Even in the dimness of the candlelight, she could see his one eye gazing at her with piercing understanding. "My dear Flora, have you forgotten what I told you?" he asked softly.

She gulped and answered, "And what was that?"

"Beauty and the beast, remember? Only be assured, this beast will never force himself upon you. I gave my word we would occupy separate bedchambers and so we shall."

A vast relief swept through her. "Do you mean it, sir?"

"I gave you my word, did I not?" Despite his continued politeness, she detected an edge of harshness in his voice. "I shall never come to you, Flora. You can count on it."

"I understand," she answered, trying to conceal the wonderful sense of relief that had just swept through her.

"So be it, then. And in the future, Flora, be honest with me. Tell me your concerns. That's all I ask." A long moment passed before Dinsmore's normal, pleasant demeanor returned and he continued in a brisk but friendly manner, "I, too, am tired, and shall retire to my own bedchamber directly." He smiled down at her. "Sleep well. I trust you'll have a pleasant night. I shall see you at breakfast."

"And what time is breakfast?"

"Whenever you like."

Before she could express her surprise, he limped from the dining room and was gone.

Flora slept fitfully that night. Not that she was afraid Dinsmore would invade her bedchamber to claim his marital rights. She believed his assurances he would not. Still, the pain in her heart would not go away. In the darkest dark of the night, she saw the truth: Richard did not love her and most certainly was not coming to rescue her. Such a foolish fantasy to ever think he would! So here she was, stuck in a strange, hostile place, trapped in a loveless marriage that would last for years and years—forever, as far as she was concerned, and it was all because of her own stupidity and rash actions.

*I shall never be happy again,* she thought. In black despair she lay tossing and turning. Occasionally she thought of Lord Lynd and how glad she was she might see him tomorrow. Such a perceptive man! And how kind, actually offering to marry her to save her from scandal. Only he, other than her sister, could begin to understand the predicament in which she had willingly thrust herself against all good advice. She wished she could talk to him. He would listen and not make fun when she expressed her anguish over her foolish actions. Not that he could do anything, not that anyone could. Just the same, she pictured his warm, sympathetic smile and thought what a comfort it would be to see him again.

Things were always supposed to look better in the morning, Flora reflected as, dressed in a blue chintz morning gown, she entered the breakfast room. Her mother used to say it was always darkest before the dawn. Well, it was not.

Her mood was as bleak as it had been the night before and she yearned for home.

Lord Dinsmore, seated at the table, looked up from his newspaper and smiled pleasantly. "Good morning, Lady Dinsmore. I trust you slept well." He nodded toward a terra-cotta marble side table. "We are informal here. Just help yourself to whatever you like."

Serve herself? How strange. What were the servants for? She had never served herself, but then, what did she care? She was still not the least bit hungry. Rather than protest, she took up a plate and took a tiny helping of eggs and sausage. As she seated herself, wondering how she could ever eat one single bite, Lord Dinsmore spoke up.

"Gillis tells me you are dissatisfied with the housekeeping arrangements."

*Baker.* How Flora wished her lady's maid had kept her silence. "Not dissatisfied, sir. That's too strong a word. It's just . . . Well, perhaps the furniture could be dusted a bit more frequently."

"Tell Mrs. Wendt." Dinsmore halted a forkful of eggs halfway to his mouth. "You are mistress of Pemberly Manor now. Mrs. Wendt is to follow your instructions, or out she goes."

*Easier said than done,* Flora thought, remembering the icy-cold look the housekeeper had bestowed upon her when they met. She had no intention of causing the poor woman to lose her position, though, and wondered how best to approach a delicate situation. Young though she was, she knew perfectly well how to run a well-ordered household. In fact, thanks to her mother's thorough training, she was confident she could turn Pemberly Manor into the consummate country estate, rivaling the very best in all England. If she wanted, she could have a perfectly run household, complete with flawless servants, all required to strictly obey rigid rules. The only problem was, to accomplish such an end, she would need to be as imperious as the queen of England—in other words, just like her mother.

*Wonderful,* came her cynical thought. She didn't want to be like her mother. Not only that, she was acutely aware that her demands for change would cause great resentment among the servants. They would look upon her in the same way the servants at home treated her mother—polite on the surface, but underneath boiling with resentment.

*Is this what I want to do with my life?*

*Do I have a choice?*

No. She had made her bed and now she must lie in it, and be grateful, she thought wryly, that her worst fears concerning her wedding night had not materialized.

Flora took a nibble of sausage, but she could hardly swallow it as she decided now was the time to tell Lord Dinsmore what he wanted to hear. "With all due respect, sir, certain improvements most definitely need to be made, and I shall endeavor to make them, starting with . . . with the servants, I suppose, and the  . . ." Oh, dear! The more she talked, the more hopeless seemed her situation, until her eyes suddenly bordered with tears. She would *not* cry! Not in front of the Hero of Seedaseer. It would be too humiliating. She gulped and tried to speak again, but her new husband, who had been listening with avid attention, raised his hand.

"Enough," he said simply. "We shall go on a picnic."

Flora was so surprised, her tears stopped. What on earth was the man thinking of? The last thing she wanted to do right now was go on a picnic. "Sir, I hardly think—"

"A picnic," he softly reiterated. "We were going riding today, remember? We shall combine the ride with a picnic. You're wound tight as a top. What you need is a meal by a quiet stream surrounded by nature's beauty, not this house and not the servants. Lord Lynd is coming, by the way, and his sister. I shall dispatch a footman to inform them of our new plan."

She was curious as to how her husband could plan a picnic on such short notice. In her experience, picnics meant Cook packing all sorts of fancy dishes to carry in not one, but several elaborate hampers. Picnics meant footmen scampering here and there, setting up tables under the trees and spreading fine linen tablecloths. Picnics meant half the serving staff coming along, all in attendance as her family pretended to enjoy themselves while brushing away horrid little bugs and insects. "I really don't think . . . It's so much trouble—"

"No trouble at all." Lord Dinsmore arose from the breakfast table and gazed down at her with a look that proclaimed his decision was final. "You've brought a riding gown?" She nodded, thinking of the wool serge gown she wore on her rare rides atop Buttercup. "Then go put it on. We leave in an hour."

Dinsmore started to cough. It was then Flora noticed a feverish flush upon his forehead and cheeks.

"Sir, I fear you're not well."

"Fit as a fiddle," Dinsmore protested, still hacking. "One more moment and I shall be fine."

When the cough finally subsided, Flora asked, "Are you all right?"

"Of course! Just a touch of 'flu.' Nothing to it."

Flora said no more, knowing the Hero of Seedaseer had his pride.

# Chapter 10

The day was full of surprises.

Flora's first surprise came when, neatly attired in her one-and-only riding gown, she stepped onto the front portico. "Where is my mount?" she inquired. On the rare occasions when she'd ridden, old Grisby, the groom, stood waiting at the bottom of the steps, ready to hand her the reins belonging to ancient Buttercup, who was already saddled, ready to go. Hardly ever did she set foot in the stable, which her mother considered most unsavory with its "uncouth stable boys and unpleasant smells."

Unpleasant? Flora loved her rare visits to the stables, where she could breathe deep of the pungent aroma of the horses, mixed with oats and newly mown hay.

"We shall proceed to the stables and saddle our own horses," said Lord Dinsmore, dressed in breeches, dark brown riding coat, and simple stock. He still looked feverish. "Ready?" he asked.

Followed by Gillis, they started for the stables. Their stroll was a pleasant one, along a narrow, winding path bordered with tall oaks and pink and white rhododendrons. In the distance she could see tangled gardens blooming with marigolds, carnations, pansies—it seemed every flower imaginable, their vibrant colors striking against the deep green background of the bordering woods. They reached the stable, where beyond, in an open field of lush green, she could see several horses grazing peacefully. In the dimness of the stable, she peered down a long row of stalls, some empty, some with the head of a curious horse peering out. "I didn't know you owned so many."

"Only a few," Lord Dinsmore answered in an offhand manner, yet she could see he was proud of his stables. "These are my coach horses." He pointed to four chestnuts groomed to a high gloss. "Prime cattle, by the way. These two matched grays pull my curricle. You'll be seeing a lot of them when you make your visiting rounds." He led her along the straw-covered walkway that divided the two rows of stalls to a stall containing a young, chestnut-colored filly. "Meet Primrose. What do you think of her?" He opened the stall door and slipped a bit in her mouth. "Here, I'll lead her outside."

In the courtyard, Flora took a long look at the little filly and immediately fell in love. Fondly patting Primrose's withers, Flora announced, "She's perfect."

"She's yours if you want her," Dinsmore said quietly.

"You really mean I can have my very own horse?"

"High time, don't you think?"

Flora returned delighted laughter. "But I haven't ridden much. When I did, it was always over Mama's objections. She made Amy and me ride the oldest horse in our stables, always at a sedate walk, by the way. Not that Mama was being mean. She was just afraid I'd get thrown and break something, preferably not my neck."

"Then I'd say it's time you owned your own horse. That is, if you want her."

"Oh, yes!" Flora joyfully wrapped her arms around Primrose's neck and buried her head in the horse's sleek chestnut mane. "Of course I want her." She knew she was acting like a ten-year-old, but she was so delighted she didn't care.

"Then let's go riding," said Dinsmore. She could tell from the warmth of his voice he was pleased. He continued, "Wait here a moment while I get my horse and the saddles." She was surprised that a man as illustrious as her husband ignored help from the stable boys and was about to saddle his own horse, hers as well. He further surprised her when he inquired, "What kind of saddle would you like?"

"What do you mean?"

"I was hoping you'd want to ride astride, not sidesaddle."

"Are you joking? A lady always rides sidesaddle."

"Do tell," he dryly replied.

"But ride astride?" What an astounding notion. She still could not comprehend. "Only little girls are allowed to ride astride."

The sound of galloping hooves interrupted. Flora turned

to see Lord Lynd, mounted atop a magnificent black thoroughbred, accompanied by an attractive, raven-haired woman of forty or so. "Good morning, Lord and Lady Dinsmore," Lynd called as he brought his mount to a spectacular, dust-rising halt. He cast a fond gaze at the woman beside him. "Lady Dinsmore, may I present my sister, Lady Beasley?"

"Widow of the late, lamented, William, Lord Beasley," Lynd's sister added in a throaty voice, in a tone so lively Flora wondered if the late Lord Beasley was much lamented at all. "I'm delighted to meet my new neighbor," Lady Beasley went on. "You must call me Louisa and I shall call you Flora, if you don't mind."

Lord Lynd laughed indulgently. "I trust you're not offended, Lady Flora. My sister is hard put to tolerate what she refers to as all that foolish formality of the *ton*."

Flora dipped a curtsy, concealing what was indeed her surprise at such informality. In the Polite World, first names were hardly ever used, except for family and the closest of friends. But why not? In the mood she was in, she was ready for anything. "Delighted to meet you, Louisa. I would be most pleased if you would call me Flora."

"Marvelous," declared the vivacious woman, her gloved hands in masterful control of the reins as her magnificent bay danced about. What a handsome woman, Flora thought admiringly, noting her rosy cheeks, confident style, and smart, periwinkle blue riding gown. Her face was tanned, as if she spent a great deal of time out-of-doors, something most certainly no self-respecting lady of the *ton* would do. *And she's riding astride,* Flora noticed. "Do you ride often?" Flora asked politely.

"You'll find my sister is glued to her horse," Lynd said playfully. "That explains why you'll never see them apart."

"Nonsense!" Louisa awarded her brother a playful swat on the arm with her riding crop. "Well, not quite nonsense," she admitted. "I do love my horses." She tipped her head inquisitively. "And what about you, Flora?"

Drawn to the friendly woman, Flora responded, "I haven't done much riding, but I'd love to learn."

"Then we shall get along famously." Lady Beasley leveled a stern gaze at Lord Dinsmore. "Well, Charles? Are we going to dither about in your courtyard or are we going on this picnic you invited us to?"

Dinsmore opened his mouth to answer, but instead fell into a fit of coughing. When at last the hacking subsided, he look wan and spent. "I fear you'd best go without me," he managed to whisper.

"But I can't leave you," Flora protested.

"We can easily postpone the picnic," added Lord Lynd.

Dinsmore stilled them all by raising a firm hand. "I insist. It's most important my new bride sees the woods today and has her picnic. Also, Louisa, I'd be most grateful if you could talk her out of her silly notion about sidesaddles." Dinsmore looked toward his butler. "Give Lynd the saddle-bags, Gillis, then help me back to my bed."

Flora watched in concern as her new husband retreated toward the house. "I trust he'll be all right."

Lord Lynd frowned. "He's not been well lately—"

"But he doesn't want our picnic spoiled, now, does he?" interrupted Louisa. "So, Flora, you don't wish to ride astride?"

"I'm concerned lest someone see me," Flora replied, realizing how immature she sounded the moment she spoke.

The beginnings of a smile tipped the corners of Lord Lynd's mouth. "You're Lady Dinsmore now. I assure you, as the wife of one of England's greatest heros, you could ride backward standing on your head if you so desired. Forget the sidesaddle. What a ludicrous notion that a lady must ride with her knees tight together. It's a ridiculous device, uncommonly awkward and uncomfortable."

"Amen to that," chimed in Louisa in hearty agreement. "Do you really care if someone sees you?"

"Well . . . Yes, I suppose I do. Aren't I supposed to care?"

Louisa leveled a wise gaze. "You might give some thought to why you should care what others think of you. I, personally, would not care to live a life based on the opinions of others." She glanced at her brother. "Do you not agree, Sidney?"

"Most heartily." Smiling, he continued. "Very well, Lady Dinsmore, I grant you, if we were going someplace where we might be seen by one of those stiff-rumps in the *ton*, then for propriety's sake, you might feel obliged to use a sidesaddle, although it's still your choice. Not today, though. We're riding deep into the woods where we won't be on display, so you needn't feel the least uneasy. Come, give it a try."

All at once, Flora's inhibitions fell away. Lord Lynd and his sister not only were bright and intelligent, they brimmed with life and good humor. What a prig she was being. How silly she must sound, worrying about the opinions of others. And really, what harm would it do? "Very well. You've convinced me."

"Excellent!" Lord Lynd proclaimed. "Wait here." He retreated to the stable and quickly returned with harness, bridle, blanket, and saddle. Flora stood watching as he easily and expertly saddled her mare. She could not help noting, too, the eye-catching shape of his lean, strong body.

Soon they were riding through the woods on a narrow trail where, through tangled hedgerows and thick growths of alder, birch, and elm trees, she caught occasional glimpses of a swiftly flowing stream. The deeper they went, the more her spirits lifted. She was thrilled with Primrose. The filly responded to her lightest touch. She was thrilled with the saddle, too. Up to now, she was resigned to riding sidesaddle. Was it not a lady's lot in life? But now she realized how awkward it was to sit sideways and twist her head around to look forward. Such an unnatural position! Her neck and back ached each time she rode. Now, with the back of the horse hugged securely between her knees, she felt comfortable and relaxed, and in much better control.

The trail widened. As Louisa rode ahead, Lord Lynd slowed his mount so that she caught up and rode beside him.

"Like the saddle?" he asked, and looked pleased when she gave him an enthusiastic yes.

As they rode along, she glanced occasionally at his profile and realized for the first time he wasn't half bad looking. True, his nose wasn't exactly straight, yet it had a noble air about it—actually, a most admirable nose. She liked his jawline, too. It was firm and his jowls didn't sag, not like many of the dandies she'd met in London who early on lost their looks because of drink and who-knew-what-other dissipations.

Not that Richard has either, she idly thought, then remembered, *Richard!* Her heart gave a little lurch. How could she have gone for minutes—perhaps the better part of an hour—enjoying herself and not thinking of him? She felt strangely disloyal. Her heartache returned as she remembered her sad situation. She thought of the many dreary years ahead when, even on a lovely day like this, she would feel sick with regret at the loss of the only man she would ever love.

They were riding along at a brisk pace, ever deeper into the thick woods, when Lord Lynd turned to her. "Getting hungry?"

"I could eat," she said, bewildered, "but where are the hampers? I assumed Lord Dinsmore had forgotten."

Lynd patted his saddlebag. "It's all in here. Ahead, there's a nice spot by the stream. We'll eat when we get there."

Flora discovered the place where the three stopped was more than a "nice spot." It was more like a fairyland glade with interlaced branches of tall oak trees forming a canopy above. Underneath, the ground was carpeted with a tangle of rich green grass, blue forget-me-nots, yellow primroses, and purple violets nestling against mossy stones that bordered the stream.

They dismounted and tied their reins to low branches. Lynd uncinched the saddles and untied the saddlebags. When he saw her watching, a wry smile touched his lips. "I'd wager this isn't the sort of a picnic you're accustomed to."

"You could say that."

"Follow us." Each carrying a saddlebag, Lord Lynd and Louisa led her to a grassy spot directly beside the bubbling stream, bade her sit on the grass, and reached into one of the bags. "We've done this so often, I can almost guess . . . Ah, yes, bread, cheese, and apples," he announced, pulling packages wrapped in linen in rapid succession from the bag. "A bit of cake for dessert, and here's my contribution to the picnic"—he reach into the other bag and triumphantly pulled out a small flask and held it up—"brandy."

"But—" she began, bit her lip, and stopped herself.

Louisa grinned. "I know exactly what you were going to say." She struck her hand to her heart and in a perfect imitation of a snobby arbitrator of the *ton*, recited, "A well-brought-up young lady does not indulge in brandy at ten o'clock in the morning! I am shocked and scandalized."

"I am horrified!" added Lord Lynd.

"Appalled!" Louisa continued. "It simply is not done."

Flora broke into laughter. "That's exactly what my mother would say."

"No disrespect, mind you," said Lynd. "It's only a nip or two. Not enough to get you foxed."

Flora contained a giggle. "I have never been foxed."

"Do tell!" they both replied, each feigning great astonishment.

As they all laughed, she realized that for the very first time since the wedding, some of her awkwardness and trepidation had faded. She remembered that last conversation with Lord Lynd at the wedding, wherein at one point his expression had clouded with anger and he'd informed her she had just thrown her life away with both hands. Today, though, he seemed perfectly pleasant and surely must have forgotten the unpleasant scene. She ate some bread and cheese. Feeling deliciously decadent, she took a sip of brandy from the small cup he'd handed her. It slid down her throat with ease, spreading a warm glow all the way. She leaned back against a rock and settled comfortably, listening to the soothing gurgle of the little stream, sniffing the sweet smell of tall grasses. For the first time in ages she felt at ease.

As they ate, they talked. She told them tales of her childhood—quite uneventful, she assured them, but they seemed keenly interested, nonetheless. In turn, Lynd regaled her with fascinating stories of his days in the military, in particular the Battle of Waterloo. She listened in awe, although she suspected he was glossing over the more horrific parts of the battle.

Lady Beasley had much to say, mostly about her obvious passion, horses. In between her fervent descriptions of the bits of blood she owned and the thrill of riding down Rotten Row on a bang-up piece of flesh, she filled Flora in on her personal life. At forty, she was widowed and had no children—obviously not a great loss since her horses were her children. Although she spoke of her late husband with respect, she did not appear to be brokenhearted over the loss of Lord Beasley, who lamentably had broken his neck during a foxhunt and died instantly.

"I've adjusted quite nicely to being a widow and shall never marry again." Louisa idly plucked a violet and brushed it under her nose. "My horses, my brother"—she threw Sidney an affectionate glance—"who is the best brother in the world, by the way, make my life complete." Louisa cast a questioning glance at Flora. "And what of you? Shall you be happy here?"

"Who knows?" Flora answered honestly. "There's the matter of running that huge household. My mother expects me to become the greatest hostess in all England. From what I hear, the first Lady Dinsmore did a marvelous job. As for me, I'm not so sure it's what I want to do. Already matters have arisen concerning the running of the household—"

"Do whatever you feel like doing," Lord Lynd interrupted.

"But I feel an obligation. Isn't that what women are supposed to do?"

"Women should do what they want to do!" Louisa stoutly declared.

Lynd asked, "Has Lord Dinsmore expressed his opinion on the subject?"

"Not really. But then, I must adhere to his wishes."

Lynd, propped on one elbow, stretched comfortably on the grass, continued. "That's the trouble with you women. You think you have no power, but you do. You must be bold enough to take it, though, and not stay a milksop all your life." He smiled ruefully. "Oops, there I go again, giving a lecture. If you want to be the greatest hostess in all England, then do so. I'm sure Lord Dinsmore won't object. But if you don't, I'd wager he won't care a groat. It's up to you. For a change, think about what *you* want, instead of what everyone expects of you." He cast her a wry smile. "And the devil take you if you continue to worry about what people think. That's what got you here in the first place, isn't it?"

"I suppose," she admitted, suddenly very much wanting to change the subject. "So how do you fill *your* life?"

He thought a moment. "These past few years I've lived quietly. My books, of course. It should be no surprise I'm a devotee of military history. Matter of fact, I'm in the midst of writing a history tome myself. After my wife died, I felt no need to entertain. Instead, I hunt, fish, and then there's my horses. I ride every day, as well as indulge myself in four-in-hand whenever possible. There's nothing like it."

"I envy you men," Flora responded. "All my life I've thought the most exciting thing in the world would be to drive a coach-and-four. How I would love to try it!"

Lynd glanced at his sister. "What do you think?"

Nodding enthusiastically, Louisa said, "Why not?"

Lynd addressed Flora. "Then try it you shall."

"You mean, you'd teach me?" Flora asked.

"Of course I mean it. Given your husband's permission, of course, although I can't imagine he'd deny it, and perhaps if he's feeling better he'll come along."

"Tomorrow!" Louisa exclaimed.

Lynd continued. "We shall hitch up my coach-and-four and go visiting, and of course we'll take you by Vernon Hill." He thoughtfully added, "You'll be climbing to the box so you'd best wear a wide skirt. Whatever you do, don't be like most women and cripple yourself with a tight-skirted gown encumbered with all those ribbons and furbelows."

She was going to learn four-in-hand! Flora was thrilled.

When the picnic was over, they mounted their horses and headed for home. "I enjoyed it," she gayly called to Lynd as he rode ahead.

He flung an amused glance back at her. "Lord Dinsmore was right when he said you needed a picnic."

*And so I did,* she mused. As their horses jogged along the trail, she realized she felt much better. Her last vestige of resentment against Lord Lynd had faded away. He did not seem nearly so distant and remote anymore, and not nearly as cynical. She'd seen an entirely different side of him during the time they'd spent by the stream. He had proven himself to be kind, considerate, and exceedingly funny, as well.

As for shaping up the household and becoming the greatest hostess in all England, she didn't even want to think of that right now. But she *must* speak to Mrs. Wendt about the dust. Perhaps dust-free furniture would be enough to appease Baker, and the rest she would consider later. All she could think about, really, was that tomorrow she would drive four-in-hand.

Arriving back at the stable, Flora was fully aware that she was under the scrutiny of both Lord Lynd and his sister as she swung, mercifully without incident, off her horse. Despite the offer of help from the groom, she removed the saddle herself. As she started to rub down Primrose, Lord Lynd appeared alongside. "Do you know, I've never done this before?" she remarked.

"Then there's no reason you shouldn't from now on," Lord Lynd replied.

Flora's spirits were high as she bid good-bye to Lord Lynd and her new friend, Louisa. What a lovely time she'd had today. How nice to know there were many more in store. Her high spirits lasted until, returning to the house, she thought of her husband, sick and awaiting her. She hastened to his bedside where she found him much better and about to arise from bed. "Did you enjoy yourself today, my dear?" he asked, taking her hand.

"The ride and the picnic were splendid. I had a marvelous time." Once again, a jolting thought struck her. *Richard*. How terrible she hadn't thought of him for hours. The thought sent her hurtling back to bleak reality. She'd enjoyed a lovely time today, but even though everyone had been exceedingly kind, nothing had changed. *I still love you*. She felt guilty, disloyal to her love. How could she actually have managed to enjoy herself with another man?

Dinsmore abruptly dropped her hand. *How could he know?* she asked herself. Had she, without realizing, tried to pull away? Trying to make conversation, she remarked, "I should imagine Lord Dashwood must have enjoyed these woods. Did he go riding often?"

Lord Dinsmore stiffened. "I cannot recall," he cooly replied.

She knew immediately she'd said the wrong thing. "Oh, dear. Should I not mention him?" she asked warily.

"I'd rather you did not."

"Is it because of the way he treated me?"

"In part. His actions were appalling. He was not brought

up to shirk his duty, I can assure you. However, this latest mischief isn't my only source of irritation. There have been other things, too. . . ." Dinsmore frowned, for a moment appearing to be lost in old, unpleasant memories. "Suffice to say, my cousin is no longer welcome in my home."

Flora's spirits plunged.  Somehow, in the back of her mind, she had assumed she would see Richard occasionally. Not that she would be party to any impropriety. It was just that she would so enjoy seeing him, if only from time to time. "Are you sure about Lord Dashwood?" she asked. "I hate to think that I'm the cause of a rift between you."

Lord Dinsmore's jaw set firmly. "The subject is closed," he said with cold finality.

"Well, then." To dispel an awkward silence, she asked lightly, "What time is tea?"

Lord Dinsmore let an uncomfortable moment of silence roll by. "You may as well know there is no time for tea. Not since Edith . . . You understand, I'm always busy running my estate, and such matters as tea are not of great import."

No tea. Well, that would change, but she'd take action later, not now. "All right, but surely you must have a set time for dinner."

"Dinner is whenever I want it to be."

"I see," she replied, not letting him know she was shocked and horrified. . . . Or was she? Certainly her mother would be. And Baker, too, of course, who was bound to think an indeterminate dinner hour represented the absolute depths of sloth and disorder. She would certainly have to do something about such laxness, Flora mused, but for the moment she would say nothing. Not tomorrow, either, because—her heart leaped with anticipation—she was going to drive four-in-hand! Next day, perhaps.

Striving for friendly conversation, she asked her husband, "Lord Lynd has volunteered to teach me four-in-hand tomorrow, along with his sister, of course. Have you an objection?"

"Of course not! I doubt if I'll be feeling up to going, but I will when I can. Meanwhile, be sure to invite them to dinner next Saturday night. Informal as always, of course."

# Chapter 11

Next afternoon, Flora sensed Baker's displeasure as she stood before her full-length mirror examining her plain, mud-colored riding gown and straw bonnet, unadorned except for the yellow ribbon tied beneath her chin. "What do you think?" she asked, knowing full well what her maid would say.

Baker's lips pursed disapprovingly. "Did you not tell me Lord Lynd and Lady Beasley are taking you visiting this afternoon and you'll be stopping by Vernon Hill?"

Flora nodded. That much was true. However, she had deliberately *not* mentioned her forthcoming lesson in four-in-hand, mainly because such juicy bits of *on-dit* had a peculiar way of getting back to her mother.

"Then I must say, madam, that your attire is most unsuitable." Baker nodded toward the open wardroom where hung Flora's beautiful new gowns. "Lord Lynd and his family are of inestimable importance. I cannot imagine why you would present yourself at Vernon Hill in *that*." Baker emphasized her last word with a look so full of scorn Flora could hardly keep from laughing. She felt sorry for the poor woman who, all her life, had been trapped in the chains of her obdurate homage of propriety. *But am I any different?* Flora asked herself, not wanting to delve too deeply into her own motivations in order to come up with a truthful answer.

As Flora stepped onto the portico, a coach pulled by four cantering horses came rolling up the circular driveway. Whip in hand, riding solo in the box, Lord Lynd brought the conveyance to a smart halt directly in front of her, the horses snorting and tossing their heads, as if in anticipation of another fine, exhilarating day on the road.

"Good morning, sir," she called. "You didn't forget, did you?"

"I do not forget such things, madam," Lord Lynd answered, a trace of laughter in his voice. As he climbed down from the box, Louisa leaned out the window from inside the coach and greeted her. "I've not tried four-in-hand, so I'm just here for the drive," she explained, adding lightly, "and since you're so concerned about propriety, I'm also your chaperon."

Intent on his lecture on four-in-hand, Lynd ignored his sister and addressed Flora, his expression serious. "First, you must realize driving a coach-and-four is not a matter of simply holding the reins and looking stylish."

"I never thought such a thing," she answered, trying to stifle her excitement and look properly solemn.

Lynd continued in his serious mode. "Before horses can be driven satisfactorily, they must be properly put together. To this end, anyone who aspires to be a coachman needs a practical knowledge of his . . . er, excuse me, *her* team, which must be harnessed and 'put to coach' as they say. So many things to remember. You must check that the pole chains aren't too slack, because if the pace is fast, there's a tendency to make the coach rock. You must make sure the load is proportioned to the power of the team, else the team cannot go as easily. Also—"

At his abrupt halt, Flora, who had been listening intently, inquired, "Why are you stopping? Have you given up? Do you think I don't understand?"

Lynd's lips twisted into a lopsided grin. "I have never before taught a woman how to drive a coach-and-four. I find it a rather . . . shall we say, unique experience."

She jammed her hands on her hips. "You think I cannot?"

"On the contrary. I do believe I was picturing the look on your parents' faces when they discover I've taught you four-in-hand. I doubt they'd approve."

"Of course they wouldn't, but aren't I married now? And out from under their control? I trust you won't let my parents stop you. Besides, Lord Dinsmore thinks it's a fine idea," she added with an adventurous toss of her head. "Mama and Papa worship him. In their eyes, he can do no wrong."

"In that case, enough of the lecture on practical matters

for now." Lynd extended his hand. "Shall we be off? Later, you'll be learning how to hitch the team. That is, if you're still interested. When all is said and done, the best way you can learn the art of driving is to sit beside me on the box seat and watch my hands."

Flora had never ridden on the top of a coach. Always before, she'd been safely ensconced inside, *where a lady ought to be,* came a faint echo from her mother.

But now was not the time to think of her strict upbringing. Now was the time to . . .

She raised her eyes to the coachman's box and concealed a worried frown. *How do I get up there?*

Lord Lynd appeared to sense her dilemma. "Shall I help you up?" His gaze dropped to her skirt. "At least you're wearing a wide skirt. That will have to do, I suppose, although I've always thought it a pity women cannot wear breeches like we men do."

Well, she wasn't wearing breeches and likely never would, so there was no sense even commenting. In fact, if ever there was a time when she didn't want to appear the helpless female, this was it. "I don't need help. You go first."

He didn't argue—one of the things she liked about him— but instead placed his right foot on the right side of the front axle and reached up to grasp the footboard. He swung with ease up to a small step attached to the side, then a higher step, then into the box. Frowning, he peered down at her. "Sure you can manage?"

"Certainly." Determined to ascend as swiftly and easily as he, she placed her right foot on the front axle. She gripped her skirt to keep it from sliding up but was forced to let go, when she gripped the footboard tightly and boosted herself a notch higher, placing her left foot on the first tiny step. A quick, overt glance over her shoulder convinced her that at least there were no servants around to gawk. She swung her right foot up to the next small step and from there slid smoothly onto the box to sit beside Lynd. "Ready," she announced in an offhand manner, smoothing down her skirt, which, to her annoyance, had traveled a slight distance higher than she had anticipated. But no matter. After all, she was a married woman. Lord Lynd would not be interested in such things.

"So we're off, then," Lynd announced. "Watch carefully. We shall circle through the village, then stop, and you shall take the reins. We shall visit Vernon Hill on our way back."

With a smart crack of the whip over the heads of the horses, they were off down the driveway. On the road, the horses burst into a canter, perfectly in step. It was as if the heavy coach behind them was but a feather at their heels.

They drove through the nearby village at a pace so quick that Flora had to hang on tight to prevent herself from being precipitated into the street as the coach twisted around the sharp corner by a cheese monger's shop and turned into the marketplace.

"Too fast for you?" Lynd called. There was a wild, excited gleam in his eye as he cast her a quick glance. "I can slow down if you like."

"Don't you dare!" Feeling totally exhilarated, loving the breeze blowing in her face, Flora called, "This is the best ride I've ever had!"

On the other side of the village, Lynd halted the coach and got it turned around. "Your turn." He placed the ribbons in her hands. "Remember, when you mount you hold the taut leads with your right hand. You must never put them down while you're driving. Now, your left hand is free to take up the whip."

"All right, then!" Flora took a deep breath, cracked the whip over the horses' heads, and they were off. The team responded gallantly as the coach fairly flew down the road, she in command. Oh, what an intoxicating feeling! How mighty she felt knowing she controlled a team of four fine bloods in her one small hand! The milestones seemed to flash by until Lynd pointed toward a driveway ahead and shouted, "We're coming to Vernon Hill. Pull to the right!"

She did so, and the coach turned down the long driveway at a fast pace. As they approached a pillared portico, she felt a moment of panic and called, "How do I stop?"

"Pull," Lynd calmly declared, pointing to the ribbons. She pulled. Horses snorting, dust flying, they came to a stop so quickly she was brought half out of her seat. She fell back laughing, aware, but not caring, that her hat dangled by its ribbons down her back and her hair, blown awry by the breeze, must look a fright.

"That was marvelous, Lord Lynd," she said.

Lynd regarded her with calm amusement. "Call me Sidney. We don't stand for formality at Vernon Hill."

"Indeed, we do not!" called Louisa as she climbed out of the coach. "Very nicely done, Flora."

"Indeed," said Lynd. "I must say, you have handed me a surprise."

Flora looked down her nose at him, feigning great disdain. "And what surprise is that?"

"I think you know. Suffice to say, it's not every day I see a lady such as you driving a great coach such as this. How daring." His eyes glowed with admiration. "How extraordinary. Even my devil-may-care sister has never attempted such a thing."

"I am only just beginning to learn, thanks to you," Flora answered modestly, pleased, nonetheless.

Lynd scrambled across her and down the side of the coach with catlike ease. Once on the ground, he turned and reached his arms to her. "Come, I'll help you down."

Thank goodness. She had never been overly concerned about modesty, but with Lynd closely watching, she was keenly aware her descent down those tiny steps from the top of the coach, especially in a skirt, was full of peril. Without hesitation, she came down partway, then allowed herself to fall, fully trusting, into Lynd's arms. She could feel his strength as he caught her and the warmth of his body as he lifted her down. Oddly, she found herself wanting to linger in his arms and felt a vague disappointment when he placed her gently on the ground and stepped away.

Once inside, Flora was impressed by the beauty of Vernon Hill, a house of Elizabethan origin, built, Louisa explained, in 1562. Flora noted it was not nearly as large as Pemberly Manor. Much better kept, though.

At tea, the three indulged in lighthearted chatter, discussing her wedding and wedding guests, the cost of horses, tenants and crops, how much wheat was expected from this year's harvest.

Flora enjoyed herself immensely, except for one unsettling observation: neither Lord Lynd nor Louisa made mention of Lord Dashwood.

Not one single word! And here she'd looked forward to hearing news of him, but it seemed as though both were avoiding the subject. Still, she found it hard to believe they could both refrain from talking of Richard. He was Dinsmore's heir, was he not? Surely Louisa knew him well, and wasn't he supposed to be Lynd's best friend? Or was he? Childhood friends, anyway. But why wouldn't Lord Lynd at least mention Dashwood in their conversation?

She, in turn, would not dream of mentioning Richard's name, lest she give herself away. She must remain patient. Surely sooner or later someone would bring up the name of Dinsmore's one-and-only heir. She'd heard no news of him since the day he jilted her. Even her family had assiduously avoided the subject. Meanwhile, disquieting thoughts crowded her mind. Not only was she concerned for Richard's welfare, her curiosity was intense. Had he married the countess? Was he still in the city? She was dying to know.

At the end of Flora's visit, Louisa said her warm goodbyes and retired upstairs. Finding herself alone in the grand entry hall with Lord Lynd, Flora realized now was her chance. Despite her better judgment, despite the risk of Lynd's eyebrow raising in that cynical, mocking little way, she took a deep breath and asked, "And what of Lord Dashwood? Have you seen him lately?"

A casual observer would not have noticed any change in the pleasantly arranged features of her host's face, but Flora, being close and facing him squarely, detected an extra-fast blink of his eyelids, accompanied by the barely discernible twitch of a cheek muscle.

"Lord Dashwood is doing splendidly," Lord Lynd replied in a velvet-edged voice that failed to conceal his pique.

She knew she should let the matter drop, but curiosity drove her on. "Did he marry the Countess de Clairmont?"

"Not to my knowledge. It appears the countess is peddling her assets in other, more lucrative markets."

Dashwood was still single! She felt a warm glow flow through her and could not help her sigh of relief and sudden smile. "Oh, really?" She had tried to sound disinterested but knew she hadn't.

Lynd regarded her a moment, his expression unperturbed. Therefore, she was startled when suddenly he burst out, "What in the name of the devil's backside are you doing?"

She flinched but recovered quickly. "I have no idea what you mean."

"Oh, yes, you do." He glowered at her. "You still love that scapegrace, don't you?"

He was hovering over her, suddenly so big, dark, and menacing she was tempted to step backward, but she held her ground. "He's not a scapegrace!"

"You're avoiding the issue. Damn!" Lynd rolled his eyes upward in frustration. "I am completely dumbfounded that you, married to one of the finest men on earth, would deign to spend so much as a passing thought upon that selfish, conceited—"

"You have already called him a scapegrace," she hotly interrupted. "Isn't that enough? I thought he was your friend."

"Friend, yes, but that doesn't mean . . ." Lynd bit his lip in irritation. "My friendship with Richard has nothing to do with the fact he should be dragged through the horse pond for jilting you."

"You let me worry about that," she retorted, not attempting to conceal her anger. "Can't you see you're wrong about Lord Dashwood? He did *not* jilt me! I'm not sure why he failed to ask Papa for my hand, but he must have had his reasons."

"I shall sum up all his reasons for you in one short word—greed! Are you so blinded by love you cannot see?"

"All I can see is that Lord Dashwood is noble, honorable, and pure hearted in every way, whereas *you,* sir, are a cad."

He stared at her in amazement. "*I'm* the cad?"

"Yes, because you're saying such beastly things."

Lynd started to answer, stopped himself, and threw up his hands. "What are we doing?" he asked softly. "I am only trying to tell you that I worry you'll—"

"I'll what?" she asked sharply. "Forget my marriage vows and run off with Dashwood?"

"If you want the truth, yes."

"That won't happen. If you knew me well enough, you would know I'd never do a thing so dishonorable. I shall always hold to my marriage vows, but that doesn't keep me from"—she looked around the entryway, making sure they were alone—"loving Lord Dashwood until the day I die."

"Ha!" retorted Lynd, all softness gone from his voice

again. "And what happens when Richard comes visiting, which he will, you know, sooner or later. How will you resist, some night after your old, crippled husband retires, and there he is, your golden lover, whispering sweet nothings in your ear, eager to take you to his bed?"

"He is too honorable ever to do such a thing!"

"Spare me. I know Richard, and I know what he'll try. And you *will* go. I know you will."

"I will not," she retorted through gritted teeth, fighting to keep down her voice.

"Oh, yes, you will." Lord Lynd settled back on his heels, crossed his arms, and regarded her with total disgust. "Imagine, the Hero of Seedaseer cuckolded by a selfish, head-in-the-clouds, dim-witted female who's stupid enough to love a rake not worthy of her little finger!"

Flora stared at him a moment, so angry she had trouble untangling her words. "Lord Dinsmore will never be a cuckold. Even if he were, why should he care? We don't have that kind of marriage."

"What do you mean?" Lynd inquired, puzzled, his voice softer still.

"We are friends, that's all."

"Friends," he scoffed. "That's ridiculous. Are you saying you two are not—?"

"We most certainly are not!"

"You won't be having children?" He looked amazed.

She answered in a scathing voice, "I may be young, sir, and inexperienced, but I am aware what causes babies, so no, I won't be having any. I repeat, Lord Dinsmore and I are just good friends and intend to stay that way."

"The coach is ready, sir," called a stable boy who had just poked his head through the front door.

Flora swiveled quickly, turning her back to her host. "I cannot tell you how wrong you are," she called over her shoulder as she hastened toward the door. She knew her voice was shaking but she didn't care. "I shall never break my marriage vows, despite what you say."

Lord Lynd followed her outside. "So what now?" he inquired. "Are you game for another lesson in four-in-hand, or would you rather sulk inside?"

*Quit now? Never!* "Of course I want another lesson."

"Wait, I'll help you up."

"I shall climb up myself," Flora proclaimed, still so angry she hadn't a care whether or not she fell flat on her face. She placed her foot on the axle, out of the corner of her eye catching Lynd watching from the portico. She extended her left foot to the first tiny step above, making no effort to keep her skirt down. *Let him look.* She stepped higher with her right foot, totally ignoring her sliding skirt. *Let him get his eyes full.* By now, a most shocking amount of leg was showing, but she would die before she'd reach to cover it.

*You are a wicked, wicked girl,* came her mother's voice from afar.

*Yes, I am,* she agreed with great satisfaction as she slid to the seat and finally, with a great show of modesty, tugged down her skirt. From beneath lowered lashes, she ventured a glance at Lord Lynd, who still stood on the steps, his face that of the perfect host, friendly but unfathomable. "Well, are you coming?" she inquired. Silently, he climbed up and took his place beside her.

She took up the ribbons and drove home at a respectable pace, neither exchanging a word. At the portico of Pemberly Manor, she climbed down, in a much more decorous manner than she'd climbed up, and tilted her head back to say good-bye. Remembering her husband's invitation, she sweetly called, "Good-bye, sir, and I almost forgot. Lord Dinsmore wants you and Lady Beasley to come to dinner next Saturday."

"My sister is busy, but I am happy to accept. It's informal, I trust."

"Informal. And thank you," she said most sincerely. "I enjoyed the lesson very much."

A look passed between them. Although his face showed no emotion, something flared in his eyes for an instant deep within. She knew what it was.

Desire.

Lynd wanted her. She was positive he did because women simply know those things. She could always tell when a man was attracted to her, an easy task when they fawned and gave her fancy compliments, but in Lord Lynd's case . . .

Despite his harsh words in the entryway just now, despite his hardly ever paying her a compliment, she knew, from the look in his eyes alone, he had a special feeling for her.

Suddenly she was ashamed. Even if Lord Lynd did lust after her, honor alone would keep him from ever expressing his feelings. So what had she just done? Acted like a jade. Taunting, teasing him with a flash of bare flesh, with no other reason than spite and wanting to hurt him for the rotten things he'd said.

She regretted, too, the look she'd just given him, a look that proclaimed, *Feast your eyes! I know you desire me, but I don't want you, and I'm angry enough to give you a peek at what you, sir, will never have.*

No matter that she had taken her revenge in one of the few ways a woman could. Her parading herself in front of him was a mean, childish thing to do. Immoral, too, considering she was now a married woman.

But what fun she'd had this afternoon! Driving four-in-hand was every bit as exciting as she'd thought it would be. She could hardly wait for her next lesson, with Lord Lynd as her instructor.

But despite her euphoria over four-in-hand, Lynd's words concerning Richard kept coming back to her.

*He should be dragged through the horse pond for jilting you.* Oh, never! Lynd simply did not understand.

*How are you going to resist, some night after your old, crippled husband retires . . . ?*

How dare Lord Lynd say such a thing! So totally untrue, so totally, totally . . .

*She is about to ascend the staircase when she feels the warm touch of Richard's hand on her arm.* "Lord Dinsmore has gone up to bed."

"I'm going, too."

"Stay!" *His fingers stroke her arm, causing little tingles.* "God, I've missed you."

"Richard, you must not."

"But I must. Oh, Flora, I love you. I shall never forgive myself for losing you. One kiss, that's all I ask. Then I shall go away."

*Before she can stop him, his arms are around her and he crushes her against him. His mouth hungrily covers hers and suddenly she's aflame, the pit of her stomach in a wild swirl.*

*She returns his kiss, eagerly, passionately. Finally he breaks away and looks down at her with his big, blue, pleading eyes. "Come to my room, my darling. Cousin Charles need never know. How could it be wrong when we love each other so much?"*

*"I . . ."*

She caught herself. What was she thinking? Was there no end to her wickedness? She thought again of how shabbily she'd treated Lord Lynd. When she found the opportunity, she would apologize for her less-than-ladylike behavior. She would even show a modicum of regret for her heated words, despite the fact that she was right, and he, not seeing Richard for the truly wonderful man he was, was completely wrong.

When Sidney arrived home, he turned the coach over to his coachman, headed inside, straight to his study, which he entered and slammed the door, servants be damned.

God's blood, what a scene! He fell into his desk chair and dropped his head in his hands. Bad enough, he'd lost his temper. He, who had always prided himself on his never-failing, moderate demeanor. He never allowed anything to upset him. He remained calm and reasonable at all times. Except today. The very thought of that harebrained girl still thinking herself in love with Richard had so shocked him, he'd become . . . no other way to put it, temporarily deranged.

Such shocking disloyalty! She didn't deserve such a fine man as Lord Dinsmore. She wasn't fit to kiss his feet.

No, not true. Smothering a groan, Sidney threw himself back in his chair and regarded the ceiling. With whom should he be honest if not himself? So he had to admit the truth: It was not her disloyalty to Dinsmore that upset him. It was the shocking, irrefutable fact that despite his hitherto unquestioned loyalty to the great Hero of Seedaseer, he, the honorable Lord Lynd, had fallen hopelessly in love with Lord Dinsmore's wife.

He had known before today that he liked her—very much, in fact. But it wasn't until this afternoon, when she'd come flying up the driveway atop the coach, bonnet bouncing on her back, its ribbons streaming, shining hair flying in the breeze, cheeks glowing with excitement, dainty hands firmly gripping the reins, that he realized how much he wanted her.

Sidney groaned and covered his eyes. No. He must not even think it. His father had raised him to be a gentleman, and so he would be, always remaining true to his code of honor. He might not like it, of course, but he must not even dream of lusting after his neighbor's wife, especially when that neighbor was one of the finest, most courageous men he had ever known.

So he must live with his love for Lady Flora tightly bound up within himself, never to be spoken of, or hinted at in any way. What rotten fortune she was his neighbor. Time and again, their paths would cross. Each time, seeing her would present a powerful temptation he must resist.

Perhaps in time . . . Surely his passion would fade.

Not now, though. He didn't even want to think about the counterfeit performance he'd be obliged to give when he dined at Pemberly Manor. He would play his part as the old family friend who had dined there many a time before, but it would be difficult. He knew because even after all his stern admonitions to himself, deep inside there was a part of him that looked forward to seeing the tantalizing Lady Flora once again, and for all the wrong reasons.

# Chapter 12

The following Saturday, when Flora greeted Lord Lynd in the drawing room, she could not help but note how handsome he looked in his dark wool cutaway coat, fairly tight breeches, and perfectly tied cravat—much fancier than what he usually wore.

Since Lord Dinsmore had not yet come down to dinner, Flora recognized the perfect opportunity for her to apologize. Still, she hesitated, noting Lynd's correct but faintly remote demeanor. Her hesitation lasted only for a moment, though. Obviously, he was thinking of their last, less than cordial, meeting. Part of it had been her fault and she really must set things straight. Now might be the only chance she'd have all evening.

She cleared her throat. Her heart beat a little faster as she regarded Lynd, sitting casually across from her, and began, "About our last discussion."

" 'Discussion?' " Lord Lynd dryly repeated. "I believe you mean argument."

"Yes, argument." He was not being very nice. "I wanted to say—"

"Don't. The whole unfortunate incident is best forgotten."

"No, it's not." She decided to forge ahead, despite his unpleasantness. "I was rude. I said things I shouldn't have."

"So you're apologizing?"

"Well, yes." Couldn't he at least smile? She hated the detached expression in his eyes.

"You're forgiven," he said, the soul of politeness. "I accept your apology." He paused, as if reluctant to continue and finally managed, "I, too, was rude."

"You're forgiven," she replied. "I'm not finished yet."

"You're not?"

There went that cynical raise of his eyebrow that she absolutely despised. "There were some things I did that were not, uh, ladylike."

He burst into laughter. "You mean the little show you put on when you climbed atop the coach?"

"I would hardly consider it a show."

"This may come as a surprise to you, but I've been aware for quite some time that women have legs underneath their skirts and petticoats." He cocked his head and blithely added, "By the way, yours are especially slim and shapely. I enjoyed the view."

"Oh!" She could feel her face flush crimson. "Here I am, trying to humbly apologize while you . . . you—"

"I what?" he demanded, still with that abominable smile on his face.

"You're laughing at me."

"Of course I'm laughing. It's difficult not to laugh when a supposedly bright young lady like yourself commits blunder after blunder."

"What blunders?" Her humbleness was fading fast. Just who did he think he was?

"You know what I mean."

"I do not! Pray, sir, enlighten me."

Lynd cast a quick glance at the door. He lowered his voice. "I have already told you what I thought of that exalted, sacred love of yours for Dashwood. What more is there to say, except I might suggest you devote some of your time to your husband?"

She awarded him an indignant glare. "My marriage is fine, thank you."

Softly he asked, "Are you still 'just good friends'?"

"Of course. Lord Dinsmore is happy with me just the way I am."

He smiled and sat back in his chair, maddeningly relaxed. "If you think that, you don't know men. You're a beautiful woman, Lady Dinsmore. Not only that, you're bright and you possess a great curiosity and courage to try the unknown. Some might interpret your behavior as rash and impetuous, but I admire you for it. Doubtless Dinsmore does, too. I don't know what sort of pact he has made with you, but I'd wager sooner or later he expects more than friendship." Although Lord Lynd's tone was smooth and controlled, she noted a sharp, sarcastic edge crept into his voice when he said "friendship." He paused, as if aware his composure was beginning to slip. More quietly he added, "You would be well advised to remove your head from the clouds. You'll never find a finer husband than Lord Dinsmore. Can't you look beyond that poor, scarred face and give him a chance?"

She thrust out her palms in an innocent gesture. "If he wants something more, why doesn't he say so?"

"For God's sake, woman, did you ever hear of pride?"

Before Flora could answer, she heard footsteps and the tap of a cane, and the subject was abruptly closed as Lord Dinsmore entered the drawing room.

"Ah, Sidney," Lord Dinsmore exclaimed, "Lady Dinsmore has told me how delighted she was with the four-in-hand lesson you gave her."

"Thank you, sir."

"No one could teach four-in-hand better than you, my boy. He's an expert, Flora. If he hadn't been born to the nobility, I'd wager he'd be king of the road by now—coachman on the Comet or the Silver Streak."

"That's kind of you, sir."

"And I trust you'll be around to give my bride many more lessons, won't you, Sidney?"

"Of course, sir."

Flora wondered if only she caught the slight hesitation before Lord Lynd gave his last response.


A few weeks later, Flora, dressed in her riding gown, was about to leave her bedchamber and go for a ride on Primrose when Baker swiped a finger across a side table, held it up, and remarked, "No dust. Your little chat with Mrs. Wendt has brought results."

"Apparently so," agreed Flora. Baker needn't know how short the chat was. "Now, I hope you're satisfied."

"Heavens, no. There is still *much* at Pemberly Manor that *begs* for your attention."

Uh-oh, she might have known. "And what might that be, Baker?" Flora asked, knowing full well what her finicky lady's maid would spout in her upcoming tirade.

"It is simply not enough." Baker's nose always twitched

when she was miffed. It was twitching now. "Much remains
in disarray. The servants *still* are not properly attired. Some
of the furniture is quite shabby—have you not noticed?
The situation is easily rectifiable, since there are some
beautiful pieces of furniture in the attic that should be
brought down, as well as portraits. And the china! Why
hasn't the French Haviland been put to use, as well as—"

"There simply hasn't been time," Flora interrupted, none
too kindly. Her husband, finally feeling better now, awaited
her, along with Lord Lynd and Lady Beasley. She was
much more interested in taking Primrose for another glorious morning ride than standing there arguing with her
maid. Still, she felt uncomfortable knowing the main cause
of her crossness was her own guilt over her indifference to
her duty. Since arriving at Pemberly Manor, she had ex-
pended little time nor energy toward becoming England's
greatest hostess. Instead, she had been riding nearly every
day, enjoying herself immensely with Lord Lynd, Louisa,
and her husband on the few occasions he'd been able to
leave his bed.

The problem was, she'd been so engrossed in riding and
four-in-hand she hadn't quite gotten around to restoring
Pemberly Manor to its former state of grandeur.

*Poor Mama will be so disappointed,* she thought, her guilt
deepening. She could hear her mother now, bragging about
her daughter, the esteemed wife of the Hero of Seedaseer,
who had used the many skills her mother taught her in
order to once more turn Pemberly Manor into one of the
most beautiful estates in all England.

*I haven't even started,* Flora thought glumly. *Except for
the dust. I've been having far too good a time for myself.*
Still, it wasn't too late. "Baker, since his lordship is feeling
better, I do believe we shall have a dinner party—make it
a week from tonight. Only a few guests, ten at the most,
including Lord Lynd and Lady Beasley, but we shall make
it a *formal* dinner party this time."

"Oh, perfect, madam, there's our starting point." The
usually staid Baker actually clapped her hands together in
delight. "We shall get out the Haviland, the silver epergne,
the—"

"Yes, fine," Flora answered, happy she had pleased her
lady's maid. "Do what you think best."

"But of course, your ladyship!" Baker answered with such an avid gleam in her eye Flora knew she'd head for the attic posthaste, as soon as their conversation was done. "But you had best speak to Mrs. Wendt," she warned. With a sweep of her arm, Baker indicated the entire mansion. "Everything must be turned out. Rugs beaten, windows washed, chimneys swept, and all that." Her perennial frown deepened. "She's not going to like it."

Flora inwardly cringed. She didn't want to confront the dour housekeeper again, even though Baker was right. The house was still shabby, dust or no dust, and needed a complete renovation. But she was Lady Dinsmore now, Flora reminded herself. She must assert herself, play the part for which she was intended. Her spirits sank at the thought. What was wrong with her? she wondered, unwilling to admit she was having too good a time doing what she pleased. What a heady experience to no longer feel constrained!

In part, she had her husband to thank. But he'd been sick much of the time and it was really Lord Lynd who had filled her days with happiness. How she had changed her opinion of him! When they'd met, she had thought him nothing more than a cynical, difficult man. How wrong she'd been! Lynd's conversation was so engaging she would much prefer accompanying him and Louisa on a ride through the woods than entertaining a gaggle of ladies at tea. There was nothing she enjoyed more than going on a picnic where they sat by a stream, laughed a lot, and discussed matters ladies weren't supposed to know about, such as military history and who was running for parliament.

But most of all, she enjoyed driving four-in-hand down a country road, hands firm on the reins, Lynd beside her, enjoying the ride as much as she.

Those terrible dark days she'd suffered through after Richard jilted her were gone. She would never be truly happy and would always mourn his loss, but still, she was fairly content with her life, and knew now she could carry on.

"Well, madam?" Baker asked impatiently.

"Er . . . Yes, I suppose I must speak to Mrs. Wendt again." She brightened. Life wasn't so bad after all! Swinging her arm high, she proclaimed, "Mark my words. Pem-

berly Manor shall rise from the ashes, Baker! We'll see to
it, won't we?"

Baker left in a state of delight. And although Flora tried
to focus on her upcoming elegant dinner party, and her
talk with Mrs. Wendt, she found her thoughts lingered on
Lord Lynd. She liked the unpretentiousness of the man.
He truly wouldn't care about the elegance of her china. He
was kind, too, and thoughtful, and witty when he wasn't
glowering at her. How fond she was of their nearly daily
rides! Along with Louisa, of course.

Flora's thoughts were interrupted by a small commotion
in the front entry hall. Moments later, her younger sister
burst into her bedchamber, smiling brightly, cheeks a rosy
glow.

"Amy, I thought you were in London."

"I was," Amy declared as she hugged her sister. "But I
had to come in person and give you the news."

*Armond.* Only he could bring such a glow to Amy's
cheeks, such a bright gleam to her eyes. Flora knew Amy
had been seeing him the past few weeks. Her heart sank
as she asked, "The duke?"

"He has asked for my hand!" Stepping lightly, Amy
twirled in a little dance of delight. "Isn't that wonderful
news? You must attend me at the wedding."

*Oh, Amy, how foolish you are.* Flora suppressed a shud-
der as she thought of the arrogant, thin-nosed Duke—so
cold, so . . . It was hard to say exactly, but to her mind, he
seemed almost sinister.

Amy gave her a rueful smile. "I know you're not thrilled
with my choice."

Flora asked, "Isn't one loveless marriage enough in the
family?"

"But who could love me? Oh, you'd never understand,
you with all your beauty and charm, whereas I . . ." Amy
drew a resigned breath, seeming to calm herself. Smiling
faintly she continued. "I assure you, I am one of the happiest girls in the world. Imagine, a *duke.* I shall be a duchess."
Playfully she tilted up her nose. "Everyone must bow and
scrape to me and call me Your Grace."

"Not I," Flora replied with sisterly scorn. She grew serious. "As if you cared about rank. What is it, Amy? Were
you so unsure of yourself you thought no one else would

have you? If that's the case, then you're wrong. Forget the duke. Tell him you've changed your mind."

"It's far too late for that," said Amy with a rueful grin. "Besides, Mama would kill me." Before Flora could form a reply, Amy dipped into an exaggerated curtsy. "My dear, esteemed Lady Dinsmore, do you realize that between the two of us we shall be the most dazzling pair of snobbish aristocrats in all London?"

Flora wanted to reply in kind to Amy's banter, but her heart was too heavy. "If only you had waited," she said wistfully. "I know you would have found someone who sees you for the beautiful person you are."

"If I have any beauty at all, it's on the inside, but men don't see what's on the inside, do they?" Amy clasped her sister's hands. Her eyes pleaded as she asked, "Can't you be happy for me, Flora? I was never as beautiful as you, or as clever, and, oh my, never as slim." Frowning, she gazed down at her short, pudgy figure. "This is nothing new. All my life, I've thought I would have to content myself with a man who married me for money, not love."

Flora forced a small smile. "Well, we cannot accuse the duke of wanting your money, can we?"

"He's rich as Croesus. Doesn't that prove he's at least fond of me? He says he is. Else why would he want to marry me?"

Why, indeed? Flora wondered if the duke might have looked beyond Amy's lack of beauty and seen her for the thoughtful, generous person she was. Not likely. Doubtless the lofty duke had decided the time had come for him to marry. Pressure from his mother, most likely. Her Grace, the Dowager Duchess of Armond, no doubt wanted grandchildren, and the duke, single for too long, had run out of excuses. And who better to marry than Lady Amy Winton, with her generous dowry and impeccable family background? But whatever his reasons, this was no time to dampen Amy's high spirits. The deed was done. There was nothing Flora could do except pretend enthusiasm, offer her support, and hope for the best.

"Amy, if you're sure, then I am thrilled for you." If she had to lie, she might as well make it a good one. "After all, the duke does have his charms. Mama must be beside herself."

"Oh, indeed, she is," Amy chimed. "Just think, you caught the Hero of Seedaseer and now I've caught the duke. I do believe Mama is at last content, knowing both her daughters are happy and set for life."

"Happy and set for life," Flora thoughtfully repeated. "I suppose we are, aren't we?" She concealed her doubts, both about Amy and herself.

Amy's surprise visit was like a breath of fresh air. Later in the day, after Flora, Amy, and Lord Dinsmore had gone for a short ride, the sisters settled across from each other in the drawing room and chatted over tea.

"I so admire Lord Dinsmore," ventured Amy. "Always before, he appeared so unapproachable, but riding today, I could see how companionable he is, how . . . Well, I never thought I'd say this, but he is charming."

"Indeed, he is," Flora responded.

Amy hesitated before she asked, "Have you grown fond of him, Flora? Oh, I hope so! And I hope by now you've forgotten all about that awful man who jilted you."

Flora looked around to make sure they were alone. "Lord Dashwood is as much on my mind as ever. If you must know, I love him still and I always shall."

Startled, Amy asked, "But what of your husband?"

"We are friends and nothing more. We don't . . . you know."

"You don't?" Amy looked amazed.

Flora proceeded to explain how Richard was "not awful" and she would always love him, how she had truly grown fond of Lord Dinsmore but could never love him, how she could not work up any enthusiasm for being the grand mistress of Pemberly Manor, but she was trying.

"Lord Lynd is coming for dinner Saturday—my first formal dinner party, by the way—but I'm not the least excited. Baker's the one who's eager to drag out the good china and silver. I could not care less."

Amy said, "It's our mother who's at fault. You know how she dotes upon such affairs, but she drives herself to distraction every time she entertains, she's so worried over every little detail."

"Is the soup a tad too cold?" Flora asked in a fair imitation of her mother. "Are the sterling nut cups not properly shined? Poor Mama can never relax."

"And by the time the evening is over and the last guest gone, she's ready to collapse."

"I should hate being that way."

"Still, though . . . I, personally, shall be ecstatic when I become the Duchess of Armond. What balls I shall give! What soirees!" Amy eyed her sister accusingly. "Just like you should be doing."

"But I hate it. I don't want to entertain. I'd rather be riding through the woods, like we were today, or practicing my four-in-hand with Lord Lynd."

"To what end?" Amy inquired. "Do you plan to be a coachman? Oops, a thousand pardons, a *coachwoman?* What are your chances of *that?*" Amy grew intently serious. "Really, Flora, I don't wish to sound like our mother, but when you come down to it, a woman has but one role in life. That's to support her husband, and that means running his household, be it large or small, in a suitable fashion, and also having children, which you, so far, have shown no inclination to do." With a tiny grin she added, "Well, how could you, if you're not . . . you know."

"But how can I when I love another man?" cried Flora, spreading her palms in frustration.

"You are being most unrealistic and you'd best reconsider." Amy squeezed a slice of lemon into her tea and stirred vigorously. "I love you dearly, Flora, but I give you this piece of advice for your own good. Don't be a rebel. Be good to your husband and stop all this daydreaming about another man. It will get you nowhere. Eventually, your husband is bound to discover how you feel and show his displeasure."

"You don't understand," Flora replied, feeling quite deflated. "Lord Dinsmore has indicated he's happy with our arrangement."

"Ha! I grant you're older than I, and smarter, but sometimes you can be *so dense!*"

"But it's true! Lord Dinsmore highly values my companionship."

Amy threw her a look of scorn. "Oh, please. He's a man, isn't he? Even I, young and inexperienced though I am, know what men want, and it's not a companion." Amy took a sip of tea and plunged on. "You might yearn to be different, Flora, but you'd best remember you're a woman, just like the rest of us, and it's best you do what's expected of you. I warrant, Lord Dinsmore wants you in his bed and he wants sons."

Flora listened in amazement. She would never have guessed her younger sister could come up with such a mature view of married life.

"And Baker's right," Amy continued. "At the very least, you should refurbish Pemberly Manor—become England's greatest hostess and all that goes with it. You'd be pleasing your husband. Mama, too."

Could Amy possibly be right? Lately she'd been so satisfied with her life, but perhaps she'd been wrong. Flora didn't even want to think about it. Perhaps tomorrow. She picked up the teapot. "I shall give some thought to what you say. Now, let's change the subject, shall we? Would you like more tea?"


Amy left for London the next day, but her words stubbornly lingered in Flora's mind. She had thought she was being a good wife, but was she? Oh, why must her world be full of difficulties when right now all she wanted was to ride her horse and practice her four-in-hand with Lord Lynd?


A week later, Flora's dinner party was a smashing success. Guests from the local gentry indulged in lively conversation, ate a superb dinner cooked by Lord Dinsmore's newly hired French chef. The food was presented on the French Haviland plates Mrs. Wendt had finally retrieved from the attic. Lord Lynd even tactfully commented upon how "especially elegant" Pemberly Manor looked that evening, a comment to which the guests all heartily agreed. Flora reminded herself to give her compliments to Baker, who the past week had worked herself to a frazzle, cleaning, hanging pictures, overseeing the placement of new furniture.

Flora should have been delighted, but by now she hardly cared how the evening went. Although she had spent the evening acting the engaging hostess, her smooth facade hid inner turmoil. Amy's remarks concerning her relationship with Dinsmore deeply troubled her, especially in the wake of what Lord Lynd had told her when last he came to dinner. They could not possibly be right, or could they?

During the course of the evening, she observed her husband in a way she never had before. As always, he was the soul of politeness and consideration. So far as she could see, no simmering feelings of passion for her lurked beneath his courteous but reserved demeanor. He'd been ill much of the time, of course. . . . Perhaps if he were feeling better . . . ?

The more she thought, the more she began to realize Lynd's and her sister's words had merit. Perhaps she hadn't been that good a wife. These past weeks, Dinsmore had been more than kind—making sure she had everything she needed, catering to her every wish, demanding nothing. She asked herself what she had done in return and could come up with nothing, except she'd had a good time for herself, and in so doing had been stubborn, selfish, and unfair.

Her thoughts filtered back to what Dinsmore told her on their wedding day: *"I shall never come to you, Flora. You can count on it."*

In her vast relief she would not be assaulted on her wedding night, she had dismissed his words, hardly giving them a serious thought. She had assumed he wanted nothing to do with her, *that way*. Now, after reconsidering, she realized he had not said that at all. He *did* want her, only she must come to him.

He was so patient, so kind. The Hero of Seedaseer deserved better.

*I shall do it,* she decided with a jerky little nod of her head that brought a quizzical glance from Lord Lynd who sat across from her.

She would consummate the marriage this very night. It was the right thing to do, and high time. Mama would be so relieved. Dinsmore would be delighted. He deserved a nice surprise. She would not, however, say she loved him, because that would be a lie. But surely he would not expect such a declaration. Instead, he would be grateful she had finally seen her duty and come to his bed.

As for Lord Lynd . . .

There he sat across the dinner table, half smiling, lazily regarding her from beneath half-lidded eyes. She wished he knew what she was thinking. The irony was, she *wanted* him to know what she was thinking And that was because . . . ?

The esteemed Lord Lynd could talk all he pleased about how she would never find a finer husband than Lord Dinsmore, how she should look beyond that pitiful, scarred face and give her poor husband a chance. Drivel! Here was further proof Lynd himself lusted after her. She knew he did, despite his efforts to push her into her husband's bed. She knew he wanted her just from the way he talked to her, probing and constantly challenging her. She knew from those penetrating looks he gave her, revealing that tiny gleam of desire so deep in his eyes it was almost buried. Not quite, though. He could not totally conceal his hunger, though she'd wager he wished he could.

What she couldn't understand was why she should even care what he was thinking. In the past, when men had lusted after her, she had simply let them know she wasn't interested and sent them on their way. There was something about Lord Lynd, though, that intrigued her no end. It was almost as if she wanted to hurt him—twist the knife, so to speak, by letting him know she planned to consummate her marriage.

Surely she wasn't even faintly attracted to Lord Lynd.

Or was she?

She would think about that later. She turned her thoughts to the matter at hand, wondering how she would let Lord Dinsmore know of her decision. Perhaps she could throw out cautious feelers when they went on their ride tomorrow. Better, tonight. She could simply knock on the door of his bedchamber, and when he opened it . . .

*"I have changed my mind, Charles."*

*Startled, his gaze sweeps over her, admiring the red satin robe she's wearing and her long, full hair falling loosely down her back. His face lights. "Oh, my darling, you don't mean—?"*

*"Yes! I am your wife, am I not? I have finally realized where my duty lies."*

*"You mean it? You don't find my face repulsive?"*

*"I hardly notice it anymore."*

*"Come in, my dear. You have just made me the happiest man in the world. . . ."*

Yes, tonight. She had nothing to fear. Her husband would welcome her with open arms.


The servants had gone to bed. In the flickering light from the candle she held, Flora saw the look of surprise that crossed Dinsmore's face as he, dressed in a blue quilted satin robe, opened his door and saw her standing in his doorway.

"Please come in." He swung the door wide. Looking mildly surprised, he inquired, "To what do I owe the pleasure of your visit at this late hour?"

She entered, and when he swung the door shut, set down her candle and turned to him. "I am here because . . . I decided that . . ." Why wasn't he helping? Oh, where to begin? "These past weeks, have I made you happy?"

The moment the words left her mouth, she knew how silly she sounded, but he didn't laugh. Instead, he took her hand, all stiffness and formality gone. "Of course you've made me happy. And you?"

"Very happy." She thought of Richard and knew she was lying. Still, no one had forced her to marry Dinsmore. She had no right to complain. "Lord Dinsmore . . ."

"For heaven's sake, we're married now. Call me Charles."

"Charles. I've been thinking . . ." Oh, how to say it? Why couldn't she just blurt out she had decided she wanted to come to his bed? *Because you really don't,* cried a little voice within her, a voice she must ignore. "So far, we have occupied separate bedchambers, but I thought . . ."

"Thought what?"

"I thought . . ." Her heart raced. Could he not make this easier for her? She felt herself getting red in the face. A big lump of words caught in her throat, and she struggled to get them out. She lowered her eyelids and managed, "I thought that perhaps . . ." In a gush she finished, "You might wish me to come to your bed."

For a long time he was silent. She raised her eyelids. He seemed to be examining her, his gaze burning into hers, as if he were trying to look into her very soul. "Are you saying you wish to make love with me?" he asked quietly.

"Yes."

"Why, Flora?"

"Because—" She had to think. Finding a solid reason was difficult when she hardly knew herself. Back at dinner when she had decided, everything seemed crystal clear, and she was so certain and proud of herself for deciding to be the dutiful wife. But now . . .

"I am your wife. I have been thinking, and . . . I have become aware of my duties."

He smiled gently. "I am flattered beyond belief. However, we had a pact, remember? I was to provide you my wealth and title. In exchange, you were to provide your charming companionship to a lonely old man, which you've succeeded in doing quite admirably."

"Thank you, but . . ." This was not going as she had thought it would. He didn't seem overjoyed at all. Confusion was setting in. She was beginning to feel unsure of herself. "Don't you want me?" she blurted.

Unperturbed by her bluntness, he said, "Tell me exactly why you came to me."

"I came because . . ." She struggled for an answer. "We've been getting along famously, or so I thought, what with the riding, the picnics, and all. And I *am* your wife, so I thought, surely you wanted me to—you know, and it was my duty to . . . to . . ."

"So you thought it was your duty," he repeated, a harsh edge settling into his voice. "Not good enough. I do not require your pity. I do not want your pity."

"But it's not that at all. What it is—"

"Not another word," he said in the same voice he must have used to command his troops.

She could not contain a gasp. "You're rejecting me?"

He pulled in his breath and, frowning, turned his face away. When he looked back, his expression had softened. "Can you not understand pride is all I have left? Don't dismiss it lightly." He reached to brush her cheek gently with the back of his hand. "You've beauty, grace, intelligence—everything a man could want. Ah, Flora, you have no idea how much I would give to have you come to me because you loved me. But that's not the case, is it? I would even settle for your coming to me out of desire, not loving me but wanting me as a woman needs a man. What I shall not settle for, not now, not ever, is your coming to me out of pity."

Flora felt like crying, she was so shaken, so utterly shocked by his rejection. "Then we shall never—?"

"Never. There is another reason, too, that I . . . Well, no matter."

She stood confused, deeply wounded, astounded he had refused her. Well, she had her pride, too. She managed a tremulous smile. "Very well, Charles. You can rest assured I shall never bother you again."

"Oh, Flora, you cannot possibly know . . ." An expression close to anguish crossed his face. His arms started to reach for her. He pressed them tightly to his sides. "Are you all right?" he asked, his composure restored. "The last thing on earth I want to do is hurt you."

She steadied herself, trying to regain her own composure. "Of course I'm all right," she managed with supreme dignity. "Forgive me. It was just a passing fancy." She retrieved her candle. "Good night, sir. I shall be fine," she said over the lump in her throat, and swept from his bedchamber, head held high. In the hallway, she had to pause because her knees shook and she felt sick in the pit of her stomach. A large portrait of Dinsmore hung on the wall. She had passed it many times before, but tonight something made her pause in front of it and hold her candle high. Until now, she had given the portrait nothing more than a cursory glance. It had simply been the portrait at the end of a long row of portraits of Dinsmore's esteemed male ancestors. They were all unsmiling, dating back to the first Lord Dinsmore, a heavyset man wearing an expression of insufferable arrogance, who glowered at the world from beneath a ridiculously long, curly, black wig.

In the current Lord Dinsmore's portrait, he stood in the time-honored manner in which military men were portrayed: resplendent in full uniform, sword at his side, carriage erect, plumed hat held under one arm. His expression matched those of his ancestors: cold, stern, unyielding. Just another boring old portrait that she'd never really looked at, and yet . . .

For the first time, Flora looked beyond the obvious and

took in the whole of the man. He had been handsome once, in fact, devastatingly attractive, with a strong, square chin, high, intelligent brow, eyes the beautiful blue of glacial ice. She could feel the vitality of him, as he stood there, tall, broad-shouldered, utterly sure of himself. One could easily tell this leader of men did not suffer fools gladly and that he exuded power, vigor, and forcefulness—all the traits women found attractive in a man. What a catch he must have been! High-ranking ladies must have been charmed into bed by the dozens.

But now . . . poor man, what a terrible comedown.

How she got back to her room without breaking down, she didn't know, but when she reached the security of her own bedchamber, all the humiliations and crushing defeats she'd suffered the past months came crashing down upon her. First Richard, now this. Never had she felt so low.

Rejected by a crippled old man!

No matter he was handsome once.

And the worst part was, it was all her own fault. How could she have been so unthinking, so unfeeling as to not recognize the man had his pride?

It served her right.

She fell on her bed and started to cry, partly out of humiliation, mostly because she realized that the last vestiges of her girlhood had just disappeared forever and she would never be carefree, impetuous Flora again. She had learned her lesson. From now on, she would be more considerate, and most certainly think twice before she unthinkingly plunged ahead and did something so utterly stupid.

How she wished she could talk to Lord Lynd! How she would love to lean her head on his broad shoulder and pour her heart out. He would no doubt be amused—probably call her a milksop and a fool again—yet she knew she'd find tenderness and understanding in the comfort of his voice, as well as his arms.

The trouble was, she might have grown up tonight, but even if Lynd lectured her from dawn to sunset about how foolish was her obsession with Richard, she knew she could not forget him.

*Oh, Richard!* Would there ever come a time when the taunting image of his handsome face didn't haunt her dreams every night? As long as she loved him, she had no control over her heart. She might tell herself how prudent, how circumspect she would be in the future, but if there ever came a time when she could have him . . .

The whole thing was impossible, of course. She was married now, and marriage was a trap from which there was no escape, not ever.

But if someday she could have Richard—on any terms, legal or otherwise, moral or otherwise—she wondered what she would do.

Lord help her, she didn't know the answer.

Next day, the smell of autumn hung in the air as Lord Lynd rode his horse behind Flora's and Louisa's. Although the ride had been planned, Flora had tried to beg off. Her husband was ill again, she said, claiming she should stay by his bed. They'd insisted Flora come along, so here she was, looking exhausted, Sidney noted. Beyond exhaustion. Something was wrong.

"Lovely day!" Louisa called as she urged her horse to a canter and dashed ahead up the trail.

"Indeed!" he called after her, then slanted a glance at Flora, who was not riding her mount in her usual carefree style, but instead seemed slumped in the saddle in a defeated pose. He reined his horse closer. "You don't seem yourself today," he said.

"I'm not," she answered almost in a whisper. At first she appeared not to want to talk, but finally with a surprisingly bitter accusation in her voice she told him, "You were wrong, sir, about Lord Dinsmore. That's all I care to say on the subject."

"Let's stop a moment." Concerned, Lord Lynd took her reins and stopped both horses at a fern-filled spot by the side of a stream. He slid off his horse and reached to help her down. She allowed his assistance without protest—unusual in itself, since Flora, always independent, took pride in dismounting with grace and flare.

After they'd settled on flat rocks, facing each other by the stream, Lord Lynd asked, "Now, why am I wrong, Lady Dinsmore?"

She tilted her nose in the air. "It's a personal matter between Lord Dinsmore and myself, and I don't care to discuss it."

*Yes, you do,* thought Sidney. Curse women and their idiotic sensibilities. "You mean, you at long last found your way to his bed and something went wrong?"

"*Must* you be so blunt?" She glowered at him. "You are rude beyond all measure."

He crossed his arms and glowered back. "It may interest you to know there are parts of the world where the sexual act is an ordinary topic of conversation, not whispered about as if it were something shameful."

She dismissed his comment with a wave of her dainty hand. "Be that as it may, we're in England now and such things are simply not discussed."

"You sound just like your mother." There, that should raise a breeze.

"Oh!" Her face scrunched in a frown. Hotly, she declared, "I am not my mother."

"I know. Forget I said that. Actually you're right. Such matters are never discussed in England, and there's the pity. As for your new . . . uh, relationship with Lord Dinsmore, may I suggest, high time?"

"Oh!" She looked as if she were ready to take a swing at him with her riding crop. Then she surprised him by bursting into tears.

Suddenly everything became crystal clear. "He rejected you," Sidney said.

"How did you—?" She looked astonished. "Oh, now you really are being rude."

Sidney felt the urge to express his opinion concerning Englishwomen and their ludicrous false modesty concerning the marital bed. However, for the moment he could not. The shock of this new revelation suddenly hit full force and he felt as if someone had kicked him in the stomach. He felt relief. Joy, almost. How disgusting! Indeed, he should be deeply ashamed over such dishonorable feelings and should instead feel nothing but sorrow that Dinsmore, his old friend and mentor, had a troubled marriage. He knew why. Of course he knew why. There could be only one answer, which he doubted Dinsmore, with all his pride, would care to share.

She ought to know.

He took a moment to collect himself, then addressed her softly. "Tell me what happened."

She cast him a look full of resentment. "Do you recall when you told me I'd be well advised to remove my head from the clouds?"

"I do."

"And how I'd never find a finer husband than Lord Dinsmore? You asked me if I could look beyond that poor, scarred face—give him a chance."

"I do recall."

"Well, I decided you were right—Amy, too. So last night, I decided I would let him know that I would . . . you know, and you know what happened?"

He could guess, but waited for her reply.

"He misunderstood! He didn't want me, Lord Lynd." Flora's face twisted. Tears brimmed in her eyes. "Oh, it was by far the most humiliating moment of my life. Worse even than when—"

Her abrupt halt did not prevent him from surmising she meant when Richard had jilted her. Sidney watched as a single tear overflowed, coursed its way through tangled, thick dark lashes, down the peachy softness of her cheek. His heart ached with sympathy, as well as guilt. If he hadn't encouraged her . . . But little had he known. The usual platitudes rushed to his lips: She shouldn't take it personally, Dinsmore wasn't feeling well and all that rot, but he was sure he knew the answer. She should know it, too. He would have to explain. God's blood, but this would be hard, telling a young, naive Englishwoman the facts of life!

"I have often thought," he said, "that along with the lessons in music, watercolors, and embroidery that you young ladies take, a course in male anatomy should be included."

She brushed at her tear with the palm of her hand. "And why do you say that?"

"Because then you would know that men have certain . . . er, problems that arise from time to time—or, to put it more bluntly, don't arise." He paused and looked at her closely. "Do you know what I mean?"

"I'm not that naive, sir."

Good. She wasn't blushing. "Then you should also know

that men are quite sensitive about such matters. Loathe to discuss them because of their pride."

"So you think . . . ?" She was gazing at him, intensely interested.

"I think such could be the case with Lord Dinsmore. Why else would he reject a woman beautiful as you?"

"Don't flatter me."

He knew he shouldn't, but he reached the back of two fingers to touch her cheek. The whole of him tingled as he ran them gently down over her delicately carved facial bones, past her exquisitely dainty nose, over her musk-rose flesh, moist from the tear, to her determined chin. "I don't flatter you. You are a desirable woman. No man in his right mind would not want you."

"Then why am I so miserable?" she cried and bent toward him. "Everything I do is wrong!"

"Ah, Flora . . ." To take her in his arms would break his code as a gentleman. . . .

But she needed him. . . .

A pox upon his code as a gentleman. He wrapped his arms around her and pulled her close. Her head dropped to his shoulder. He felt the movement of her breathing, heard a gentle sniff as she fought her tears. He could feel his heart hammering in his chest—felt the arousal that *he* most certainly had no trouble with, but above all else, he must not lose his grip. She needed his comfort and advice, not his lust. But, oh God, how good to feel the seductive curves of her body in his arms at long last!

Flora felt a marvelous sense of contentment as she snuggled in Lord Lynd's powerful arms. She would not allow herself to cry. Tears were a weakness she wanted no part of, but still . . . How wonderful to let go, just once, and drink in the comfort of his nearness. Thus, they stayed, she didn't know how long, until finally she looked up and found his gaze upon her, soft as a caress. "You must think me very weak and very silly," she said.

"Far from it." He let her go and moved away, but not too far. "I suspect soon you'll have a heavy burden to carry, my Flora, but you're strong. Naive, perhaps"—an amused twinkle lit his eye—"but I've not a doubt that you, with your stubbornness and fierce determination will prevail." He took her hands. "Rise above the hurt. You must know

Lord Dinsmore loves you. Always remember, the most important thing in life is to learn how to give love and how to let love come to you."

Flora was astonished at the sudden sense of serenity she felt upon hearing his words. How right he was. How selfish of her to be thinking of no one but herself when her thoughts should be with her poor husband.

As the sounds of a cantering horse grew louder—no doubt Louisa's—Flora stood and smoothed her skirt. "Thank you, Lord Lynd. I feel better."

"Fine, then." He stood with a casual air. "Shall we get back to our horses?"

"Good idea." She tried to sound casual, too, and not let him know how, for one moment there, her senses had spun nearly out of control when she'd been in his arms and smelled the warmth of his flesh. It had been, she was loath to admit, absolutely intoxicating.

# Chapter 13

## London

A few nights later, Sidney was dining alone at Watier's when he heard a familiar voice call his name. Looking up, he concealed a frown. "Good evening, Richard," he said none too cordially. He had hoped to avoid his old friend during his latest stay in London.

Richard, jovial as ever, clapped him on the back. "Why didn't you let me know you were in London?"

"Just arrived." *Just escaped* was more like it, Sidney mused. That last meeting with Flora had been so excruciating—so downright painful—he'd been forced to place himself as far away from her as possible.

"May I join you?" Richard sat down uninvited and regarded Sidney's plate. "Ah, the *Filet de Rouget au Basilic*. An excellent choice. So tell me the latest."

Sidney concealed a resigned sigh. "What 'latest' are you referring to?"

"The latest about my cousin, of course, and his new bride. Carry on. I am all ears."

"As a matter of fact, I was their guest at dinner a few nights ago."

"Cousin Charles is well?"

"He's fine. It's a pity you're estranged, else you could find out firsthand."

A look of deep concern crossed Richard's face—most unusual for him. "It appears I am persona non grata at home, although I most certainly don't deserve his ire. The thing with Lady Flora was not my fault, actually."

"Why is it nothing is ever your fault?" Hearing the sharp edge to his voice, Sidney advised himself not to show his disgust. To his surprise, his friend refrained from giving one of his usual unctuous answers. Instead, he frowned and remarked, "I'm in trouble."

"You? Surely you're jesting."

"Yes, well . . ." Richard bit his lip. "It's Dinsmore. You know how displeased he is. I'm concerned about my inheritance."

"You're the one and only heir, aren't you? What is there to worry about?"

"Oh, I know he'd never disown me, but . . ." Squint lines of worry bracketed Richard's eyes. For a moment he actually looked desperate. "The entailments, Sidney! If he had a mind to, he could tie up my land for my entire lifetime."

"So?" Sidney took no pains to conceal his exasperation. "Bear in mind, the estate's not yours yet and won't be for some time, God willing. Besides, why should you care if it's entailed? You're not planning on selling off the family land, are you?"

"Matter of fact, I am." Richard squirmed uncomfortably in his chair. "Not all of it, but some. If you must know, I'm under the hatches."

"No surprise. I've heard you've been tossing away money at White's with both hands."

"Yes, well, even the best player is subject to the whims of fortune. I plan to cut back."

"What about the countess? Rumor has it you're in her good graces again."

Richard nodded dubiously. "There's still the possibility, I 'spose. Trouble is, the woman's impossibly erratic. Flits from one man to another."

"You must be shocked by such infidelity."

Richard, who usually enjoyed a touch of irony, did not respond in kind. "Have your little joke, but I tell you I'm getting close to desperation. I used to laugh at those poor wretches who got so deep in debt they were forced to flee England. I'm not laughing anymore." Richard's eyes went wide with anxiety. "That could be me, Sidney! At the rate I'm losing money, I, too, could be living all alone in some miserable foreign country, cramped in some squalid garret, cold, starving, spending my declining years in abject poverty."

"Are you saying—?" Despite himself, Sidney began to feel compassion for his friend.

"I am saying I *must* get in Cousin Charles's good graces again. If I don't, Lord knows what he'll do. Which leads me to ask . . . I'd like a favor."

He might have known. "If you want me to speak to Lord Dinsmore, the answer is no. You and I are still friends, despite your abominable behavior, but if you want me to persuade your cousin what a fine fellow you are, I'd sooner choke."

"Hmm." Gazing into space, Richard beat a worried tattoo with his fingers upon the linen tablecloth. "Flora, then." He shifted his gaze to Sidney. "Is she pining away for me?"

Curse the man! "Last I saw her, she was happy as a lark, enjoying married life immensely."

"Even so, I doubt she's forgotten me. I do believe I shall enlist her help. Surely she'd put in a good word for me with Dinsmore." Richard's face brightened. "Of course she would! After all, she was madly in love with me, and not so very long ago. I suspect she still is, no matter what you say. Game girl that she is, she'd cover her heartbreak."

Sidney was forced to show a sudden interest in his *Filet de Rouget,* taking a long moment to reply while he bridled his anger. At last he was able to reply smoothly, "And how do you plan to ask her? She is, after all, buried in the country, and you're not welcome at Pemberly Manor."

Richard smiled smugly. "Amy's wedding. I've known the duke for years. He'll see to it I'm invited."

Unbelievable! How low could a man sink? "You really are a cad."

"Why so touchy?" Richard gave him a perceptive gaze. "You like her, don't you?"

"Lady Flora Dinsmore is not only beautiful, she's witty, wise, vivacious . . . everything a man could want in a woman. Why you ever gave her up is beyond me."

Richard abruptly dropped his fork to his plate. "You love her!"

"My feelings for Lady Dinsmore are my own concern, not yours." Sidney awarded his unscrupulous friend a long, hard stare. "You hurt her once. Don't do it again. If you do, you'll have me to deal with."

An uncomfortable laugh escaped Richard's lips. "Well, I must say! I was only going to ask the woman to say a kind word about me to my cousin. It isn't as if I planned to run off with her."

"See that you don't," Sidney replied, not smiling. Seldom did he make a threat, but never, in all his life, had he meant a threat more than this one.


The wedding reception for the Duke and Duchess of Armond was well underway at the duke's palatial home on Arlington Street. Flora, dressed in a lavender satin gown heavily embroidered around bodice and hem, and a lavender paisley shawl, stood in a quiet corner. Casually waving her white ivory fan with a white-gloved hand, she gazed out at the crowd of milling, chattering guests, all elegantly dressed, all members of the *ton*. She wondered if Lord Dashwood might be there. Naturally her own family would not deign to invite him, but Richard was a good friend to the duke, and the duke might very well have extended an invitation. For days she'd been telling herself she didn't give a fig whether Dashwood came to the wedding or not. Even so, she couldn't keep her gaze from sweeping the crowd, searching for the man she had loved and lost. Instead, she caught sight of her sister, looking beautiful in an overdress of pink over a heavily embroidered white satin slip. Her lovely bridal veil was fastened with a brooch of pearl and pink topazes. She wore white satin slippers and white kid gloves.

*All brides are beautiful,* Flora thought as Amy approached, her eyes like stars, cheeks a rosy glow.

"Oh, Flora, I'm truly a duchess now," Amy exclaimed.

"That's wonderful," Flora told her sister with forced cheerfulness.

She didn't fool Amy, who lowered her voice and asked, "Tell me I didn't make a mistake."

Flora hesitated. Catching sight of the tall, elegantly dressed duke as he mingled with the guests, she noted how he held his needle-thin nose contemptuously high and never lost his faint, superior smile. Even on his wedding day he maintained his God-like demeanor! Her feelings were mixed. On the one hand, she felt sisterly pride that Amy had managed to snag the Duke of Armond. On the other, she felt a faint chilling fear, recalling the dark rumors she'd heard concerning the duke's private life. She could not shake her sense of foreboding, but there was nothing for it now but hope for the best. "Isn't it a bit too late to be concerned about mistakes?" she whispered back lightly. "Stop worrying and enjoy yourself, Your Grace. Want me to curtsy a time or two? That should make you feel better."

"Oh, hush!" Amy replied, her humor restored. She looked over the crowd. "See, there's Lord Dashwood! I didn't know *he* was invited." Amy slanted a gaze at her sister. "I do hope his presence won't upset you."

"Not in the least." *Richard. He is here!* Flora felt a sudden joy. There, he'd caught sight of her. Her heart started beating a wild tattoo as he stepped toward her.

Amy used her folded fan to tap Flora's arm. "You had best be careful." She gave a warning glance and moved away.

By the time Richard stood before her, Flora's pulse was racing and her knees felt weak. Speechless, she stared up into those well-remembered azure blue eyes.

"Lady Dinsmore," Richard said with an elegant bow, "how delightful to see you again."

"What a pleasure to see you, Lord Dashwood." Flora curtsied, praying she wouldn't fall over in a faint. *Don't make a fool of yourself,* called a little voice. After what this man with his little-boy charm had done to her, she shouldn't even speak to him, let alone act like an awkward schoolgirl in his presence. She should say a polite good-bye right now and walk away, but her feet refused to cooperate. Too late. He broke into that irresistibly devastating grin of his, and she knew she was lost in a romantic cloud yet again.

"It's so good to see you, Flora, truly. I . . ." The grin disappeared, replaced by an expression of contrition mixed with sorrow. He looked as if he were about to break into tears. "What happened . . . The reason I . . . God, I'm sorry. You'll never know how sorry."

"You should be," she forced herself to say.

"I am. In fact . . . Oh, Flora, I miss you so. I know it's too late, but if only . . ." In an anguished voice, he went on, "Till the day I die, I shall regret what I did to you. Can we still at least be friends?"

Her heart went out to him. If they'd been alone, she

would have fallen into his arms. "Of course we'll be friends, but nothing more."

"Of course!" he cried, looking absolutely wretched. "All I ask is that I might have the privilege of seeing you from time to time. It will be torture, knowing I can never have you, but I promise, I shall never touch you. You have no idea what I've gone through. If only Cousin Charles . . . Ah well, I doubt he'll ever speak to me again. I don't blame him."

Flora wished she could disagree, but Richard was only too right. "Indeed, he is angry at you."

"Do you think he could ever forgive me?" All contrite, Richard continued. "Since losing you, I've reformed. I would give anything if I could make him see how I've changed."

Flora's mind raced. She was reluctant to give advice to a man as experienced as her husband, yet his bullheaded attitude toward his heir seemed most unreasonable. Poor Richard obviously had reformed and should not be made to suffer. "Perhaps I could speak to him."

Richard's face lit with joy. "Could you? I would be eternally grateful if you would. Dinsmore needn't worry. My love for you transcends the physical. I shall worship you from afar for the rest of my life."

"Oh, Richard!" He did love her! Her heart swelled with happiness. She would carry his words forever. She wanted desperately to feel his arms around her, but fate decreed such bliss was never to be. As Richard said, their love must transcend the physical. If he could make the sacrifice, so could she. She tilted up her chin and managed to say dispassionately, "I shall talk to him soon."

After Richard left, Flora could hardly contain herself. The thought that he might soon be welcome again at Pemberly Manor left her dizzy with delight. Not that she would ever commit even the slightest impropriety. Indeed, not! How circumspect she would be, how extra thoughtful of her husband. Her relationship with Richard would be strictly respectable, totally correct. Their love was a precious and private understanding, never to be revealed.

Just then, she noticed the broad shoulders of Lord Lynd in the crowd. Soon he approached, but instead of his usual smile, his face wore a strange expression.

"Good evening, Lady Dinsmore." His manner was cool, formal.

"Good evening, Lord Lynd. Is something wrong?"

"I note you were talking to Dashwood."

She met his accusing eyes without flinching. "As a matter of fact, I was."

"Damn!" he near exploded. "What did he want of you?"

"If you must know, Lord Dashwood is truly sorry for his past conduct. He's desperate to reconcile with his cousin."

"And you—" Lynd rocked back on his heels, crossed his arms, and glared. "Don't tell me you've offered to assist."

"What if I have?" She spoke with as reasonable a voice as she could manage. "Lord Dashwood asked for my help, so of course I plan to speak to my husband. Surely you cannot fault me for wanting to reconcile the two."

"But don't you see—?"

"Haven't we been through this?" she retorted. "You've already called me a selfish, head-in-the-clouds, dim-witted female. What's left?"

Flora watched in silence as Lord Lynd waged some sort of battle within himself. Words seemed to rise to his lips, but he kept struggling to suppress them. "What a fool you are," he finally said.

"I most certainly am not!"

"What a whey-faced little milksop."

"What have I done?"

"You have no idea, do you?"

She jammed a hand to her hip. "Enlighten me."

His usually pleasant face suffused with anger. "Why waste my time? How can I deal with such fuzzy-headed thinking? You are so entranced by the saintly Lord Dashwood, nothing I say could possibly change your mind."

She fought the need to defend herself but couldn't resist. "You misread my motive. There's nothing personal in my offer to help, and I resent your implication."

His lip curled. "Can you look me square in the eye and tell me you have no feeling for Dashwood?"

"I . . ." Damnation! Faced with his cold, knowing stare, she could not lie.

"I thought not." His face regained its mask of composure. "I had best take my leave, but before I do, here's a warning. Think what you're doing, my dear Lady Dinsmore. Your husband may be old and crippled, but he's still a man to be reckoned with."

"I . . . I am outraged!"

"Be outraged. Just don't cuckold him."

How could Lynd be so blind, so without feeling? He *must* be made to understand. "You, sir, are so lacking in delicacy you would never understand that the love Lord Dashwood and I have for each other not only transcends the physical, it tends toward the purely spiritual, something *you* would never understand."

"Good God, spare me such slop." Lynd stepped back and bowed. "Good day, Lady Dinsmore. I wish you luck with your purely spiritual love that transcends the physical."

She glowered at him. "I won't need any luck."

"Oh, yes, you will." Lynd turned on his heel and left her standing alone, seething with anger. How dare he question the pure, chaste love she felt for Lord Dashwood? Did he not realize her conduct would always be beyond reproach? Suffice to say, Lord Lynd was despicable and she never wanted to speak to him again.

Days later, back at Pemberly Manor, Flora and Lord Dinsmore were having dinner when Dinsmore remarked, "You are not your usual cheerful self today."

Flora knew he was right. Not only was Amy's unfortunate wedding much on her mind, she did not look forward to the conversation she planned to have with her husband. Actually she wanted desperately to help Richard, but she was afraid her true feelings for him might show. "I'm fine," she said.

"I hardly think so." Dinsmore threw her a look of concern. "Something's been bothering you these past few days. Can you tell me what?"

This was the moment. It was now or never. She hated to use her so-called feminine wiles, but she had no choice.

"I do believe I shall have a house party. We shall invite the gentry from the countryside, as well as friends from London. Mrs. Wendt has worked hard, as well as Baker. It would be the perfect excuse to make the servants finally get new uniforms."

"A fine idea," Dinsmore said indulgently.

"Will you give me a list of what guests you'd like invited? I shall add it to mine."

"Gladly."

Now was the time to mention Richard. She must broach the subject extremely carefully. "Charles?" She suddenly took a great interest in buttering her bread. "I've been thinking about your rift with Richard. Surely you want it healed someday."

Dinsmore set down his wineglass with extra firmness. "Richard is not welcome at Pemberly Manor."

"Oh, I know, Charles, and you have good reason."

"His treatment of you was abominable."

"True. But I hardly think of it." Flora smiled at her husband, well aware of the dimples that formed in her cheeks when she did so. "What upsets me now is my fear I've caused the estrangement between you two."

Dinsmore shrugged. "Richard has not grown up to be the heir I had hoped for, for many reasons, not only his treatment of you."

"Still, I feel responsible. And I feel bad because I know you miss him, and I'd wager he misses you."

Dinsmore stroked his chin, regarding her thoughtfully. "Richard has disappointed me in many ways. Still, he *is* my only flesh and blood." He smiled wryly. "I would have wished otherwise, but that's another story."

"Then let him come home. We shall invite him for our house party. Surely you don't wish to remain estranged."

After a moment, Lord Dinsmore broke into a laugh that held a twist of irony. "You are aware, are you not, Flora, how you can twist me around your little finger? Very well. Richard shall come home again. I cannot say I forgive him for all his peccadillos. I do not. However, I miss the boy, and if you won't be upset, then go ahead, invite him."

"Splendid," she cried. "I was so hoping you two might be friends again."

After Flora left the dinner table, guilt weighed heavily on her shoulders all the way to her bedchamber. She'd been downright devious, inventing the house party simply as an elaborate ruse. Never again, she vowed, would she be so duplicitous, but at least something good had come of it, and Lord Dinsmore would soon reconcile with his

cousin. However, despite her noble resolve, certain
thoughts she should not be having kept creeping, uninvited,
into her head. . . .

"Welcome, Lord Dashwood. How lovely to see you at
Pemberly Manor."

"Ah, Flora . . ." He is staring at her with such longing in
his eyes she cannot mistake his feelings. "It's going to be
deucedly difficult, staying away from you."

"I know. I feel the same."

"My darling, must we?"

"Honor decrees we must. We have no choice. . . ."

How thrilled she would be, seeing the love of her life
again! What joy to gaze into his blue eyes, inhale again the
heady aroma of his musk-heavy cologne. Ah, just to be in
his presence!

But such thoughts were foolish and forbidden. If nothing
else, her parents had taught her right from wrong and what
was honorable and what was not. Her thoughts were not
honorable. Worse, to make her thoughts a reality would go
against everything decent she had ever learned. Sternly, she
promised herself there would be nothing between them, not
a gesture, not a glance, not so much as the blink of an eye.

And Richard, being the man of high integrity that he
was, would feel likewise.

She could blame no one but herself and her impetuous
nature for rushing into a loveless marriage. Certainly Dinsmore was not to blame. He had been nothing but generous
and kind. She knew she would yearn for Richard until the
day she died, but she would be loyal and true to her
husband.

# *Chapter 14*

During the weeks that followed, Flora threw herself into readying Pemberly Manor for the upcoming house party. So much to be done! Forty guests, all of whom would expect nothing less than royal treatment, would require a well-trained servant to be available day or night, at the tug of a bellpull, to grant their every need. Upper and lower servants, cooks, grooms, stable boys—all must be trained and ready. Rooms must be renovated and cleaned; proper uniforms needed to be selected and stitched for the servants; elegant invitations had to be sent and menus planned. Unused for years, the grand ballroom, a shambles when Flora arrived, needed to be made ready for the crowning event of what portended to be a glorious weekend.

Flora was grateful for the distraction, although she was so busy she was forced to forsake her leisurely daily rides. Now, with only one day left, her compensation was the sense of pride she felt over the transformation of Pemberly Manor. There was still much to do, but at last the old Tudor mansion stood nearly restored to its former glory.

No thanks to the housekeeper, Mrs. Wendt, who battled her every step of the way. Whenever Flora gave an order, no matter how tactfully, resentment lurked in the older woman's eyes. She had a habit of unnerving Flora by saying with a sniff, "The *first* Lady Dinsmore never did it that way." Finally Lord Dinsmore overheard and set straight his recalcitrant housekeeper.

"You have a new mistress now, Mrs. Wendt. Do as she says or I promise you, if you persist in this disobedience, you'll be dismissed and out the door in a twinkling."

After that, the housekeeper sullenly obeyed, but Flora knew she'd made an enemy.

"Even Baker cannot complain," Flora told Lord Dinsmore as they stood in the middle of the empty ballroom that had recently been in a state of ruinous disorder. Now the ceiling, delicately carved in a classic Georgian design, had been repainted; the Ionic columns complementing the four corners of the room had been restored to their former alabaster white; the graceful Palladian windows, dulled by years of dirt, were sparkling clean; the many years' accumulation of soot and ashes on the cavernous, stone-carved fireplace had been removed, transforming it into a classic showpiece once again.

"Not half bad," remarked Lord Dinsmore, gazing at her fondly. "You've done a remarkable job, my dear. Your mother will be pleased."

Flora suppressed a wince. "I fear Mama's been looking over my shoulder the whole time," she said ruefully, heartily wishing for the day when she wouldn't think to seek her mother's approval.

"You must relax and enjoy your weekend," said Lord Dinsmore, sensing her discomfiture.

Flora grimaced. "Have I thought of everything? Only one day more and the guests will arrive. I do hope they'll have a good time."

Dinsmore smiled indulgently. "Of course they will. Hasn't the vivacious Countess de Clairmont accepted? Not a dull moment when she's around. Then there's your parents, your sister, and the duke—a fine guest list, including Richard." He smiled. "It'll be good to see him again. I've missed him."

*Not as much as I,* Flora thought, then chided herself for thinking of Richard yet again. She vowed to keep her thoughts pure and chaste the entire weekend and devote herself to her guests.


Next day, the guests began to arrive, including Richard. Driving his curricle, he rolled to his usual daredevil stop early Saturday and alighted under the porte cochere looking smashingly handsome, as usual. Whatever doubts Flora might have had concerning the rift were dispelled when Lord Dinsmore hailed his heir on the steps with a warm hug.

"It's good to be back, sir," Richard said when he pulled away, his blue eyes gazing with deep sincerity into his cousin's. "I've changed, you'll see. I've missed you." He gave Flora no more than a quick greeting and brief nod, but she understood. Above all, they must conceal their feelings.

Soon after, the Countess de Clairmont arrived with her entourage of servants and two London dandies who seemed to serve no purpose but to fawn and simper over her. And no wonder, Flora thought. The vivacious Frenchwoman was not only rich and beautiful, it was obvious her spectacular wardrobe came straight from Paris.

To Flora's surprise, Lord Lynd arrived. She had not seen nor heard from him since their unpleasant discussion at Amy's wedding. Considering the awful things he'd said, she had assumed he had chosen to avoid her, but here he was, greeting her in the entry hall with a bow and a smile.

"What a pleasure to see you again, Lady Dinsmore."

She couldn't believe his cordial manner. He was acting as if she were his dearest friend. She looked around to make sure no one was listening. "And why would you say that," she murmured, and added with a bite, "considering I am but a whey-faced little milksop."

He showed no discomfit but bowed again, quirked an eyebrow, and replied softly, "True, but a charming whey-faced little milksop."

"You are despicable. Why did you come?"

"I received an invitation."

"Well, of course I invited you, but after our conversation at Amy's wedding I didn't think you'd come."

"Nonsense. You seem to forget Lord Dinsmore is like a second father to me. Besides"—this time it was Lynd who looked around, then lowered his voice—"Richard is here, is he not?" She nodded. "I find the prospect of observing the frustrated lovebirds irresistible. Love unrequited, how sad. Or will it be?"

She gasped and could feel the blood rushing from her face, aware she must be turning pale. "I . . . I . . . How can you say such a terrible thing? I would never—"

"Never?" His smile was infuriating. "We know what goes on at these country house parties, do we not?"

She drew herself up. "Sir, you are insulting me, and I . . ." A lump rose in her throat. So unfair! How could she defend herself when he spoke the truth? Tears sprang to her eyes. Only it was *not* the truth! He had no way of knowing she would never, *never* . . .

*What have I done?* Sidney wondered as he saw the pain in Flora's soft violet eyes and realized he'd caused it with his goading. Coming here was a terrible mistake. Ever since the night of Amy's wedding, when he'd called Flora a fool and a milksop, his thoughts of her had been tearing him apart. No longer could he deny his love for her. No longer could he put her out of his mind, even though he was well aware his love was hopeless. Doubly hopeless, what with both a husband and Richard, the man she truly loved, an insurmountable barrier between them. The word *lovesick* described him. Just like a green schoolboy. He had tried desperately to erase his thoughts of her but found it impossible. The only sure way to rid himself of Lady Flora was to take a knife to his brain and cut her out.

Now he'd hurt her. Why hadn't he stayed home? He'd tried, but knowing she was close by, he was like a moth to the flame. "Forgive me," he said, fighting to keep some semblance of dignity. "I had no right to say those things."

She blinked back her tears. "Why did you, then?"

*Because I love you, Flora. Because I'm insane with jealousy and would want to kill the bastard if he so much as laid a hand on you.* "Just my churlish nature coming out."

She gave him a thoughtful smile. "You're not churlish, Lord Lynd. You are one of the most even-tempered men I know, so I can't imagine why you said what you just said."

"Sorry." She would never know how sorry—how she'd just wrenched his heart. "Am I forgiven?"

"You won't say those things again?"

"God strike me dead if I do."

She smiled that dimpled smile of hers that drove him mad. "Then I forgive you. I hope you enjoy the party."

*Enjoy the party? Good God!* "I am certain I will, Lady Dinsmore."

With a polite bow, Sidney turned and walked away.

Although she had been shocked by Lord Lynd's initial hostility, Flora had no time to dwell on his insulting words. At least he'd apologized. By the time of the ball Saturday night, the forty house guests, plus the cream of the local gentry, had not only arrived, the party was lively and everyone appeared to be having a marvelous time. Flora was flooded with compliments.

"You've done wonders with the house, my dear!"

"Haven't seen Pemberly Manor look this good in years."

"I am extremely proud of you," said her mother.

At another time, Flora would have been greatly pleased by her mother's rare compliment, but since Richard's arrival, all pleasure had left her. He had not said one word to her. Worse, whenever she looked in his direction he looked away. She tried to tell herself she was being unreasonable. After all, she had expected his behavior toward her to be circumspect in the extreme. She had *wanted* it that way, but now that it was, a little circle of pain surrounded her heart and she wanted to cry. She had never dreamed he would completely ignore her. At the back of her mind she'd expected they could at least find a quiet corner for a cozy tête-à-tête, most discreet, naturally, and highly proper.

She tried to console herself with the notion that Richard's aloof behavior was easily explained. He was ignoring her in order to cover his love for her. To that end, he was even forcing himself to flirt openly with several female guests, particularly the Countess de Clairmont, who seemed delighted at his attentions. Flora felt ashamed of her weakness. She must try to be as noble as Richard. There were times when she couldn't keep her eyes off him, though. One time, when she was stealing a surreptitious glance, she caught the housekeeper looking at her strangely.

"Is anything wrong, Mrs. Wendt?" she asked.

"Nothing, your ladyship." The housekeeper moved away, but not before Flora caught a triumphant, malicious gleam in her eye. *She knows,* Flora thought disconsolately, and the thought made her most uneasy.

When Monday arrived, and most of the guests had gone, Flora knew her country house weekend had been a smashing success. The ball lasted until the wee small hours of the morning and was enjoyed by all. The food, prepared by the French chef recently acquired by Lord Dinsmore, was uniformly delicious. Male and female guests, who had pursued their amusements both together and apart, all claimed to have had a marvelous time. The gentlemen had hunted hare and fowl and practiced shooting on Dinsmore's special shooting range. The ladies gossiped, wrote letters, played cards, and drove about the neighborhood paying calls.

Flora's parents were about to depart. "Simply marvelous," Flora's mother said as she climbed into their coach. "You are truly well on your way to becoming an outstanding hostess."

"How nice," Flora murmured, not caring at all. She knew she was being foolish, but Richard's neglect had spoiled the whole weekend.

"Lord Lynd didn't stay very long, did he?" her mother continued. "Such a strange man."

Lord Dinsmore spoke up. "Lynd gave me his regrets. Said he'd a few urgent matters to attend to at home."

Not likely, thought Flora. She'd been so wrapped up in her concern over Richard, she'd hardly given Lynd a thought.

A sense of desolation seized her as her parents' coach drove away. For the past weeks she had thought of nothing but the house party. Now that it was over, she realized that being England's greatest hostess held no appeal to her at all. So nothing was left for her except the prospect of dreary years ahead. No babies . . . a loveless marriage . . . *no Richard.*

"Are you all right?" asked Lord Dinsmore as they reentered the entry hall. "You seem pensive, but I can't imagine why. Thanks to you, our party was a huge success. Not only that, I've reconciled with Richard. That should make you happy. He'll soon be coming back."

Of course! Flora suddenly felt better. For propriety's sake, Richard had ignored her this weekend, but there were many more weekends to come. *I shall see him soon again,* she thought, her spirits soaring. She could only love him from afar, but whatever small scraps of time she could have with him she would cherish for a lifetime.

The servants spent the day cleaning up the disarray left from the weekend. It was late afternoon when Mrs. Wendt approached Flora, who sat reading in the drawing room.

"What shall I do with this, your ladyship?"

Flora dropped her book to her lap. "With what?"

"This." The housekeeper extended her palm. On it lay an emerald and diamond earring.

Flora recalled the glittering necklace that matched the earring and immediately knew the owner. "It belongs to the Countess de Clairmont. Where did you find it?"

The housekeeper's lips spread into a thin smile. "In Lord Dashwood's bedchamber. In his bed."

Flora felt herself turn numb. "Are you sure?"

"Oh, indeed, my lady. She spent her nights there." The housekeeper raised a sly eyebrow. "At least the maids were grateful for one less bed to make."

Flora simply stared, blank, amazed and deeply shaken until at last the many years of her mother's strict training took hold, and she remembered she must never reveal her feelings in front of a servant. "That's a valuable earring, Mrs. Wendt." Flora made her voice frosty and aloof. "Give it to his lordship. He can put it in his safe until such time as it can be returned."

"Of course, madam." Mrs. Wendt quickly left the room, but not before she let Flora see her little smile of triumph.

Richard and the countess . . .

Together in his bed . . .

Making love . . . *How could he?* Flora was struck by a nearly unbearable swell of pain. She felt the tears coming but held them back. She must get to her bedchamber. Nothing was left for her but to throw herself on the bed and sob her heart out.

# Chapter 15

In the weak sunshine of a late autumn afternoon, Sidney rode, deep in thought, atop his fine new Arabian. With no particular destination in mind, he idly followed a meandering trail through the forest, reflecting, in a rare moment of introspection, that God had made a mistake and that in the scheme of things, he wasn't meant to be born a nobled, leisured member of the aristocracy.

He should have been born poor. If he had, he would surely be a coachman. At this very moment he could be high atop the box of the Quicksilver, flicking his whip over the heads of a crack team of six as the coach wheels flew down the road. He would be totally content. Of a certainty, there'd be no room in his life for pining over the loss of an unreasonable, stubborn woman who, for entirely unfathomable reasons, had married a crippled old man while in love with the world's worst scoundrel.

If not a coachman, then a sea captain. Right now, he could be standing on the dipping bow of a sleek clipper ship, wind whipping through his hair, sailing into a golden sunset, headed for lands far away, where no one had ever heard of Lady Flora Dinsmore.

He hadn't been himself lately. In the past he'd taken his responsibilities seriously, at least since his father died and he'd taken over the management of Vernon Hill, working many wearying hours. Now he took long rides through the woods every day, not giving a groat whether Vernon Hill thrived or fell into ruin. For a full two months, since the night of Lord Dinsmore's ball, he'd been assailed by an inexplicable restlessness, accompanied by a sense of futility that left him without so much as a whiff of ambition. Some, he supposed, would call his condition a malaise of the heart, but he refused to believe such nonsense.

Sidney halted his mount by a rushing stream and swung from the saddle. He tied the reins to a low branch, pulled off his coat, and sat dejectedly on a rock warmed by the sun. Had she ever been here? She would enjoy a spot as beautiful as this. But perhaps she had. More than once he'd caught sight of her riding her mare through the woods, sometimes with Dinsmore, sometimes alone. He could have hailed her, but he always refrained. Had, in fact, made a conscious effort to keep out of her sight. Better that way. Since the night of the ball what more could he say?

Most definitely, he should go away someplace. Travel. Take a long journey to a far-off spot where somehow, in some as yet undecipherable manner, he could forget about her. A foolish notion, of course. Why was he trying to fool himself? The truth was that he, the unflappable Sidney Bruxton, was not only hopelessly in love, he could not bear to leave her, and what utter folly was that? She lived but two miles away, yet she might as well live on the moon. He would not see her. She was not part of his life anymore, and yet . . . an enigmatic sense that hovered deep within himself kept crying out to him, *Don't leave. Don't let her go. She'll need you someday.*

"Why Lord Lynd! Fancy meeting you here."

*Flora.* He looked up to see her sitting astride her horse, the skirt of her simple brown riding gown spread gracefully around her. No hat. Her hair a soft cloud about her shoulders. He concealed his surprise, quickly arose, and gave her a slight bow. "Lady Dinsmore. I didn't hear you."

"I know." There was a trace of laughter in her voice. "I hadn't meant that you should."

"Sneaking up on me?"

"I instructed Primrose to tiptoe."

"For shame."

"For shame, indeed, sir. You are the one who should be ashamed."

He caught a tantalizing glimpse of lace petticoat as she slung her leg over the saddle and dismounted. Despite himself, his pulse raced; he felt a tug in his groin. "And why should I be ashamed?"

"Because you have made yourself a stranger at Pemberly Manor. Mercy, we haven't seen you since—"

"The ball."

She tethered her mare and turned to face him, holding her riding crop at a jaunty angle. "Yes, the ball. Two whole months ago."

"Come sit," he said.

As she walked toward him, he noted the same enchanting blush of roses colored her cheeks; the same youthful capriciousness sparked in her eyes; yet something new had been added, something he couldn't quite define. For a moment he was baffled, before he finally realized the flighty young woman cavorting in the waves at Brighton had vanished, for all eternity he should wager. Now a subtle aura of maturity surrounded her. "I've been busy," he said, taking up his coat. He spread it over the rock and gestured for her to sit.

"Not that busy," she snipped. She sat where he'd spread his coat and crossed her dainty feet, carefully spreading her skirt about her. "Do you stay away because of Lord Dashwood?"

If only it were just that! He could almost laugh, thinking how shocked she'd be if she knew the torment he'd gone through since the night of the ball. "I've been busy," he said again.

She looked up at him with an expression of candor. "Are you angry with me?"

"I was never angry at you. Just disappointed."

She lowered her dark, curly lashes and thought a moment. When they flew back up, he saw an accepting light vivid in her violet eyes. "Everything's different now, and it's partly thanks to you."

"Really? How?"

She bent forward and lightly placed two fingertips on his arm. "I shall never forget what you told me once about love. Do you recall?"

"I don't recall." Fire scorched through his body from the spot she'd touched.

"You said, 'Always remember that the most important thing in life is to learn how to give love and how to let love come to you.'"

"Now I remember."

"I heard what you said, sir. This might surprise you, but I listened, and, well . . . It made a difference in my life." A tiny, knowing smile played on her lips. "You'll be happy to hear Lord Dinsmore and I are the best of friends. Also, I'm sure you'll be happy to hear that I've . . . well, I do not associate with Lord Dashwood."

"You mean you've actually come to your senses?"

"Oh!" She looked as if she were ready to take a swing at him with her riding crop. Then she surprised him by bursting into laughter. "You do love to goad me, don't you? Well, I refuse to be goaded today. I'm in too good a mood."

Had she finally found her way to Lord Dinsmore's bed? Sidney wondered. But no, she would have said. He took a moment to collect himself, then addressed her softly. "Can you tell me why you've finally gotten Dashwood off your brain?"

She bristled, as he knew she would. "That's none of your concern. But since you ask, any feelings I once had for him are most definitely terminated."

"Definitely terminated, eh? Exactly what do you mean by that?"

"I mean, I consider him the lowest of the low, besides being a rakehell, a scapegrace, and utterly worthless. Furthermore, if he lay dying in the street, I would pass right by and try to refrain from spitting on him."

"My, my." Sidney raised an eyebrow. "I get the impression you're not as fond of him as you once were."

She caught his subtle humor and could not suppress a smile. "You could say that."

*Thank God she's over him,* he thought as he turned the conversation to inconsequential matters. They chatted until she said, "I had best get back. I'm concerned for Lord Dinsmore. It's his lungs, I fear. He has a cold and won't stop coughing."

Sidney frowned with concern. "Yes, you should get back. I'll get Primrose."

Flora watched, admiring, as Lord Lynd went to untether her mare. She had never seen him with his coat off, and she did have to admire how the muscles of his broad chest rippled beneath his plain white shirt. Come to think of it, she had indeed seen him without his coat: that day on the beach at Brighton when he and Richard had been wearing their bathing costumes. She hadn't really seen him, though. That day, fool that she was, she'd had eyes only for Richard.

Sidney brought Primrose to a halt in front of her. "I'll give you a boost," he said.

In a twinkling she was astride her mount, impressed by the way he'd lifted her as if she were a lady's plume. He stood close, steadying Primrose, who'd gotten restless and was fidgeting about. "Thank you," she said. "You are most kind. And I do so appreciate your advice to me that day. It's made all the difference in the world."

"Be careful riding home. My regards to Lord Dinsmore."

Her gaze locked with his. A force beyond herself compelled her not to look away, as good manners dictated she should, but to hold her gaze steady and look deep into his warm, dark eyes. Her pulse quickened when she saw that for once his customary veil of indifference had lifted, permitting her a rare glimpse into the deep well of his innermost feelings. She had never imagined Lord Lynd would reveal such raw, honest emotion, but there it all lay, open for her to see: a pulsing mixture of love, desire, frustration, and heartrending tenderness. Shaken, she finally looked away. Nothing less than love could explain such a look, but what were her own eyes saying? What exactly were her feelings for Lynd? Until lately she'd hardly given him a thought, what with Richard being constantly on her mind. Now, however . . .

His look had shaken her, but whatever her feelings, she knew she must cease such errant speculations immediately. "I am most grateful for your advice, Lord Lynd," she said with great politeness. "I shall give Lord Dinsmore your regards."

"Good," he replied, regarding her with cool detachment. The revealing moment was gone, the veil of indifference lowered once again.

"I trust you will come visit us soon." She, too, could be detached.

"Of course."

"See that you do." With a little smile she nudged Primrose and started away.

During the following weeks, Lady Rensley's visits to Pemberly Manor became increasingly more frequent, a circumstance which, before Flora's change of heart, would have displeased her no end, considering the way her mother constantly hovered about, worrying about the correctness of everything Flora did. Now, however, Lady Rensley's critical tongue was stilled. She had nothing but praise for her prodigious daughter who had married the Hero of Seedaseer and brought Pemberly Manor back to its former glory. Even Amy, married to the duke, had slipped from favorite status to second best, an event that caused both sisters secret mirth.

Not that Amy had been all that mirthful of late, Flora noticed. When Amy came to visit, always alone it seemed, never with the duke, she seemed more subdued and withdrawn each time.

Lord Lynd and Louisa had also taken to visiting frequently. All animosity, or whatever tension had been between Flora and Lynd was gone. Lord Dinsmore delighted in his visits and went riding with them when he was able. As time passed, though, he was confined more and more to his bed.

Even Richard showed up occasionally, appearing without warning, rolling up in grand style to the front entrance in his curricle. Wearing a mask of politeness, Flora assiduously avoided him. Only once did her mask fall away, one day when he found her alone, reading on the window seat in the library.

"So, my dear Lady Dinsmore!" Richard proclaimed as he strode across the room. "Finally I've caught you alone."

She caught her breath as she lowered her book. She must give herself time to act casual. "There is hardly a reason for us to be alone, sir," she replied, proud of her cool demeanor.

Richard sat next to her on the broad window seat and took her hand. "Dear Flora, I get the definite impression you're avoiding me."

"I am."

An innocent look of amazement crossed his face. "But why?"

This was so difficult. If she could, she'd leap up and run away, but his grasp was tight, and, oh, how the touch of his hand caused her pulse to race! Even now, when she was totally through with him, she could feel a tug of attraction between them. "I have nothing to say to you, sir," she said defiantly. Further words leaped to her mouth. She decided not to say them, but they poured out anyway. "Did you think your liaison with the countess would go unnoticed?"

"What?" He looked amazed. "You mean . . . ?"

"I mean the house party. I mean those nights you entertained the countess in your bedchamber."

Startled, he sat back. "Who told you such a thing?"

"One of the countess's earrings was found in your bed."

"Ah, Mrs. Wendt," he said softly, almost as if to himself. "The woman never liked me." He gazed at her aghast. "Nor you, either. You believed her?"

"Why would she lie?"

He abruptly arose and looked down at her, burning accusation in his eyes. "I would never have thought you would be influenced by the idle gossip of servants. Apparently I was wrong."

"You mean you didn't—?" she began, but never finished. Richard had turned on his heel and walked away.

That night, Sidney entertained Richard at dinner at Vernon Hill. Sidney had not invited him, but when his old friend showed up at his doorstep, what could he do?

As it turned out, he enjoyed most of the evening. Richard, at his charming, convivial best, shared the latest London *on-dit,* both the hilarious and the scandalous. Now, as the two shared after-dinner brandies and cigars, the conversation turned to the residents of Pemberly Manor.

"I discovered why our dear Flora has ignored me these past months," said Richard, looking not the least concerned.

"And why is that?" asked Sidney.

"Remember the house party? That harridan housekeeper, Mrs. Wendt, claims she found the countess's earring in my bed. Told Flora. Now she thinks I was bedding the countess the whole time."

"Well, you were, weren't you?"

Richard gave an elaborate shrug. "That's beside the point. Actually, I don't care a groat what Flora thinks, since she won't be mistress of Pemberly Manor much longer. I s'pose you've noticed Dinsmore is in fragile health."

Sidney was taken aback. "Fragile health, perhaps, but Flora's been taking good care of him."

Richard chuckled with a dry, cynical sound. "The most caring wife in the world is not going to improve those wheezy lungs of his or take away his hacking cough." He peered at Sidney intently. "You *have* noticed that cough, have you not?"

Sidney felt a sudden chill. "What are you saying?"

"Well, naturally, I don't want him to die, Sidney, so you needn't look at me as if I were some sort of ghoul." Richard took a long sip of his brandy and sat musing a moment, swirling the contents of his glass. "Still, when the time comes, and it might not be too long, I shall be making other arrangements for his widow."

"What arrangements do you mean?" asked Sidney, once again surprised by this selfish, unpredictable man.

"I shall send her off, of course. She can always return to her parents. Otherwise, as you know, Dinsmore owns several small estates, all of which I shall inherit. I thought, perhaps, that small estate in Scotland would be suitable. Not nearly so grand as Pemberly Manor, but"—a sour smile spread across his lips—"what is?"

Sidney set down his glass so hard a bit of brandy splashed over the top. "That's cruel. Lady Dinsmore adores Pemberly Manor. Those months she spent renovating—"

"Spare me," said Richard, raising a laconic hand. "I want Pemberly Manor all to myself. For one thing, I plan on entertaining lavishly. I picture my friends coming down from London in their fancy coaches. Think how impressed they'll be when they catch that first grand glimpse of Pemberly Manor as they roll up that tree-lined driveway. I shall have balls, foxhunts, hawking, hunting—all that is amiable. No host in England will provide a grander affair than I! Even the countess will be impressed—that is, if there's no grieving widow around to spoil the fun."

"And Flora? You'll just throw her out?"

"Of course not," Richard replied indignantly. "Did I not just say I'd find a place for her? Don't forget *I* am the heir to the estate. Dinsmore could not disown me even if he wanted to." He eyed Sidney triumphantly. "I shall have it all, and when I die, my son inherits everything."

"You don't have a son."

"Ah, but I will." Richard beamed. "The countess has expressed a burning desire to become mistress of Pemberly Manor. She's sure to marry me now." He frowned. "Another thing, too. My funds are at low ebb. Soon as Dinsmore . . . er, leaves us, I shall sell off part of the land and voilá! my debts are gone."

"Lord Dinsmore never intended—"

"A pox on what he intended!" Richard suddenly scowled. "You do realize, what I said was in confidence."

Sidney vehemently responded, "Lord Dinsmore loves Flora with all his heart. He would be distraught if he knew of your despicable plan."

"But you won't tell him, will you? You won't tell him because you're a man of honor and men of honor don't tattle on their friends. And I *am* a friend, Sidney." Grinning, Richard bent closer. "Saved your life once, if you recall."

Sidney shut his eyes a moment. Lord Dinsmore *must* be warned. Above all else, he would not want Flora ejected from Pemberly Manor. But on the other hand . . .

Richard was right. Sidney was indeed a man of honor. Never could he betray a confidence, most especially that of an old friend who had once saved his life.

There was only one acceptable solution: Lord Dinsmore must live to a ripe old age and most certainly not die anytime soon. *That should stop your evil plot,* he thought, glaring at his friend with devilish satisfaction.

Only one thing was wrong. Much to Sidney's dismay, he, too, had noticed that Lord Dinsmore had not been in the best of health lately.

*But he can't die now.*

# *Chapter 16*

On a chill December day, Lord Dinsmore, feeling much improved after a long bout with "flu," decided to go visiting, despite an impending snowstorm. The storm struck while his coach was heading for home, causing a biting cold wind to whip across the land and snow to choke the roads. At one point, the coach stuck in a drift and Dinsmore was obliged to assist the coachman in digging out the wheels. In the process, he caught a chill.

Two days later, feverish and coughing, Lord Dinsmore took to his bed.

Next morning he took a turn for the worse. Soon, having heard the news, his friend and good neighbor Lord Lynd arrived. He remained closeted with Dinsmore for over an hour and left wearing an expression of grave concern.

Later in the day, Sir Charles Quigley, Dinsmore's solicitor, arrived to discuss what appeared to be important matters behind closed doors. His visit culminated with the butler and housekeeper being called to the sick chamber to witness signatures on new documents, including a change in his lordship's will.

Next day, Lord Dinsmore lay, weak and feverish, fighting for each breath. Flora sat by his side, gripping his hand, her face drawn tight with concern.

"You *will* get better, Charles." she said. "You must fight! I cannot lose you now."

Dinsmore gazed at her so lovingly it wrenched her heart. "Dearest Flora," he began in a voice but faintly audible, "you have given me more joy these past months than I've had in a lifetime. If only . . ." His eyes closed. She watched helplessly as her husband seemed to drift away. Gently she squeezed his hand.

"If only what, Charles?"

Dinsmore opened his eyes, appearing to have gathered his strength again. "If only you could have known me when I was young. I was strong as a bull . . . stubborn, convinced I could conquer the world. Quite the handsome buck, too, before . . ." A fit of coughing racked him. "Back then, you would not have been compelled to dream of someone else."

So he knew! Shocked, she couldn't speak. Guilt assailed her. Because of her new attitude, she'd been happy these past few months, with only one dark cloud hanging over her. Richard's golden image still appeared in her mind in moments of weakness. But never did she dream her husband would guess her guilty secret. Now she wept, knowing she was wrong, vowing if Charles should live, she would never dream of another man again. "Oh, Charles, I am so sorry—"

"You mustn't cry," Charles whispered. "Our marriage hasn't been all bad, has it?"

"Oh, no," she vehemently agreed. "These past few months have been the happiest of my life. You gave me a horse and let me ride it. I've learned I could eat breakfast when I pleased—do what I pleased—stop living my life according to all society's silly rules. Why, I've even learned four-in-hand!"

"Thank Lord Lynd for that." Dinsmore managed a faint smile and gripped her hand. "You'll marry again—soon, I hope, and to Sidney."

"Not Richard?" she asked, surprised.

Dinsmore's scoffing laughter was interrupted by a fit of coughing. "You and Sidney will have fine sons. You two will see to it they are men of strength and honor, not like . . ." He sighed and closed his eyes again. When he opened them, he said sharply and clearly, "Watch out for Richard."

There went that stab of pain in her heart again. Despite her anger over the countess, she had hoped Charles would completely forgive his younger cousin, recognize his many fine qualities. "I'm not sure I know your meaning," she said and bent close to hear his answer.

"Yes, you do."

At another time she might have argued. Now, she sat waiting for Charles to speak again.

He did not. Instead, Charles Fraser, the Earl of Dinsmore, Hero of Seedaseer, fell into a deep coma and only hours later slipped the bonds of earth and was gone forever.

## London

Dressed in a black bombazine gown of supreme dullness, plain black bonnet resting on her head, Flora huddled in the corner of the mourning coach, one of a procession of black-decorated coaches that were wending toward St. Paul's Cathedral for the funeral of the Earl of Dinsmore.

"This is not right," exclaimed her mother, who sat next to her, garbed in equally dull black. She stuck her head out the window and peered directly ahead at the first mourning coach. Beyond it, the hearse rolled along at a slow, dignified pace, drawn by six horses covered with black velvet. "Flora, I cannot imagine why you should be delegated to the second coach in line. You were his wife, for pity's sake!"

Flora sighed and stared out the window. "It makes no difference."

"Indeed, it does!"

"Mama, let it rest," said Amy who sat across. "If the new Lord Dinsmore wants the first coach to himself, then so be it. Flora doesn't care, so why should you?"

"I really don't care," said Flora, forcing herself. It was an effort just to talk, let alone involve herself in any kind of argument. She was faintly surprised when, earlier, she'd discovered Richard had decreed he should ride alone in the first mourning coach and relegated her and her family to the second. If her father were here, he would stand up for her, but he was ill today and couldn't come. Even Amy's husband, the duke, might have helped, but he was at his hunting lodge in Scotland. At another time, she would have been deeply hurt over such an obvious slight. Now it didn't matter.

Her mother peered out the window again, this time to the rear. "There must be at least fifty mourning coaches. Truly a fitting tribute to Lord Dinsmore." She gave a triumphant little sniff. "With all the dignitaries here, I'd wager Lady Constance Boles's coach is well toward the rear."

Flora exchanged glances with Amy, both silently lamenting their mother's compulsion to consider her social standing no matter where she was, even her son-in-law's funeral. "I doubt the position of her carriage has much to do with rank, Mama."

Her mother ignored her comment. "And just look at the crowds of people," she crowed. "They line the streets." In a kindly gesture, she patted Flora's hand. "But of course everyone loved the Hero of Seedaseer."

Flora wished her mother would stop talking. *Charles gone.* Oh, how she wished she'd been kinder to him! If only she had loved him as he had loved her! But at least she'd come to know him better during his last months. If she had not made an effort to be as loving as she possibly could, she would feel even worse, if that were possible. Still, his deathbed intimation that he knew what her feelings were for Richard had increased her misery a thousandfold. Exactly how much he knew, or had guessed, she would never know.

*Please, just let me get through this,* Flora thought in silent prayer. All she wanted in the world was to survive the funeral without falling apart, then hasten home to the warm, welcoming shelter of Pemberly Manor. Although she'd lived there but a year, she thought of it as her home, not only for now, but forever, as far as she was concerned.

"So what will be your living arrangements?" asked her mother. It was as if she had read Flora's mind.

"The same as before, I should imagine." Her mother's question had surprised her. "I never thought—"

"Perhaps you should think," her mother tartly interrupted. "Pemberly Manor belongs to the new Lord Dinsmore now. Not that you're without resources. Be thankful your father negotiated a fine marriage settlement in your behalf, what with jointure and pin money. Still, as you very well know, land and houses go to the heir."

"It really doesn't matter who owns Pemberly Manor," Flora replied. "In my wildest imagination I cannot picture Richard throwing his cousin's widow out, or being less than the soul of generosity in any way."

"Hmm," said her mother, sounding doubtful. "What you should do, Flora, is move back with your father and me."

*Never!* She would lose the bit of freedom she had gained

if she moved back with her parents, although she'd never say so. No question, the new Lord Dinsmore would allow her to stay, Flora assured herself. Nearing the cathedral, she forgot the depressing conversation with her mother.

As they ascended the steps of St. Paul's, Lady Rensley nudged her. "Here he comes at last. High time!"

Richard appeared, garbed to funereal perfection in total black, including a special black mourning cloak. All shiny gilt buttons and buckles had been removed from his clothing. To complete his aura of mourning, he had replaced his usual pleasant expression with one of the severest gravity.

"Ah, Lord Dinsmore," said her mother, "are you not impressed with the immense size of the crowd? There's no doubt your cousin was greatly beloved and honored."

Richard bowed, rather briefly, Flora thought. For the first time ever, her heart didn't leap at his sight. She sensed there was something different about him. At first she couldn't think what it was, except it seemed as if now he carried a mantle of remoteness about him, tinged with more than a touch of arrogance. "Ah, Lady Rensley," he replied, a touch condescending. "Of course there is a crowd for my dear, departed cousin. I shall escort you all inside. Lady Dinsmore, protocol decrees you shall sit with me during the services."

Protocol decreed? How formal he seemed! How very cold, as if she would not be by his side if it weren't for protocol.

"So you're the new Earl of Dinsmore now," gushed Lady Rensley. "How fortunate your grandfather once held the title, else you'd not be able to assume your cousin's illustrious name." Amy nudged her. Finally realizing she was sounding much too chatty, Lady Rensley switched her expression to one more solemn. "My deepest condolences, of course. What are your plans, sir?"

Richard's expression turned even more solemn, if that were possible. "I shall need months to recover from the lamentable loss of my dear cousin Charles. Thus, I shall retire from London and return to Pemberly Manor, where I plan to spend the next few months in prayer and meditation."

"And my daughter?" Lady Rensley asked. Flora inwardly winced. Was there no question too outrageous for her mother to ask? But before she could admonish her mother, Richard turned his attention to her again.

"How soon do you plan on moving back with your parents?"

Thunderstruck, Flora was forming her shocked reply when Richard continued. "Not that you need rush, madam. Take all the time you need. Although . . . Actually, I'd like to leave London as soon as possible and reclaim my home. Do you suppose you could be out by the end of the week?"

Before Flora could begin to answer, a hand shot out of the crowd and gripped Richard's arm. Flora saw it belonged to Lord Lynd, a most unsmiling Lord Lynd with a look of lethal calmness in his eyes.

"Ah, there you are, Richard." Lynd briefly bowed to Flora's family and directed his next remark to her. "Lady Dinsmore, my deep condolences." Still with a most uncompromising grip on Richard's arm, he remarked, "Shall we go inside, Lord Dinsmore? I need a word with you at once."

Following the funeral services, in the mahogany-paneled offices of Sir James Quigley, Sidney and Richard seated themselves in front of the large, polished oak desk.

From under bushy white brows, the white-haired, shaky-handed solicitor regarded Richard with compassion. "You have my deepest sympathy. I was struck by the huge crowds that attended Dinsmore's funeral this morning. He was a fine man. A great—"

"Yes, yes," Richard interrupted impatiently. "Lord Lynd tells me there have been some last-minute changes pertaining to my cousin's estate."

Richard bent forward as the elderly man cleared his throat while fumbling through a pile of papers. He selected one and held it up. "Er . . . a slight change. Dinsmore called me to his side the day before he died. He . . . The thing is, Richard, he's entailed all your land."

Richard stared at Sir James. "All of it?"

"I fear so. What that means, of course, is that—"

"I cannot sell it?"

"I fear not."

"That's . . . That's monstrous! Why would he do such a thing?"

"I am only his solicitor. You would know the answer to that better than I."

"Then how shall I pay my debts?" Richard sprang from his chair and glared at the solicitor. "I cannot abide this, Sir James. Can you not set this aside? My cousin was ill. He didn't know what he was doing."

Sir James held the papers higher. "Signed and witnessed, Lord Dinsmore. Yes, he was ill, but I respectfully advise you he gave every indication of being sound of mind."

"Damnation!" Richard sank into the chair again. "At least I shall still inherit Pemberly Manor. The revenues from the estate should amount to something, at least." He scrutinized the peculiar expression on the solicitor's face. "Is there something wrong?"

"One other thing." The solicitor cleared his throat again. "Your cousin changed his will. You will not inherit Pemberly Manor."

"What!"

"He left it to his second wife, Lady Flora Dinsmore."

"He can't do that!" Richard rose in a rage and stomped about. "By God, am I not the closest male relative? Pemberly Manor is mine by right of progenitor."

"Exceptions can be made, as I'm sure you know."

"This is unacceptable!" Richard pointed an accusing finger at Sir James. "Rest assured, you haven't heard the last of this. I shall take the matter to the Chancery Court."

Sidney, who had sat silent throughout, detected a twinkle deep within the solicitor's faded old eyes. "You are free to do what you want, sir," said Sir James with studied patience. "I should warn you, though, you'll have an uphill battle if you choose to go against the will of the Hero of Seedaseer."

"Where are you going?" Sidney asked his still-furious friend. They had just left Sir James's office and were riding along Bond Street in Richard's curricle.

"Straight to White's, where I shall gamble all night and drink myself into a stupor," came Richard's unequivocal response.

"No need for that," Sidney answered. "You've still got the title, the land, and estates all over England. Ireland, too, as I recall. You simply cannot sell anything, that's all."

Richard stared at Sidney as if a startling thought had just occurred to him. "You knew about this, didn't you?"

Here came the moment of truth, thought Sidney. Best to face up, get it over with right now. "Not only did I know about it, it was I who told Dinsmore of your plan to evict Flora."

Richard's mouth dropped open. "I've lost Pemberly Manor because of you?"

"If you want to look at it that way, yes," Sidney replied bluntly. "You were going to throw her out, weren't you? Rather a cruel thing to do. So I could not, in all good conscience, remain silent. That's why I informed your cousin. That's why he entailed his land and changed his will."

"You betrayed me!"

"You deserved to be betrayed. Stop the carriage. I want to get out."

"What are you doing?" Richard asked as he pulled the curricle to a halt.

Sidney sprung to the ground with one swift motion and looked back up at his childhood friend. "I have never betrayed a friend before and never had the dimmest notion I ever would. Now you, with your arrogance and greed, have caused me to break my code of honor. I agonized before I came to my decision, but in all good conscience, I could not stand by and see you hurt Flora again."

Richard broke into scoffing laughter. "I always suspected you were mad for her. This proves it. So how does she feel about *you,* my faithless friend? Has she ever shown you the slightest interest? Has she ever looked at you with those dreamy eyes of hers, all smitten with love? Ha! She looks at me that way, Sidney. If you've deluded yourself otherwise, you're a fool."

"Good day, Richard." Sidney turned, waving his hand in a gesture of dismissal. He started to walk away, knowing he should be angry at his friend's callous words. Instead, he felt as if he'd just had the wind knocked out of him. Everything Richard said was true. While Flora was married to Dinsmore, Sidney's feelings were irrelevant. He had placed them under lock and key with stern instructions to himself not ever to examine them. But now that Dinsmore was gone, never-voiced feelings were surfacing. Flora was free of her obligation. Perhaps, after a decent period of mourning, she might possibly—

"I could get her back, you know!" called Richard from his curricle. "I have only to snap my fingers and she'll come running."

Sidney spun around. "Flora knows you for what you are. You're the fool, if you think she'd ever take you back."

"Really?" Richard asked mockingly. "You know she's still in love with me."

"Do tell." Sidney raised a skeptical eyebrow. "If memory serves, when we last talked of you, Flora described you as the lowest of the low, besides being a rakehell and utterly worthless. As I further recall, she added that if you lay dying in the street she would pass right by and try to refrain from spitting on you."

Richard shrugged. "She was a trifle peeved."

All humor left Sidney as a cold wave of dread flooded over him. "She's done with you."

"Don't be too sure, old friend," Richard called lightly. "Hope you find a hack!" With a laugh, he snapped the reins and drove away.

After the funeral, before she returned to Pemberly Manor, Flora found the opportunity to talk to Amy alone. "What's happened to you?" she asked. "You look positively radiant, despite all the gloom of a funeral." She had noticed Amy walked with a lighter step, possessed a satisfied gleam in her eye.

Amy bent close and whispered confidentially, "I'm in love!"

"With the *duke?*"

"Of course not. We lead separate lives now. He has his women, or whatever is his pleasure. As for me, he's made it clear he doesn't care what I do, as long as I'm discreet."

"I don't believe it."

"But it's true." A brilliant smile lit Amy's face. "At last I've found the man I shall love forever. Edward's a poet.

He's a third son, quite poor, but I love him and he loves me."

For a moment Flora was too stunned to reply. "I can hardly find the words to ask it, but what if—?"

"I should find myself with child?" Amy adamantly shook her head. "That won't happen. I wouldn't dream of breaking my marital vows. Ours is a spiritual love. When we're together, Edward reads me poetry. Don't worry, I know what I'm doing."

Did she? Flora doubted her sister. The words *reckless* and *dangerous* poised on the tip of her tongue, but she decided not to say them. From her own experience with Richard, she knew the futility of giving advice to a woman who was caught in the all-consuming throes of unconsummated passion.

# Chapter 17

Seated in the drawing room at Pemberly Manor, Lord Lynd and Lady Beasley regarded Flora with warm sympathy in their eyes. "Are you sure you're all right?" asked Louisa.

Seated across from them, Flora was pleased that her two dear friends had not subscribed to the old theory that widows wished to be alone with their grief. Since Lord Dinsmore died, they had visited often.

An ember crackled in the fireplace. Flora idly watched the small shower of sparks cascade into the ashes beneath. From outside, she heard the wind whistling. Through the large bay window, she saw the steady fall of snow. But here by the fire with her dear friends, she felt snug and content, despite her ongoing grief at losing Charles. "I so appreciate your being here," she said. "Don't think I haven't noticed how you visit nearly every day, despite how busy you must be."

Lord Lynd regarded her quizzically. "I trust we haven't worn out our welcome."

"Oh, no!" she protested sincerely, smoothing the skirt of her plain black mourning gown. "What would I have done without you? Rattling around in this big house"—she made a sweeping gesture—"memories of Charles everywhere I look. Your visits keep me sane."

"Visiting is our pleasure," said Louisa, casting a knowing glance at her brother.

After they left, Flora sat by the fire, reflecting upon how delightful she found the visits and how much she looked forward to seeing him each day—well, both of them, of course. His interest in her welfare knew no bounds. He was helpful, too, in other ways, and he had given her all sorts of good advice in handling the matters of Dinsmore's estate.

There seemed only one prickly area between them. It

occurred whenever the new Lord Dinsmore's name was mentioned. "Have you seen him?" Lord Lynd would ask occasionally.

She always answered she had not and didn't expect to.

Recently he asked, "And what would you do if he suddenly appeared at your doorstep?"

She shrugged. "Be polite, I suppose. He has written several times—polite little notes asking if he might call. I haven't answered, but I suppose if he appears uninvited on my doorstep, I surely wouldn't turn him away. After all, he's just lost his cousin. That, plus the shock of finding all his land entailed, then losing Pemberly Manor, must have been considerable. I most certainly wouldn't add to his misery."

She sensed Lynd's relief at her answer. He was certainly an expert at concealing it, though. Actually, her answer left her uneasy. Despite her protestations, thoughts of the perfidious Lord Dashwood—oops! now Lord Dinsmore—managed to steal into her consciousness more than she would have wished. Each time they did, she chastised herself. Her days of daydreaming were over. Even if they weren't, she was a fool to waste a second of her time on a man who cared for her so little he would have cast her from her home, had not Charles changed his will.

Later, Lady Rensley arrived from London and came bustling in. "Hello, Flora, dear. Are you still mooning about? Weeks have gone by, my dear, and I know you must still wear your mourning, but perhaps you might at least consider coming to London, where I could arrange discreet dinners that would at least put you again in the social swim. Lady Boles says—"

"We've been over this before, Mama. I shall stay right here. Don't expect me to change my mind, because I won't." Flora refrained from adding that, thanks to Charles, as well as Lord Lynd, she was through with letting other people run her life and telling her what to do. Consequently, she had no concern for Lady Boles's opinion, or her mother's either, for that matter.

"I have something to tell you," said Lady Rensley, seating herself, her eyes bright with excitement.

"What?" Whatever her mother was going to say, Flora had a feeling it wouldn't be good.

"Yesterday the new Lord Dinsmore came to call," Lady Rensley grandly announced.

"Do tell." Flora managed her remark with great casualness, but inside she felt a jolt. "What did he want?"

"My dear girl!" Lady Rensley clasped her hands in front of her and bent forward, eager to impart her news. "The man loves you dearly. He's devastated that you refuse to see him. Have you really ignored his letters?"

"Indeed, I have." Flora was doing her best to appear indifferent, even though her heart was racing. Could it be true that Richard loved her? But what if he did? She bade herself keep in mind all the awful things he'd done. "How could he love me after the way he's acted? Excuse me, Mama, but I don't believe anything he told you."

"Lord Dinsmore claims it was all a misunderstanding. He came to me because you've ignored his letters and positively *begged* me to intercede on his behalf. Can't you allow him a visit? He desperately wants to talk to you."

"What is the point?"

"So he might explain. Really, Flora! Why must you be so hard on the man?"

"Why do you care?"

"You know I've always had a soft spot in my heart for him, from the day we saw him standing on the beach. Not only that, he's still the best catch around, despite his little peccadillos."

"Peccadillos! He's one of the most notorious rakes in London, Mama. He drinks, gambles—"

"Don't they all? I sense the man's ready for marriage. Half the girls in London are after him. Mark you, he won't be single long, so you'd best grab him while you can."

"They can have him," Flora replied with disdain. "How can you possibly think he's such a great catch?"

Lady Rensley cocked an eyebrow. "If you married him, he would gain control of Pemberly Manor. Then he'd be out of debt and all would be well."

"Damnation, Mama. Has he cast a spell over you?"

Lady Rensley gasped. "Daughter, your language!"

"Well, you made me say it." Flora stood and faced her mother, fists clenched at her sides. "In the first place, I have no intention of marrying again, not anytime soon and perhaps never. Second, if I did marry again, it would not be to that conniving liar. In fact, if I were to marry anyone, it would be"—a name came quickly to her mind—"I would marry Lord Lynd, who is twice, three times the man Dinsmore is."

"Humph!" came her mother's skeptical reply. "Lynd has shown no interest in marrying again, whereas our new Lord Dinsmore—"

"Oh, stop it," commanded Flora. "Really, Mama, I won't hear another word about how wonderful he is, because he's not."

Lady Rensley's face fell. "Then you won't see him?"

Despite her determined resolution, Flora hated to disappoint her mother. "Can't you see how I feel?" She waited. Her mother stared blankly. "No? I guess you don't. Well, I'll tell you a secret. I used to daydream a lot. Foolish dreams. The most foolish was my fantasy that Lord Dashwood was my golden prince"—she laughed ironically—"when in reality, he was my impossible hero. Thanks to Charles and Lord Lynd, I know better now. They made me realize I'd lived my whole life doing what I was supposed to do, not doing what I really wanted to do. I was miserable. My only escape came through fantasies." She paused and tossed back her head. "A pox on society's rules. From now on, I shall do as I please, not what you, or Papa, or anyone else tells me. I plan to lead a quiet life here at Pemberly Manor. I need nothing more, and that includes fantasies."

"I've never seen you like this before," said Lady Rensley, frowning in bewilderment.

"I'm a different person now."

"I have no idea what you're talking about. Do you really want to spend the rest of your life as a widow with no children? All I know is, Lord Dinsmore says he's changed. Surely you could condescend to see him and give him the chance to explain."

Flora sighed in frustration. Nothing she'd said made the slightest impression on her mother. "All right, I'll see him, but don't expect anything to come of it, because nothing will."

Lady Rensley's face lit again. "Splendid! I shall get word to him immediately."

"There's no rush," Flora said, knowing her mother would return to London post haste to deliver her message.

She was right. Lady Rensley left shortly after, leaving her daughter in a turmoil of mixed feelings. Flora's good sense told her no matter how much Richard begged and cajoled, she would remain firm and reject him. But what about her heart? *No, you cannot even consider forgiving him,* cried the little voice of reason that dwelled within her. And she wouldn't, Flora firmly concluded. Absolutely not.

Days later, in the drawing room of Pemberly Manor, in front of a roaring fire, Flora received her visitor, the new Lord Dinsmore. The two made a somber picture as Flora, attired in black, sat stiffly in the middle of the sofa, with Dinsmore, also in black, sitting across. She was shocked by his appearance. Not only was he noticeably thinner, but his hair, usually so meticulously arranged, was slightly disheveled, as if he'd run a careless comb through it and nothing more. The twinkle in his eye had disappeared. Lines of strain etched his pale, drawn face, making him look downright haggard.

Poor Lord Dinsmore, how he must be grieving for his cousin Charles!

She rang for tea. They chatted of inconsequential matters. Finally Richard surprised her by saying in a voice most humble, "Thank you for seeing me. You are most kind."

"My pleasure." She was amazed at his unassuming new attitude, so much so she decided to speak her mind. "I must admit, I am surprised."

"In what way?" he asked quietly.

"Aren't you angry?"

He frowned in puzzlement. "Why should I be angry?"

"This." She made a sweeping gesture. "Don't you feel cheated of your childhood home? Aren't you furious with your cousin for not leaving Pemberly Manor to you?" She touched her palm to her chest. "Aren't you furious with me?"

The old Richard would have laughed. This new Richard carefully set down his cup of tea and regarded her with eyes full of pain. "Which brings me to why I came here today. I've come to beg your forgiveness. I want nothing more than to make amends, if I possibly can, although I fear there's no way in the world you could forgive me."

She met his directness with her own. "There isn't. The day of the funeral your behavior was appalling."

"I know I hurt you. God knows, I didn't mean to. I shall not make excuses, but I want you to know part of what happened was truly a misunderstanding."

"Really?" Sick anger swept through her as she thought of his actions that day. "Do you deny you wanted me to leave Pemberly Manor?"

"I do deny it." His troubled eyes gazed directly into hers. "Of course I didn't want you to leave. But can't you see? I was sick with grief that day—hardly knew what I was doing. I wrongly assumed you would want to return to your parents. My words came out wrong." He shook his head in a self-deprecating manner. "I made a mess of it. The last thing on earth I wanted was for you to leave. That's because I . . ."

He bit his lip, hung his head. "I cannot say it. I have no right to say it."

"Say what?" she asked, knowing full well she shouldn't ask, but how could she not?

"You're in mourning. I shouldn't even be here."

"Say it."

"I love you, Flora." His face twisted with suffering. "I've loved you since that day we met on the beach. Since then, my love has grown until I can't eat, can't sleep. My life is unbearable, knowing what I've done to you, knowing I can never have you."

Shocked, she set her own cup on the side table. What to say? Words spun in her head. One thing she had to know. "What about the countess? If you love me as you claim, then why—?"

"It was a lie, Flora! Can't you see that?"

"You mean you didn't entertain the countess in your bedchamber three days running?"

"That's exactly what I mean. If you obtained your information from Mrs. Wendt, you must remember she's no friend of yours, or mine. I don't wish to sound ungallant, but the countess came uninvited to me that night. I was quite surprised and, I assure you, made haste to get rid of the woman. No doubt Mrs. Wendt saw enough to get the idea in her head she could cause all sorts of mischief. But

I swear to you, Flora, I am innocent! If only you could find it in your heart to understand."

She was so overwhelmed she couldn't speak, just stared at him amazed. "I . . . I didn't know," she whispered.

"Well, you know now."

Suddenly he was on his knees in front of her, gazing up at her with pleading eyes. "*Please* forgive me! I'm begging you on bended knee. *Please!* I love you, Flora. I want you desperately. If you don't forgive me I'll never get over it. I'll . . ." His voice broke. He buried his head in her lap. "I need you, my darling! I am lost without you!" came his muffled cry.

Flora gazed down at the noble head, now so humbled, with its golden curls in disarray. He had treated her so shabbily, and yet . . .

"I was terribly hurt by what you did."

He gazed up at her again. "I know, and I'm humbly sorry. Won't you give me the chance to prove I would never, ever, treat you in such a shameful fashion again?" He shook his head in desperation. "Oh, I know you're in mourning. It's much too soon even to think of marriage, but at the proper time I want to marry you. I want to spend the rest of my life adoring you—and only you. I swear, I shall never look at another woman again."

Flora gazed into Richard's desperate face. An errant curl had fallen over his forehead. She felt a keen urge to reach for it, brush it away. At first, she resisted, knowing if she did, she'd be lost forever to this feckless man who had existed as a hero only in her fantasies. But he *was* real. And he *was* sorry—had even humbled himself, gotten on his knees. And he loved her. Her hand stole out. She was helpless to stop it. Her fingers touched the golden curl and shoved it back. "Oh, Richard," she murmured. "I hardly know what to say."

"You needn't say a word." He arose and sat beside her, took her hand, looked deep into her eyes. "Just give me the chance to redeem myself. That's all I ask. You won't be sorry. I promise."

She tried to remind herself of all the bad things, but how could she under his searing, heart-wrenching gaze? He was so sincere, so truly regretful. *He's been misunderstood,* cried the little voice. Lord Lynd was wrong. He did not understand Richard the way she did. Even her mother perceived his nobleness, his honesty, despite—what did she call them?—ah, yes, his little peccadillos. And that's all they were. Nothing serious. No man was perfect.

He drew closer. "Is there any hope for me? If there is not, I promise you I shall leave immediately—never bother you again. But if somehow you could forgive me . . ."

"I forgive you, Lord Dinsmore." Lovingly she laid her palm upon the dear cheek that was pale because of her. How could she have doubted him? "You know I care for you."

Uttering a cry of joy, he brought her hand to his lips and covered it with kisses. "You won't be sorry."

"We must wait." For some reason, she didn't want him to kiss her now.

"Yes, yes!" he replied impatiently. "The proscribed amount of time, whatever suits you. Then we'll marry and you'll be mine, my darling, all mine."

*Dreams do come true,* she thought, and wondered why she wasn't quite totally suffused with joy.


Within the hour after Richard proposed, he left in high spirits for London, exceedingly pleased his little plot had worked even better than expected. Begging on bended knee was not to his taste, but a clever ploy nonetheless, even though . . . He glanced down. . . . No, by God, not the slightest stain marred his black breeches. How he detested wearing mourning. Ah, how he yearned for his tight yellow pantaloons! But what luck Flora had capitulated. No, not luck. He should give himself more credit. What brilliance! He must share his triumph with his old friend, Lord Lynd. As his curricle rolled to a stop at the front portico of Vernon Hill, he experienced a brief moment of uncertainty, recalling how Sidney had stormed off in high dudgeon when last they met. *But I'm the one who should be angry.* Richard vividly recalled his and Sidney's visit to the offices of Sir Charles Quigley, wherein he discovered all his land had been entailed. Now he must let Sidney know his plans to succeed were in motion and nothing could stop him.

His childhood friend seemed not angry in the least, although now, as they sat chatting in the study, Richard reflected his old friend's greeting had not been overly warm. "I've just come from Pemberly Manor," Richard told him. "Checking on the grieving widow."

Sidney eyed him suspiciously. "What are you up to?"

Richard innocently spread his palms. "Nothing. Except"—he tried to remain solemn, which was difficult, considering he felt like shouting his victory from the rooftop—"do you remember when I said I had only to snap my fingers and our dear Lady Dinsmore would come running?"

Although Sidney remained silent, the sudden tautness of his face said it all. In fact, was it Richard's imagination or had his friend turned a bit pale? "Of course you remember," Richard jovially continued. "It's true, you know. I'm back in her good graces." In triumph, he crowed, "We talked marriage, Sidney! Nothing official, of course. We shan't become betrothed until the proper time, but just think! Pemberly Manor will be mine after all."

After a long silence, Sidney said, "Congratulations," in a rather strangled voice that sounded totally unlike him. Perhaps, Richard observed, it was due to the fact he seemed to be speaking through clenched teeth.

After that, the rest of the visit fell flat. To Richard's chagrin, his old friend became so uncommunicative as to be boring. No fun at all, actually, so he left shortly after he arrived. As his curricle rolled toward London, he wondered why Sidney had not been his usual wry, amusing self. Perhaps he really did have feelings for Flora. But what if he did? She was only a woman, after all, and what were women for but to be used for man's pleasure and convenience?

Surely nothing more.

For a long time after Richard's departure, Flora sat by the fireplace alone, examining her feelings, waiting to be illuminated by the glow of happiness that would surely wash over her at any moment. Richard loved her, she told herself over and over again. Why did she not feel the intense love for him she had felt before? She thought back to that terrible day he had jilted her. How she had anguished! How she would have given anything in the world if she could regain his love. Now, miracle of miracles, Richard was hers again. She decided the impact of this marvelous turn of events simply hadn't sunk in yet. Naturally it would take time. She wasn't herself, what with the death of Charles, but given time—in fact, any moment now—her heart would sing with delight and she'd be blissfully happy.

Next day she was still waiting for bliss to strike when she began to wonder why Lord Lynd had not paid a visit at his usual time. Hardly a day passed that he didn't drop by, with or without Louisa. Flora had to admit she'd come to look forward eagerly to his visits, which had become a highly enjoyable part of her daily routine.

The day passed. She waited in vain. An uncomfortable thought struck her: had Lord Lynd discovered she and Richard had reconciled? Could he possibly be furious? Oh, surely not. He was simply busy, that was all.

The next day came and went without a word from her neighbor and good friend. By the next day she was forced to acknowledge her growing suspicion that Lord Lynd knew the truth. She could easily imagine how Richard, in the spirit of friendship, might have stopped by Vernon Hill to celebrate his good news on his way back to London.

So be it then, she told herself firmly. Why was she wasting her time thinking of Lord Lynd when she should be dreaming of her future life with Richard? Ah, how blissfully happy they would be! He, of course, would be utterly devoted, the perfect husband. . . .

*She lies in bed, watching fondly as Richard climbs in beside her, bends to kiss her. Fondly she regards his dark, craggy face, runs her fingers through his thick straight black hair. . . .*

*He looks up . . .*

No, no, no! How did *that* happen? It wasn't Richard's fair visage she was looking into, but the wise, dark eyes of Sidney, Lord Lynd. Really! Why was *he* intruding into her fantasy? Why couldn't she focus on Richard?

How exasperating.

Another day came and went and no Lord Lynd. She began to feel sick with worry at the thought she might have lost his friendship. Her impulse was to hitch the curricle and drive to Vernon Hill to see him. No, a terrible idea. Louisa was in London, thus couldn't be used as an excuse, and Flora had been taught from childhood that a lady did

not, under any circumstance, visit a gentleman in his abode.
Such an action was considered so extremely brazen that
even she, liberated from society's rules as she was, could
not bring herself to do it.

A letter! Better yet, an invitation, which good manners
decreed he could not ignore.

The new Lord Dinsmore forgotten, she sat at her black
and gold lacquered writing desk and penned,

> My Dear Lord Lynd,
>    I have missed your friendly visits these past few days
> and trust all is well. You are invited for tea tomorrow,
> Thursday, at three o'clock. I look forward to your visit.
>                              Most sincerely,
>                              Flora Dinsmore

Done and sent, Flora thought as she handed her sealed
missive to the footman and directed him to deliver it without delay to Vernon Hill.

Next day, after sending a brief and proper note of acceptance, Lord Lynd appeared promptly at three o'clock. Flora
arose as Gillis announced him and he strode purposefully
into the drawing room.

Smiling, Flora dipped a curtsy. "I am so delighted to see
you again."

Lynd did not return her smile. "I have a few things to
say. You won't be so delighted when I finish, I can assure
you."

Fear knotted inside her. "What do you mean?"

"I am about to inform you why I haven't visited these
past few days. Also, why you won't be seeing me again."

Flora's knees went weak, not only because of his words
but because of the icy gleam in his eyes. "I gather something is wrong."

"What an astute observation. One question. Is it true
you've allowed Dinsmore back in your good graces?"

Under his withering gaze, she hated to answer but knew
she must. "Yes, but you see—"

"I don't see."

Why was he being so cold and unforgiving? In truth, he

was back to his old, cynical self again, only more so. She asked, "What are you trying to tell me?"

"I would not have told you anything at all, my dear Lady Dinsmore, had you not sent your ridiculous invitation to tea. We could have gone our separate ways, no one the wiser. But since you ask"—a corner of Lynd's mouth lifted with disdain as he set fists to hips—"you've given me the perfect opportunity to bring to your attention what a fool you are."

Resentment boiled within her. "That's an insult."

"I meant to insult you. How could you love such a profligate? It's beyond idiocy."

Loyalty to Richard came flooding back. "You misunderstand him. Lord Dinsmore has given me perfectly reasonable explanations for all he's done."

"I understand every move Richard makes, so save your breath. It's you who don't have an inkling as to his true character."

"I do, and I love him."

"Love is blind. If I didn't believe that before, you just proved it."

The conversation was getting out of hand. She would try a more conciliatory tone. "Won't you miss our visits?" she asked. Judging from the blaze of fury in his eyes, she knew immediately she'd said the wrong thing.

Suddenly he gripped her arms so tightly her breath escaped in a startled gasp. His curt voice lashed at her, "Yes, I'll miss our visits! What I won't miss is having to witness a seemingly intelligent woman such as you throw her life away on a worthless rake."

This was unbearable. "Lord Lynd," she cried, "I've never seen you act this way before. I had no wish to offend you. These past few months I've enjoyed your visits immensely. I think of you as a dear friend and I—"

"Friend?" he rasped. "I was more than a friend. I was the man who would have loved you, cherished you, taken care of you for all our lives. But you couldn't see that, could you? You, with your silly head full of your golden-haired prince." He put her away from him and regarded her with eyes that glowed with a savage inner fire. "He'll eventually treat you like dirt, you know, only you're too besotted to see it."

"I think it's time you left," she cried. She tried to struggle from his grasp but he held her like a vise.

"I'll leave gladly," he replied, his breath coming hard. Cynically he asked, "But don't you think I've earned a farewell kiss?"

"Get out!" She tried again to wrest herself away, but to no avail. He pulled her roughly toward him. His mouth came hard on hers, covering it hungrily, relentlessly. She pounded his shoulders with her fists, but it was like hitting a brick wall, and he paid no heed. His mouth remained on hers, warm, caressing. Almost at once her fists stopped their pounding as she became acutely aware of how tightly she was molded to the contours of his lean body. Would he ever stop? Did she want him to stop? All she knew was that his cruel, searching mouth demanded a response. Soon, almost of their own volition, her arms crept around his neck. Feeling a stirring deep within her, she forgot any thought of resistance and met his kiss with her own. Umm, how warm he was, how nicely she fit in his arms! She quivered at the sweet tenderness she felt and would have gone on, forever if she could, lingering, savoring every moment, but suddenly he broke from their embrace.

His breath was ragged as he stepped back and gave her a mocking bow. "It's time I left. My apologies for my— shall we say, inappropriate—behavior." His voice hardened. "You have my word, it won't happen again."

She stood trying to catch her breath, barely clinging to her composure. "I . . . I don't know what to say."

"What is there to say except you'll see no more of me? Good day, madam. I wish you good fortune, which, I assure you, you're going to need."

"But . . ." She started to say more, but it was too late. The next instant, Lord Lynd was gone.

# Chapter 18

A few weeks after Lord Lynd's disastrous visit, Flora suspected something was troubling Amy. She sensed her sister's unhappiness the moment Amy arrived at Pemberly Manor for a visit, thinner still, her cheeks bereft of their usual rosy glow, her face taut with lines of stress. Amy said nothing, though, and at lunch showed her concern over Flora.

"Are you happy?" she asked from across the table.

"You know I love your visits," Flora replied, deliberately misconstruing what Amy meant. She regarded Amy with concern. "You're not yourself. Tell me what's wrong."

"I know you love my visits, but that's not what I meant," said Amy, ignoring Flora's question. With a significant lifting of her brows she asked, "I meant, are you happy Lord Dinsmore proposed? I thought you'd be ecstatic, but I don't see any signs of it."

"I truly am thrilled," Flora protested. "But it's only been a few weeks since he proposed, and I *am* still in mourning, after all. You know we must wait at least a year."

"Indeed, else imagine the scandal. At least Mama's keeping quiet."

Laughing, Flora responded, "She had better this time. Really, I'm fine. Richard's been coming down from London nearly every week. He's been wonderful, simply brimming with charm and solicitude, cheerful, full of affection—everything I always wanted from him. I'm blissfully happy, and I can hardly wait to show it."

"Hmm," came Amy's faintly skeptical reply. "What about Lord Lynd? He was so attentive for a while, but where has he been lately? I haven't seen him since—"

"Lord Lynd and I had a disagreement," Flora cut in sharply. "You won't be seeing him, not at Pemberly Manor, anyway." Flora braced herself. If Amy pursued the subject, she would be obliged to explain. She never kept secrets from her sister, but she fervently hoped she wouldn't be obliged to discuss Lord Lynd. Whenever she thought of him, a kind of desolation struck her heart. She felt bereft, though she couldn't explain why. "And how are *you* doing?" she asked Amy, hoping to distract her. "Are *you* happy? I must say, you don't look it."

For a time, Amy remained silent, biting her lip in deep thought. Finally she said in a voice little above a whisper, "Something terrible has happened." She stared at Flora, gray eyes wide with fear. "I am in the family way, and the Duke is not . . . not . . ."

At first Flora's mind refused to register the significance of Amy's words. When it did, she could not conceal her consternation. "You mean to say the duke is not the father?"

"Oh, Flora!" Tears trembled on Amy's eyelids. "I've gotten myself into a terrible fix. There's not the faintest possibility Armond could be the father. When he's not spending his time hunting, he's with one of his mistresses. He doesn't have the slightest interest in me. We haven't shared a bed in months."

"Even so," Flora responded, "how could you have deceived him?"

"He made it clear he'd lead his life and I could lead my life as I chose, long as I was discreet." Amy's tears spilled as she cried, "But a baby is not discreet! I cannot fool him. He'll *know*. He'll divorce me at the very least. I'll be disgraced forever, and so will the family."

Flora leaped to her feet and hastened around the table to put her arms around her sister. "Was it that poet? The one who's a third son and poor?"

"Yes, Edward." Breaking into sobs, Amy buried her head on Flora's shoulder. "I loved him. I couldn't help myself."

"Well, I can certainly understand that," said Flora, gently patting Amy's arm. "What do you plan to do?"

"What can I do, other than throw myself into the Thames?"

"You mustn't even think it!"

"What choice do I have? When I told Edward, he acted

as if he hardly knew me. He said there was nothing he could do and we shouldn't see each other again."

"So much for your poet and his undying love," said Flora, reflecting upon the perfidy of men. Actually, there was nothing Edward could have done. She wouldn't say it to Amy, but at this point, his defection was of no import. She, Flora, was the only person in the world who could help Amy. She couldn't bear to see her beloved sister in such a state of despondency without doing something. But what? After she pondered a moment, one answer came to mind—not her own idea but a solution she'd heard more than one lady of rank had utilized. "How many months along are you?"

Amy sniffed and wiped her eyes. "Two and a half, I think, perhaps three."

"Good. Then there's time to make our plans. You and I shall slip off to Italy. There you'll have the baby and no one the wiser."

"No!" Amy protested. "I cannot allow it. How could you possibly get away? You have Lord Dinsmore to consider now."

"It's useless to argue, Amy." With a fine show of enthusiasm, Flora launched into her plan. "It's all so simple. I'm the grieving widow, remember? What I need is a change of scene. For the sake of my health, which has suddenly turned *quite* fragile, I must escape this cold and snow and set sail for a warmer clime. Like Italy! You see how it all fits together? Naturally, I must have my sister along for companionship. That would be you. And it would take . . . let's see, six more months, at the very least, before my full recovery."

The look of desperation eased in Amy's eyes. "You really think it would work?"

"The duke will never know, nor Mama and Papa. Nobody need know except us and, of course, Richard. I shall be obliged to confide in him. I'll need his help."

"Then . . ." Amy's tears had ceased. Her face flooded with relief. "We could stay at some remote village in the Italian countryside. When the baby is born . . . Oh, dear." She looked as if she was about to cry again.

"You'll have to give it up," Flora said gently. "There's no other choice."

Amy lifted her chin bravely. "I know. It'll be hard, but

I'll do it. We'll find a good home for the child, then return to England, no one the wiser."

"Exactly," Flora answered, pleased she'd found the answer to Amy's dilemma. "We'll take Baker along."

Amy sighed. "Must we?"

"She's dull, but trustworthy." Flora smiled wryly. "She also knows how to keep her mouth shut."

After a much-needed laugh, Amy asked, "But what about Lord Dinsmore? Won't he object to your being gone so long?"

"Don't worry. I'm sure he'll be most helpful and understanding once I explain. I'll tell him tomorrow. He's coming down from London, driving that fancy new coach he just purchased. I'm returning with him. I want to visit Mama and Papa, and Richard plans to take me to the Royal Italian Opera House. Will you come back with us? While there, I'll make arrangements for our journey to Italy."

"I'll send my coach back today," Amy replied and ruefully added, "I'm so sorry I've spoiled your plans."

"Don't be silly," Flora assured her. "I know I shall love sunny Italy. And what difference will it make? Richard and I can't be married for several months yet. It'll all work out for the best."

Later, when Flora was alone, she reflected upon how truly she'd spoken when she told Amy she was happy. Richard had indeed been wonderful. In the weeks since he proposed, she had grown increasingly eager for the day when they could announce their wedding plans.

But Amy's mention of Lord Lynd had been most disquieting. Lately, whenever Flora imagined Richard and herself finally married, gloriously happy, at long last sharing a bed, her fantasy quickly faded, because each time she was in the midst of a passionate kiss with Richard, she found herself kissing Lord Lynd. His intrusion was most dismaying. Worse, each time, hard though she tried, she could not switch her thoughts back to Richard, but instead fell into the tingling remembrance of how Lynd's mouth came down hard and masterful on hers that day in the drawing room, when he'd been so angry. She could not stop thinking about how she, helpless to resist, had melted into his arms after fighting him off for an embarrassingly short time—in truth, not more than a moment. She kept telling herself she should be ashamed for thinking such wanton thoughts, but instead, something wild smoldered within her whenever she thought of those impassioned moments. Insane though it was, she found herself yearning to see Lynd again. She was determined to forget him, though. And well she should, she sternly reminded herself. Lynd had made no attempt to see her since that day he'd coldly stated his reasons why she wouldn't be seeing him again.

And besides, wasn't she going to marry Richard, the man of her fantasies? Had they not recaptured their true bond of love? How could she not feel the same way she'd felt on that glorious night in Vauxhall Gardens?

*What's wrong with me?* she wondered.

The next day, Richard arrived from London. Ordinarily he drove his curricle, but on this occasion, when he would be carrying Flora, Amy, and Baker back to London, he personally drove his newly purchased coach, constructed of ash and mahogany, painted a dark green and primrose with the Dinsmore crest grandly displayed on either side.

Flora heard the coach jangling up the driveway and reached the portico in time to see Richard in the box, gripping the ribbons in fine style, looking absolutely dashing atop the box in a many-caped coat and tall beaver hat.

Anxious to speak to him alone, she ushered him into the study shortly after his arrival. "I have something to discuss with you concerning Amy," she said as she firmly closed the double mahogany doors and turned to explain.

". . . And so you see," she finished minutes later, "I must accompany Amy to Italy. I hate to be away from you so long, darling, but"—she spread her palms—"this is for dear Amy. In all conscience I cannot do less."

A long silence passed in which Richard, who had remained stone-faced during Flora's recitation, seemed to draw himself up. "Absolutely not," he said finally.

Flora was taken aback. "What are you saying?"

Richard's ordinarily friendly blue eyes now seemed full of remoteness. "Have you gone daft?"

"Well, no, I'm not—"

"How could you even consider such a ridiculous scheme?"

"I love her. She's my sister!"

"She's a harlot," Richard's curt voice lashed at her. "Has she not cuckolded the Duke of Armond? And you defend her? I am astonished!"

Flora felt herself grow crimson. Not in her wildest imagination had she expected a hostile response from Richard. "You don't understand how the duke has treated her. You don't see—"

"Silence!" he commanded in a strident voice she'd never heard before. "No wife, or any future wife of mine shall ever go traipsing off to Italy in such a fashion. Is that understood? I forbid it."

His mention of *forbid* hit her hard. Since she'd married Lord Dinsmore, she hadn't had to contend with that word. "Your cousin—"

"My cousin was a fool, but even he would not have countenanced such a scheme. So Amy wants to hide her disgrace in Italy? Fine! Let her go. Send Baker with her, but you, my dear, are staying home."

Flora could hardly breathe, let alone think logically under Richard's wrathful scrutiny. "And if I don't?"

"Then the marriage is off."

Flora stared dumbfounded at her future husband. Where was the merriment in his eyes? His charming smile? This couldn't be happening, but stunned and sickened, she knew it was. Her entire future revolved around this man. She couldn't give him up! But when she thought about poor, desperate Amy, she knew she could give but one answer. "Much as I love you, my obligation to my sister comes first. Under no circumstances would I desert her."

Richard's eyebrows shot up in amazement. He looked positively stunned. "You . . . You would give me up for that hoyden?"

"*Don't* you call her names! Yes, I would."

"Well . . . Well, damnation!" Richard ran his hand nervously through his hair. He pondered a moment before he continued in a quiet, more reasonable voice. "Can't you see this is all a misunderstanding? Perhaps I should have told you, but lately I've been thinking we should throw caution to the winds—not wait to be married. Tongues would wag, but what of it?" He gave her a look of heartrending tenderness. "Can't you see how desperately I want you? I don't want you going off to Italy. I want you here, as my wife."

Although relief flooded through her, Flora felt uneasy. It was as if she'd called his bluff. "Then you do understand?"

He spread his arms expansively. "Come, let me hug you. This must never happen again." When she was in his embrace, he continued. "Do you know we've had our first quarrel? Of course, go to Italy. I won't like it, but I shall wait—forever if I must."

What a relief to be in Richard's arms again! Flora decided she would forget this little scene ever happened. He had been upset, that was all, and with good reason. She'd experienced a dreadful moment when she thought she was seeing the real Richard for the first time, a selfish, shallow Richard.

Thank goodness, she'd been wrong.

Next morning, a flurry of snowflakes brushed Flora's face as she stepped out on the portico along with Amy and Baker. Richard's coach awaited, their luggage already strapped on top. Richard, bundled in a greatcoat, beaver hat, and a warm scarf that covered much of his face, already sat in the box, atop.

Concerned about the several inches of snow on the ground, Flora called to him, "Are you sure we should go?"

He called down, "Why not?"

"The snow. We might get stuck."

"Nonsense! The roads are perfectly safe. A bit of snow won't hurt us. Don't be so hen hearted! Get in."

Against her better judgment, Flora climbed into the coach, trying to reassure herself that if Richard said the roads were safe, then they were safe, and she shouldn't worry. Easier said than done. The northeast wind seemed to be veering around to every point of the compass. Snow was falling heavier by the minute.

She decided to say nothing more, fearing she might offend Richard again, and that was the last thing she wanted after last night's quarrel. Besides, she knew she must show her trust in her future husband. He was head of the family now. She must respect his judgment.

They started out and hadn't gotten a mile before Flora started worrying in earnest. It was freezing cold, the wind sharper than ever. The snow, heavier now, flew past them sideways, almost horizontal. "Lord Dinsmore must be miserable up there," she remarked as she drew her cloak closer.

Huddled in blankets, Baker dourly remarked, "Why he does it as a hobby is beyond me. I've heard tell of coachmen freezing to death in the box, as well as guards and outside passengers."

"But I'm sure that doesn't happen often," said Amy.

"Amateurs!" scoffed Baker. "These noblemen who think they know four-in-hand! If you ask me—"

"No one's asking you, Baker," said Flora, interrupting wearily. "Lord Dinsmore knows what he's doing. We'll be fine."

The coach kept going slower and slower, through ever-higher drifts until it barely moved. Finally it stopped completely. In another moment, the door flung open and a shivering Lord Dinsmore climbed in. "My God but it's cold as death out there!" He stripped off his gloves and vigorously rubbed his hands. "Can't see two feet in front of me. There's ice beneath the snow. Horses slipping all over the place. Won't worry about them running off. They're good as stuck."

Flora asked, "Do you think we should return to Pemberly Manor? We haven't gone all that far, have we? Or, for that matter, Vernon Hill is ahead. Perhaps we could take shelter there until the storm—"

"Certainly not!" His male pride obviously wounded, Richard threw her a look of scorn. "There's no need to ask for help. I said I'd get us through and so I shall."

"I have every confidence you will." Flora knew better than to argue. Perhaps he could use some help, though. She had no desire to leave the relative warmth of the coach but felt she should volunteer. "Let me help. You know Lord Lynd taught me four-in-hand, and if I could be of assistance—"

"You?" Richard's voice was scathing. "You're only a woman." He looked amazed. "Sidney might have taught you a bit of four-in-hand, but don't think for a moment you know enough to drive this coach."

Wishing she hadn't asked, she sat back and said no more. Richard lingered a few more minutes, warming himself. At last he announced he was ready, exited the coach, and disappeared atop. Flora heard him yell a curse, along with, "All right, now! Off you go!" At last, after a repeated cracking of the whip, the coach started to move. It was going at a reasonable pace again when suddenly she felt it skid sideways. She held her breath as the coach came to a sudden stop, then tilted, as if it had gone into a ditch. At that same moment, Flora heard a desperate cry. In horror, she watched from her window as Richard fell past her window and landed on his side in the snow.

"Everyone stay here!" Flora yelled and swung open the door. Snow stung her face. A biting wind cut through her as she hugged her cloak closer about her and stepped into a snowdrift.

Richard lay moaning. Thank God he wasn't dead, she thought as she knelt beside him. "Are you all right?"

"Couldn't hold on when the coach tipped," he gasped, obviously in pain. "Fell. God, my shoulder!"

"You can't stay out here. Come, you must get inside or you'll freeze."

Both Amy and Baker joined her. Between the three of them, they managed to lift Richard back into the coach. "Watch my shoulder!" he kept calling. He lay back against the squabs, gripping his shoulder, obviously in great pain. "I know it's broken," he said.

Flora solicitously hovered over him. "We'll get you to a doctor as soon as we can."

"We'll stay here until help arrives," he announced with another moan. "I cannot go atop again."

Baker protested, "But, your lordship, what if no one comes along? If we stay, we'll freeze."

"Can't help it . . . Can't drive." Richard seemed on the verge of fainting.

Baker was right, Flora thought with a sinking feeling. The undeniable facts were clear: The temperature was dropping. If they stayed here they would indeed freeze. But Richard was helpless. In a moment of fearful clarity she realized there was only one solution. "I shall get us out of here," she quietly announced.

"Impossible," replied Richard, wincing in pain. "We're in a ditch . . . horses floundering . . . can't be done."

"Oh, yes it can," Flora firmly replied. "Do you think I'd just sit here and let everyone freeze? No, I've got to try."

Over Richard's objections, Flora collected blankets and took his scarf to wrap around her face. She said to Amy and Baker, "Come help me. We'll see if we can free the wheels. Then you get back inside."

Bracing themselves, the three stepped from the coach and circled around it, fighting constantly against the biting wind and stinging snow. At first, the situation looked hopeless. The coach had indeed slipped off the road and tipped into a ditch. The team of four horses was foundering in the snow. "But look," Flora called. "The horses aren't quite in the ditch. If we can shovel the snow away from the wheels, they'll be able to pull the coach out."

Sharing the one shovel from the coach, the three soon cleared a path for the wheels. "Now get back in," Flora called to Amy and Baker over the howl of the wind. "I'll do the rest."

Clutching her cloak and blankets around her, the scarf covering her face from chin to nose, Flora climbed to the box and took up the ice-covered ribbons in her right hand, the whip in her left. Could she do this? How different this was from those sunny afternoons when she and Lord Lynd had gone four-in-handing! *You can't. You can't!* cried the little voice.

*But I can because I must.*

"All right! Wo-ho, so-ho then!" she called, cracked the whip over the heads of the horses, and snapped the reins. At first the coach refused to move. She tried again, calling louder, cracking the whip with increased vigor. At last the coach moved. Soon they were out of the ditch, back on the road.

Remembering the lessons Lord Lynd taught her, she firmly grasped the ribbons and drove the coach straight ahead to the first shelter she could think of, Vernon Hill. Snow blinded her eyes so that she could barely see. The cruel wind bit straight through blankets, scarf, and cloak, benumbing her with cold. Ah, to feel the warmth of the coach again! But she wouldn't give up. Four lives, including her own, were in her hands. She would freeze to death right there in the box before she would surrender to the cold.

With the snow almost totally obscuring the landscape, she nearly missed the entrance that led to Vernon Hill. At the last moment, she spotted it and turned up the driveway.

With the last of her strength, she halted the horses at the front entryway and climbed down, almost losing her balance in a drift of snow.

Shaking with cold, she staggered to the door and pounded with her fists with all her might. Finally it opened and there stood a startled butler. Snow fell from her cloak as she stepped inside and saw Lord Lynd approaching. "Oh, it's so good to see you, Lord Lynd," she called as she fell into his arms, wet, cold, shivering, happy they were all still alive.

The next few hours were a blur. She remembered Lord Lynd summoning his footmen to carry Richard to bed, ordering housekeeper and maids to see to Amy and Baker. She vaguely remembered how he personally carried her to an upstairs bedchamber, slipped off her shoes, waited outside while the housekeeper helped her remove her wet clothes. When she was safe under warm blankets, Lynd returned, frowning with concern. She especially remembered his reaction when she, through chattering teeth, poured out the story of how she'd managed to free the coach from the ditch and drive it to Vernon Hill.

"How courageous of you," he exclaimed. "How brave! Not many men could have done what you did. You have my utmost admiration."

After he'd left, Flora slept for a time. When she finally awoke, she dressed and asked after Richard. Told he was awake, she hastened to his side and found him propped in bed, wearing a nightshirt, his arm in a sling.

"You look much better," she said, as she sat by his bed and took his hand. "I am so relieved. Is your shoulder still painful?"

"Of course it's still painful," Richard answered petulantly. "Not like before, but bad enough. I am amazed at you."

"Really?" She prepared for another compliment, hoping he would not be too effusive when he thanked her for saving his life.

Suddenly he glared up at her, eyes hard and filled with dislike. "Don't you ever do that again."

She was dumbstruck. "Do what?"

"You mean you don't know?" he inquired, voice loaded with sarcasm. "When you become my wife, I shall expect you to act in a ladylike manner at all times. If you ever take the reins of a coach again, I shall divorce you on the grounds that you've acted like a hoyden."

"But . . . but . . ." she sputtered. "I saved our lives."

"Nonsense. Had you not been so impetuous, I've no doubt help would have arrived. Your blatant bid for attention was for naught. You've done nothing but disgrace yourself."

Flora stood silent, her thoughts churning, until at last something clicked in her mind. *I don't love you, Richard,* she thought in a moment of clear revelation. She should have known it yesterday when he was so nasty about Amy. Why hadn't she seen before that he wasn't her golden prince but just another petulant, spoiled dandy who cared for no one but himself?

How could she have been so stupid? What a waste of her fantasies! But lately her fantasies had been about . . .

*Lord Lynd!* Her heart swelled with a feeling she'd never had before as suddenly she found herself looking through the world with different eyes. *I love Lord Lynd.* He was no golden prince, but who wanted one? Despite his bluntness and cynicism, he was generous and kind. He had loved her once, and she'd ruined that. No doubt, he could never love her again after seeing how foolish she'd acted. Still, she remembered her shivers of excitement that day he kissed her. . . .

Oh, yes, she wanted Lord Lynd! And not just because he was generous and kind, but for reasons she blushed to think about. Well, she'd have her fantasies, if nothing else.

"Well?" Richard asked impatiently.

She forced herself to return to the matter at hand. "Well, then," she said. "Since you feel I've disgraced you, you had best not marry me."

Richard smirked. "Oh, we'll marry all right, and in future you'll do as I say."

Fury almost choked her. "I won't be marrying you, Lord Dinsmore."

"Oh, yes, you will."

"You couldn't drag me to the altar."

"You'll come willingly," Richard answered with an infuriating smile.

What did he mean? Something sinister, she suspected, but she couldn't think what. Concealing her anxiety, she asked, "Will you tell me why?"

"Because if you don't, I shall go straight to the Duke of Armond and tell him about Amy."

She gasped aloud. "You wouldn't!"

"I would and I will."

"You would ruin my sister's life?"

"Oh, come now, Flora, be reasonable. I *am* fond of you, you know. You won't have such a bad life. You want babies, don't you? Rest assured I'll give you plenty. I'll be good to you, I promise, and you'll still be the grand hostess of Pemberly Manor."

"Pemberly Manor is mine," she retorted.

"So tell me, do you think more of Pemberly Manor than your sister?" He awarded her a knowing smile. "I think not. You may fight me all you want, but in the end you'll come 'round. You *will* marry me. You have no choice."

"We always have a choice," she softly said. Her anger had faded. Somehow she'd managed to regain her composure, as well as her pride. She thought of Lord Lynd—his kindness, his genuine admiration over what she had done, so devoid of hypocrisy and pretense. He hadn't minded she was a woman. She was no threat to his manhood, not like . . .

She regarded the man who was once her hero. She had thought him charming, but it was easy to be charming when you were a noble, and rich, and life was pleasant. Given a crisis, his true colors emerged. Thank heaven, she finally saw him for what he was. Now she could hardly abide the sight of him and knew that beyond the shadow of a doubt she could never marry him.

*But what can I do about Amy?*

Lord Lynd's words came back to her: *That's the trouble with you women. You think you have no power, but you do. You must be bold enough to take it, though, and not stay a milksop all your life.*

Was she a milksop? she asked herself and had to answer yes. *But where is my power? What can I do?*

Suddenly she knew. It would mean sacrifice, but life was full of sacrifice. Besides, she had her pride and honor, so what more did she need? "Richard, I shall never marry you."

"Then I shall go straight to the duke."

"No, you won't. I propose a compromise." She took a deep breath, knowing her world was about to change forever. "You give me your word you won't go to the duke and I'll give you Pemberly Manor." She waited. He remained silent, as if astounded. "Well? It's what you wanted, wasn't it?"

He finally found his voice. "You mean you'd actually give up Pemberly Manor?"

"When all is said and done, it's only a pile of stones and mortar. There are things I value more."

"Where will you go?"

"Do you care?" Back to her parents, she supposed, but he needn't know that.

Richard's face wreathed in a smile. "I believe you do mean it. Splendid. I agree. I'll have my solicitor draw up the papers." He reached for her hand. "We can still be good friends, you know."

She thrust her hand behind her. "How do I know I can trust you? Until now, you've done nothing but deceive me."

Richard drew back. "My dear girl, you wound me! You know I have a fondness for you, as well as Amy. Besides, what benefit would I receive if I hurt your sister now?"

Flora considered a moment. True, Richard was shallow and selfish, but he wasn't a cruel man, nor vindictive. Also, if he had nothing to gain, doubtless she could trust him. "So be it, then," she said in a voice cold as ice. Without a backward glance she hastened from his bedchamber.

She had used her power and it had worked! Now, there was one other matter of importance to take care of. During the course of her discovery that she didn't love Richard, she had discovered many things about herself. How pigheaded she had been! How utterly blind! *I love Lord Lynd.* She could not deny her feelings any longer. From the start, he had loved her—she could see that now. He'd stood by her, helped in every way he could while she, head in the clouds, committed folly after folly. What irony that she'd finally realized Lord Lynd was the man she truly loved, only when it was too late. He had made it abundantly clear he wanted nothing more to do with her. But was it really too late? Perhaps if she went to him this minute and poured her heart out . . .

*"Lord Lynd, I have made a terrible mistake. It isn't Richard I love, it's you. It's been you for a long time, but I just didn't realize. Can you forgive me? Can you forget the past? Can you find it in your heart to give me another chance?"*

*"Ha! Are you daft? I loved you once, but I wiped you out of my mind and heart a long time ago. Get out of my sight, you harebrained woman. I want never to see you again. . . ."*

Hopeless! There wasn't a chance in the world he would ever forgive her. Still, she'd tell him anyway. After all she'd put him through, she owed him that much. She descended the stairs. Perhaps he was in the drawing room.

Flora found Lord Lynd standing, his back to the drawing room fireplace. "So you're feeling better now," he said.

"Oh, much!"

"Fine, then," he said rather stiffly. "In case you're wondering, I shall make arrangements for your return to Pemberly Manor as soon as the snow lets up."

"You have been most kind." She heard his response—a faint, derisive sniff. "I don't blame you."

"Don't blame me for what?" he asked.

"For a lot of things." Here was her chance to pour out her heart, but the words stuck in her throat.

"Such as?" he inquired indifferently.

"Well . . ." It was now or never. After all, the worst thing he could do to her was throw her out. So what did she have to lose? "You said once I had committed blunder after blunder. Do you recall?"

"You are the queen of blunderers." He regarded her with hooded eyes. "What are you getting at?"

"Well . . ." She gathered her courage and plunged on. "I have just realized I have indeed committed blunders, the biggest being my supposed love for Richard."

"Supposed?" he asked cynically. "It seemed genuine to me."

"What I'm saying is, I don't love him anymore. In fact, I think now I never did. He was some sort of fantasy."

"So you don't love Dinsmore," he said dismissively. "Anything else?"

"Yes. I love you."

There, she'd finally choked out the words. She stood, hearing her heart pound, feeling the blood rush to her face. Here came the part where he'd laugh and tell her to get out.

Except for one near imperceptible quiver, he had hardly moved. Still stood with his arms behind him, just staring as if he could hardly believe such idiocy. "And when did you decide this?" he finally asked.

"I think I knew it all along. You've been wonderful to me. You've been there when I needed you."

"How flattering. So has your mother."

Oops, *here* was the part where he was going to throw her out. Yet, he hadn't. She should leave this instant, save herself further embarrassment, but she had more to say and she'd say it, even if it killed her. What was it that he'd said about power? Time to put his advice to additional use. She walked to where Sidney warmed himself by the fireplace and stood in front of him, just inches away. With a direct gaze upward into his imperious dark eyes, she said, "Do you remember that day you kissed me? I liked it, and I'd like very much if you'd do it again."

"Don't," he said, arms still behind him. "You've wounded my heart too many times, Lady Dinsmore. I can't—"

"Yes, you can." With great deliberation she pressed her palm to the front of his dark woolen waistcoat. Lightly, she slid it upward until her fingers traveled over the folds of his cravat to his clear-cut jaw. He immediately tensed.

"Stop!" He caught her hand in a grip like iron. "I cannot believe you're through with him!"

"But I am. Look into my eyes if you don't believe me. I have much to tell you." She pulled at her hand. He let go. Her fingers continued their travels, now the other hand, too, until she cupped his face. "Listen," she said, rising on tiptoe. "I love you with all my heart, Lord Lynd. I know I was a fool, but can't we talk about it later?"

A faint light twinkled in the depths of his beautiful dark eyes. "Don't think we won't," he said, as with a ragged breath he swept her into his arms.

Klaang angled away from that building and went for the silver tower to the side. It was windowless and tall, suggesting an inner confusion and a possibility of darkness in which to conceal himself.

The door was large enough for him, made of thin metal and bracings. He pushed it shut and slammed the rod that obviously bolted the door.

Would Suliban be stopped? Klaang stepped back into the darkness and looked at the door. A thin sliver of light around the perimeter proved the door was not tight. Suliban would flatten through it.

He had seen the disgusting sight before. He began to feel his way around, and found a ladder.

By the time he heard the Suliban dislocating their skeletal structure to melt under the door—actually, he heard their shuffles as they reassembled, but in his mind he saw the meltdown—he was bursting out another door, high in the silver tower. Another roof!

Yes, he had seen this nearby small building, and now it was here to help him! He held his breath, and leaped.

# ENTERPRISE™

## *Broken Bow*

A novel by Diane Carey

Based on *Broken Bow*
Written by Rick Berman & Brannon Braga

Based on *Star Trek*®
created by Gene Roddenberry
Based on *Enterprise*™
created by Rick Berman & Brannon Braga

POCKET BOOKS
New York   London   Toronto   Sydney   Singapore

This book is a work of fiction. Names, characters, places, and incidents are products of the author's imagination or are used fictitiously. Any resemblance to actual events or locales or persons living or dead is entirely coincidental.

POCKET BOOKS, a division of Simon & Schuster, Inc.
1230 Avenue of the Americas, New York, NY 10020

STAR TREK is a Registered Trademark of Paramount Pictures.

This book is published by Pocket Books, a division of Simon & Schuster, Inc., under exclusive license from Paramount Pictures.

ISBN: 0-7434-7062-1

First Pocket Books printing June 2003

10 9 8 7 6 5 4 3 2 1

POCKET and colophon are registered trademarks of Simon & Schuster, Inc.

For information regarding special discounts for bulk purchases, please contact Simon & Schuster Special Sales at 1-800-456-6798 or business@simonandschuster.com

Printed in the U.S.A.

Parts of this novelization were written aboard the topsail schooner *Pride of Baltimore II* during the American Sail Training Association Great Lakes Tall Ship Challenge of 2001.

D. Carey
Ship's Cook

# ENTERPRISE™

## *Broken Bow*

# Prologue

THERE WAS NO WIND, YET THERE WAS A RUSH. THE starship was fast, faster than anything, ever. That was the rule. Just from the speed, the bad guys would be too scared to pick a fight. When they saw it go, then, all of a sudden, just magically couldn't see it anymore, they'd know to back off.

*Back away, because I'm going. I'm going . . .*

". . . where no man has gone before."

*Prrrrsssshoooom!*

Sure, it was just a paintbrush, but it made the perfect sound, the soft whisk of a starship's super-engines, just the way Jonathan heard it in his head, over and over, the way Dad described the sound—the rush of possibilities. Anything could happen! Space—the final frontier!

"Doctor Cochrane would be proud of you," Dad

3

said, instead of *give me the brush before you paint your own nose*.

"I know the whole speech by heart," Jonathan said.

"Watch out! You're painting over the cockpit windows."

Jonathan Archer glanced up at his dad and muttered, "Sorry," and drew back the paintbrush. Before them on the porch table, where Mom hated them to spill anything, was a good reason to spill. The ship was almost finished—a shipbuilder's scale model, one of a kind, because Dad was the builder. Jonathan knew he was the only kid on Earth, in the whole universe and even on Mars Colony, who had a model like this. It was only his because Dad didn't need it anymore, not for planning, anyway.

Jonathan surveyed the ventral plates and complained in his head that the dove-wing paint didn't quite match the gunmetal of the nacelle housings.

But the model wasn't suffering any, except for maybe a little overshoot from his brush on the starboard side. Jonathan was more embarrassed that he might keep the crew from seeing some important thing in space. And let the captain down. Captains had to be able to see everything and know everything. It was the crew's job to help him. *Someday I'll be a heck of a crewman, on this ship! I'll make sure the captain knows everything. He won't take a step without me*.

The boy pressed his lips together and didn't say

that out loud. He knew what he wanted, and he would get it. Decision made.

Sunlight poured through the sunporch windows. San Francisco's skyline glittered and enhanced the light shining on the model of the starship. Jonathan was an important person, because otherwise, why would somebody as famous as his father let him work on the actual builder's model of the starship?

*Star*ship . . .

For a few minutes he and his dad were silent as Jonathan put touches of the darker gray on the featureless white nacelles. He saw his dad's hand twitch, itching to take the brush away and do this himself, but Jonathan leaned closer, signaling that he was determined to be careful and get it right. This was one of those things parents were just croaking to do themselves, but knew they'd be bad kid-raisers if they didn't let their kid try. So Jonathan was ahead. He was almost ten, and he had parents figured out.

"When's it gonna be ready to fly?" he asked his father.

"Let the paint dry first."

"No, I mean *your* ship."

Dad shrugged, but his eyes gleamed. "Not for a while . . . it hasn't even been built yet."

"How big will it be?"

"Pretty big."

Jonathan immediately began weighing comparisons in his head. As big as a Starfleet troop transport? As big as the Universe Planetarium?

"Bigger than Ambassador Pointy's ship?"

Dad opened the can of blue paint and Jonathan dipped the brush.

"His name is Soval," Dad said, "and he's been very helpful, and I've told you not to call him that. Get the leading edge of the nacelle."

Nacelles . . . the magic of faster-than-light drive! Zephram Cochrane's big discovery would take men to the stars—*us*, on our own, without any help from pointers. We had it before they found us, so we could take credit for getting ourselves into space. That was fair. We were coming, and they would have to live with it.

"Billy Cook said we'd be flying at warp five by now if the Vulcans hadn't kept things from us," he dared.

He knew he was venturing into sensitive territory now, but an explorer had to gamble.

"They have their reasons," Dad said, holding back. Then more slipped out. "God knows what they are. . . ."

Jonathan lowered the paintbrush so fast that the stick hit the edge of the table and spat a blue decoration on the ship's stand. He turned sharply, bluntly. "What? What reasons? You always say that! You always say, 'They must have some good reason,' but you never tell me what. I'm ten, and it's time!"

Dad tried not to laugh, then chuckled anyway, and bobbed his brows. "You're nine."

"Nine and three-quarters! If I'm old enough to ask, then I'm old enough to get told something, and not just, 'Well, it's mysterious.' Why won't they help? We would help them! *I* would help!"

Dad's smile faded to something else. He leaned forward, hunched his shoulders, and gazed directly, in a way that made Jonathan feel important.

Then, all at once, Dad started talking—but *really* talking, really saying something, as if he had started speaking to another grown-up all of a sudden.

"I haven't been very fair to you, have I?" he considered. "Treating you the way the Vulcans treat humans . . . the way they've treated me. . . . I've been assuming that I'd be the one to decide when you were ready to know things, assuming you don't have anything to offer because you're . . . you're . . ."

Jonathan flared his arms and spat the word. "Primitive?"

The interruption got just the reaction he wanted. Dad smiled, rolled his eyes, flushed pink in the face, and got embarrassed. For an instant, Jonathan felt as if he looked a lot like his dad— the sun-dipped brown hair, the same brown eyes, pretty good smile that crinkled his eyes, friendly face, not enough of a tan. And the same flicker behind the gaze, like maybe they were both smarter than the next guy about certain things, even if the next guy was each other.

"Primitive . . ." Henry Archer murmured. It was a mocking word, one the Vulcans used a lot, till it was more like a joke.

The sadness in Dad's face, though—it hurt them both. Jonathan shrugged a little, not knowing what to say, but his feelings *were* hurt. His dad had done everything a human could do to prove that we were ready for space, just as good as the Vulcans or whatever slimers were out there, and still the pointers wouldn't teach the important stuff, like they thought we were just puppies in clothes who couldn't learn. They knew how to swim, but wouldn't teach us. They wanted humans to half-drown, like some kind of punishment, then learn to swim on our own, and if we almost drowned, well, then they'd step in, maybe, and be heroes for saving us. What kind of friend is that, to think your friends are less than you in the universe? Some friends. Couldn't they see, just from working with people like Dad and Zephram Cochrane? When Starfleet came around, didn't they get it that we were serious? Didn't they see how much we *wanted* to go? Couldn't *they* learn? Couldn't they *dream?*

So who was primitive, and who wasn't?

*If I can make a person like Dad be honest with me, then I can do it with other people, too. I'll think about this later, and figure out what I did right. Then I'm gonna use it on somebody. I'll make the Vulcans talk!*

*And I'll make them say they're sorry to you, Dad. Because they should be.*

As if hearing Jonathan's thoughts, Dad stood up and tapped the lid back on the blue paint. Then he reached for Jonathan's hand.

"Come on, son."

Jonathan took a leaping step, because he knew. "Where're we going?"

"To the Spacedock." Dad drew a long breath and nodded in agreement with himself. "It's time for you to see the real thing."

# Chapter 1

*Thirty Years Later . . .*

OKL'HMA!

*Failed! I have smashed my craft, and now I flee to live!*

*Die here? In rows of weeds and seeds? This is no way to die! Suliban! The savage pawns must not have what I know. Escape is not cowardice! Run!*

Thus he ran from the smelling wreck of a noble craft that had carried him so far, whose flawed intakes he had not been able to mend in time. The wreck would distract them. It was Klingon to its core and it would serve till the end, spewing a curtain of smoke to hide him in the stalks.

Who was on this planet? Who had made the stalks into rows as tidy as a *mOghklyk's* spine plait? What beasts were here who built the land into squares, the buildings into squares, and the fences into squares? Were they also square?

Klaang ran, ran like a fear-driven child, but with anger also, which kept him leaping harder with each step. The gravity here—he could run faster than on Qo'noS. His bulky body served better here and seemed young again. He knew he was big, even for a Klingon, but here he sensed an advantage. Suliban animals would lose him in this weed field.

Then the blasts began, and he knew he was wrong. The stalks beside him burst into flame and withered, blackened. A glance over his shoulder told him they were after him even through the smoke and weeds. He saw their mottled faces, heard their weapons, and sensed their insult.

"Hah!" A burst of new energy, driven by the stink of burning plants, drove him faster toward the square buildings he had seen as his craft rushed overhead to its death. A good death in battle for a good old craft, to go ferociously into the dust and flame with scars of Suliban attack. The future would know about it.

The Suliban weapons spat bitter fire at Klaang as he ran. The alien countryside lit up in great expanses. Ridiculously, he tilted toward each shot; escape would be preferred, but if there was no escape, he wanted to die boldly. He was running to save the mission, after all, not himself. His conscience and his duty were in conflict.

But to die with Suliban disruption in the *back*—who would tell how it really had been for him? Why he died with wounds in his back?

Could he run backward?

He was about to try when a port opened in the nearest building and an alien emerged, bright in the face and round in the body, with hairless chin and narrow shoulders and cloth on its head. Shock broke across its expression, and it disappeared back into the swinging port.

Klaang angled away from that building and went for the silver tower to the side. It was windowless and tall, suggesting an inner confusion and a possibility of darkness in which to conceal himself.

The door was large enough for him, made of thin metal and bracings. He pushed it shut and slammed the rod that obviously bolted the door.

Would Suliban be stopped? Klaang stepped back into the darkness and looked at the door. A thin sliver of light around the perimeter proved the door was not tight. Suliban would flatten through it.

He had seen the disgusting sight before. He began to feel his way around, and found a ladder.

By the time he heard the Suliban dislocating their skeletal structure to melt under the door—actually, he heard their shuffles as they reassembled, but in his mind he saw the meltdown—he was bursting out another door, high in the silver tower. Another roof!

Yes, he had seen this nearby small building, and now it was here to help him! He held his breath, and leaped.

His soles slammed onto the tiny roof, breaking the plated material that warded off weather. In his mind, he endured a quick guess about what kind of weather would come to a place like this.

Then he was on the ground again. He lost balance for a moment as he spun around and drew his disruptor. Now! He would get a shot at them! They were inside that port he had just come from, trapped in the metal tower! A disruptor shot would charge those metal walls and force the Suliban out the other end, where Klaang would be waiting for them!

He leveled his disruptor and fired a single salvo at the open portal he had just come from.

Rather than a simple charge, what came out was a gout of sheer fireball. The tower rumbled at its base, then blew to splinters with a great throbbing roar.

Explosives! Why would these aliens keep volatiles in a field of stalks?

Klaang staggered, shocked, blown backward by the unexpected detonation. He stared at the instantly burning wreckage and wondered why a simple tower would get a noble death, just for hiding volatiles.

But the Suliban would have no more interest in him. Not those two Suliban.

*"Top ryterr!"*

Momentarily confused, Klaang stumbled and turned to see the slope-shouldered alien now standing two steps from him, with a weapon aimed at Klaang's breastplate.

*"Aymeenut!"* the alien cried.

Klaang tried to make sense of the sounds, which seemed to have some Klingon inflections, but he made much more of the stance. *"Rognuh pagh goH! Mang juH!"*

Would the alien understand his warning?

The alien's face crinkled. *"May'v nodea mityer sning, muttay gerrentee i nowow tuze iss!"*

Why had this creature interfered in the quarrel of others? What kind of people were these? In a rage of insult and irritation, Klaang slapped his thighs and ranted, *"HIch ghaH! Oagh DoO!"*

He was about to spit out his further opinion, when the alien proved him completely wrong by opening fire.

An energy stream bolted from the weapon and caught Klaang in the chest. As he sailed through the light and bright air to the place where he would die in the stalks, he silently thanked the interesting alien for a wound in front. At least future ages would know he hadn't died running.

# Chapter 2

*Starfleet Spacedock*
*Earth orbit*

Spacedock was a technological wonder. Built in space of geodesic parts assembled on Earth and expanded to full size in space, the shimmering silver dock soared in orbit around a glowing blue planet marbled with white clouds, an image almost religious in its mystical beauty. Within the enormous open structure buzzed a tiny workpod, moving like an insect around the elegant gray-blue body of the planet's first faster-than-light deep-space cruiser.

Together, as the pod maneuvered around the orbital inspection pod and under the rim of a gigantic blue-gray saucer, the two men inside watched through a small ceiling portal as a string of hull bolts breezed past in orderly fashion.

"Well, Trip, ol' boy, it's an unwritten law in these parts that every starship's got to have a country boy on board or it ain't going to fly right."

"You're making fun of me," Engineer Charles Tucker noted.

"Darn right I am, pardner." Captain Jonathan Archer smiled, completely content in the moment. "If I didn't take it out on you, I'd probably go ballistic in the face of some Vulcan dignitary or an admiral or a ship's cook or somebody important."

"Are you saying I'm not important!"

"Why would I say that? You're the country boy."

"Can an engineer tell a captain to shut the heck up?"

"Sure. 'Shut the heck up—' "

"*Sir!*" they finished together. Their laughter rang through the cramped cockpit. Sounded good. They didn't hurry to stop.

Archer held his gaze on his younger friend a few moments longer than necessary. Tucker was trying to be nonchalant about the new ship's imminent launch, but the veil was thin. He was just as excited as Archer, but Archer didn't feel obliged to hide his near-giddiness at just being here, skimming across this ship, at this time in history. The two weren't quite nine years apart in age, and between Archer's boyishness and Tucker's pretending to be a grown-up at least half the time, Archer figured that put them pretty close. Of all the newly assigned crew, they'd been together the longest, from the design stage to fitting-out of the new warp-speed ship. The new ship hovered above them in Spacedock, as comfortable as an eagle in its aerie, being tended, coddled, and preened by devoted minions in extravehicular suits, none quite as consumed with wonder as the proud captain himself.

"I wish Dad could've seen this. . . ."

At his side, Tucker let his bright grin soften to a misty understanding. "Everybody does, John. Some things just aren't gonna come out fair. I don't think anybody in Starfleet'll ever quite forgive the Vulcans for stalling."

"The worst part is how they pretend they didn't," Archer commented drably, "as if we're too silly to know the difference. I've been waiting thirty years for them to open up, and it's never really happened. They just keep dangling that carrot."

With one hand on the helm controls, Tucker held out the other palm and said, "But look what we've done anyway. There she is!"

Archer smiled, heartened, and drew a deep breath. "Yes, there she is. . . ." He gazed for a moment at the underbelly of the meaty, stubborn-looking ship's wide saucer section, then turned a grateful regard to Tucker. "With you around, who needs a ship's doctor?"

"We do." Tucker whirled the inspection pod around sharply as they came to the neck section and speared downward toward the nacelles. Beneath, the planet Earth gleamed mightily in a sheen of sunlight that made Spacedock glitter. The old Earth and the new ship moved together through the solar system that had given them both life. Magic!

"The ventral plating team says they'll be done in about three days," Tucker offered when he saw where Archer's eyes were leading.

"Make sure they match the color to the nacelle housings."

"Planning to sit on the hull and pose for postcards?"

"Maybe." Archer smiled again, and sighed happily. "God, she's beautiful. . . ."

"And fast! Warp four point five on Thursday!"

Archer shivered with awe. "Neptune and back in six minutes! Let's take a look at the lateral sensor array."

Before the last syllable was out, the pod vectored ninety degrees on its port seam and spun aft, dropping fifty feet like a stone. Only at the last second did Tucker wheel out of the fall.

Archer closed his eyes and swallowed a moan. These stupid utility pods—smaller than they had to be, and definitely faster than they had to be.

"If I didn't know better," Tucker chided, "I'd say you were afraid of flying."

"If I'm afraid of anything," Archer said, "it's the scrambled eggs I had for breakfast."

"Pretty soon, you'll be dreaming about scrambled eggs. I hear the new resequenced protein isn't much of an improvement."

Archer skewered him with a meaningful look. "My number one staffing priority was finding the right cook. I think you'll be impressed."

"Your galley's more important to you than your warp core. That's a real confidence builder!"

"You're a great engineer, Trip, but a starship runs on its stomach. Slow down—there. Those are the ports that buckled during the last test. They need to be reinforced."

Tucker released the controls, picked up a padd and a stylus, and scribbled notes to himself, checking the numbers on the hull plates and poking the identifiers on a schematic of the section that came up on his padd. With one passion competing with another, the pod drifted sideways and—

*Ponk*—struck the body of the new ship, then made a lazy yaw to starboard.

"Sorry . . ." Tucker kneed the controls and the pod stiffened to a more stable position.

Archer pressed forward in his seat and craned to look out the viewport. "Great. You scratched the paint."

Tucker took a breath to make his presence

known, but the com chirped and cut him off. He tapped the button. "Orbital Six."

"*Captain Archer? Sir?*"

Oh, well, they'd found him. Arched leaned back. "Go ahead."

"*Admiral Forrest needs you at Starfleet Medical right away.*"

He looked at Tucker, but the engineer just shrugged.

"Very well," Archer called to the com. "Ask him to stand by. I'm on my way."

"*Thank you, sir.*"

Tucker was still looking at him, even though he was also now spinning the pod out of the presence of Spacedock and heading toward the planet. "Who's sick?"

Archer shrugged. "It can't be personal. Everybody I care about is up here."

"Come on, John," Tucker sighed. "Don't be bitter. Not today."

"Don't worry, I'm not. It's just the truth. A little truth never—"

"You and the truth. Can't we have a little old-fashioned social disguise from our captain? Fool us some? Lull us into complacency?"

Archer laughed again and dropped a hand on the engineer's arm. "Tucker, you are *plenty* complacent enough! Speed up, will you?"

"But the approach vector limit here is—"

"They can give me a ticket. Whatever Forrest's

got, I want to get it over with and get back here while the getting's good."

"That's a lot of 'gettin', Captain. I'm on it! Hang on!"

"Trip! Holy—!"

"Who was chasing him?"

"We don't know. They were incinerated in the methane explosion, and the farmer's description was vague at best."

"How did they get here? What kind of ship?"

"They were using stealth technology. We're still analyzing our sensor logs."

"I'd like to see those logs."

"The Klingons made it very clear. They want *us* to expedite this."

"It happened on *our* soil."

"That's irrelevant."

"Ambassador, with all due respect, we have a right to know what's going on here!"

"You'll be apprised of all pertinent information."

"And just who gets to decide what's pertinent?"

Jonathan Archer knew exactly what was going on before he ever entered the ICU at Starfleet Medical. There were five voices—Admiral Forrest and that other funny little admiral who always reminded him of Grandpa's golf partner . . . Admiral Leonard was his name. Commander Williams as well. The other two—well, he knew Ambassador Soval's voice well enough, curse him, and the other was clearly a Vulcan, too. That snooty tone of voice, the precise diction, and the shield of parentlike solemnity—Archer almost made an unpleasant sound, but decided to just walk in instead. Probably the same effect.

He was still in civilian clothes, but he didn't care. If they wanted formal, they could invite him to a dinner party, not demand that he interrupt his shakedown inspection to visit a sick—

What the hell was that?

Big, that's what. And noticeably hairy. And toothy. The massive humanoid form was hooked up to just about every contraption this place had to offer. Life support? Was it dead?

"Admiral," he spoke directly to Forrest and made eye contact with the other two humans, deliberately leaving out the two Vulcans, who now gazed at him with mixed disapproval.

"John, I think you know everyone," Forrest mentioned, whether it was true or not.

"Not everyone." Archer studied the big sick guy through the isolation window.

Admiral Leonard tried to help. "He's a Klingott."

"A Klingon," one of the Vulcans corrected.

Archer looked at the Vulcan, picking up an underlying joy in correcting a human admiral. Now he remembered this one. Ambassador Tog? Tos?

He started to say something, possibly rude,

when a movement behind the two Vulcans caught his eye. Another Vulcan. A woman. Wasn't anybody going to introduce her? Or were the Vulcans so advanced that courtesy didn't involve women?

He decided their protocol was their own problem, and put his attention back with the Kling-On.

"Where'd he come from?"

"Oklahoma."

"Tulsa, right?" Archer moved closer to the glass.

"A wheat farmer named Moore shot him with a plasma rifle," Forrest filled in. "Says it was self-defense."

"Fortunately," Tos added, "Soval and I have maintained close contact with Qo'noS since the incident occurred."

Archer turned. Oh, what the heck—just ask. "Qo'noS?"

"It's the Klingon homeworld," Admiral Leonard said, proud that he could pronounce it now.

Forrest eagerly added, "This gentleman is some kind of courier. Evidently, he was carrying crucial information back to his people—"

"When he was nearly killed by your 'farmer,' " Soval stuck in.

Uh-oh. Archer's back stiffened. He knew that tone, that inference. *Your farmer*. Good thing he was well enough educated to understand the subtle nastiness as wielded by the pointy among us.

He turned, faced them all, tilted his head just a little, and waited for the other shoe to drop.

Carefully Admiral Forrest finally admitted, "Ambassador Soval thinks it would be best if we push back your launch until we've cleared this up—"

"Well, isn't that a surprise?" Archer snapped. He looked directly at Soval with what he hoped were his father's eyes. "You'd think they'd come up with something a little more imaginative this time."

Soval's face was impassive. "Captain, the last thing your people need is to make an enemy of the Klingon Empire."

"If we hadn't convinced them," Tos filled in, "to let us take Klaang's corpse back to Qo'noS, Earth would most likely be facing a squadron of warbirds by the end of—"

"Corpse?" Archer broke in. "Is he dead?"

That would change things, but he had no idea how. What was an alien agent or courier doing bumbling about on Earth anyway? If Archer understood the general layout of this part of the galaxy, Earth wasn't particularly easy to stumble onto, which was why nobody had stumbled here until Zephram Cochrane sent up his big flare.

The Vulcans were annoyed at his questions, but Archer wasn't about to be swayed by that. Where was it written that humans had to be polite and accommodating to Vulcans and everybody else, but nobody felt obliged to be polite back?

Starting today—

He stepped past Soval and Admiral Leonard to

the ICU door, opened it, and cued a passing physician. "Excuse me—is that man dead?"

Though in hospital garb, the physician was some kind of exotic alien breed, nothing Archer recognized, but his delight at getting to work on this patient was downright human. "His autonomic system was disrupted by the blast, but his redundant neural functions are still intact, which—"

"Is he *going* to die?" Archer pestered. Yes or no. Just yes or no.

"Not necessarily."

Close enough.

Without amenity, Archer turned back to the five musketeers. "Let me get this straight. You're going to disconnect him from life support, even though he could recover. Where's the logic in that?"

"Klaang's culture finds honor in death," Soval explained. "If they saw him like this, he'd be disgraced."

"They're a warrior race," Tos added. Unlike Soval, his hair was still free of gray, but his face was heavily lined; Archer got the impression that the current situation had deepened his furrows. "They dream of dying in battle. If you understood the complexities of interstellar diplomacy, you would—"

"So your diplomatic solution is to do what they tell you? Pull the plug?" Archer heard his temper rising in his tone. Why not? Diplomacy was one thing, but letting a being die in the name of honor was quite another. Perhaps Klaang would be disgraced if his people saw him now ... but what about giving him a chance to recover? So the Klingons carried the notion of a noble warrior's death to an extreme—all it did was guarantee that they'd be at war with somebody all the time and they'd fight each other if they couldn't find some stranger to fight. And the Vulcans called Humans primitive? But this they respected?

"Your metaphor is crude, but accurate," Tos said.

"We may be crude, but we're not murderers." Archer turned a cold shoulder to the Vulcans and faced Forrest. "You're not going to let them do this, are you?"

And he asked in a way that made them all understand that *he* wasn't going to let this happen and the admirals could help if they wanted to. As he waited for their decision—whether to agree with him now or in a few minutes—he glanced at the enormous form on the ICU bed, its legs hanging off the bed from the calves on down. This Klingon hadn't even had the chance to die in battle. He'd crashed and was running. What kind of battle death was that? Better he live and pick something better.

Maybe a hand-to-hand with Tucker. Or Soval. Yeah ...

Soval leaned a little toward them. "The Klingons have demanded we return Klaang immediately."

"Admiral?" Archer prodded, ignoring the ambassador.

Forrest fidgeted. The sight enraged Archer. That the Vulcans and Klingons could reduce a Starfleet admiral to nervousness—some things just shouldn't happen. It was time they stopped happening.

"We may . . . need to defer to their judgment," Forrest attempted, trying to make everybody happy.

Archer looked hard into the admiral's eyes— looked beyond them, at the mental image of the Klingon's great body, stilled by death; at the mental image of the aged Henry Archer's slumped shoulders, bowed not so much by the passage of time as by the loss of a dream.

"We've deferred to their judgment for a hundred years," Archer snapped.

"John—"

"How much longer?"

His bluntness did the trick, not to mention the clarification that he really wanted an answer. This wasn't rhetorical. He was making a demand not for himself, not for Klaang or the new ship, but for Earth, to establish itself a stake separate from the Vulcans. If they wouldn't come up to the plate, Earth would come up without them. Archer was ready. Why weren't these others? When would there be a better chance to demonstrate what humanity was all about, among these people who thought silly things were important? How you died instead of how you lived, for instance.

The Vulcan female stepped forward, quite suddenly, right through the two elder ambassadors. She was the only one with the guts to say what she was thinking.

"Until you've proven you're ready."

Archer bristled. The Vulcans kept chanting that mantra, but they were never interested in letting Earth people do anything that might just prove readiness. Who did these stiffs think they were anyway? Interstellar schoolmarms?

"Ready for what?" Archer asked, even though he knew. Hell, everybody knew, but he wanted to make her say it.

"To look beyond your provincial attitudes and volatile nature." The elegant female had a firmness in her eyes. She was playing his game. She darn well comprehended the triteness of her own declaration. Maybe she was waiting to see how far Archer could be pushed.

"Volatile?" Archer mocked with a little lilt. "You have no idea how much I'm restraining myself from knocking you on your ass."

Eyebrow raised, she looked at him in near enjoyment—was that right? There was a glint in her eye, despite her mosaic stillness. He got the idea she might not like what she heard, but did like hearing it. Very few humans talked back to Vulcans . . . yet.

This Vulcan seemed subtly different from the other two—almost as if she were able to imagine Archer actually trying to knock her down—and finding humor in what would, of course, be the inevitable result of any human attempting to overpower any Vulcan.

He pivoted back to Forrest. "These Klingons are anxious to get their man back. Fine. I can have my ship ready to go in three days. We'll take him home. Alive."

"This is no time," Soval interrupted, "to be imposing your ethical beliefs on another culture."

Archer just cast him a look of deadly irony, and waited while Forrest turned to Leonard.

"Dan?" Forrest asked.

"What about your crew?" Leonard asked. "Your com officer's in Brazil, you haven't selected a medical—"

"Three days. That's all I need."

Okay, everybody always said "Three days," so Archer had picked it out of a hat, hoping they'd think it had a good ring.

"Admiral," Soval protested. No doubt he was having nightmares about a crew full of Neanderthals shooting through space into "civilized" areas like the Klingon cul-de-sac.

"We've been waiting nearly a century, Ambassador," Forrest said at last. "This seems as good a time as any to get started."

"Listen to me," said Soval, his voice noticeably louder. "You're making a mistake."

Archer's reply was calm, but there was no mistaking the condescension. "When your logic doesn't work, you raise your voice? You *have* been on Earth too long."

The debate was over. Forrest had found what might be his last tidbit of resolve and made a decision. Archer felt a sense of relief. The Klingon would survive; and the *Enterprise* would survive her first launch and deliver him back to his people.

The Vulcans, realizing that Forrest's resolve could not be shaken, departed in stoic silence—not before the female shot him a curious glance.

Archer almost smiled, but managed to bury it. Score one for the amoebas.

Forrest waited until they were gone, then winked at Leonard and spoke to Archer. "I had a feeling their approach wouldn't sit too well with you, John. Don't screw this up."

Archer restrained his comment. The last part must be meant as a joke, because nobody would say it to a captain and be serious. Maybe Forrest had invited him here just to provoke this very outcome. Possible? Was there some deck officer in the old boy yet? Better give him the benefit of all doubts and not fiddle with success.

Archer just smiled and pretended to get all messages.

As Forrest, Leonard, and the rather bewildered Williams exited the ICU window chamber, muttering a discreet continuation of the whole argument, Archer moved to the glass partition and rapped a knuckle on the window. The alien physician and a couple of nurses flinched, looked at the equipment, then noticed Archer motioning.

He gestured to the alien. *Psst. Come here.*

The young alien paused. *Me?*

The labyrinth glowed dimly with mysteries and technology provided by even more mysterious presences. The room was bisected by a huge archway that contained unexplained energies, a rippling barrier between here and elsewhere, unidentified, a crossroads between the concrete here and the vague there.

Silik stood on one side, in the here, at the podium that sent pulses of energy through the archway to identify him. He was Suliban, a senior of the Cabal, here reduced to childhood by the being who floated on the other side of the archway. The creature there was as unidentified as the place from which he broadcast himself. They were a mere arm's length away, but they were separated by the ages. Silik felt the privilege of his position eaten up by the smallness of his power.

"Where's Klaang?" the milky being in the portal

spoke. There was a preecho that obscured the creature's words. Even his form was obscure, though he had a head and arms and legs like Silik, like most of the creatures who had achieved intelligence in this galaxy. But perhaps that creature wasn't in this galaxy. Anything could be true, and Silik was at this person's disposal for facts or deceptions. As he stood here, a lifetime's achievements in the Suliban Helix were subordinated to this glowing individual beyond the archway.

"The humans have him," Silik provided bluntly.

"Did you lose anyone else?"

"Two of my soldiers were killed." His jaw grated tight at this report. "One of them was a friend. Can you prevent it?"

Coldly, the creature said, "Our agreement doesn't provide for correcting mistakes. Recover the evidence."

The preecho was both intoxicating and maddening. These ghostlike creatures had all the advantages. They had technology, which they dangled before the Suliban, a chance for enhancements far beyond the foreseeable future of technology. They wanted to tamper with things. The Suliban were their conduit. Silik wanted what they could give, but he disliked catering so much to them without any return of respect.

What choice did he have? They had all the power, and all of time on their side.

"I will," Silik said. "I promise you. When will we speak again?"

The figure beyond the archway seemed to enjoy this part of their conversation whenever it came. He liked speaking of time as a plaything, as his pet. Silik could only stand by and be told yet again what he had heard before.

"Don't be concerned with when," the ghost said.

And the creature vanished, without the slightest hint of ceremony. The radiant energy subsided to a simple haze. The archway disappeared.

Once again Silik was alone in the labyrinth, thinking about losses and gains, and wondering which the Suliban would have in the end.

# Chapter 3

"MR. MAYWEATHER, DON'T STAND TOO CLOSE TO that contraption, please, lest we lose a bit of you."

"Don't worry, Mr. Reed. I'll be tending all the bits of me."

"Mmm . . . to be sure. New technology is always perfect from the start."

Malcolm Reed held his concern in check, but was quite prepared to drop his Lord Nelson persona and knock Travis Mayweather right off that platform if any bit began to sparkle. Such a nightmarish miracle, this. "All right, now you really must stand clear. We're receiving a clearance to—what's the word they decided upon? Ream?"

"Beam." Mayweather's cocoa complexion glowed a little in the overhead prism lights that would soon show themselves as more than conveniences.

"Amazing, the group dynamics assessments they undertake to select descriptive terms for the unimaginable."

"I heard they went through 'scramble,' 'heat,' 'dissemble' and 'spear,' before they found one that wouldn't scare people. 'Beam' sounds so peaceful and sunny—"

"Not quite what's going on here, is it?" Reed sighed at the awesome complexity of this contraption.

Travis Mayweather, though, was giddy with pleasure at the new might of their science. He had just come aboard, and the glaze of awe had yet to take a scuff. It would be his privilege to be the first command watch helmsman of this ship, and he knew his name would probably go down in a few history books. Reed contained his approval with proper British reins, but was secretly pleased at a shipmate's delight and fulfillment.

Mayweather looked particularly stylish in the Starfleet dark-blue jumpsuit, with its geometrically drawn shoulder piping. Reed liked the uniform design. Simple, comfortable, easy on the eye, yet just military enough to make everyone stand properly. He wished they would bring back hats.

In any case, soon they would all be fulfilled, for they were all privileged. As armory officer, Reed's duties would be rather less glamorous than Mayweather's, but had the potential to be more satisfying in the large picture. Ah, well, time would tell whose stories might live on. Until then, it was their charge to make this interesting gadget functional to their purposes.

He stepped to the control island and flipped a toggle.

"Very well, dockmaster, we're ready for you to engage the transporter."

*"Roger, shipboard. Are you standing clear of the platform?"*

Reed glanced at Mayweather, who backed up two more steps and shrugged. "That's affirmative." He, too, stepped back, but commented, "Either this gentleman is paranoid or psychic. Both useful traits, I should imagine."

The hairs on his skin began to shiver even before the lights on the platform changed. The transporter chamber quickly became a receptacle of patterns and flashes that made Reed wish there were some kind of partition to protect them. This thing *must* be giving off some kind of ray or contaminants. How else could it work? So much scrambling energy simply had to radiate.

But they said it didn't. The royal "They."

He and Mayweather watched, each guarding his expression, as containers of various sizes formed inside the chamber, bathed in glitter and fanfared by an earsplitting whine.

"Let's hope something's done about that

squawk," Mayweather commented over the noise.

"I shall send a memo." Reed glanced about and scanned the control island after the whine had stopped and the lights had faded. He didn't really believe it was completely safe to stand up there. What if someone hit the wrong button on the other end?

He controlled his apprehensions and led the way onto the platform, which now contained a clutter of cargo kegs that moments ago had been miles away. Despite the skittishness of the contraption and the doubtful nature of its methods, the transporter was indeed a magical gift from humanity to itself, a fulfillment of dreams from travelers from ages untold. To wish to be there . . . then to *be* there . . .

"I heard this platform's been approved for biotransport," Mayweather said as he pushed the receiving authorizations on the side of each container.

"I presume you mean fruits and vegetables," Reed drawled.

"I mean armory officers and helmsmen!"

Reed accommodated him by touching his own uniform front with an expression that said *Moi?* "I don't think I'm quite ready to have my molecules compressed into a data stream."

"They claim it's safe."

"Do they indeed . . . well, I certainly hope the captain doesn't plan on making us use it."

"Don't worry. From what I'm told, he wouldn't even put his dog through that thing."

Reed opened a canister and was engulfed in frustration that changed the subject. "This is ridiculous. I asked for plasma coils. They sent me a case of valve sealant. There's no chance I can have the weapons on-line in three days."

"We're just taking a sick man back to his homeworld. Why do we need weapons?"

"Didn't you read the profile on these Klingons? Apparently they sharpen their teeth before they go into battle."

Mayweather shrugged. "Then don't let them get close enough to bite you."

"Personally," Reed opined, "I suspect it's all rubbish and lore. After all, with whom do they do all this battling they speak of? And who supports this constant tactical front? Someone must do the sewing, cooking, construction, repair, and run a supply line, correct? Someone must cobble the soldiers' boots, as they say. One should think they must have some other flammable race which also prefers to battle constantly, or they would have to simply battle with everyone they meet. Sooner or later, someone will have shown them their own heads."

"You really think it's a myth?"

"Oh, yes. One simply can't behave that way without ultimately coming up against a bigger dog, sharpened teeth or no."

"And a more disciplined dog, sir?"

"Why, of course. Discipline ultimately beats all Celts and Huns. It's the British way."

Mayweather rewarded him with a stream of laughter as they exited the mystical transporter room and hurried down the corridor, through a scaffold of working crewmen engaged in the hustle of making the ship ready in record time. No one had been ready for the captain's morning muster. Three days? They wouldn't be ready, but there would be a passable pretense of readiness.

"No doubt Mr. Tucker will reassure me that my equipment will be here tomorrow," Reed went on, satisfied with his performance for the day. He continued, imitating Trip Tucker's Southern drawl. "Keep your shirt on, looo-tenant."

Mayweather wasn't listening. "Is it me or does the artificial gravity seem heavy?"

Reed took a few measured steps. "Feels all right . . . Earth sea level."

"My father always kept it at point-eight G. He thought it put a little spring in his step."

"After being raised on cargo ships, it must've felt like you had lead in your boots when you got to Earth."

"Took some getting used to—"

"Excuse me." Though Mayweather took a breath to say more, Reed was on to something else, for he had spotted a crewman about to tune the power conduits to the lower levels with his magnetic coil reader. "You may find that if you re-balance the polarities, you'll get that done quite a bit faster, crewman."

The midshipman glanced at him.

"Thank you, sir," the young lady said, not meaning it.

"Very well. Come along, Mr. Mayweather."

As the two men continued hurrying down the corridor, Mayweather cast a glance back and chided, "What was that all about? She didn't need the help, y'know. Did you enjoy a little venture into superiorizing?"

"Yes, I did. Of course, it also helps that everyone in earshot got a little jab that we are indeed in a genuine hurry."

"Ulterior motives. Sneaky."

"Anything for king and country."

"Listen, Malcolm," Mayweather began, more quietly, "If I didn't thank you for recommending me for this assignment, let me do it right now."

"Oh, all I did was drop a syllable or two into the captain's ear. Your record spoke for itself. All your life aboard spaceships, able to fly nearly any make or model—"

"There's no model like this one."

"No, there isn't. So take heart, for there's nothing against which to compare you. No one will know whether you're mucking up at the helm or not. Wait—engineering is *this* way. Always bear to starboard below deck eight."

"Starboard, aye. But thanks anyway."

Reed nodded. "We shall see."


"Okay, Alex, give it some juice!"

Trip Tucker danced his own kind of ballet through the outcroppings and knotholes of the cramped engineering deck, a complex scaffold made to support experimental technology of the most skittish kind. This was the red-light nerve center of the new ship, busy and tightly fitted, a place where a thousand adjustments had been bolted on where they were needed, from circuit breakers to flow quenchers, some just to see if they helped at all. Tucker swung and dropped, hooked and monkeyed through the arrangement rather like a child on playground equipment or a zoo monkey on the run. Malcolm Reed winced as Tucker's foot slid on a rung, but the engineer succeeded in barely keeping a heel-hold with the other foot and hovered in place to check whatever he was doing.

"Beautiful!" he cried to someone among the many crewmen rushing around this area. "Lock it off right there!"

His voice, so high against the chamber's ceiling, carried an echo. Reed, with Mayweather at his side, stood watching Tucker in his engineering flight suit dance about the ladders and support structures for the mighty and prelegendary warp core. Reed felt a fresh rush of pride. He had first heard of the *Enterprise* project when he was no more than a lad, and for years he had worked for the day when he would be one of the chosen few. Now, to actually be standing here, to see the engines being prepared for the first launch ... it was quite close to overwhelming, but Reed composed himself firmly and reminded himself there was work to be done.

He did, however, take note of the grins that lit up Tucker's and Mayweather's faces.

"Look at him," Reed commented. "The very embodiment of glee."

"I would be, too," Mayweather sighed, "if this baby were all mine the way it belongs to its chief engineer."

"Oh, or its primary watch helmsman, I dare say. Don't sell your role short. You are the first, after all."

"You're determined to make me self-aware at the wheel." A bright smile broke within Mayweather's face. "But you're right—it's giving me butterflies to realize what I am, and where I am. Do you think all the men who came before us on ships felt like this?"

"Unless they were shanghaied." Reed muttered his comment, then realized he had failed to fan the mystique. "Ah," he added, "but each age has its *Enterprise* ... and always has. This is ours, for all our own people, and any other who wishes our friendly hand."

Mayweather accepted the heartfelt sentiment. "Or our firm fist."

"Amen to that."

The two stood together, in their ship, among shipmates, and embraced this moment of charm.

A dash of spritely humanity came as Trip Tucker swung downward toward them, finally to slide down the handrail of the last ladder and land with a thunk on the deck not ten steps away, proudly eyeing the warp core. At last he pulled out an engineer's cloth and relieved a smudge of its misery.

"I believe you missed a spot," Reed charged.

Tucker turned, and seemed immediately proud, then eyed Mayweather.

"Commander Tucker," Reed introduced, "Ensign Travis Mayweather."

Tucker stuck out his hand eagerly. "Our space boomer!"

Mayweather seized the hand and tried to return the enthusiasm—helmsman and engineer, the right and left hands of any ship—but he couldn't keep his eyes off the stunning warp core.

"How fast have you gotten her?" he asked, finding a compromise that excited them both.

"Warp four! We'll be going to four point five as soon as we clear Jupiter. Think you can handle it?"

Reed buried a grin at the two children who had

found each other in the midst of fantasyland, each wanting to do the other's job, just for a few minutes.

"Four point five . . ." Mayweather gazed hungrily at the power source, openly awed and not ashamed to show it. Unthinkable speed, indescribable power, soon to be in his hands.

"Pardon me," Reed interrupted, "but if I don't realign the deflector, the first grain of space dust we come across will blow a hole though this ship the size of your fist."

Tucker snapped back to business. "Keep your shirt on, Lieutenant. Your equipment will be here in the morning."

"What's taking so long?"

"There was some problem at central dispatch with Spacecrate Incorporated's shipment manifest. The crate with your stuff in it got waylaid in transit, and it's being rerouted."

"By whom? Who signed that reroute order?"

"Some guy at the dockmaster's office."

"Seems odd . . ."

"That's what we get for trying to hurry things up—they get more late."

"But the shipment was confirmed for this afternoon," Reed protested. "I got the bill of lading. How do these things occur? Inefficiency?"

Tucker shrugged. "We've had six foul-ups already, and it's not even breakfast. You're not the only one."

"All involving shipments?" Travis Mayweather asked.

"All but two, which were misinstallations of critical parts for the motive power system. I'm having to watch my engineers like a mama lion."

Reed frowned. "Who made these misinstallations?"

"Don't know. We're trying to trace them, but nobody seems to know where the work orders are coming from. Just confusion, is what I think."

"Well, I don't care for that at all . . . where's the captain?"

"Oh, him?" Tucker shrugged again. "Where would you be if you had just ordered your ship fitted out with a seventy-two-hour readiness deadline and you didn't even have a deflector or a command staff? He's in Brazil. Where else?"

*"Ghlungit! tak nekleet."*
"Very good. Again."
*"Ghlungit! tak nekleet."*
Ah, the sound of learning. Jonathan Archer came up on the doorway of his target classroom and noticed that he'd been doing a lot of eavesdropping lately. Gotten a lot of information out of it, too. He paused for a couple of moments and listened, trying to pick out which language the students were repeating to their teacher. The process was heartwarming, but quickly becoming obsolete, as most of the races humanity met as it

moved into space had learned English just as quickly. They were probably more accustomed to dealing with foreign languages—but, on the other hand, Earth has more than her share of languages, so humans had been used to this sort of thing, too, for eons. Of all the planets Archer had heard of, both rumors and confirmed, Earth had by far the widest range of cultures, races, dialects, and languages. Though the Vulcans and others liked to pretend otherwise, Earth was the most cosmopolitan and diverse planet in the charted galaxy.

But diversity didn't suit Archer's purpose at the moment. He needed one narrow thread of talent. It was in that room.

He heard her voice. A charmingly high— "small"—voice, almost a child's voice, but strong and confident at leading the mumble of students through tedious repetitions of alien pronunciation.

"Tighten the back of your tongue," the charming voice suggested.

Then somebody choked.

Oh, it wasn't a choke. Probably alien poetry. Who knew?

Archer was looking forward to having Hoshi Sato's spirit and cheer on his bridge. Good thing, because she would be there about half the time, and most command watches, as the ship's communications officer. The station was a relatively new posting, never before located on the ship's bridge itself, but this was a correction of a problem. The communications officer had turned out to be far more important to the moment-by-moment workings of a ship in space than anyone had expected, even when nobody was talking to anybody. It would be Hoshi's responsibility not only to make sure the crew heard every command, but that all the systems in the ship were communicating with *each other*, from sensors to the red alert Klaxons. Hoshi was also in the command line, simply because the com officer always had firsthand knowledge of exactly what was happening.

Then she spotted him lurking in the back of the room. Her youthful face screwed up with concern. The captain never showed up without a reason, and that meant she would be leaving with him. She knew it, he could tell, but he could also see protest rise in her almond eyes. She would try to talk him out of whatever was about to drag her away.

Archer watched her. She was already disappointed, upset, just from seeing him here. Her right eye got a little tighter.

He was dressed in casual civilian clothes, but they were no disguise: Hoshi would know at once that he was on official business; in fact, he was sure she had already guessed what she was about to ask.

He would have expected no less of her quicksilver linguist's mind. It was one reason he wanted her as part of his crew.

"Keep trying," the young lady said to her chanting pupils. She kept her eyes on Archer. "I'll be right back."

As if stepping through a looking glass, she came out of the classroom and skewered him with a pure glare. "You're not here, are you, sir? Not *here*."

Her voice was musical and happy despite her annoyance. Archer smiled. "Well," he said, "you're here, so I had to come . . . here."

"Outside, please."

Outside was a jungle garden. For all its wildness, it was, in fact, artificial. Everything here was native to Brazil, but had been brought here and nurtured in this domed university under controlled environments. The eerie part was how real it all looked. The only telltale element was the smell. No rot.

"I need you," he stated bluntly as she stepped out before him on the constructed pathway.

"You promised," she moaned. "I took this job because you promised I could finish. There are two more weeks before exams. It's impossible for me to leave now."

Archer managed not to groan at her flimsy excuse. "You've got to have someone who can cover for you." He avoided commenting that it was just a foreign language class and she might have to re-arrange her priorities to a more galactic mental-ity. No, probably not the thing to say right now.

"If there were anyone else who could do what I do," she said, "you wouldn't be so eager to have me on your spaceship."

She had him there.

"Hoshi," he began, but didn't finish quickly enough.

"Captain, I'm sorry. I owe it to these kids."

He almost laughed, though managed to keep from it again. Kids? She was hardly a crone her-self. And there were other things at work besides devotion to this particular cluster of students, who would be scattered far and wide in a matter of weeks.

"I could order you," he attempted, just to see what kind of a rise this would get.

"I'm on leave from Starfleet, remember? You'd have to forcibly recall me, which would require a reprimand, which would disqualify me from serv-ing on an active vessel."

He shrugged. "I need someone with your ear."

"And you'll have her. In three weeks."

This angle was all wrong and wouldn't work, Archer knew. She was a sweet and benevolent person, intelligent and clever, but she was lousy at lying, and this was a lie. Nobody was quite this ir-replaceable. There were plenty of teachers out there who could gargle in front of a group and get them to repeat it. This wasn't the first time she'd put him off. She was afraid. They both knew she didn't want to go out on an experimental ship on a mission that could turn dangerous on a whim. Hoshi wasn't the pioneer type.

How could he broach the reality? Tell her she was right to hesitate? He wanted to open up and reassure her that being scared of scary things wasn't the same as being a coward.

Except for one thing. She wanted to be out there speaking languages, not down here teaching them, and he knew it. Time for the heavy artillery.

From his breast pocket he took a small device and clicked it on, letting a stranger's voice speak for him—a Klingon voice, speaking the garbled ancient language never heard on Earth before a few days ago.

The tension left Hoshi's brow. Something else replaced it. "What's that?"

"Klingon. Ambassador Soval gave us a sampling of their linguistic database."

"I thought you said the Vulcans were opposed to this!"

"They are. But we agreed to a few compromises."

Hoshi fell silent and listened to the recording gacking and gleching and k'tonking merrily in Archer's hand. Archer kept his lips clamped on any encouragements. He had to give her something worth being scared for. She didn't want to teach—she wanted to *do*. Teachers were always the last to use new information. Hoshi would want to be the first.

Yes, yes?

She was leaning a little closer to his hand. "What do you know about these Klingons?"

"Not much," he tempted. "An empire of warriors with eighty polyguttural dialects constructed on an adaptive syntax—"

"Turn it up."

The Klingon voice got louder. What a language. Sounded like this guy was throwing up.

"Think about it. You'd be the first human to talk to these people," he trolled. He lowered his voice, hunched his shoulders, and leaned toward her. "Do you really want someone else to do it?"

Her eyes flickered like butterflies. She backed off a step, then two, and looked at him without turning again to the speaker in his hand. "Why are you rushing me?" she asked. "What do you *really* want?"

"I want people around me who I already trust," he admitted.

"Because? The mission's so simple . . . deliver a sick man home. Why do you need to trust anybody the way you're saying?"

He shifted on his feet, wobbling into a perfectly formed fern, and decided that if he could force her to be honest, then he should be, too.

"Because something's wrong."

"Nothing's happened yet," she said. "What could be wrong?"

Archer gazed down at the little device, its alien voice of the unavoidable and complex future.

He clicked it off.

"I don't know yet."

# Chapter 4

"TRIP, DOESN'T ALL THIS STRIKE YOU AS TOO MANY things going wrong?"

Charlie Tucker frowned at Jonathan Archer's question as the two of them peered out the small ready room's viewport at this side of Spacedock. "What difference does it make what I think? What do *you* think?"

"Don't parry. Just tell me."

"Well, you rushed us into readiness and we're still not ready, but that meant cutting a lot of corners . . . things are bound to tangle some—"

"This much?" Archer settled on the edge of his desk. "Doesn't this strike you as excessive? Something going wrong with almost every shipment of ordnance of any kind? Messages garbled, timelines confused, shipments misdirected—maybe I'm just being overly cautious."

"Paranoid, you mean?"

"I want it to work, Trip."

Tucker smiled briefly. "Well, I think we all want that, Captain. Although I can't speak for our science officer." He paused, weighing his words. "Since when do we have Vulcan science officers?" he said at last. Tucker's complaint was more of a moan, and there was much more to the statement than he was saying outright. *Vulcans who hadn't earned a place at the top of the team. Rank she hadn't earned, trust she hadn't earned, on a ship she'd never touched, dealing with science her people won't share—a perfect perch from which to keep even more secrets.*

So Archer gave him the bald truth by way of an answer. "Since we needed their starcharts to get to Qo'noS."

Seeming almost in physical pain, Tucker rolled his eyes. "So we get a few maps . . . and they get to put a spy on our ship."

His disdain was justified, to Archer's mind, which made this all the worse. They were selling rank and influence at a pretty low price, on top of the plain risk of a randomly appointed executive officer. Bad judgment, and he couldn't pretend it was anything less.

He looked away from Tucker, out at the bright Spacedock, which would no longer protect them after today. He felt cheapened, as if he'd bent too far backward, and the people feeling the ache were his crew.

"Admiral Forrest says we should think of her as more of a 'chaperone,'" he attempted. Pathetic. Fancy words couldn't massage the gift of authority to someone who didn't deserve it. If anything happened to him, nobody would be taking orders from a "chaperone." The figurehead could very quickly go to supreme power and the crew would be obliged to obey. And he had told Hoshi he only wanted people around whom he trusted. What would he say to her about this?

"I thought the whole point," Tucker rasped, "was to get *away* from the Vulcans."

"Four days there, four days back, then she's gone. In the meantime, we're to extend her every courtesy."

Trip Tucker groaned low in his chest. "I dunno . . . I'd be more comfortable with Porthos on the bridge."

Archer smiled sorrowfully at the idea, and searched for something that might give Tucker a boost. He was interrupted before he began by the door chime. His spine snapped straight. "Here we go . . . come in."

No time to let the red flush go out of his face or the burn out of Tucker's eyes.

There she was, coming in from the bridge on which she didn't really belong. As if to rub in the insult, she was wearing a Vulcan commissar's uniform. Or would it be worse if she were wearing a Starfleet uniform?

She offered Tucker not so much as an elevator glance, and handed a padd to Archer. "This confirms that I was formally transferred to your command at 0800 hours. Reporting for duty."

He took the padd and gave it a cursory once-over, because she expected him to. He took the moment of silence to listen to the steam coming out of Tucker's ears, and hoped it would wane. When he looked up at T'Pol, her nose was wrinkled, her neck stiff, and her eyes shifting back from a brief shot around the room.

"Is there a problem?" he asked.

"No, sir."

"Oh, I forgot." He glanced at Tucker, then over to the couch, where Porthos lay sleeping with three of four paws in the air and his snout off the edge of the cushion. "Vulcan females have a heightened sense of smell . . . I hope Porthos isn't too offensive to you."

He pushed an inflection on the word "females," just enough to prickle her if she could be prickled. The Vulcans were always prancing about how they had heightened this and heightened that, so he winged her with one. His goading seemed to ease Tucker's posture. The engineer relaxed some and took joy in this discomfort for the pretender.

"I've been trained to tolerate offensive situations," T'Pol announced.

Tucker perked up. "I took a shower this morning . . . how 'bout you, Captain?"

T'Pol eyed Tucker, and held her breath as long as she could.

"I'm sorry," Archer began, pausing just long enough for her to think he might be apologizing for stinkiness. "This is Commander Charles Tucker the Third. Sub-Commander T'Pol."

Tucker jabbed his hand out toward her. "Trip. I'm called Trip."

T'Pol took a slight breath. "I'll try to remember that."

Oh, enough. Archer allowed himself an annoyed sigh and plunged into the core of Tucker's very legitimate problem with all this.

"While you may not share our enthusiasm for this mission," he said to T'Pol, "I expect you to follow our rules. What's said in this room and out on that bridge is privileged information. I don't want every word I say being picked apart the next day by Vulcan High Command."

If she happened to be insulted, he declared to himself and silently to Tucker, then her irritation would be due payback for her rudeness. The Vulcans prided themselves on their social decorum, but they were among the most discourteous people Archer had ever met. Truly sophisticated people treated others with more respect just as a matter of course, until given much better reasons otherwise than the Vulcans possessed. Humans had certainly demonstrated that Earth wasn't going backward, wasn't standing still, and wouldn't be impeded by snobbery, so why not help? Like Hoshi, the Vulcans didn't want to take any risks. Unfortunately, they also wanted to act superior about their own reticence.

Archer didn't feel like letting them anymore, and he finally had the influence to make good.

"My reason for being here," T'Pol began, feeling the pressure, "is not espionage. My superiors simply asked me to assist you."

"Your superiors don't think we can flush a toilet without one of you to 'assist' us."

"I didn't request this assignment, Captain," she went on, "and you can be certain that, when this mission's over, I'll be as pleased to leave this ship as you'll be to have me go."

She flinched suddenly. Porthos had moved off the couch and was at her leg, sniffing her knee.

"If there's nothing else . . ." she said stoically.

"Porthos!" Archer scolded—but he had waited five seconds longer than he would've with anyone else on the business end of that soppy nose.

The dog cast him a glance, then moved back to his couch.

"That'll be all," Archer said.

T'Pol seemed for a moment to be unsure whether he was addressing her or the beagle. Good.

Over there, Tucker had sidelined himself, with his arms folded and his shoulder blades pressed against the viewport, and said nothing as T'Pol turned and left the ready room, heading to the bridge, which she now had a legitimate right to occupy.

The door slid shut. The ready room fell to silence, except for the faint whirring of the vents with a gush of fresh air. When Archer turned, Tucker was watching the vent port with an accusatory glower.

"What do you think?" Archer asked.

"I think I ought to lube that fan."

"About *her*, Trip. What do you think about T'Pol?"

"I think she likes us as much as I like her, and welcome to it."

Archer eyed him, Tucker eyed back, and after a moment they both blurted, "*Sir.*"

Archer laughed, and was relieved when the engineer finally did, too. They were stuck with the situation, and began here and now to make the best of it. Command didn't mean everything necessarily went Archer's way. This was one of the examples of how the new ship and this whole mission really weren't all his yet. He hadn't proven himself. The ship hadn't. Maybe later both would have the influence to tell offensive interlopers and political hacks to find some gravitons and go fly a kite. That time hadn't come. He made a silent vow to himself and to Tucker that it certainly would.

"You think she's really a spy?" he asked.

"Probably," Tucker said. "If you think she's not going to go back to whoever and tell them how we handled ourselves, then you're more naive than I know."

"No, I'm kinda hoping she does that, actually."

"Me, too. Do I think she's here to steal technology or sabotage the ship or screw us over somehow to botch the mission . . . well . . . no, I don't guess I figure that. Yet."

"It's not enough of a mission to botch," Archer agreed. "We're delivering a guy from here to someplace else. Returning a Klingon national to his home space. It's a gesture of good will, and also to show what we can damned well do on our own, with or without anybody else's favors." He reached down to scratch Porthos on the top of his head, in the little bump where the dog brain was kept, and wished himself the same kind of peace. "The Vulcans may be queasy about helping us, but I honestly don't think they're out to hurt us. I don't think they'd actively wreck our advancement, once we prove we can get there—"

"Maybe you're naive after all," Tucker interrupted. "How many times have you heard them say how we're 'not ready' to go out into the galaxy, or how they're waiting for us to 'prove we're worthy' of the company of others, and all? What if they don't think we're 'worthy' yet and they decide to slow us down some for our own good? I mean, John, I'd be lying if I told you that woman doesn't make me nervous, being here all of a sudden, out of nowhere. Serving as a senior officer! Why would she have to be a senior officer if they just want to keep an eye on us? Don't think there's nothing to that. I'd be peekin' over my shoulder if I was you."

Archer's expression changed. He felt his face grow tense. "Is that a serious recommendation? You think my life could be in danger?"

"With her in that position and the Vulcans thinking we're bad news, hell, yes. Vulcans can be just as devious as anybody, and you'd have to be a sponge to think they couldn't."

Archer nodded charitably. "No, any intelligent being can deceive. It goes with the braincase. Sue me if I'd rather think better of them till proven otherwise."

"Not me. I'll look over your shoulder for you."

"But if we don't give them the benefit of the doubt, then we're doing to them what they do to us, always assuming the worst. I'm not ready to do that yet."

"Guess I'm not as nice as you." Tucker shook his head. "You don't *know* her, John."

Archer sank onto the couch next to his dog, without really relaxing. "No, I don't know her. Not yet." Then a surge of conviction struck him, and his eyes flicked up to meet Tucker's. "But, Trip . . . she doesn't know *me* either."

With a sigh, Tucker indulged in a grim, daring smile. "Not yet."

# Chapter 5

THE SPACEDOCK OBSERVATION DECK WAS AWASH with dignitaries, invited guests, officers, ambassadors, muckety-mucks, and would-bes. Starfleet brass rubbed elbows with Vulcan emissaries, clusters of pundits, power-grabbers, and publicity wonks, all here on a day's notice. Some showed obvious signs of jet lag and more than a little confusion at the sudden acceleration of launch.

Admiral Forrest was speaking already, even though not everyone was seated yet. They were really hurrying this along.

Jonathan Archer was glad of it. At least they took his determination seriously. He hadn't even called sickbay to make sure the transfer of the Klingon had gone well and the guy was still alive.

He glanced at his sides. Trip Tucker was beside him, and after him was Lieutenant Reed.

On Archer's other side were the newly arrived helmsman, Mayweather, and Hoshi and the Vulcan, T'Pol. He'd feel comfortable but for her presence among people he trusted. Even Mayweather was an associate from two of Archer's previous ships. The only stranger was the Vulcan woman, and she made them all uneasy.

Archer tried to bury his concerns, doubts, and the sniggering insult at having her here with these people who had embraced the faster-than-light program with far more devotion than the Vulcans could muster. He tried to suspend his thousand immediate concerns and do his ceremonial duty—pay attention to Admiral Forrest's bountiful pontifications from the podium.

"When Zephram Cochrane made his legendary warp flight ninety years ago," the admiral was saying, "and drew the attention of our new friends, the Vulcans, we realized that we weren't alone in the galaxy."

The crowd obliged with applause, stretching moments into minutes.

"Today," continued Forrest, "we're about to cross a *new* threshold. For nearly a century, we've waded ankle-deep in the ocean of space. Now it's finally time to swim.

"The warp five engine," the admiral went on, "wouldn't be a reality without men like Dr.

Cochrane and Henry Archer, who worked so hard to develop it. So it's only fitting that Henry's son, Jonathan Archer, will command the first starship powered by that engine."

Forrest nodded to Archer. The crowd applauded again as Archer and his command staff stood up and moved away from their seats. Archer kept his eyes from meeting anyone's. The applause should be for Dad and nobody else. Archer knew he was catching the glory by reflection only, and wondered how many other bits of fallout from his father's work had bolstered him in his own climb to command. That couldn't be ignored, and it would be unfair of him to claim otherwise. Bitterness set in again. He would happily have become a shuttle conductor if only Dad had received the honors he deserved and the right to see his ship launched while he was still alive. This was too little, too late.

Damn Vulcans.

He led his crew toward a set of doors while the admiral kept talking.

"Rather than quoting Dr. Cochrane, I think we should listen to his own words from the dedication ceremony for the Warp Five Complex, thirty-two years ago. . . ."

A large screen took over the crowd's attention as it came alive with archival footage of a very elderly Zephram Cochrane, the father of warp drive, giving a speech in front of a throng of scientists, including Henry Archer, a long time ago. Ironically, Archer remembered being present at that speech, before he was even seven years old. Even then he had realized the import of what he was hearing.

"On this site," the crotchety Cochrane began, "a powerful engine will be built. An engine that will someday let us travel a hundred times faster than we can today. . . ."

Archer led his crew through the breezeway to the airlock attached directly to the ship. As they moved, the speech was piped through to the bridge.

The bridge was a compact command center, austere and spartan, mostly steel-walled, with a source of light from hidden panels overhead. There were no carpets or amenities, just various stations with bucket seats, and a maze of gauges, dials, and little scanner screens. In the middle was the captain's chair, to which Archer dutifully moved while the universe watched.

"Imagine it," Cochrane's voice thrummed. "Thousands of inhabited planets at our fingertips . . . And we'll be able to explore those strange new worlds, and seek out new life, new civilizations. . . . This engine will let us go boldly where no man has gone before."

Barely conscious of it, Archer noticed his own lips moving to the words. He stopped and cleared his throat. Everybody was waiting for him now.

"Detach mooring umbilicals and gravitational supports," he ordered. "Retract the airlock and disengage us from the Spacedock. Confirm all break-offs. Internally metered pulse drive, stand by."

"Impulse drive standing by, sir," Mayweather responded. "All sublight motive power systems ready."

At Archer's side, T'Pol appeared. But she didn't repeat any orders, as would a practiced Starfleet officer. She didn't interfere at all. Perhaps she felt as out of place as they thought she was. She took the science station with reserved grace, but seemed out of place and unhappy.

Frozen vapor swarmed through the Spacedock, as if a dragon had breathed across dry ice. Archer leaned forward in the command chair. Around him, the crew was tense and expectant. On the engineering tie-in screen to his left, he saw Trip Tucker standing before the throbbing warp core, looking like an eaglet about to fledge.

In Archer's mind, his father's hand worked the control unit of a model ship, smiling warmly at a little boy who believed in him completely. Every man could do much worse in life than to have a little boy believe completely in him. The father's hand came down, and passed the control unit to a boy's tiny palm. The boy inserted the unit into the model ship.

"Take her out," Archer said finally. "Straight and steady, Mr. Mayweather."

"Ladies and gentlemen," Admiral Forrest's voice overlaid Archer's words. "Starfleet proudly presents to the galaxy . . . the faster-than-light long-range cruiser, *Enterprise!*"

Applause rang and rang in Archer's ears. A shiver went down both arms.

The lean and masculine ship, rugged in construction and blatantly field-ready, undecorated and proud of it, began to move slowly forward, throbbing with power to her innermost bones. Spacedock peeled back from his view and disappeared behind him, like so many memories. Everyone else expected her to be back in eight days, but Archer had other ideas. If the ship stressed out well and he could play his cards right, she wouldn't see a Spacedock for the next six months.

They'd made it. They were out, and with two hours to spare. Now all those dignitaries could go back to bed. Archer forgot them immediately. His eyes were on the forward screen. Open space.

He found his voice again and tapped the chair com. "How're we doing, Trip?"

Behind Trip Tucker's voice, the warp engines pulsed at full power. "Ready when you are," he responded. Sounded both excited and nervous.

"Prepare for warp. Mayweather, lay in a course," Archer said, and glanced at T'Pol. "Plot with the Vulcan starcharts . . . direct course to the planet Qo'noS."

Mayweather's eyes flicked toward T'Pol, but he studiously managed not to look at her. He worked his navigational controls, which only now, as they cleared the solar system, received clearance from the access-classified starcharts brought by their new executive officer.

"Course laid in, sir."

That was it. Never again would the Vulcans be able to hide the location of the Klingon planet from Earth. Sounded like a prime tourist destination, didn't it? Yes, folks, spend your next holiday spitting and howling in the galaxy's newest vacation wonderland!

"Request permission to get underway?" Mayweather looked at Archer.

Archer snapped out of his thoughts. Warp speed . . . high warp. This was it.

He looked at T'Pol and asked silently for confirmation of the course.

She sensed his eyes and looked up. "The coordinates are off by point two degrees."

Mayweather glanced at her, embarrassed and angry. Something about the way she said that . . .

But Archer wasn't about to let her spoil the moment. "Thank you," he said quickly, and waved casually to Mayweather. "Let's go."

"Warp power," Mayweather uttered aloud, though he didn't have to. "Warp factor one . . ."

The ship surged physically. There was a snap of light, and the crescent of Earth was left behind as if by magical invocation. The whole solar system was suddenly no more than a whim.

"Warp one accomplished," Mayweather confirmed.

Archer made eye contact with everyone around him . . . first T'Pol, who had no more criticisms. Then Reed. He seemed weary, but British propriety kept his shoulders back and tension in check, and he gave Archer a nod of generous encouragement.

Archer smiled, then looked at the little screen with Trip Tucker shepherding his engines. "Trip? You okay?"

"Ready and willing," Tucker responded, but never looked away from the glowing warp core.

"Go to warp factor two."

"Warp two," Mayweather choked.

Another flash, another surge, and the ship shouldered into a multiplicity of speed. Stars blurred. Space itself began to bend to the ship's will.

"Warp two accomplished, sir."

"I like the feeling," Archer offered. "Everybody stable? No jumps in the readings?"

No one spoke up.

"Warp factor three."

Though Mayweather didn't respond, his hands worked on the helm. Another flash. The surge this time was smoother, and in a moment they had made warp three.

"Good," Archer commented. "Everybody take a breath. Check your stations. Hoshi, do a shipwide sweep."

"Shipwide, aye," Hoshi responded, her voice tight. She was terrified. Giving her something to do was sound operational practice. He'd have to make sure she wasn't idle at times like this.

"Let's have warp four, helm."

He barely felt his own voice. Pushing it, yes. He should've cruised at warp two for a day. He didn't feel like waiting. He wanted the first log entry to read immediate high warp.

Somebody gasped, but he wasn't sure who. Probably Hoshi. Couldn't be T'Pol, right? Or Reed.

Not that it mattered. They were all gasping on the inside.

"Respond to me, Travis," Archer steadily insisted.

"Oh . . . yes, sir. Warp factor four, aye. Sorry."

"No problem at all. Doing fine. Feels pretty good, actually. Hear that warp hum? I like that."

His casual conversation seemed to help them all. The power systems whined some at this higher challenge. Lights flashed on several consoles, but nobody called an end to it. Anyone, at any station, could have stopped the progress with an alarm warning. Unless they were at battle stations, even Archer would have a hard time explaining pushing beyond stress once he got a stop warning from one of the crew, almost anywhere on the ship.

No one spoke up. In fact, they were eerily quiet. Hoshi's communications board flickered with green lights from systems deep in the ship's fibrous flanks.

"Warp factor four," Mayweather uttered, "accomplished, Captain. All systems report stable. Helm is steady."

"Trip?"

On the engineering monitor, Tucker finally turned to meet Archer's expectant eyes. "We're all-go down here, Captain. Flow over the dilithium crystals is even. No flux on the power ratios. She looks good."

"Congratulations, Trip . . . everybody. Let's cruise at warp four for a while and see how she does. All hands, standard watch rotation for the next twenty-two hours. T'Pol, how would you like to try the con on for size?"

She looked up, startled. Yes, he'd managed to fluster her. Clearly she hadn't expected to take command at all. She knew she was just some kind of figurehead here and had probably hoped to stay pretty much to what she knew at the science station.

But if the rest of the crew had to endure trials, then so did she. After all, she could've stayed on a nice Vulcan boat if she wanted passivity.

Archer stood up, offering the hot seat.

T'Pol's eyes narrowed. She sensed a trap. Perhaps it was. Under the cloying eyes of the crew, she stood up and moved to the center of the bridge and took the command chair. What choice did she have?

"Good," he said. "Why don't you join me for dinner at change of watch? We can get to know each other. Put the crew at ease, if nothing else."

She eyed him. Just who was suspicious of whom?

"Thank you," she said, not giving anything away.

Choreographing his movements carefully, Archer stepped away from the center and moved to the exit hatchway. The tall, airtight swinging hatch was almost big enough to get through without ducking—almost. He paused before leaving the bridge, turned, and looked at the expanse of space spilling out before the newest Earth ship, named *Enterprise*, as she flashed along on her invisible racetrack.

"We made it, Dad," he murmured. "Couldn't have done it without you."

And in his mind, the model spaceship streaked for the clouds.

# Chapter 6

VISCOUS PINK FLUID TWISTED IN A JAR. TINY CORK-screw organisms flitted through the pink like birds in an eternal microsunset. The jar turned, but the liquid and the flitters pretty much stayed the way they were, enjoying their brainless dance.

"Love what you've done with the place. . . ."

Jonathan Archer turned the jar again, watching the little life-forms squiggle.

"Those are immunocytic gel worms," Phlox explained happily. "Try not to shake them."

The quirky alien was in a perfect fantasy here in the ship's minimal sickbay. He had ultimate say over everything. Suddenly he was the senior medical officer on a ship. That didn't happen every day.

Archer paused and watched as the funny fellow

arranged, like an old-lady apothecary, dozens of jars, tools, and definitely non-Starfleet-issue medical paraphernalia onto the Plexiglas shelving behind the doctor's computer center. As he handed Phlox the pink jar, Archer turned his attention to the unconscious Klingon lying on the biobed. He wanted to ask how this fellow was doing. Alive? Almost alive? Would he be able to stand up and walk out of here when they reached Qo'noS?

Or would Archer be forced to hand over a semi-corpse to the Klingon reception committee? Not his first choice. He didn't think they'd much like it, either.

He held back the questions. The Klingon was stable, wasn't going anywhere, and he wanted Phlox to feel at ease enough to do a good job. He'd pulled the Doctor out of a secure position at Starfleet Medical, where he had plenty of others making decisions to support him and he had a support system to lean on. Here, even though he didn't seem to know it yet, things would get a lot harder, and fast.

"So, what'd you think of Earth?" Archer asked pointlessly, just to get things rolling.

"Intriguing," Phlox said with enthusiasm. The stocky, round-faced Denobulan exuded warmth and ease, along with a distinctly eccentric charm, as he bustled about sickbay. "I especially liked the Chinese food. Have you ever tried it?"

Handing off articles from the packing box on top of the desk, Archer shrugged. "I've lived in San Francisco all my life."

Of course, San Francisco had a Chinese restaurant on every third corner, just like any other American city, but he sensed Phlox wanted to have something on him.

"Anatomically, you humans are somewhat simplistic," Phlox said, probably not realizing he was being insulting. "But what you lack biologically, you make up for with your charming optimism. Not to mention your egg drop soup. Be very careful with the blue box."

Gingerly, Archer passed him a funny-looking box with breathing holes punched in both lateral sides. Inside, something skittered that made him almost drop the container. "What's in there?"

"An Altairian marsupial. Their droppings contain the greatest concentration of regenerative enzymes found anywhere."

"Their droppings?"

"If you're going to try to embrace new worlds, you must try to embrace new ideas."

"Ah."

Archer just nodded, annoyed that everybody seemed to be taking classes in etiquette from the Vulcan Institute of Creative Condescension.

"That's why," Phlox went ignorantly on, "the Vulcans initiated the Interspecies Medical Exchange. There's a lot to be learned."

But Archer had stopped paying much attention. Instead, he wandered to the ward and stood over the Klingon. Was he breathing?

"Sorry I had to take you away from your program, but our doctors haven't even heard of a Klingon."

"Please!" Phlox blurted. "No apologies! What better time to study human beings than when they're under pressure? It's a rare opportunity! And your Klingon friend . . . I've never had a chance to examine a living one before!"

"Ensign Mayweather tells me we'll be to Qo'noS in about eighty hours." Archer turned to the intern. "Any chance he'll be conscious by then?"

"There's a chance he'll be conscious within the next ten minutes," Phlox said. "Just not a very good one."

"Eighty hours, Doctor," Archer told him. "If he doesn't walk off this ship on his own two feet, he doesn't stand much of a chance."

"I'll do the best I can." The alien smiled infectiously—and his smile got bigger, bigger . . . bigger . . . weirder . . . "Optimism, Captain!"

Trip Tucker climbed through the ship's cramped crawl space, a laddered passage meant pretty much for maintenance, not really for daily use. Preoccupied with thoughts divided between the ship, the captain, and the Vulcan, he didn't even realize he had company until a boot heel scraped his shoulder. He turned and looked above him.

There, in an open gap between two ladders, Ensign Mayweather was enjoying his off time by squatting on what really was the ceiling. In space, of course, there was no real ceiling, but just an artificial feeling of up and down created by spinning gravitons.

"You're upside down, Ensign," he mentioned.

Travis Mayweather blinked at him. "Yes, sir."

Tucker got the idea he'd interrupted a meditation session or something.

"Care to explain why?" Tucker asked. He really meant *how*.

"When I was a kid, we called it the 'sweet spot.' Every ship's got one."

" 'Sweet spot'?"

"It's usually halfway between the grav-generator and the bow plate." He pointed to a thin conduit crossing below them. "Grab hold of that conduit. Now swing your legs up."

Tucker took a grip on the conduit, but couldn't quite muster the nerve to jump off the ladder, the only stability between him and three decks looming below.

"Swing your legs," Mayweather encouraged.

"Wow . . ." Tucker gulped as an unseen force took hold of him with the slightest encouragement and gave him support as he twirled in sudden zero-G. He still had a grip on the conduit, just in case.

"Now, let go," Mayweather said.

One hand, then the other . . . he laughed at the sensation. Just like basic training! He spun and pirouetted merrily, tucking his legs and stretching them out again.

Then he bumped his head on the ceiling next to where the helmsman sat.

"Takes practice." Mayweather reached for him and helped him find a stable sitting position. "Ever slept in zero-G?"

"Slept?"

"Like being back in the womb."

Tucker paused and eyed him. "Captain tells me you've been to Trillius Prime."

Mayweather nodded. "Took the fourth, fifth, and sixth grades to get there. I've also been to Draylax, and both the Teneebian Moons."

"Mm . . . I've only been to one other inhabited planet besides Earth. Nothing there but dust-dwelling ticks. I've heard the women on Draylax have . . ."

The helmsman nodded drably. "Three. It's true."

"You know that firsthand?"

"Firsthand, secondhand, and thirdhand."

Mayweather shot him a sly glance; Tucker couldn't tell whether he was joking or serious.

"Guess growing up a boomer has its advantages," he said, avoiding a comment about how a cow has four. They shared a silly smile.

"The Grand Canyon?"

"No."

"Big Sur Aquarium?"

"Sightseeing was not one of my assignments."

"All work and no play . . . everyone should get out for a little R and R now and then."

"All our recreational needs are provided at the compound."

Well, wasn't this rather like having a dinner conversation with a block of granite.

What was it about Vulcans and common courtesy? Maybe humans should just cut their losses and learn to be stiff and rude.

Little blessings . . . the door chimed and got Archer off the hook of making small talk with a person with whom he should have an awful lot to talk about. He'd known captains and science officers who talked nonstop for the first five watch rotations, just to get to know each other.

Not this time.

"Come in," he said thankfully.

Charlie Tucker strode from the mess hall into the captain's private mess chamber. It was a pleasantly appointed room with a table for four, six if they squished, warmly lit by two candles provided by the captain's steward as a first-meal gift. There was no food yet, but only a basket of breadsticks between the candles. Tucker came all the way in to let the door close and declared, "You should've started without me."

"Sit down," Archer said, afraid he might get away.

Tucker clumped into a chair beside Archer and snatched up a breadstick. Noisily he began to gnaw, paying special attention to the sesame seeds.

T'Pol raised her chin and looked down her nose at him—literally and figuratively—in clear disapproval of the eating habits. Archer smiled. How else *was* there to eat a breadstick except with some noise and breakage? You had to burn a few dilithium crystals to get power, after all.

Archer extended the basket of breadsticks to T'Pol. She obligingly took one and placed it dead center on her plate, then looked at it as if expecting it to explain its intentions.

"T'Pol tells me she's been living at the Vulcan Compound in Sausalito," Archer attempted.

"No kidding," Tucker blurted. "I lived a few blocks from there when I first joined Starfleet. Great parties at the Vulcan Compound."

T'Pol didn't respond, but picked up her knife and fork and began dutifully sawing at the breadstick on her plate. It crumbled almost immediately, and sprayed the tablecloth with crumbs.

"It might be a little easier," Archer suggested, "using your fingers."

"Vulcans don't touch food with their hands." Refusing to be defeated, she paused primly to study the recalcitrant breadstick with a distinctly scientific air; Archer suppressed an inkling of amusement.

"Can't wait to see you tackle the spareribs," Trip Tucker commented as T'Pol changed her approach to the breadstick.

She held it down with the fork, and began to deliberately saw at it with the butter knife, but she glanced forbiddingly at Tucker.

"Don't worry," Archer said. "We know you're a vegetarian."

As if conjured, the steward entered from the galley passage with three plates of food. Two meat, one grilled vegetables. Archer was suddenly glad he'd remembered that little detail at the last minute. Vegetarians on ships had caused complications for ship's cooks for centuries, not to mention allergies and other special needs. Plain baked beans instead of pork 'n' beans. Having aliens aboard would certainly change even more galley plans. T'Pol was all of those.

"Looks delicious," Tucker commented. "Tell the chef I said thanks."

The steward nodded and simply exited.

Archer and Tucker began to eat enthusiastically, but T'Pol ignored her food and continued methodically sawing at the breadstick.

"You humans claim to be enlightened," she said, "yet you still consume the flesh of animals."

Archer caught Tucker's annoyed glance, but got the idea the engineer was enjoying something about this predicament.

"Grandma taught me never to judge a species by their eating habits," Tucker mentioned.

Ah, yes, infinite diversity, Vulcan style.

" 'Enlightened' may be too strong a word," Archer pushed on, "but if you'd been on Earth fifty years ago, I think you'd be impressed by what we've gotten done."

"You've yet to embrace either patience or logic," T'Pol accused. "You remain impulsive carnivores."

"Yeah?" Tucker blurted. "How about war? Disease? Hunger? Pretty much wiped 'em out in less than two generations. I wouldn't call that small potatoes."

"It remains to be seen whether humanity will revert to its baser instincts."

"We used to have cannibals on Earth." Tucker leaned closer to her and wagged his eyebrows. "Who knows how far we'll revert? Lucky for you this isn't a long mission."

"Human instinct is pretty strong," Archer supported. "You can't expect us to change overnight."

At this special moment in their relationship, T'Pol succeeded in snapping the breadstick with a rather tidy final cut. She slid the piece onto her fork. "With proper discipline, anything's possible."

She then ate the piece, as if that were really something worth showing off.

Archer managed not to groan. If this turned out to be the only level on which they could converse, then the whole ship was in trouble. He had honestly hoped to be able to communicate with T'Pol as an equal, and to speak frankly of his concerns regarding Ambassador Soval's attitude toward the *Enterprise*'s launch. He had even hoped—foolishly, he realized now—to discuss the importance of creating an atmosphere of mutual respect between Vulcans and humans.

This seemed so unproductive . . . and it really wasn't why he had asked her here, or Tucker either. Wasn't there *some* way to break through to her?

They ate in silence, which seemed to suit T'Pol perfectly well. Apparently Vulcans didn't take meals as social lubrication. This was more like church. It even had the nasty glances from the naughty kid.

Just when Archer thought his head would blow off, Tucker shifted on his seat and asked, "So, Miss TeePol, how long you been on Earth?"

"A few weeks, this occasion. I am not permanently living there."

"Yeah? Where'd you go to school?"

"At which level?"

"Well . . . the latest level."

"I am Ambassador Soval's apprentice in interplanetary sociopolitical studies."

"Really? Got any military training? Like, ever piloted a ship before?"

"Trip," Archer cut off. "She doesn't have to pilot the ship. We have helmsmen for that. She'll get through the next eight days just fine with our support system."

*Don't badger.* Tucker got the message and fell silent again.

T'Pol finished her vegetables and immediately stood up. "Thank you for inviting me to your meeting. I shall return to my post. I have many studies. I must acquaint myself with the vessel in order to be an effective senior officer."

Archer got to his feet—something he really didn't have to do as commanding officer—and escorted her to the door. "I hope this is only the first," he said graciously. "Thank you for coming, Sub-Commander."

"Yes, Captain. Enjoy your evening."

And she was gone. Archer stared for a moment at the closed door.

"Not bad," Tucker commented, "for an 'impulsive carnivore' such as yourself, Captain."

Archer shook his head in wonderment at all this. "But you notice how forgiving they are of anything the Klingons do, no matter how savage. Humans are unenlightened, but Klingons are 'diverse.'"

"Uppity hypocrites. What a surprise."

"Hey, don't underestimate her. She did, after all,

conquer that primitive breadstick with superior discipline."

Tucker laughed.

"Oh, give her some credit," Archer allowed. "At least she knows she's not familiar enough with the ship to be effective yet, and she admitted it. That's not all bad."

"You're bending," Tucker warned. "No bending allowed. Vulcans never bend for us, remember?"

"Are you ready to go to warp four point five?" Archer asked, changing the subject to something they both liked much better than Vulcans.

"Already?" Tucker sat bolt upright. "It's only been—what?—ten hours!"

Archer gave him a sly look and a dangerous grin. "What are we waiting for?"

Tucker seemed to be stricken numb. "I don't know . . . I guess I'm used to bureaucrats and sleepy admirals making the progressive decisions. Twenty memos and a month of means testing, feasibility studies, and role definition."

"We don't define roles here anymore, Trip. We make a list, cut it in thirds, and give everybody a piece. Let's gather the operative minds and take the bridge."

"Delta Watch'll be disappointed."

"They can stay on duty. We're not dismissing them. We're just horning in."

Archer put down his suffering chicken leg. "Come on. I've had it with sitting around being socially unacceptable. Let's do some serious shaking down."

Ten minutes later they were on the bridge, with the primary crew mustered. Malcolm Reed was already on the bridge for some reason. Hoshi showed up a little groggy—she'd been asleep—and Mayweather appeared only a moment after her.

The on-deck bridge crew was uneasy with the appearance of the primary watch, but seemed reassured when all they had to do was stand aside for a few minutes. Any irritation was quickly swallowed in the anticipation of going to warp four point five so many hours early. They could massage their egos later—at higher warp—and enjoy it a lot more.

"Let's all check our readouts," Archer ordered as he took the command chair. "Sing out if you see any irregularities. How have the ratios been?"

"Steady as a stone, sir," Mayweather reported, checking his tie-in to the engineering deck. If anything went wrong down there, he'd be the first to see it on his console, with T'Pol a fast second.

At the science station, she said nothing. Archer could tell, even so, that she disapproved of this early risk.

Well, it wasn't too early for her to have a dose of what made humans tick, other than fresh meat. Archer paused a few moments and listened to the ship. The bleeps and whirrs, the soft hum of warp drive, the twinkle of systems constantly diagnosing themselves. He wanted to memorize those sounds as they were now, doing the right things, feeling the right amounts of energy flow, so he could tell when they didn't sound right.

"Everything seems okay to me," he said, and looked at Mayweather. "Why don't you try four-three?"

Mayweather's shoulders tightened as he worked his helm controls. The sound of the ship made a slight change in pitch—the engines, increasing everything on an incremental level, across the board.

No calls from Tucker . . . so far, so good.

"Warp four point three, sir," Mayweather reported.

They waited and listened. Would something happen?

Or had it just happened, and this was it? This was the sound of success.

"Not much of a change," Reed observed.

"I don't know," Hoshi spoke up. "Does anybody feel that?"

Archer looked at her. "Feel what?"

"Those vibrations . . . like little tremors."

T'Pol cast her a cool glance. "You're imagining it."

Archer thought about what they had said. His science officer neither saw nor felt anything, but his motion-sensor super-ear did.

Of course she did, right? There were bound to

be tiny increases in everything. They had just gone from really fast to really-really fast. They had just shortened their trip by several hours, even on the galactic scale. That was a lot of change.

Sure she felt something.

Mayweather was looking at him.

Archer nodded. "Bring us to four-four, Ensign."

This time the ship shuddered, and everybody felt it. Sounds thrummed from deep places with the new acceleration. Vibrations racked the deck under their feet.

Hoshi grabbed the sides of her seat. "There! What do you call that!"

"The warp reactor is recalibrating," T'Pol explained coldly. "It shouldn't happen again."

But an alarm went off at Reed's tactical station.

Hoshi jumped. "Now what?"

"The deflector's resequencing," Reed told her. "It's perfectly normal."

T'Pol eyed her own board, but said, "Perhaps you'd like to go to your quarters and lie down."

Hoshi cast her a provoked glance. *"Ponfo mi-rann,"* she said. Vulcan for "butt out"?

Archer watched the women. They were, more or less, a microcosm of the whole crew and all his problems.

"I was instructed," T'Pol responded, "to speak English during this mission. I'd appreciate your respecting that."

Archer interrupted, "It's easy to get a little jumpy when you're traveling at thirty million kilometers a second. Should be old hat in a week's time."

Another alarm tone broke over his words, causing Hoshi to flinch again, but Archer just struck the com panel. "Archer."

"This is Dr. Phlox, Captain. Our patient is regaining consciousness."

"On my way," he said. "Hoshi."

She snatched up her translator padd and joined him eagerly as he headed for the lift. Once the doors had closed and the lift rushed downward into the body of the ship, Hoshi scowled, "I don't like her."

"Why not?" Archer asked.

"Mostly because she doesn't like me."

"Good judgment. You—not her. Besides, I don't think *anybody* likes her much. Of course, she doesn't care whether she's liked. She won't be here that long."

"She wouldn't care anyway."

"You need to relax, Hoshi. This ship is on the cusp of exploration. If you want to speak to aliens and learn new languages, this is the place to be. You'll like it after a while."

"I've just never felt anything like that before. There *were* vibrations that didn't feel right."

"I don't have a doubt of it," Archer offered passively. "The ship's bound to have plenty of instabilities. It'll be our job to track them down, one by one. That's why they call it a 'shakedown.' But you have to do some shaking to get the optimal results."

She sighed and looked like a lost puppy. "Why do all the interesting things have to happen so far from solid ground?"

Archer smiled. Her statement had an ancient ring of truth about it and set his mind to imaginings.

He took her arm gently and squeezed it. "Now, just take things a little slower. Take cues from the people around you instead of the machinery you don't understand."

She looked up at him. "What do you mean by that? What about the people?"

"Most of us have been on ships a lot more than you have. One of the oldest secrets of success on board is to do what the old-timers do. If we sleep, you sleep. If we take a shower, you go take a shower. Eat when we eat. And when things seem scary, take cues from those who've been through scary things before. Stand back and stand by."

"Stand back and stand by," she repeated, tasting the precious advice.

"Right," he said. "In time, you'll be the one the rookies are watching for cues. No matter what the legends say, nobody's born to this."

Though she still appeared doubtful, she did

step out of the lift with more confidence. In fact, she led the way to sickbay. Archer took that as a step up.

Even before the door opened to the medical area they could hear the loud growling of the Klingon, like some kind of werewolf on the prowl.

The alien was even more imposing in person than he was just listening in the corridor. Sitting up now, he was absolutely huge. If he stood he would top seven feet. Even sitting he was eye to eye with Archer. Wisely, the doctor had tied him down.

Klaang barked and snapped furiously. *"Pung ghap HoS!"*

Archer flinched at the rage of a strong warrior only inches from him, and was suddenly glad of the security guard, very nearly six-foot-five himself, armed with a plasma rifle and eyeing the delirious Klingon with a hungry glower.

Hoshi was picking and poking at her translator padd, frowning at the information on the tiny screen.

"What's wrong?" Archer asked.

"The translator's not locking onto his dialect. The syntax won't align."

Major faux pas—unaligned syntax.

*"DujDaj Hegh!"*

"Tell him we're taking him home," Archer said simply.

Hoshi struggled over the words, but she hesitated. The language seemed, to Archer's ear, to be little more than coughs and hacks.

After a moment, she tried. *"Ingan ... Hoch ... juH."*

*"Tujpa'qul Dun?"*

She frowned. "He wants to know who we are." She didn't add the obvious trailer "I think," even though it was implicit in her tone.

Archer nodded, an equally simple gesture.

Hoshi turned to the Klingon. *"Qu'ghewmey* Enterprise. *PuqloD."*

*"Nentay lupHom!"*

Hoshi repeated one of the words for her own benefit, then concluded, "Ship. He's asking for his ship back."

Or maybe he was asking to take possession of this one? Archer was reluctant to give him any kind of answer, because neither one would make the Klingon any happier.

"Say it was destroyed."

*"SonchIy."*

Klaang erupted in a raving protest and roared, *"Vengen Sto'vo'kor Dos!"*

Puzzling over this, Hoshi cocked a hip and screwed up her expression in confusion. "I'm not sure ... but I think he's saying something about eating the afterlife."

"Try the translator again." Frustrated, Archer tried to contain his impatience.

She worked with the padd. It didn't help.

"I'm going to need to run what we've got through the phonetic processor."

*"MajOa blmoHqu!"*

Archer turned to her again, but Hoshi could only offer, "He says his wife has grown ugly."

He sighed. If the best translator he knew couldn't do any better than this, what kind of primitive garble were they dealing with? What he needed was a Klingon who spoke English.

"I'm sorry, Captain," Hoshi said quietly. "I'm doing the best I can."

He was about to give her a word of comfort when Phlox interrupted.

"Excuse me," the doctor butted in as he took a scan of the Klingon. "His prefrontal cortex is hyperstimulated. I doubt he has any idea what he's saying."

*"Hljol OaOqu'nay!"*

"I think the doctor's right," Hoshi said. "Unless 'stinky boots' has something to do with all this."

The ship shuddered under them, sending Hoshi wobbling against the Klingon's bed. She shimmied away and Archer caught her arm and pulled her farther. The guy had spiked leg bands, after all.

"That's the warp reactor again, right?" she asked softly.

*"OaOqu'nay!"*

Archer hurried to the nearest wall com. "Bridge, report on that."

"We've dropped out of warp, sir," T'Pol's voice announced with a shiver of electrical static. "Main power is—"

A burst of static. The com went dead. The lights flickered suddenly—then, consoles all around sickbay began to go dark, one by one!

# Chapter 7

ARCHER INSTANTLY CROSSED TO THE COM BOOSTER and played with the controls, but all he could get was a ghost of the action on the bridge.

"T'Pol! Respond!" he attempted. "Tucker! Anybody?"

The com chittered, but there was no sense to it. "It might be the sensors going dark," he muttered, thinking aloud. As he spoke, the sickbay went finally to total darkness. The Klingon raged on his bed. The security guard shambled about, though he didn't know what to do. Archer heard them, sensed them, felt Hoshi's rising fear, but couldn't see a thing.

The com was completely dead. The ship was dark.

In his mind, he saw the action going on all over

the ship—crew automatically going to stations, the procedures of emergency and safety snapping into place. He imagined them calling for him on the croaked com system. He felt the ship's power depleting rapidly, felt the drag on his body as speed dropped. Around sickbay, Phlox's zoo of pet alien organisms chirruped and whistled either in confusion or ecstasy.

"Where are the handheld lights?" he demanded. "Phlox!"

"I don't know, Captain. I haven't inventoried those yet."

"They've got to be in a drawer or a cabinet. Feel around. We can't do anything if we can't see. Hoshi, look around for the beacons. Guard, you, too."

"Aye, sir," the guard rumbled.

Despite her fear, Hoshi started moving. He heard the clap of cabinets and drawers. A few moments later, she was the one who found them.

Instantly, sickbay glowed with red lights. Klaang continued to bellow his maddening protests.

Archer paused and forced himself to think. "Auxiliary power should've kicked in by now . . ." When the Klingon growled and spat again, louder now that nobody was paying attention to him, Archer added, "Do you know how to tell him to shut up?"

More nervous by the second, Hoshi swung to Klaang. "Shut up!" she shouted.

But it didn't work. Diplomacy just wasn't the way today, was it?

"Sedate him if you have to," he snapped to Phlox. "I need to get to the bridge!"

"Captain!"

He whirled at Hoshi's shocked cry. She was moving her beacon across the lateral bulkhead.

Why was she doing that?

Without waiting for him to ask, she hissed, "There's someone in here!"

Archer glanced around the poorly lit room. "Hoshi . . ."

"I'm telling you, there's someone—"

She stopped moving. Archer followed her beacon to the wall again—

A humanoid form!

Like a chameleon, the form had taken on the appearance of the background, complete with certificates and alien life-forms in jars on the shelves! It was barely visible, but now that he focused, there was no mistaking the intrusion.

Once discovered, the creature leaped from its hiding place back into the shadows.

On the biobed, Klaang fell to bizarre quiet. "Suliban!" he growled.

Archer spun, flashing his own beacon across the wall, trying to rediscover the—what was the word? Suliban . . . well, he didn't need any help translating that. Boogeyman.

Another one! Perched high on the wall like a spider! But this one wasn't camouflaged like the other. This one had blotchy skin, almost tie-dyed, with eyes that were clearly evolved for some kind of night vision.

"Crewman!" Archer shouted.

The guard's rifle snapped up just as the Suliban leaped to the ground and met a third one darting from the shadows!

The guard fired. Plasma bullets flashed through the room in quick stroboscopic flashes. Now the action turned to rapid cuts illuminated by the strobes. Klaang yanking around in frustration and shouting in Klingon . . . Hoshi cowering low to avoid the gunfire, scanning erratically with her beacon . . . the guard swinging around to take aim again at something he sensed behind him—

And one of the Suliban leaping onto the big boy. The guard hit the deck, and so did his plasma rifle. The weapon rattled and skidded away.

Archer lunged toward the weapon, hoping he was going in the right direction, but lost his handheld beacon as he struck the deck. Hoshi's beacon was gone now, too. Was she hurt?

The rifle fell into his hands, like a warhorse seeking a rider, and he whirled it toward the nearest Suliban. Taking an instant to be sure he wasn't shooting at his own people, he opened fire.

The Suliban was hit, and flew backward into the wall.

At Archer's right elbow, Klaang stared upward and spat an accusation. Suliban directly overhead! The creature dropped from the ceiling! Archer felt the hard strike of a heavy body on the back of his head and neck. He was driven to the deck under a crushing weight, the plasma rifle trapped under his ribs.

The room went dark again—and very abruptly silent. The silence was scarier than the chaos and rifle shots had been.

Hoshi's little tremor squeaked from under the biobed.

"Captain . . . ?"

Archer tried to roll over. This time he felt no resistance. Whatever had been on top of him was now gone. As he got to his knees, a surge of power thrummed up through the skeleton of the ship under his knees and hands. One by one, the consoles began to flicker and light themselves.

Warp power! It was coming back!

*Good boy, Trip . . .*

The guard was just sitting up, dazed. Phlox rushed to help him. Under the biobed, Hoshi found herself crouched beside the dead Suliban and squirmed suddenly away.

Archer staggered to his feet and looked around as the lights came back on all the way.

The biobed was empty. The Klingon was gone.

And so were the two Suliban interlopers who had survived the past few moments.

Violation. And kidnapping.

Not such a good day after all.

# Chapter 8

A SHIPWIDE SEARCH HAD TURNED UP NOTHING. THEY weren't onboard. Still, Klaang and the things he called Suliban had gone somewhere, because they weren't here anymore.

Jonathan Archer paced the bridge, agitated. His ship had been breached, the engines temporarily shut down, then just as mysteriously repowered again; intruders had found their way both onto the ship and back off without being tracked. None of that made him feel very good at all.

"We've got state-of-the-art sensors," he complained angrily. "Why in hell didn't we detect them?"

Around him, the bridge crew was virtually sheepish with lack of answers. "Mr. Reed thought he detected something right before we lost power," T'Pol said, as if she really did want to help this time.

Archer whirled on Reed, who was working his tactical and security console. After a moment, the lieutenant offered, "The starboard sensor logs recorded a spatial disturbance."

Trip Tucker leaned over Reed's shoulder. "Looks more like a glitch."

"Those weren't glitches in sickbay," Hoshi noted sharply.

Archer turned to Trip. "I want a complete analysis of that disturbance."

Trip responded by heading for the door, and Archer returned to Reed.

"Where do we stand on weapons?"

"I still have to tune the targeting sensors," Reed admitted unhappily.

"What're you waiting for?" Archer snapped at them.

Reed wasted no time in following the captain's implicit order; he and Tucker at once headed for the turbolift.

"Captain," T'Pol began, crossing toward him.

He ignored her and swung instead to Hoshi. "The Klingon seemed to know who they were. See if you can translate what he said."

That word . . . *Suliban*. Was it a Klingon word? An accusation or warning? Or was it what Archer thought it was—the name for those creatures?

"Right away," Hoshi said, and also turned to go.

"Captain," T'Pol attempted again.

Finally, with no one else to chew out, order around, or grouse at, he turned to hear what she had to say.

"There's no way you could have anticipated this. I'm sure Ambassador Soval will understand."

"You're the science officer," Archer blurted. "Why don't you help Tucker with that analysis?"

"The astrometric computer in San Francisco will be far more effective."

"We're not going to San Francisco, so make do with what we've got here."

"You've lost the Klingon," she said. Though she sounded reasonable, he still heard that familiar superior attitude in her voice as she finished, "Your mission is over."

He leaned toward her, broiling under the surface. "I didn't 'lose' the Klingon. He was taken. And I'm going to find out who took him."

"How do you plan to do that?" she asked reasonably. "Space is very big, Captain. A shadow on your sensors won't help you find them. This is a foolish mission."

"Come with me."

What he really meant was something along the lines of getting her ass in here, but luckily he still had a little hold on the reins of decorum. He stepped into his ready room and almost instantly whirled on her.

"I'm not interested in what you think about this

mission. So take your Vulcan cynicism and bury it along with your repressed emotions."

"Your reaction to this situation," she protested, "is a perfect example of why your species should remain in its own star system."

He closed the small distance between them in an openly hostile manner. Did they have body language where she came from?

"I've been listening to you Vulcans tell us what *not* to do all my life," he fumed. "I watched my father work his ass off while your scientists held back just enough information to keep him from succeeding. He deserved to see that launch. *You* may have life spans of two hundred years. We don't."

T'Pol was affected by his words, perhaps more by his passion, but she didn't back down.

"You *are* going to be contacting Starfleet," she said, "to advise them of the situation."

"No, I'm not," he said with a warning glower. He hoped his message was clear, because clarifying further wouldn't be either polite or pretty. "And neither are you. Now get the hell out of here and make yourself useful."

With nothing more to say, she had no choice but to simply leave. He couldn't imagine Reed or Tucker welcoming her help or even her presence in their work. That was her problem, something she had set up for herself with her own lack of manners.

Archer stalked the ready room—which wasn't

much of a stalking space at all, but only a tiny excuse for an office where the captain might be able to be alone once in a while. He didn't really like it here, but was determined to get used to it. The space came in handy just now, as a good place to chew out the sliver under his fingernail—namely, T'Pol.

Bitter and impatient, he struck the com on his desk. "Sickbay, Archer. Phlox, I'm coming down there and I want some answers ready when I arrive. Make them up if you have to, but give me something."

Sickbay never responded. He never gave Phlox the chance.

Within moments he was stalking the corridors instead of his ready room, thumping down through the tubes and access ways directly to the sickbay deck. It wasn't exactly faster than the turbolift, but at least he wasn't standing still while the box rushed him around the ship. He didn't lose many seconds, and he managed to use up enough frustration that, by the time he plunged through the doors into sickbay, he was ready to listen.

Dimly lit except for the surgical lamp shining down on the dead intruder, sickbay was almost like it had been during those terrible moments of attack. Phlox's gloved hands were busy inside the opened chest of the dead creature. He picked enthusiastically through the entrails as Archer watched, unmoved.

"Mr. Klaang was right about one thing," the doctor said. "He's a Suliban. But unless I'm mistaken, he's not an ordinary one."

Archer's throat tightened. How could he tell that this Suliban was special if he had no experience with what an ordinary Suliban was? And he didn't feel much like taking biology lessons. Were there short answers?

"Meaning?"

"His DNA is Suliban . . . but his anatomy has been altered. Look at this lung. Five bronchial tubes. It should only have three. And look at the alveoli clusters. They've been modified to process different kinds of atmospheres."

"Are you saying he's some kind of a mutant?" Archer asked, going for those short answers as deliberately as possible without discouraging information he might need.

"Yes, I suppose I am. But this was no accident, no freak of nature. This man was the recipient of some very sophisticated genetic engineering."

Like a kid in a candy store, Phlox almost giggled with delight at his discovery. He activated a tiny instrument with a thin red beam and shined the light on the Suliban's dappled face.

"Watch this."

He moved the light, revealing that the skin had changed color, perfectly matching the hue and intensity of the red light.

"Subcutaneous pigment sacs."

He tapped a control on the little instrument and the color of the light changed to blue. He shined it on the Suliban's clothing this time, instead of its face. The clothing also adapted to the new color. The clothing?

"A biomimetic garment!" Phlox piped, delighted.

Archer didn't even bother trying to control his amazement. The skin he could understand. How did these people make their clothing biological enough to do the same thing?

"The eyes are my favorite," Phlox went on. He lifted an eyelid on the corpse, exposing a superdilated pupil that glowed nearly phosphorescent. "Compound retinas. He most likely saw things even your sensors couldn't detect."

*Like my sheer anger?* Archer thought. Even a dead guy should be able to pick that up.

"It's not in their genome?" he asked.

"Certainly not. The Suliban are no more evolved than humans. Very impressive work, though . . . I've never seen anything quite like it."

*No more evolved than humans. Yeah, we're still practically microbes compared to all you demigods out there.*

Determined to raise the veil of ignorance even if he had to kick somebody out of the way, he asked, "What do you know about them? Where do they come from?"

"They're nomadic, I believe," Phlox said, apparently not catching the fact that his captain was about to reach down his throat and pull the information out physically if it didn't start coming faster and more voluntarily. "No homeworld. I examined two of them years ago. A husband and wife. Very cordial."

The word stuck in Archer's craw. He couldn't imagine cordiality at this particular moment, from the Suliban, from himself, or anyone else. He didn't even want any.

"Look, Doctor," he began tersely, "I'm not in a pleasant mood. I don't want to hear about anything nice or cordial or even intriguing right now. I want to know where the Klingon went, how the Suliban got onto this ship, and how they got off it. Something tells me they didn't jump out a space hatch and go for a random free-float. They went some-*place*. I mean to find out where. None of the answers to those questions is bound to be nice, so you don't have to feel obliged to smile or twinkle at me anymore." He jabbed a finger at the body on the bed. "You have the only piece of concrete evidence we own. I'm giving you my permission to get ugly. If you have to set up candles and a Ouija board and bring this corpse back to life, I want to know how they did what they did today on my ship. Do I have to say any of that a second time? Good."

Trip Tucker had the distinct displeasure of working side by side with the Vulcan female at the sensor data station in main engineering. Still, it gave him a chance to see what she knew, just how much of a token she was in practice. That Vulcans had a strong science base in their education and also their natural predilections couldn't be denied. Hiding a spy as a science officer became the convenient and most obvious trick. There was too much about this woman that was just plain obvious.

Working made Tucker feel better. No matter what they did, he hadn't been able to find any systems failure or fall-off. The intruders had flickered the power flow just enough to do what they wanted to do—steal the Klingon—then let everything come back without damage. No damage at all.

As glad as he was that no damage had been done to the ship, Tucker still couldn't understand how the kidnappers had managed to sneak aboard the vessel, steal the Klingon, and elude detection. Now *there* was some technology he'd love to take a look at.

"How about this?" he pointed at the newest flush of data on the sensors.

"It's just background noise," the Vulcan's monotone voice stated. "Your sensors aren't capable of isolating plasma decay."

"How can you be so damned sure what our sensors can do?"

"Vulcan children play with toys that are more sophisticated."

Tucker stopped what he was doing and took a moment to reflect on this, which was just a plain fake-out. She knew better, and worse—she knew *he* knew better. Either she was playing, or enjoying another insult.

"Y'know," he began, fed up, "some people say you Vulcans do nothing but patronize us, but if they were here now . . . if they could see how far you're bending over backward to help me . . . they'd eat their words."

Her dark eyes barely registered that he had said anything at all. "Your captain's mission was to return the Klingon to his people. He no longer has the Klingon."

"I realize he's only a simple Earthling," Tucker responded acridly, "but did it ever occur to you that he might know what he's doing?"

She was silent. Of course, he'd put her in a bad position. Even impolite Vulcans knew better than to openly criticize a commanding officer's decision before that decision had played out. At least not too much.

Tucker laid off the snide tone and tried something else. "It's no secret Starfleet hasn't been around too long . . . God knows you remind us of it every chance you get, but does that mean the man who's been put in charge of this mission doesn't deserve our support?" He waited a moment to see if his words got a rise out of her. "Then again," he added resentfully, "loyalty's an emotion, isn't it?"

She looked at him, and he could tell a response was forming—what would she say? Under that stony facade and the gloss of having a "mission" of her own, what did she really think of Jonathan Archer? He knew, of course, what she'd been told, probably all her life, about humans and Starfleet and Earth culture, because she parroted it mightily. Still, anybody or any race who didn't embrace something new—new people and relationships— would eventually just sit down and finish dying.

Before she could say anything, though, Captain Archer stalked in, obviously annoyed and impatient.

Who could blame him?

"Any luck?" he demanded.

Tucker glanced at the Vulcan. "Not really."

T'Pol had a longer version. "My analysis of the spatial disturbance Mr. Reed saw indicates a stealth vessel with a tricyclic plasma drive."

"If we can figure out the decay rate of their plasma," Tucker said, "we'll be able to find their warp trail."

"Unfortunately your sensors weren't designed to measure plasma decay."

Both men looked at her with varying degrees of resentment. She didn't mean the "unfortunately" part.

Tucker didn't make any comment. But the new communications officer walked in behind Archer and stopped short, looked around engineering at the massive pulsing warp core and the over-whelming complexity of consoles and scanners. Apprehension showed in her eyes.

She sidled toward them on the farthest side of the deck. "Are you sure it's safe to stand so close to that?" Her tone was half-joking, but only half.

"What've you got?" Archer asked sharply.

"I've managed to translate most of what Klaang said. But none of it makes any sense." She handed him a padd.

The captain took it and read the screen. "Nothing about the Suliban?"

"Nope."

Archer now turned to T'Pol and skewered her with a glare. "That name ring a bell to you?"

"They're a somewhat primitive species from Sector 3641. But they've never posed a threat."

"Well, they have now."

Tucker snickered at her. Yet another "primitive" species for the Vulcans to chide? Did she think of the Suliban the way she thought about humans? If so, were they more capable of subterfuge than she gave them credit for?

"Did he say anything about Earth?" Archer asked Hoshi.

She shrugged. "The word's not even in their database."

Archer eyed the padd again. Tucker watched him, and wished he could help.

"It's all there," Hoshi said weakly. "There were

only four words I couldn't translate . . . probably just proper nouns." She wanted to help, too, but Archer's problem wasn't improving.

The captain strode away a few steps, contemplating what he saw on the screen. "Jelik . . . Sarin . . . Rigel . . . Tholia . . . Anything sound familiar?"

T'Pol hesitated, uneasy. Seemed her goals were at cross-purposes. Or worse, maybe they weren't.

"T'Pol?" Archer sternly pressed.

She paused again, glanced at Tucker, who was careful to give her one of those get-cracking looks.

"Rigel," she finally began, "is a planetary system approximately fifteen light-years from our present position."

Tucker watched and held his breath. Of course, Earth had known about the blue giant Rigel for generations, and other stars like Altair and Arcturus, but this was the first he'd heard of settled planets there.

"Why the hesitation?" Archer challenged.

Tucker almost blurted *ah-hah!*—but he held back. Archer looked as if he might be ready to pull this gal's eyebrows off if she didn't give, and quick.

Realizing she was about to knock the stick off his shoulder again, she decided to shell out.

"According to the navigational logs salvaged

from Klaang's ship, Rigel Ten was the last place he stopped before crashing on your planet."

Though Archer's face flushed with new anger, he plainly wasn't surprised. "Why do I get the feeling you weren't going to share that little piece of information?"

"I wasn't authorized to reveal the details of our findings."

There it was—the problem in a nutshell. "Our" and "your"—"we" and "they." She was here, but she wasn't yet on the team.

Tension mounted. Archer shared a pointed glance at both Tucker and Hoshi. Tucker held his own expression in careful check, not knowing which side of this teeter-totter would be the best one to be on. Should he fan Archer's anger and therefore his strength of will, or should he mollify the situation and hunker down for more efficiency?

Better not choose right now. The captain would signal soon enough which direction he wanted to go.

Controlling himself valiantly, Archer was scarier now than if he'd been yelling. He glowered at her like a cat.

"The next time I learn you're withholding something," he warned, "you're going to spend the rest of this voyage confined to some *very* cramped quarters. Understood?"

T'Pol's expression was hard to read, but she

didn't have any snotty remarks. In fact she said nothing at all.

Archer hit the wall com. "Archer to helm."

"Aye, sir," Mayweather responded from the bridge.

"Go into the Vulcan starcharts and find a system called Rigel. Then set a course for the tenth planet."

"Aye, Captain, right away."

Turning to T'Pol, Archer strictly said, "You're going to be working *with* us from now on."

She paled a little, but owned up to her reasons. "I'm sorry you feel slighted. But I agree with Ambassador Soval's restraint in giving Earth too much information. Perhaps the last thing we need is another volatile race in space with warp power. You may easily go out and get yourselves killed. It may be a mistake to have helped you so much, to give you so much before you are ready."

"So *much?*" Archer barked. "You'd better use the next portion of your long lifetime to go back over the records and see just how much we've done on our own, in spite of your cultural cowardice."

"Cowardice?" Her eyes widened.

Over to the side, Tucker smirked and pressed his lips flat with delight.

Archer closed the step between him and her. "I've been thinking about Vulcans all my life. You've been in space a long time, and suddenly the game is complex. Vulcans are logical, but it won't be enough. You've been advanced for a thousand years, and suddenly you're being over-run by us rabbits. The clock is ticking. All sorts of species are moving out into the galaxy. Maybe you don't need another volatile race out there, but guess what—they're everywhere. The galaxy will be driven by passion, not prudence. You haven't been holding back because you think we're so primitive—if you thought that, you wouldn't be bothering with humanity at all. Being logical allows you to say, 'That is a new idea; therefore it hasn't been proven; therefore I don't have to pay any attention to it.' "

"Shall we give you the knowledge to rush out into the galaxy and cause chaos?" she gulped. "Humans claim some right to know that which has been earned by others—"

"We never said that. You offered. On the galactic scale, thirty years this way or that is nothing. When you see somebody is ready to walk, why hold back? There's more going on with you people."

He narrowed his eyes and unplugged the flood-gate he'd been saving for Soval all these years.

"You're not the cutting edge anymore, are you?" he badgered. "In a thousand years, why has Vulcan progress been so slow? And here comes Earth, making wild advances in less than two hundred years. You're dragging behind, and now you need us more than we need you. Why else would you want to come and teach the apes how to sew? I think all this is happening because you're plain scared of being out there alone anymore."

Stunned, T'Pol parted her lips again. Nothing came out this time. She never blinked, as if staring at a flashing billboard declaring his words to the known galaxy. He was saying the Vulcans were doomed. Nobody had the guts to say that to their faces.

Archer backed off now, but pointed at her with a determined finger. "You get on that warp trail. And you'd better find something or be able to explain why not in *very* clear terms. Dismissed."

T'Pol blinked almost as if he'd slapped her. She turned on her heel and exited without a word, taking a cloud of confusion along on her shoulders.

Hoshi squirmed a little and said, "I'll . . . I'll keep learning Klingon."

"Good idea."

He handed her the padd.

When Archer and Tucker were alone in the steadily pulsing warp chamber, the captain finally allowed himself a moment of quiet contemplation. He flexed his shoulders, took a deep breath, and let his arms sag. He really wanted to talk to his father.

Instead, there was Trip Tucker, offering him a sympathetic and curious gaze.

"Maybe now we know why we had so many quirks and misdirections with the last three days before launch," Archer contemplated. He turned to lean on the console that had provided such little information.

"You think they infiltrated before we left Earth?" Tucker said.

Archer shrugged. "I don't know. It's a possibility. Getting off the ship is far less problematic than getting on, but where they went presents us with a goading mystery. I don't like goading mysteries."

"Yes, you do," Tucker drawled. "They had a ship following us, and they went over there."

"If we can find the trail, we'll follow them. If not, I'll go to Qo'noS anyway and start there. Klaang's mother might know something."

Tucker shook his head in worried respect for the sheer gall of that plan. "Why would these Sulibans want to blow our chances to make nice with the Klingons?"

"Might not be it at all. For all we know they might have a personal grudge against Klaang."

"Or . . . maybe they want to ruin our chances to make nice with the Klingons, John."

Archer smiled cannily to reassure him. "I'm not missing that one, Trip, believe me."

Tucker shifted on his feet. "You were pretty

hard on Lady Jane. You never had your own pet Vulcan to kick around before, did you?"

"No, and I mean to be harder on her. She's about to discover what the term 'short leash' means."

Appreciatively Tucker nodded and bobbed his brows. "Probably smart, now we know for sure she's been hiding information from us on purpose."

"She'd better knock it off, too." Abruptly, Archer turned grim. "She's my science officer now, not Soval's patsy. She'll learn that lesson over the next week if I have to tattoo it on her tongue."

"Good thing it was you chewing her out instead of me. I'd have punched her in the nose."

"She'd hit me back," Archer said. "And she'd probably break my jaw."

Tucker grinned, though rather drably. "She, uh . . . she came on the ship about the same time as all our little troubles started . . ." He broached the subject, then let it hang there. He didn't seem to have quite the conviction for a direct accusation.

Archer accepted what the engineer was saying. The idea wasn't new to him. He'd be silly to ignore it. "We'll wait and see. Vulcans are reserved. They don't converse. She's just learning about us. As Vulcans go, she's very young. I get the feeling she's as much in the middle as we are. She could be just echoing what she's been taught all her life, and doing what she was told to do. Just a feeling, though." Archer offered him another smile, a little different from the one before. "Anyway, I won't ignore your concerns. In the meantime, you organize a landing party. Make T'Pol part of it."

"Do I have to?"

"It'll show her which team she's on. And Hoshi and Reed. And Mayweather's spent his whole life in space dealing with merchants and travelers. Let's use what we have and get this done."

# Chapter 9

HUMANS WERE GETTING HELP FROM THEIR VERSION OF "future" people—the Vulcans—who had advanced technology to give. Was it so unwise for Silik's people also to have assistance?

Yet he was troubled and made to feel small by the future beings. Like strangers on the shore, they gave gifts without reasons, asked for trust without substance. Why? If only to play for affection, everyone gave gifts for reasons. Certainly these people had no need of Suliban affection.

Silik stood before the Klingon, Klaang, who was constrained in a medical chair, sitting upright, monitored by the two Suliban physicians. Tubes and devices of bizarre natures were hooked into the Klingon's body. He was bathed in the blue glow of the temperature light, and lolled with the groggy results of having been thoroughly drugged.

"Where is it?" Silik persisted in the Klingon's native language. He had asked the question three times before.

"I don't know." Klaang responded for the fourth time.

"We're not going to harm you. Tell me where it is!"

"I don't know."

Frustrated, Silik looked at the physicians. "Are you certain he's telling the truth?"

"Absolutely certain," one of them answered, and he seemed to believe it.

Silik bent forward toward Klaang. "Did you leave it on your ship? Did you hide it somewhere? Is it on *Enterprise?*"

Klaang's enormous head rolled to one side. "I don't know what you're looking for."

As he realized this line of questioning had solidified and would offer no progress, Silik thought about different approaches that might shake the Klingon's mind.

After contemplating for a moment, he attempted, "What were you doing on Rigel Ten?"

"I was sent to meet someone."

"Who?"

"A Suliban . . . female . . . named Sarin."

At last—the first bit of useful information.

"And what did Sarin give you?"

"Nothing."

But Silik now had a tidbit upon which the day might turn. From a single name, he had an idea of where to begin.

He turned away from the Klingon and to the physicians charged, "Keep him alive while I'm gone!"

## Enterprise
## E-deck

"Once we've tied down, we'll be descending into the trade complex. It's got thirty-six levels."

Archer paused and looked at T'Pol, indicating that she should take over. The crew should become accustomed to hers as the voice of the science officer.

"Your translators have been programmed for Rigelian. However, you'll encounter numerous other species. Many of them are known to be impatient with newcomers. None of them have seen a human before. You have a tendency to be gregarious. I suggest you restrain that tendency."

"You forgot to warn us about the drinking water," Tucker complained as he belted his jacket and took one of the communicator/translator devices she was handing out to the landing party.

Archer didn't make any comments. If she was going to keep sniping at them with sentences like that, then she deserved what she got back. Beside him, Tucker, Reed, Mayweather, and Hoshi Sato were veritably twitching with anticipation. A new planet! Strange new worlds.

T'Pol didn't even get Tucker's comment. She went on to the next thing. "Dr. Phlox isn't concerned with food and water. But he does caution against intimate contact."

Archer glossed over that one, disliking the idea of treating his command staff like cadets on leave. "The Vulcans told us Klaang was a courier. If he was here to get something, then whoever gave it to him might know why he was taken. That was only a few days ago," he added optimistically, "and a seven-foot Klingon doesn't go unnoticed. T'Pol's been here before, so follow her lead."

He gave her a glance of what he hoped was confidence.

"Where do we rendezvous if we find something?" Hoshi asked.

"Back at the shuttlepod. And no one goes anywhere alone. From what I've heard about this place, it's an alien version of an Oriental bazaar. Don't stop to buy trinkets. Ask simple questions, get direct answers. If you don't like what you hear, move on. There are a lot of people down there, or versions of people. Don't get swallowed up. Watch each other. Clear?"

Whether it was or not, they were on their way. The six-seat subwarp shuttlepod was functional, but not really comfortable, and the trip down to the planet seemed longer than it was.

Mayweather brought the pod into the atmosphere and found himself bucking snow-torn slopes and high winds.

"Approaching what appears to be a landing deck." He squinted out the windshield. "I see a trail of lights. Runway, possibly."

"I'd say this spaceport accommodates all kinds of craft," Archer confirmed, just to make them all feel better. They might be strangers here, but they were coming to a place that was used to strangers. Coming into a cosmopolitan spaceport would be much easier to tolerate than invading a tribal clutch or a village.

In fact, when they finally found the landing pad in the whipping veils of snow, their shuttle turned out to be the smallest thing around, in a swarm of dozens of ships coming and going at the same time. The sight was eerily familiar to anyone who recognized a travel center. Something about it was reassuring to Archer, as they approached and were received as a matter of course. No fanfare, no ceremony, no warnings or threats.

Beacons and trails of blue and yellow landing lights branched out in patterns both distinguishable and not, at least enough to get them down safely. T'Pol used her knowledge of this place to secure a parking spot where the shuttle-pod had a chance of not being plundered, and they immediately disembarked and broke into teams.

Trying to appear casual, Archer went first to the dockmaster's control tower. After all, something had to come and go from here with Klaang aboard. He certainly hadn't popped in out of thin air, so there had to be a trail.

He and Hoshi were ushered through a tubular construction with lots of bridges into a central control area with windows on every side, couched by banks of controls and broken every few seconds by the sweep of a beacon from the runways. The dockmaster himself was a huge burly alien preoccupied with traffic.

"Pardon us," Archer began, hoping the translator didn't get it wrong. "I'm Captain Jonathan Archer of Starfleet."

"Who? What planet is that?"

"It's not a planet. It's an organization. The planet is Earth."

"Good for you. The visitor's center is on Quintash Plaza."

"Thanks very much. Before we go, would you answer a few questions for us?"

"There's a manual on the wall in the corridor. Read it," the alien rumbled. "Next time, approach from the mountains. Less crosswind."

"Thank you again . . . I'd like to know whether a Klingon vessel of any kind came through here about five or six of your days ago."

"Five or six days? Do you realize how much traffic we process in a single day?"

"You must keep records," Archer suggested, glancing at Hoshi. "This was a one-man Klingon scoutship."

"What species are you?"

"Human. We're called humans."

As if congratulating him, an alarm went off and lights flashed on the dockmaster's console. The dockmaster hammered on what might have been a keyboard, then checked a monitor.

"Elkan nine, raise your approach vector by point two radiants!"

When the alarm stopped, the dockmaster hammered something new into the keyboard and the monitor changed.

"It was *seven* days ago. A *K'toch*-class vessel."

"Does it say who he was here to see?" Although the question was probably out of line or classified, Archer took his best shot at getting what he wanted.

"What it says is that he arrived at docking port six and was given a level one biohazard clearance."

Archer kept from clapping his hands—he would never have given up information like that just for the asking! At least this guy had no such guardrails. "You don't seem very interested in what people do here."

"Our visitors value their privacy," the dockmaster said, even though he had just handed over information Klaang probably never wanted known. "It wouldn't be very *tusoropko tuproya plo* business they're in."

Archer flinched at the sudden change in sounds and looked at Hoshi, who busily adjusted the communicator/translator.

"It's all right," she said. "Rigelian uses a pronominal base. The translator's just reprocessing the syntax."

Archer took her word for it, grateful for her expertise.

"Do you have any records of a Suliban vessel coming in around the same time?"

"Suliban? I don't know that word. Your device must still be malfunctioning."

The dockmaster went back to his work, turning his idea of a shoulder to the newcomers. If the body language of a mollusk was anything Archer could trust, he got the idea the alien was all done talking. Had he asked the wrong question? Or the exactly right one?

He motioned to Hoshi and thanked the unresponsive dockmaster before leading the communications officer out into the corridor.

"He's lying," she told him immediately.

"I know. But he has no reason to tell us anything. He's probably more scared of whoever wants him to keep silent."

"Why would he be?"

"You saw the Klingons and the Suliban. They're both a little more rugged than you and I appear to be. Whose threat would you take more seriously?"

"Then we still don't know anything."

"We know for certain that Klaang was here."

"We knew that before, didn't we?"

"Yes," Archer agreed. "But now, if I read my dockmasters correctly, somebody else will know we're here looking for him. Let's go down to the Plaza and appear obvious, shall we?"

The main downtown area was an ancient, towering, weatherworn complex that seemed to have been constructed over several decades. Architectural styles ran the gamut here, as did the age of the buildings. In some cases, new structures were built right on top of old ones, without bothering to demolish. The city was swirled on the outer reaches with inhospitable subarctic terrain and constant winds and snows. Plumes of steam blasted constantly from geothermal vents that kept the buildings from freezing.

Within the city itself, things were about twenty degrees warmer than the spaceport complex, just from the tightly clustered buildings and narrow streets, which didn't allow the arctic blasts to dominate. Haze hung in the air, perforated by shafts of artificial light. Myriad species went about their private business, moving in and out of concealed and sometimes locked trading alcoves. Some were in uniform, others in indistinct robes or layered with jewelry. Many carried weapons.

The flavor of the old West was palpable.

"This place reminds me of somewhere," Archer commented, glancing at a mammoth carpet-haired beast of burden with legs like tree stumps and the smell of a pig farm. "If it were a desert, I'd swear I've been here before."

"And I'd worry about your taste in vacation spots," Hoshi murmured, flinching from a slimy individual who passed by on their left.

Alien insects came to investigate them—large insects the size of birds on Earth. They hovered, and one perched on Hoshi's head for a moment, but became quickly disinterested.

"They don't seem harmful," Archer shored her up.

Hoshi shivered. "Jellyfish don't *seem* harmful either. But don't stick your hand under one."

"Look—this must be the Plaza." He led the way to a vast, cavernous thoroughfare of bridgelike walkways that crisscrossed each other well into the sky and for miles in three directions from where they stood. The concourse was poorly lit, just enough to walk by. As Archer looked out over the incredible complex, he began to worry for his

other crewmen. This wasn't the kind of place anyone wanted for a first venture into the galactic
wilds.

"Shouldn't we call the captain?"

Travis Mayweather's question was fraught with
doubts and misgivings. Quite normal.

Malcolm Reed, on the other hand, blithely followed their alien contact into the trade complex,
climbing to the fifth level with a quiver of excitement in his stomach. Around them chattered a
cacophony of strange sounds and a sea of deep-
green lighting.

"Maybe we should wait," he said to the ensign.

Mayweather hunched his shoulders and called
to their very odd guide. "How much longer?"

"It's not very far," the alien called over his—was
that a shoulder? "I promise you."

"Are you sure his name was Klaang?" Reed
asked again. "Couldn't it have been another
Klingon you saw?"

"It was Klaang. I'm certain. I'll show you exactly where he was."

The alien's confidence was encouraging. His
unwillingness to describe where he was going,
however, was not, and Reed had his doubts. They
kept moving.

"I think somebody's following us," Mayweather
said, glancing behind them.

"Nonsense. You're just uneasy."

"Then why are the shadows moving in my periphery?"

"They're alien shadows. They probably have arms as well."

"Funny, sir."

"Of course."

"Look at that!" Mayweather pointed ahead of them as the lights changed—literally—to red.

Alien music pervaded the air just above the comfort range for conversation. In an archway off to one side, two mostly undressed alien women squirmed and writhed to an unusual rhythm. It almost sounded Eastern European, but Reed dismissed that as coincidental. Between the women was a thin lantern with dozens of butterfly-type creatures flitting around the light.

As he and Mayweather watched, rapt by the sight, the women squirmed closer to the lantern. One of them tipped back her head and emitted an eight-inch tongue that snared one of the butterflies.

An instant later, the second woman did the same. Were they competing?

Only now did Reed and Mayweather realize they had been joined by a gathering of other spectators to watch the butterfly dance. The crowd seemed to run the course from arousal to disgust. Reed felt an odd mixture of both sensations: the sight was curiously compelling, the females' movements at once sensuous and rapacious.

At the same time, he began to suspect that their guide had no intention of leading them to Klaang, and in fact had no knowledge of the Klingon's whereabouts; his suspicion was immediately confirmed.

"Would you like to meet them?" the alien man offered, waving a large narrow paw at the women. "I can arrange it."

Mayweather grimaced. "Was this where you saw Klaang?" he persisted.

"No, no, not here. I'll show you where. But first, you should enjoy yourselves! Which one would you prefer?"

"We're here to learn about the Klingon," Reed reiterated, though he found himself watching the women and the . . . "Are those real butterflies or some kind of hologram?"

Mayweather took his arm. "We should get going, sir."

"Yes . . . absolutely. You're right."

They moved down the tubelike arcade of erotic dalliances from topless fire-eaters to costumed performers of every stripe. Reed slipped in front of the alien man who was supposed to be guiding them and began to ignore the fellow's gestures of this way or that. Obviously he was more of a tour guide than an informant.

"Gentlemen, gentlemen!" the alien called, sud•

denly desperate. "Perhaps you'd prefer to watch the interspecies performance?"

"You don't know anything about Klaang, do you?" Mayweather bluntly accused.

"Of course I do, but there's no reason to hurry, is there?"

"Interspecies performance?" Reed asked.

"Lieutenant," Mayweather called wearily, "this man has no intention of helping us."

Reed nodded. "Perhaps another time."

Disappointed, their guide sagged in several places and disappeared into the crowd. Reed and Mayweather moved in a completely different direction, just in case the fellow held a grudge.

"I can't believe we fell for that."

Reed shrugged; he failed to share Mayweather's embarrassment. They'd made an honest go of trying to locate Klaang, and it wasn't their fault the alien had had a different agenda. Besides, the exotic image of the women replayed itself in his brain; he was still trying to decide if the jewel-colored butterflies had been real insects or holograms. "We *are* explorers."

Trip Tucker had gotten himself paired off with T'Pol. Not the most natural of buddy systems, but he wanted to keep an eye on her. If she had a chance at subterfuge, this would be the place.

She was over there, speaking to a uniformed

alien—maybe a security hireling or this place's version of a constable. He looked just as seedy as everybody else here. Tucker felt like maybe he should've let himself get five o'clock shadow before he came.

He didn't like it here. It was dirty and unfriendly. Nobody trusted anybody. Nobody deserved trust. Too many people, too little square dealing.

All he could do was wait. They had agreed on a game plan. She would do the talking and he would do the watching.

He was sitting among a weird assortment of beings, waiting, and hating every minute of it. The place was smoky, smelly, and dim. He'd never see a knife coming at him.

And over there was this alien infant, screaming its tentacles off. He couldn't help but keep looking at it. Most of the "people" here ignored what was going on, but the loud squawling drove Tucker to wincing.

The alien mother kept tweaking a complicated breathing apparatus on her child's nose. Ear. Whatever it was. Tucker thought at first the mother was trying to get the kid to stop crying, but every time she twisted the device, the child went into greater and greater distress.

Why was she taunting him? It? Was this some kind of bizarre alien mothering ritual? Drive your child crazy with suffocation and it'll behave?

He shifted in his seat and glanced at T'Pol and the constable. How much longer was she going to take? She seemed to be doing all the talking. What good was that?

The mother twisted her child's breathing device again. The poor thing howled in agony.

A few people around him shifted just from the noise, but no one interfered. What kind of people were these? To stand by and witness child abuse without a flicker? This was what awaited humanity in the open galaxy?

Here came T'Pol. She motioned to Tucker, who quickly got up and hurried across the field of feet and tails to her side. By the time he reached her, she was already speaking into her communicator.

"T'Pol to Archer."

On the com unit, the captain responded almost immediately. "Go ahead."

The wail of the distressed child cut off any chance at conversation. Tucker turned to the mother, unable to control himself any longer. "Hey—"

T'Pol ignored his concern and continued speaking to the captain. "Central Security claims to have no record of Klaang. But they told me about an enclave on level nineteen where Klingons have been known to go. Something about live food."

"Where on level nineteen?" the captain asked.

"The easternmost subsection. By the geothermal shafts."

"I'll meet you there as soon as I can. Archer out."

The alien child was hysterical now. Tucker's innards squirmed as the mother disconnected the breathing tube entirely. The child was suffocating!

Tucker bolted forward. "What are you doing! Leave that kid alone!"

T'Pol was right after him and seized him by the arm. "Don't get involved."

"Do you see what she's doing? He's going to suffocate!"

"They're Lorillians. Before the age of four, they can only breathe methyloxide." She paused, watching the mother and child as the little one began finally to grow quiet and begin breathing on his own, without the device. "The mother is simply weaning her son."

Tucker inhaled deeply in empathy. "Could've fooled me. . . ."

"Humans can't refrain from drawing conclusions," T'Pol scolded. "You should learn to objectify other cultures so you can determine when to interfere and when *not* to."

Tucker glanced back at the child. He knew he'd made a mistake, but that was all it was. He didn't like being lectured.

He followed her into the open stretch of walkways and tubes leading toward the upper levels. "Well, hey, Sub-Commander," he told her, "next time I see somebody backing you into a corner and taking a switchblade to your ribs, I'll know to wait a few minutes just in case it's a dance. Do you feel like somebody's following us? I feel like we're being watched. Do you get that feeling? I do. . . ."

"Do you think they're all right?"

"No way to know yet."

"They don't like each other."

"I don't think T'Pol would let anything happen to Tucker, no matter how they feel about each other."

Archer led Hoshi through a forbidding trade complex much more desolate and eerie than the central cluster. Deep grinding noises from the power generators far below echoed through damp floors that creaked under their feet. He kept Hoshi close behind him as they skimmed past rows of burping geothermal ducts that constantly vented violent shots of steam.

And they were completely alone.

"Isn't an 'enclave' supposed to have people?" Hoshi nervously asked.

" 'Enclave' can mean a lot of things," Archer comforted, but he kept his eyes open. The place looked empty, but that also could mean a lot of things.

"T'Pol said something about 'live' food," Hoshi went on, quite spooked. "I don't see any restaurants. . . ."

Archer started to answer, but drew up short instead as a flicker of movement caught his eye in the industrial distance. Klingons!

"Excuse me!" he shouted. "Hello! Excuse me!"

The Klingons moved away from them.

"Hoshi!" he snapped.

She flinched, then shouted, "*Ha'quj jeg!*"

But there was only silence. The movement stopped. The shadows sagged back to stillness.

"They looked Klingon to me," she said, suddenly breathless and completely jittery.

Archer grunted a dissatisfied response and snapped up his communicator. "Archer to T'Pol." After a moment, when no answer came, he repeated, "T'Pol, come in."

Anxiety rose as no answer came. Hoshi shivered at his side. "Maybe we should get back to where there are more people. . . ."

"There are plenty of people right here."

He drew his plasma pistol. The movement frightened her.

"Stay behind me," he warned.

They moved into the deep purple shadows along the path leading to where the Klingons had disappeared. Above, a spiderweb of age-old metal drums, bridges, archways, and tubes threaded the darkness. Steam billowed from the geothermal ducts, obscuring every step before they took it.

There was someone here. He felt the shifting

gazes of the shadows and pounding machinery. Silence would be better than this constant grinding and drumming.

They passed too close to a geothermal duct just as it blew its top. A mushroom of gray-white steam burped from the depths and separated Archer from Hoshi for a critical instant.

He glanced behind, but she was lost in steam.

A piece of a shadow burst toward him—Hoshi's hand flashed in the cloud and she screamed, only steps from Archer, but though he reached out, she slipped away.

He whirled full about and took aim—what could he do? Shoot her?

In that instant of hesitation, he was attacked from two sides by a now-familiar dappled team who moved like insects. Suliban!

His pistol flew from his hand at a single blow. His fingers went numb, and he stumbled. He lashed out with the other fist and landed a solid strike on a surface that collapsed—a lung or stomach—and seconds turned into punches. One of the attackers fell back.

The other, though, made use of his partner as a distraction. Archer spun to keep fighting, but his arms were yanked behind him so violently that he gasped with pain and arched his back. In the steam, Hoshi cried out again. At least she was alive!

Frantic, he let out a kick, but failed to connect.

His hip twisted. A shot of pain rushed up his side. His attackers took the advantage. With a single gasp of protest, Jonathan Archer was dragged into the dark depths as if swallowed by a giant burrowing animal.

# Chapter 10

A STEAMY MAZE . . . VERTICAL, DIAGONAL, HORIZONTAL tubes, bridges . . .

Archer fought to stay conscious. One of the Suliban must've landed a blow on his head or neck. He strained to see Hoshi. She was behind him, but no longer safe there.

They had succeeded in making their presence known, whether that would turn out to be good or bad. Rather than finding someone, they had succeeded in being found. He took that as progress.

They were being pushed right along at a daunting pace for his aching thigh. He forced his leg to keep moving. Couldn't let it freeze up on him. Might have to run.

One of the two Suliban who pushed them along had his plasma pistol. He caught glimpses of it, just enough to tempt him every few seconds. He wanted the weapon back, and pummeled himself mentally for losing it to them. He had handed his enemy an advantage. Rule number one broken.

Sweat drained down his face. The surroundings were getting hotter and steamier, though the Suliban didn't seem affected at all—

What was that? An energy field?

Archer blinked as a fizzing light half blinded him. He fought to adjust.

T'Pol! And Trip—in a box of some kind, with a force field locking them in. Like Hoshi, alive. Now that he knew for sure they were being stalked, Archer got a burst of relief at seeing them. Where were Reed and Mayweather?

He winced as the Suliban operatives yanked him to a stop. Hoshi bumped his right arm. One of the Suliban worked a handheld device that caused the energy field to snap down. Then that same Suliban reached for Hoshi.

Archer tried to get between them, but there was no fighting the strength of the individual who had him by both arms behind his back. This one had figured out that Archer's leg was hurt and he could be held off balance.

As the Suliban with the device pulled Hoshi inside the chamber and left her with T'Pol and

Tucker, Archer noticed that these two weren't dressed the same as the two who had infiltrated the *Enterprise*. Of course, that didn't mean they weren't the same two. He couldn't tell from their mottled faces, or make out any individuality at all.

Archer waited to be put inside. Instead, the Suliban stepped out and raised the electrical shield again. From inside, Tucker stepped forward toward Archer, but there was no hope to break through the force field. T'Pol gave him no such concern. Instead, she seemed to be saying with her eyes *I told you so*.

Angry and aching, Archer let himself be led away without further struggle. He sensed a chance for answers now, if not the ones he wanted.

What would be done with his crew? Would they be interrogated? Pressured?

The Suliban pulled him down a conduit to some steps, then down the steps. He had to duck twice, bumped his head once on something he never saw, and was drawn through three locked doors and a small hatch. Thoroughly disoriented by the time they stopped, Archer found himself in a chamber with beds, computers, piles of clothing, tables and chairs, and clutter.

He looked around critically and got an idea about this place. He knew a secret subversive base when he saw one. Were the Suliban dissidents? Against whom?

Or more pointedly, were *these* Suliban dissidents?

The two Suliban finally let him have his arms back. Without a word or gesture, they turned and left him alone in this chamber—which probably meant there was no easy way out. Judging from the way they came in, he might be lost down here for weeks before he found his way to the surface.

"You're looking for Klaang," a female voice said in perfect English. "Why?"

Archer turned, looked. Neither of the Suliban had come back or spoken. Who had?

"Who the hell are you?" he demanded coldly.

The shadows behind a stack of boxes shifted. A woman stepped out. Strikingly lovely and definitely human, the woman strode toward him, studying him as she came.

"My name is Sarin. Tell me about the people who took Klaang off your ship."

"I was hoping you could tell me," Archer reversed. "They looked a lot like your friends outside."

She stepped toward him. "Where were you taking him?"

"How come you don't look like your friends?" he asked, instead of giving her anything.

She was uncomfortably close now. "Would you prefer I did?" she asked in a sultry tone.

She was pale-skinned, pale-eyed, with dark hair drawn tightly back and mostly hidden beneath a hood that framed high, sculpted cheekbones and full lips. Archer noted the beauty, but let his anger eclipse any sense of attraction.

Stick to business.

"What I'd prefer," he attempted again, "is that you give me Klaang back."

"So you could take him where?"

"Home. We were just taking him home."

Sarin was now inches away. Less. She seemed to be gauging him. He was returning the favor.

"You'd better be careful," Archer murmured. "I'm a lot bigger than you are."

She moved until they were very close and her breath brushed his cheek. "If you're thinking of harming me, I'd advise against it."

She ran her hand along his jawline.

"What're you doing?" he asked, as if he didn't know.

"Why were you taking Klaang home?"

"Y'know," he said instead, "under different circumstances, I might be flattered by this, but . . ."

Sarin came up on her toes and pressed her lips to his, forcefully and with purpose. Archer coolly accepted what was happening and bothered to relax enough that she might get discouraged sooner. With his ship on the line and his crew in a cage, he didn't much care how seductive she wanted to playact.

She got whatever she wanted—or didn't—and stepped back rather abruptly. Her face began to melt.

A moment later, she was Suliban. Archer grimaced in disgust.

"That's never happened before," he offered.

"I've been given the ability to measure trust," she said, "but it requires close contact."

Maybe next time they could just shake hands. He tried to imagine her smooching T'Pol, and shook that image away before it took hold.

"You're Suliban," he said, giving her a pretense of the shock she was probably going for.

"I *was* a member of the Cabal," Sarin said, "but not anymore. The price of evolution is too high."

"Evolution?"

Carefully, she moved away, no longer meeting his eyes. "Some of my people are so anxious to 'improve' themselves that they've lost perspective."

"So you know I'm not lying to you," Archer vectored back to the point. "Now what?"

"Klaang was carrying a message to his people."

"How do you know that?"

"I gave it to him."

"What kind of message?"

"The Suliban have been staging attacks within the Klingon Empire," she told him. "Making it appear that one faction is attacking another. Klaang was bringing proof of this to his High Council. Without that proof, the Empire could be thrown into chaos."

"Why would the Suliban want that?" Archer asked, following her and keeping her from turning away. He knew guilt when he saw it, and was determined to get answers before she changed her mind or had an attack of regret.

"The Cabal doesn't make decisions on its own," she went on, more anxious to tell him things. "They're simply soldiers fighting a temporal cold war."

"Temporal? You've lost me."

"They're taking orders from the distant future."

The announcement stopped Archer in his tracks. He ended up leaning on his bad leg, enduring shots of pain through his hip, but the strange concept held him still. "What?"

In his periphery he saw a movement on the ceiling and flinched. Only a shot of steam from a crack.

Temporal cold war . . .

Sarin turned fully to face him, now firm with conviction. If she had harbored any doubts, they were gone.

"We can help you find Klaang," she said

quickly. "But we don't have a starship. You'll have to take us with you!"

A blinding flash of blue light discharged between them. A computer station at Archer's elbow exploded into shards and drove him sideways. He reached for Sarin and pulled her out of the blast area.

Another weapon blast struck even closer. Two Suliban skittered across the ceiling, firing weapons at them!

It didn't take a genius to understand that the secret base had been breached and these weren't the same two Suliban who had brought him here.

Sarin's Suliban came streaking in from a doorway, firing as they ran, but the other Suliban seemed to have physical advantages. They skimmed the walls and ceiling like insects.

All hell broke loose. Archer dragged Sarin toward the way they'd come in, assuming she would have the sense to lead him out through those tubes—

"Get us out!" Archer choked.

In fact, she had a shortcut. Five seconds later, they were out in the main access level, being sprayed by geothermals and burned by the fritzing electrical screen that blocked off the *Enterprise* landing party. Behind them, the battle raged—Suliban against Suliban.

One of Sarin's operatives fell dead just inches

behind Archer, while the other exchanged hand-weapon fire with the two attackers. Sarin raised a weapon now that Archer hadn't even known she possessed, and began returning fire, blocking blast after blast that might've taken Archer's head off.

Sarin's other operative followed them out, rushing frantically along a bridge, firing as he went. He blasted one of the two attackers, but was caught in crossfire and killed by the second invader.

That left Archer and Sarin on their own—and Archer had no weapon! His team was armed, but they couldn't get through the force field. He had to break that force field!

The Suliban attacker, the remaining one, had the same idea. He drove Archer and Sarin into hiding with his wild firing, then opened on the force field with the *Enterprise* crewmen behind it. They dove for cover, but there wasn't any. All they could do was crouch with each other as the field disrupted in blinding displays of free energy.

At Archer's side, Sarin took the initiative and stood clear. She fired openly at the attacker's body and blew him off his feet. With that window of opportunity, she rushed to the control panel of the force field and worked it with some kind of code.

The field fell! The crew flooded out, Tucker first. T'Pol pushed Hoshi before her.

Sarin yanked open a panel that turned out to be a locker. She started handing the crew their plasma pistols!

Archer briefly connected with Tucker—just a reassuring glance—and they were off running.

"Where is your vessel?" Sarin asked.

"On the roof! Docking port three!"

"Captain!" Hoshi cried, and pointed at the underside of a diagonal conduit high over the ground. Two more Suliban, defying gravity, crawled along the pipe!

"This way!" Sarin called.

As she led them in a completely confusing direction, one of the Suliban dropped and landed only a pace from Archer.

He lashed out, and the Suliban sprang out of reach and out of sight with a heightened agility that startled even Sarin.

But here were two more Suliban—dressed like Sarin's associates. *On our side?* Yes! They were firing at the other Suliban!

How many people were in Sarin's subversive splinter group? Right now Archer wanted dozens, hundreds.

Flashes of weapons fire illuminated the distance. The Starfleet team plowed forward after Sarin, ducking and running, navigating the wild jungle of pipes and buttresses.

Sarin reached a massive vertical tube, hit a control, and opened a hatch that Archer was relieved to see, because there was no way to climb this monolith. A large pipe opened before them. Inside was a circular platform a few feet above the deck. Archer spun to pile Hoshi into the hole while Tucker acted as rear guard.

What about Reed and Mayweather?

He reached for T'Pol.

Weapons fire streaked in from hundreds of feet away.

"Trip!" Archer called, and shoved the engineer onto the platform, then piled in after him. Under them, the platform began to rumble and shift with the rush of thermal energy. Sarin was doing something with a control box. Was this an elevator?

"Come on!" Archer waved, but his voice was snatched away by a thermal rush.

Sarin moved toward the platform. She reached out to climb aboard. A blast struck her square in the back.

A Suliban stood across the area, his weapon trained on her. He fired again just as his eyes met Archer's.

Sarin fell hard. The points of impact on her back glowed and sizzled as they burned their way through her writhing body.

Archer launched off the platform, followed by Tucker. Tucker provided covering fire and drove the Suliban back while Archer knelt at Sarin's side.

The Suliban took cover behind an outcropping

of twisted pipes, but he was more persistent than the others and didn't run. Archer's mind flashed on his moment of contact with the single Suliban, and he recognized something in this individual's eyes, his manner, his drive. Unlike the others, who had ducked and hidden with more relish than they had fought, this one had a stake in whatever was happening.

Archer glanced over again and memorized the patterns of dappling on this Suliban's face.

But beneath his hands, the female Suliban was dying.

"Find Klaang," Sarin murmured raggedly.

Mercifully, she lost consciousness as the wounds in her body continued to glow, burn, and grow, eating her from the inside out.

"Trip!" Archer bolted to his feet. He hoped it would be quick for Sarin. He could give her no more now.

He motioned for Tucker, and together they jumped back onto the trembling platform. Archer slid the hatch shut.

The moment he did that, the platform blasted upward through the shaft, driving them to their knees, propelled by a rolling pillar of steam.

In seconds the hot steam was blown away by an arctic blast. Archer forced his eyes open and saw snow blanketing the landing dock. They'd made it!

The platform shot up and stopped a full two

feet over the dock. The Starfleet team was thrown into a pile, but alive. Steam blasted out in all directions under them, billowing into the frozen air.

Still covered with sweat, Archer pulled his team into the frigid snow. "Let's go!" he called over the whine of wind and blowing ice.

"Where's the pod?" Hoshi called.

"Over here!" Tucker waved and pointed.

T'Pol, though, called louder over the wind and pointed in a different direction. "No, this way!"

Archer weighed the two options, then picked T'Pol's direction. She was the only one who had ever been here before. He made the bet and pointed. "Come on!"

As the four of them headed toward an obscured shape with two lights that might indeed be the shuttle, Archer bent against the wind, endured the sweat freezing on his cheeks, and brought the communicator up, flipping it as he ran. "Lieutenant Reed, this is Archer! Come in!"

*"zzzzzzkkkkkgggggaaazzzk."*

"We're up on the roof! You need to get up here as quickly as possible! Where are you? Emergency evacuation! Reed!"

The communicator buzzed frantically. Someone was definitely trying to get through to him. Where were they? How deeply had they wandered into that steamy maze?

The storm was getting worse. The landing

deck was turning into a skating rink. Archer fell twice, Tucker once, and the women stumbled into each other like skittering ducks before the shuttlepod took shape before them in the white fume.

Unintelligible sounds continued to burst from his communicator. He left it open, hoping to hear something that would give him a clue he could follow somehow to get Reed and Mayweather out of the complex, and all of them away from these attacks.

Suliban soldiers appeared only seconds after Archer and his shipmates skidded onto the frozen deck. Time seemed to crawl when a blast rocketed past him.

The wind began to clear. Blowing snow flattened into a sea, and the docking platform opened before them—empty! The obscured shape had been nothing but an approach shield!

"Great!" Hoshi blurted.

"Like I said," Tucker shouted, "it's over there!"

Another blast of weapons fire sliced the air. Archer ducked and ordered, "Weapons!"

They had to cross the deck again. And now the Suliban had found them! Even in the now-rising snowstorm, Archer caught a glimpse of his determined counterpart, the one Suliban who wouldn't be put off, and whose resolve gave substance to the others behind him.

But there was distance between them. Archer

was resolved, too, and worked to use the blowing snow as a shield. If it could obscure a whole platform, then he could make it obscure his team.

"Down! Get low, everybody! Form a single file!"

He tried to imagine what the Suliban would be seeing. Lower—lower—and keep moving steadily. Sporadic movement would gain more attention.

They kept searching for the shuttle, this time following Tucker through the storm of snow and weapons fire, firing all the way. Deep red plasma bullets streaked across the platform toward the place where the Suliban shots were coming from. Though the Suliban were moving toward them, Archer sensed they were being held back by his and Tucker's shots. T'Pol was more reserved, taking shots more carefully, but she, too, was succeeding in driving them back. Hoshi was just skittering like a bird across the ice, intent on their target. She had a weapon, but she also knew she was of little use with it. Probably smart to let the trained officers handle that detail, Archer noted as the moments rushed past.

His single-file trick was working. Suliban shots were going wild behind them. Then they corrected their error forward, and the team was forced to scatter. Hot blue beams cut between them, driving them away from each other.

A darkened form, sheeted and blistered with ice, suddenly flashed with blue energy before them. The shuttlepod! The Suliban weapons fire lit up the skin of the pod and gave the Starfleet team a clear beacon to safety.

T'Pol circled around Archer and pounded on the shuttle window. Why was she doing that?

The emergency hatch began to crack open, popped out a few inches, and swung wider. Air gushed with equalization and temperature change.

Archer tried to reach the shuttle, but a crackle of blue energy raked the hull and drove him back into the swirling snow. His face and hands were numb with cold now. Where was Hoshi? He'd lost sight of her!

The Suliban were closing in. He knew that without even looking. He'd be doing the same thing.

"Hoshi!"

"Captain?" her voice was weak, but not far.

Shivering now, he forced his legs to keep moving away from the shuttle and toward her voice. Behind a wall over there, Tucker was firing steadily at something he could obviously see. The cover gave Archer time to find Hoshi in the roiling white storm. Without saying anything, he took her arm and pulled her along back the way he had just come.

Where were his footprints? He had just come this way, but the trail was already erased.

A mechanical roar directly overhead shook him to his boots. He pushed Hoshi down and tried to see what new method of attack the Suliban had invented. An aircraft—an alien craft launching from the port! Only its running lights showed through the blowing snow. Its great gush of thruster exhaust caused a frozen hell down here.

Archer pulled his eyes away from the transport overhead and squinted through the miasma toward the place where the Suliban shots had come from.

They'd stopped. The Suliban were driven down by the thruster exhaust. But the exhaust did one favor here and executed a problem over there— T'Pol was directly under the exhaust. The force knocked her off her feet and blew her across the deck. She had been near the shuttlepod and now she was way over there, shifting and dazed, alone, unarmed.

The Suliban soldiers and their leader rose out of the exhaust stream as the big ship moved away from the pad. They saw T'Pol. A clear target.

"Get to the ship!" Archer shouted at Hoshi over the wind.

Luckily she wasn't the heroic type and did as he ordered.

Archer thrust himself up on his aching legs

and made himself obvious. He snapped his pistol up just as the Suliban leader noticed him. Without looking for cover, he ran furiously across the tarmac, directly toward the Suliban, firing as he ran.

One of the Suliban was struck by a lucky shot—lucky only because most of his plasma bullets were being sucked sideways by the wind vortex on these open flats. One more down.

The leader and the other soldier took cover. Archer reached T'Pol's weapon, scooped it up without missing a step, and kept on with his direct assault.

"Go!" he called to her.

"*Enterprise* needs its captain!" she called back. "Give me the weapon!"

"I said, *go!*"

To her credit, she hesitated another moment. During that moment he struck her with a look so forceful that she must have realized she wouldn't be changing his mind. This was no time for a discussion.

Archer broke the contact, raised the second weapon, and began firing both as T'Pol ran behind him toward the shuttle.

He glanced back to gauge her progress and saw the shuttlepod hatch open again for her. Reed was reaching for her! Archer spotted Mayweather warming up the helm. They were already aboard!

A flush of relief numbed Archer's whole body. His team was intact!

As Reed pulled T'Pol inside, Archer moved backward toward the shuttle, firing constantly. The pistol in his left hand began to cool. Losing power!

The Suliban leader waved his hand. The Suliban broke apart from each other, forcing Archer to divide his target. The leader had figured out what to do, a simple but effective maneuver.

Archer was closer to the shuttle now, close enough for a good leap if he could only turn around, but he had to keep shooting. He aimed slightly to his left at a moving form.

From his right, a blue shot streaked in. His leg folded under him, burning and quivering. A moment later, the blinding pain struck full out.

A tangle of movement confused him. Reed, right overhead, firing into the snow!

Trip Tucker appeared at his side and pulled him through the hatch. Archer did everything he could to save himself and them from further torment, but he could barely think over the searing pain in his thigh. His thoughts piled together. Nothing made sense. He dug his shoulder into Tucker and accepted the support from his friend, who could do nothing for him, not here, like this.

"The starboard thruster's down!" Mayweather spat.

"Ignore it." T'Pol, almost excited. "Take us up."

Hoshi's face appeared in his closing periphery. She looked small, distant.

"Open a channel." T'Pol again.

The surge of acceleration made Archer's mind swarm like bees in the sky. The lower half of his body sizzled, as if he were being fried in a skillet. He tried to move, to sit up—

"Sub-Commander T'Pol to *Enterprise*."

"Go ahead," the voice on the com responded.

"We'll be docking in a few minutes. Have Dr. Phlox meet us in decon."

"Acknowledged. Is someone wounded?"

Archer tried to speak, to protest that he could stand, work, take them back to the ship, and go on with their mission to find Klaang . . . the Klingons . . . he had to . . .

"Your pitch is too low. Bring the nose up."

The pod rocked and turned in the wind. The port nacelle struck a branch and skidded into the snow. No, it was sand . . .

"It's okay. You've almost got it. Try again."

The ship skittered on the sand and rose over open water, airborne again, wavering.

"I can't do it!"

*Dad, I can't keep the ship in the air! Why can't I do it right?*

"Yes, you can. Take her up, straight and steady."

The ship skidded into a sand dune, bruised and lifeless.

"Damn!" Archer gushed.

Dad came to his side.

"You can't be afraid of the wind," he said. "Learn to trust it."

Archer turned and looked up onto the dune. T'Pol stood watching him and his father as they worked the model ship and tried to make it fly. What was she doing here?

"The captain is injured," she said. "I'm taking command of the *Enterprise*."

Dad didn't seem surprised. Why not?

# Chapter 11

"You're not in command yet. Don't get ahead of yourself."

"The captain is incapacitated. My action is logical."

"That's what you think."

Trip Tucker shed his wet field jacket and dumped it on the hangar deck beside the scarred and steaming shuttlepod, leaving him in a clammy, snowcaked uniform. He watched with dismay as the medics disappeared into the turbolift with the captain on an antigrav gurney. Things weren't supposed to be this way. While Tucker's rational mind had always accepted the fact that space was fraught with danger, it had never sunk in emotionally that he might have to face the specter of good friends and shipmates—

least of all Jonathan Archer, who had always seemed impervious—being wounded or worse.

What kind of bolt had struck him? The wound had been chewing away at itself all the way back here, as if burning from the inside out. Tucker's innards twisted at the memory of it, of Archer's face as consciousness faded, giving the only relief from what must've been torture.

He wracked his mind for signs that the whole episode had been a trap engineered from inside this ship. Had T'Pol given Archer false information about the Klingon's activities? Everything stemmed from her. Now she was an inch from making the next command decisions.

"He saved your life," he told her. "You owe him a buffer zone. Give him time to come out of the sedatives they just gave him."

"Dr. Phlox is working on the wound," T'Pol said. "The captain will see to himself, as we all must. Command responsibility is now mine. Even you cannot dispute it."

"Watch me. I'm going to check on the captain."

He started toward the exit.

"You haven't been scanned for contaminants," T'Pol called. "Tucker! The safety of the rest of the crew!"

That stopped him. Damn, it did. He couldn't much comment on her responsibilities if he didn't oblige his own.

"Hell, all right . . ."

* * *

"Is this really necessary?"

Tucker shifted his feet uneasily as he and T'Pol stood side by side in the decon chamber, still in their wet uniforms, now bathed in ultraviolet light.

Dr. Phlox was here instead of sickbay—probably a good sign for the captain.

"The other scans were negative," he said. "You two, unfortunately, were exposed to a protocystian spore. I've loaded the appropriate decon-gel into compartment B."

Tucker groaned and began to strip out of his uniform. Beside him, T'Pol did the same.

"Tell Mr. Mayweather to prepare to leave orbit," T'Pol said to the doctor.

"How's the captain?" Tucker bluntly reminded, insisting that she not forget the weight of what she was about to do.

"I'm treating his wound," Phlox said.

"Will he be all right?"

"Eventually."

A metal slat slid shut, cutting off Tucker and T'Pol from the rest of the ship. They each turned to a locker, opened it, and deposited their contaminated uniforms inside. Tucker tossed his in. T'Pol used the hook.

Tucker stripped down to his shorts. T'Pol wore a form-fitting but utilitarian gray combination of tank top and undershorts.

Without comment she turned to him, handed

him a beaker, and they began spreading the goop
on each other. The phosphorescent gel gleamed in
the ultraviolet light, illuminating their skin with
an otherworldly glow.

"Correct me if I'm wrong," Tucker began, "but
aren't you just kind of an 'observer' on this mission? I don't remember anyone telling me you
were a member of Starfleet."

"My Vulcan rank supersedes yours," she said.

He bristled. "Apples and oranges. This is an Earth
vessel. You're in no position to take command."

"As soon as we're through here, I'll contact Ambassador Soval. He'll speak to your superiors, and
I'm certain they'll support my authority in this situation."

Tucker clamped his lips. If she made the call,
this mission was over.

"You must really be proud of yourself. You can
put an end to this mission while the captain's still
unconscious in sickbay. You won't even have to
look him in the eye."

"Your precious 'cargo' was stolen," she said irritably. "Three Suliban, perhaps more, were killed,
and Captain Archer has been seriously wounded.
It seems to me this mission has put an end to itself. Turn around."

"Let's say you're right," he went on, reining in
his combativeness just long enough to get this
out. "Let's say we screwed up, just like you always
knew we would.

"It's still a pretty good bet that whoever blew that hole in the captain's leg is connected somehow to the people who took Klaang."

"I fail to see your point."

"Captain Archer deserves the chance to see this through. If you knew him, you'd realize that's what he's about. He needs to finish what he starts. His daddy was the same way."

*But he never got to finish. That was your fault, too, you people.*

"You obviously share the captain's belief," she said, "that my people were responsible for impeding Henry Archer's accomplishments."

"He only wanted to see his engine fly," Tucker countered. Surely T'Pol could not believe that the Vulcans hadn't been responsible for holding Henry Archer back. "They never even gave him the chance to fail. And here *you* are, thirty years later, proving just how consistent you Vulcans can be."

They fell silent as each took a towel and began wiping off the blue gel, now that it had set into a film.

"Tell you the truth," Tucker continued after a few moments, "we don't know why you're here. There's nothing to 'observe,' so who stuck us with you? But you notice we accepted you. Nobody's been giving you dirty looks, 'cept maybe me once in a while. That's how we silly humans are. We trust first, and ask each other to come up to it. Maybe you don't."

T'Pol pulled the congealed film from her lips and cheeks, and revealed soft puckering around her eyes. Worry? Guilt?

"You know nothing about me," she protested without much enthusiasm.

Tucker grunted with the irony of her statement. "Funny, isn't it? We trust you anyway. Odd, silly humans . . . You can follow along behind every Vulcan who came before you, but I don't hold much for that kind of life. I wonder if you've got the steel to go off on your own. Maybe . . . The captain must see *something* in you, or he wouldn't have accepted you in his command line. He didn't have to do that, you know. What do you think he saw? Youth? Grace?"

"Those aren't command traits," she said. This time her voice was very quiet.

"Hell, no, they aren't," Tucker shot back. "Not even your 'Vulcan' rank is enough to get you what you've got here. You wouldn't have it if Jonathan hadn't given you the chance you're denying him. We're 'only' humans . . . but we gave you the same trust we give each other. Now the captain's asking you to return it. You got the guts?"

She didn't respond. She had cut herself off from the conversation.

Tucker reached into another locker and pulled out a fresh T-shirt. "I guess we'll see," he said.

The ship was flying now. Pretty against the sky.

Jonathan Archer opened his eyes, gritted his teeth against a sudden shot of pain, and looked down at his legs.

He was lying, partially reclined, on a biobed. Dr. Phlox was at work on his thigh wound, removing what looked like a disembodied liver from the leg.

Underneath the liver, the wound was reddened, but sealed.

"Very nice," Phlox commented. "Very nice. Your myofibers are fusing beautifully!"

Archer moved his arms and flexed his neck muscles. "How long have I been . . ."

"Less than six hours. I thought it best to keep you sedated while the osmotic eel cauterized your wound."

Phlox appreciated his glossy little pet, then deposited the thing into a pot of fluid.

Archer looked at the creature, now happily swimming around, and reserved judgment. "Thanks."

He started to ask about the landing party— was everyone else all right? But Trip Tucker and T'Pol entered, answering part of his question here and now.

"How're you doing, Captain?" Trip asked immediately. Relief showed in his face to see Archer awake and lucid.

"That depends," Archer said. "What's been going on for the last six hours?"

Tucker didn't say anything. What did that mean?

T'Pol raised her chin a little and announced. "As your highest ranking officer, I assumed command while you were incapacitated."

Archer's stomach sank. "Are we underway?"

Tucker nodded.

To T'Pol, Archer coldly accused, "You didn't waste much time, did you?"

She didn't respond, but turned to Phlox. "Is he fit to resume command?"

"As long as he returns for more eel therapy tomorrow."

Archer ignored her and looked at Tucker. "How long till we get back to Earth?"

"Earth, sir?"

Was that a hint of a smile?

T'Pol turned back to them. "We're currently tracking the Suliban vessel that left Rigel shortly after you were injured."

Skeptical and surprised, Archer asked, "You got their . . . plasma decay rate?"

"With Mr. Tucker's assistance, I modified your sensors. We now have the resolution to detect their warp trail."

"What happened to 'This is a foolish mission'?"

"It *is* a foolish mission," she insisted. "The

Suliban are clearly a hostile race with technology far superior to yours. But, as acting captain . . . I was obligated to anticipate *your* wishes."

Well, well, well. Had something changed in Archer's dreams? "As acting captain," he echoed, "you could've done whatever the hell you wanted to do."

Her cheeks flushed olive—just enough to notice—but she didn't offer any explanations or comments on what he had just said to her.

"I should return to the bridge," was all she said.

"Dismissed."

Archer had more to say, but he let her go. Whatever had happened, it was hard enough on her to buck the Vulcan trend. Renewed hope surged up. He hadn't lost the mission yet.

Trip Tucker waited until the door closed, then looked at Archer. With significance, he said, "Modifying the sensors *was* her idea, sir."

Archer let his head sink back on the cushion. "Why would she do that? Go against the wishes of whoever designed her position here?"

"It just might be," Tucker said with a twinkle, "you're having more effect on her than they are. Whoever *they* are."

"Have you and Reed found out anything?"

"She's clean and normal right up until she gets the scholarship that put her in Soval's office. Then, her records start getting real terse and kind of vague."

"Could be just the logging style of that office," Archer mentioned. "Details never were very important to Soval."

"Or it could be a masking technique," Tucker said. "Got to admit, I was knocked over when she decided to pursue."

"It's not what a spy would do, is it?"

"No . . . sir, could it be she's a spy and even she doesn't know it?"

"If she doesn't know it, then I don't care one way or the other. As long as she knows who she works for here and now."

Tucker paced around the end of the bed. "She might work for you . . . except we picked up log echoes of several messages going back and forth between Soval and Admiral Forrest just before she was assigned."

Archer narrowed his eyes in thought. "I didn't think Soval and Forrest had that much to say to each other."

"You think they're up to something?" Tucker asked. "And she's the something?"

"Or *we're* the something. All of us, together. I know Forrest. He's not likely to have me watched. If he agreed to a Vulcan plant, there must be a different reason. Completely different."

"They wouldn't tell you?"

"I'd be the last person they'd tell. Trip . . . what do you think of this . . . maybe the Vulcans really don't know if they can be around humans and function for decades upon decades. Maybe **Soval** finally wants to know, once and for all, if we can exist together in hostile space and come out productive."

"You mean they're testing us?"

Archer thought about that, then dismissed it. "I doubt it. They know everything there is to know about humanity. All you have to do is look at history. It's all there. We don't hide anything, even the worst things. Humans aren't a mystery. But . . . *Vulcans* are still a mystery, even to each other. They don't step out of that box very often, and they're about to be kicked right out. It could be they're testing themselves. And they're using her to do it."

"T'Pol's the guinea pig?" Tucker blurted. "They want to see how *she'll* do? I'll be damned!"

"And it worked," Archer said. "Her technical expertise and ability to stay cool, side by side with my irrational leaps of anger and whatever else I've got . . . it worked. We came out of our first big test as a human-Vulcan team."

"I'll be damned . . . How can you confirm any of this?"

"I probably can't. All I can do is keep going forward with nothing to hide. A spy's no good if you've got nothing to hide."

"How 'bout that . . . T'Pol's the lab animal. What do you know!" Tucker slapped the end of the bed with a victorious hand, then recoiled. "Sorry! Did I hurt you?"

Archer leaned back, put his arms behind his head, and luxuriated. "Trip, I don't think anybody can hurt me anymore today."

"What are the symptoms of frostbite?"

Hoshi Sato picked at her fingertips. Behind her complaints, the sensor console was making a strange and frantic *ping* every few seconds.

Lieutenant Reed didn't offer her a sympathetic glance, but did explain, "Your appendages blister, peel, turn gangrenous."

"I think I have frostbite."

Ah, well. He moved closer to her, glad he didn't have to cross in front of T'Pol in the command chair. "Let me see . . . Dr. Phlox may have to amputate."

Hoshi frowned. "I never had to worry about frostbite in Brazil."

Before he could respond, the *pings* became suddenly more frantic and closer together.

"They're getting too far ahead of us," Ensign Mayweather said, watching the helm with frustration.

"Match their speed," T'Pol said flatly.

Mayweather glanced helplessly at Reed, then declared, "I'm not authorized to go beyond four-four."

T'Pol tapped a button.

"Engineering," Tucker's voice answered.

"Mr. Tucker, would you please give the helmsman permission to go to warp four point five."

"It's okay, Travis. I'll keep an eye on the engines."

Reed watched Mayweather, but couldn't tell whether the helmsman liked or disliked what he was now doing. The ship surged under them, physically and with great confidence. The *ping*ing slowed down to a normal rhythm and volume. The sensors were much happier.

There was a certain irony in T'Pol's being the one to give the order to go to four-five. Reed tried not to be affected by such trivialities, but some rites of passage should belong to the captain alone. Yet, without consideration, the Vulcan woman had seized the privilege for herself. And the glory, if any came?

He respected the uniform, as he must, but her presence here was the culmination of a dire prediction by Trip Tucker. Tucker's instincts had proven correct, or partially. In fact, this woman had bothered to execute the captain's plans instead of her own.

Still, his investigation had turned up a strange trail of communiqués culminating in her assignment here. The captain had chosen not to question the trail, but to push them all farther down it. Now T'Pol was, perhaps, still being manipulated, but by Jonathan Archer.

Very nice. Reed rocked on his heels. Very nice indeed.

"Archer to bridge."

Reed relieved Hoshi of the need to use her poor fingers by pushing the intercom himself. "Yes, sir, Reed here."

"Tucker says we just accomplished four-five. I'd have liked to have been there for that."

T'Pol glanced at Reed, but let him do the talking.

"You are here, sir, in all our spirits. We wouldn't have been here at all if not for you."

"The farther in the future they are, the more crazy and dangerous it is that they would be doing these things. While it has marginal effects on people here, it could completely change their own time. So what do they want?"

Jonathan Archer took tentative steps as he circumnavigated the table in his office. His leg was tingling from the knee to the hip. Still not good.

"Trip . . . give me a hand."

Trip Tucker rushed to him from the couch and eagerly helped him back into the office chair. Beside them, stars streaked by the portal at high warp. Archer felt out of commission, wearing only his T-shirt and nonreg trousers, but he knew he had to give himself another hour to come out of the doctor's funny sedative. He seemed to have the time. They were in hot pursuit, but only matching the speed of the people they were pursuing. They didn't, after all, want to catch them—not quite yet. They wanted to be led somewhere first.

Warp four point five . . .

"It's possible there's something about time travel we don't understand," Archer suggested.

"I'd say the odds for that are good," Tucker grumbled as he stuffed a pillow under the captain's bad leg and bothered to fluff it. He straightened and surveyed his work. "Feel better?"

"Fine, I'm fine, Trip, thanks. Is it somebody more advanced than we are," Archer contemplated, "trying to change the near past? Or are they in the far distant future? I'd like to ask T'Pol what she thinks. Do I dare?"

"I wouldn't," Tucker bluntly announced. "She's always enjoyed a rigid thought process. Today I think you shook her with your free-roaming methods. Throw time tampering into the mix? I'm scared enough for both her and me.

"Higher level physics break down rationality," Tucker continued. "Progress at that level comes from intuitive leaps, like Einstein imagining what it was like to ride a beam of light."

"No Vulcan would do that," Archer said. "It's not possible to ride a beam of light."

Tucker lowered his chin. "It is now."

Archer smiled. "They think emotionalism, unchecked, will destroy. It's made them afraid. But look at Hoshi. She's terrified every time something happens, but she keeps moving. She always moves to the next step, past the point of fear. Humans might go off in forty wrong directions, but the forty-first might take us someplace new."

Tucker contributed, "Vulcans never want to get off the trail."

"Well," he began instead, "you can sit inside and watch through the window while children play in the street, and say how they might get hurt out there. You can be the little old ladies of the galaxy, but you don't have any fun, and before long nobody talks to you. The Vulcans have wrapped it in a shell of elegance. If I told her that, what do you think she'd say?"

Tucker's face screwed up as he tried to pretend a Vulcan point of view. "Probably something about men in Earth history like Stalin and Li Quan—they were given the power to get anything they wanted, measured by their idea of 'fun.' "

"Good point. I think we agree it's dangerous for these beings from the future to help the Suliban, but it's not so different from an advanced race like the Vulcans coming and helping Earth. If it's so risky, why are they helping us at all? They didn't help the Klingons, did they?"

"No, nor anybody else, if I read the subtle side correctly. I've never heard a single Vulcan talk about any other race they shepherded."

Tucker laughed. "I'll ask her that one myself."

Archer nodded, agreeing with the sentiment but not the plan. "The idea of time travel itself is, on its face, illogical. Isn't it?"

"No," Tucker seized. "She'd have to agree with me on this. The illogical doesn't exist in science. There is something we don't yet understand that allows time travel to take place."

Archer troubled to understand what Tucker had just said, and for a moment forgot about T'Pol. Instead, he found himself remembering Sarin. "If travel backward in time can take place, then causality doesn't exist. If causality doesn't exist, where is logic? 'A' plus 'B' causes 'C.' "

"But causality *does* take a beating at a level of quantum physics. It seems to break down at certain points. Are we discussing whether or not time travel is possible?" Tucker asked. "Or why anybody would be stupid enough to try it?"

"Both," Archer said. "First, is it possible, and second, why would anybody do it, because you can go back and destroy yourself very easily. If I go back and stop an Austrian farmer in the mid-1800s and ask him directions while he's on his way to the market, he gets to the market five minutes later, and misses meeting the woman he was supposed to marry. She passes by. Because they never met, Adolf Hitler is never born. World War II never happens, or happens later for other reasons, and the technological rush of the mid-20th

century is delayed thirty or forty years ...
Zephram Cochrane doesn't have the infrastruc-
ture he needs to invent warp drive, and we never
meet the Vulcans."

"Instead of meeting the Vulcans," Tucker
picked up, "we meet the Klingons instead. By
now, the Klingons are dominant on Earth and
using Earth as a toehold in this whole section of
the galaxy."

"A butterfly flaps its wings in Africa," Archer
murmured, "and there's a typhoon in China the
next spring. This idea that anyone can engineer
the future by screwing up the past—"

"John," Tucker interrupted, "could it be possible they *want* to screw up their own time? Are
they insane, maybe?"

Archer didn't have the answer, but the question made him think of something else. "Or ...
are they reacting to something? Are these people
from the future being forced to action, the way
Vulcans and humans are forced to put weapons
on our ships because there are hostile powers
out there? Are they being forced to tamper with
the past to stop somebody else from tampering?"

"Sure *seems* insane."

"I wish I could talk to these people for five minutes ... if we have no way of knowing, how can
we act?"

"With you laid up, there won't be any action.

T'Pol—she'll just say since we have no basis on which to act, then you should do nothing."

"That's the difference between us," he reminded. "Since we have no basis, I'll act on what I *do* know. They took the Klingon, they have no right, and we're taking him back."

Archer bristled at his own conclusion and looked at Tucker for the support he knew would be there. This whole episode had been anything but proactive. Instead of making things happen, they had been involved in a scheme of making things *not* happen.

He wanted to change that.

"I just have one thing," Tucker slowly added. "What's the moral imperative to protect the future?"

"None," Archer said with a jolt of enthusiasm. "It hasn't happened yet."

The ship shuddered under them suddenly, cutting off the conversation.

"Captain . . ." Tucker made a tentative step toward the door.

"Sure, Trip, go mind your engines. Thanks for helping me work through this. If we know some questions, we'll have a way to recognize the answers when they come."

"I love the concrete! Call if you need me." Embracing that which he *could* control to some degree, Tucker was gone in a flash.

When he was alone, Archer looked out the window at the streaks of stars they were passing at remarkable new speeds. *We're here, Dad . . . warp four point five.*

He cleared his throat and touched the nearest computer link. "*Enterprise* starlog, Captain Jonathan Archer. April sixteenth, 2151 . . ."

Starlog.

"No, no—delete that. Begin recording . . . Captain's log, April sixteenth, 2151. We've been tracking the Suliban's ship for ten hours, thanks to our science officer, who came up with a way to tweak the sensors—computer, pause."

He let his head drop back and spoke aloud to the nearest sympathetic ear. "I save her life . . . and now she's helping us with the mission. One good turn deserves another? Doesn't sound very Vulcan."

He stopped mumbling, thought about what he had just said, what he and Tucker had talked about before, and about the future—all the different possible versions.

"Resume log."

The computer bleeped to assure him it was recording.

"I have no reason to believe Klaang is still alive. But, if the Suliban woman was telling the truth, it's crucial we try to find him. Computer . . . pause."

His back was aching in this position. He pulled Tucker's pillow out from under his leg and sat up.

Sitting down just wasn't getting him in the right frame of mind. With care, he pushed off the chair again and put new pressure on his leg.

He moved across the room to where Porthos lay digesting a fine nonvegetarian meal. He scratched the dog's nose thoughtfully. "Have you ever known a Vulcan to return a favor? No, neither have I."

So he and Tucker were right—there was more going on with T'Pol than just guilt about his risking his own life to save hers. Officers, soldiers, shipmates did that for each other all the time. He couldn't believe selflessness was so new to Vulcans that they had only found it here. They'd been in space a long time, and you can't do that without a scaffold of cooperation and generosity toward each other, whether you admit it's there or not.

He scratched the dog and thought about his conversation with Tucker about time tampering. He wished he could discuss it with T'Pol, because he needed a cool head when it came to such long-range theoreticals, but all his internal alarms stopped him.

"Resume log. I still haven't decided whether to ask Sub-Commander T'Pol about this temporal cold war ... my instincts tell me not to trust her—"

He paused. Something had just changed. The vibrations coming up through his injured leg were different from a few seconds ago.

He looked at the window. The stars were changing. The ship was falling out of warp!

"Computer, pause. Archer to T'Pol. Report!"

"If you're feeling well enough to come to the bridge, Captain," her voice called with a thread of tension, "now would be a good time."

# Chapter 12

THE TEMPORAL ARCHWAY GLOWED AND SIZZLED AS IF in anger. the barrier of energy blocking the way to the future, and also providing a window to it, now glared fitfully in its cylindrical housing. The murky, milky figure of the future being stood passively, but Silik could tell the individual was displeased.

"Did Sarin give them anything?" it asked.

"I don't know," Silik said, both truthful and impatient. He didn't like being made responsible for dangerous things of such undefinition.

"What do you know?" the figure demanded.

"They followed us here."

"Looking for Klaang? Or for you?"

"I don't know. But I'll destroy them before they locate the Helix."

The being was still for many seconds. When it spoke again, the words curdled Silik's blood to his very core.

"We didn't plan to involve the humans, or the Vulcans. Not yet. Sarin's message cannot reach Qo'noS. If the humans have it, you must stop them."

"It's a gas giant."

Archer settled into his command chair as T'Pol stepped out of it, and eyed the big orange mass on the viewscreen—a gargantuan planet of mostly gravity and dust holding each other together on a vast scale.

"From the looks of it, a class six or seven," he muttered.

"Class seven," T'Pol confirmed. "The Suliban vessel dropped to impulse a few hours ago and altered course. Their new heading took them through its outer radiation belt."

"We've lost them?"

Reluctantly, she nodded.

"Move us in closer."

Mayweather glanced at him, then worked to obey that order. Archer pushed out of his chair and paced, working his leg to keep it from stiffening up. Phlox's pet liver had done a good job. He felt twinges, but no loss of strength.

The ship moved closer toward the radiation belt of the orange gas giant. The planet loomed large and imposing on their screens, causing warnings to go off on several stations, but not the right ones.

"Anything?" he asked.

"The radiation's dissipating their warp trail," Reed reported. "I'm only picking up fragments."

Archer gave T'Pol his hunting-eagle glare. "You finished helping us?" he challenged.

She went to Reed's station and eyed the graphics, then hit a control. One simple click.

On the main screen, an enhanced picture of the giant appeared, this time with a fragmented ion trail faintly traced in colors, being broken up by the winds.

"Lieutenant," she said, "run a spectral analysis of the fragments."

Reed hit a series of controls in specific order. On the graphic, a sequence of numbers appeared near each fragment, all different.

"There's too much distortion," Reed complained. "The decay rates don't even match."

"Calculate the trajectory of each fragment."

He looked a bit dubious, and glanced at Archer, who nodded. "You heard her."

Reed clearly hadn't a clue what she was looking for, but he did as he was bidden.

T'Pol, while Reed worked, turned and met Archer's eyes. For the first time they seemed to be thinking the same thing.

The graphic now displayed telemetry for each

fragment. Archer nodded at T'Pol, who moved to another station and began doing the work for herself.

"Recalibrate the sensor array," Archer authorized. "Narrowband, short to midrange."

"Measure the particle density of the thermosphere," T'Pol added.

Archer looked at her again. "Those fragments weren't from the Suliban ship."

T'Pol confirmed, "They were from fourteen . . . and all within the last six hours. I believe we've found what we're looking for."

Despite her reticence until now, she had a lilt of victory in her voice.

Archer dropped a hand on Reed's shoulder. "How are your targeting scanners?"

"Aligned and ready, sir!"

"Bring weapons on-line and polarize the hull plating."

The crew jumped to action all over the bridge. That was no by-the-book order!

Armed conflict during the shakedown voyage!

"Lay in a sixty degree vector," Archer said calmly. "We're going in."

# Chapter 13

EVERYONE WAS AT HIS STATION. THE APPEARANCE OF them there was beginning to gain a rhythm in the captain's mind. He had started knowing which person he was addressing without turning to see who was there. He felt their tension without any words to confirm it. He knew what they were feeling and sometimes thinking.

Intensity could do that.

The *Enterprise* moved through disruptions of gaseous energy and storms the size of whole planets. Her running lights cut through the dense layers, but it was still strangely similar to that ice cyclone on Rigel Ten.

Hoshi's little voice at his side had a new tremor in it when she spoke this time. "Sensor resolution's falling off at about twelve kilometers . . ."

Archer leaned forward. "Travis?"

Mayweather worked feverishly. "I'm okay, Captain."

The ship trembled and rolled—full swings her entire beam-width from side to side. Even her massive power was nothing against the natural monstrosity of a gas giant. This was a terrible risk, something Archer knew would take weeks of exploration, testing, and measurements in another circumstance.

He wanted to know what the ship could do. This would tell him.

T'Pol worked almost anxiously at her console. "Our situation should improve. We're about to break through the cyclohexane layer."

The orange color gave way to an even denser layer of roiling blue liquid. The blue color, normally peaceful, seemed even angrier than the outer atmosphere, and more eerie. It was also more solid, slamming the bow every few seconds with powerful strikes. The ship trembled so hard that Archer held himself in place with both hands.

"I wouldn't exactly call this an improvement," Archer commented.

"Liquid phosphorescence," T'Pol explained. "I wouldn't have expected that beneath a layer of cyclohexane."

The ship rocked sideways again, then took a hard drop forward.

Hoshi hunched her shoulders and hung on until her knuckles turned white. "You might think about recommending seat belts when we get home."

"It's just a little bad weather," Archer assured.

The roiling on the main screen thinned and changed again.

The console near Hoshi suddenly cried out— *peep peep peep peep!*

"We've got sensors!" she called at the same pitch.

"Level off," Archer ordered. "Go to long-range scan."

"I'm detecting two vessels," T'Pol reported, "bearing one-one-nine mark 7."

"Put it up."

Hoshi worked her board. The viewscreen changed to show two Suliban ships moving away in the distance. The little vessels were unique to Archer's eyes, about twice the size of shuttle-pods.

"Impulse and warp engines," Reed reported.

"What kind of weapons?" Archer asked.

"We're too far away."

"Sir," Mayweather broke in, "I'm picking up something at three-forty-two mark 12 . . . and it's a lot bigger!"

The viewscreen shifted as Hoshi worked faster.

"All sensors," Archer instructed T'Pol. "Get whatever you can!"

Before them on the changing screen, a huge complex came into focus. Was it a ship? Or buildings? Archer couldn't tell, but it was massive. It had to be free-floating, because this gas giant had no surface.

"Go tighter."

The screen zeroed in closer. The complex was indeed some kind of moving object, made of hundreds of Suliban ships interlocked to form a massive spiraled space station. A few individual cell ships engaged and disengaged from the mother complex.

"Biosigns?" he asked.

"Over three thousand," Hoshi reported. "but I can't isolate a Klingon, if there is one—"

A jolt rammed the body of the ship.

"That was a particle weapon, sir," Reed reported, too little and too late.

Hit again!

"Bridge!" a call came in from Trip Tucker. "We're taking damage down here! What's going on?"

"Just a little trouble with the bad guys," Archer assured. His tone was confident, and even though Tucker did not reply, Archer decided the engineer's next intake of breath was a bit calmer. Somehow the Suliban didn't scare him so much anymore. The fight with them on the planet had equalized things. T'Pol was wrong—the Suliban weren't so much more advanced than he was. Maybe the mystery had gone away, or maybe he was concentrating on the bigger badder guys from the future who could use such as the Suliban as a tool.

"I suggest returning to the phosphorous layer," T'Pol called over the *boom* of the next hit.

"Take us up," Archer obliged.

The ship rapidly ascended, leaving the attacking cell ships behind with admirable grace. The Suliban cells quickly homed toward the main complex.

"Captain," T'Pol called.

Archer joined her to stare at the eye-level readout on one of her monitors. "What've you got?"

"It appears," T'Pol began, "to be an aggregate structure, comprised of hundreds of vessels. They're held in place by an interlocking system of magnetic seals."

Archer stared at the structure, fascinated. Each hexagonal ship fit into the greater structure like one cell in a honeycomb . . . a honeycomb that could come flying apart into a swarm of hundreds of ships in an instant.

"There!" Hoshi yelped. "Right there!"

Biodata tumbled across the main screen over a small section of the Suliban aggregate.

"These bioreadings are not Suliban!" she added.

T'Pol looked at her. "We can't be certain they're Klingon," she warned.

"Even if it is Klaang," Archer accepted, "we'd have a tough time getting him off of there."

Reed turned in his chair and broached a touchy subject. "We could always try the transporting device. . . ."

"No," Archer quietly said. "We've risked too much to bring him back inside out. Would the grappler work in a liquid atmosphere?"

"I believe so . . ."

"Bring it on-line. One more time, Mr. Mayweather. Take us down to proximity range."

"Proximity range, sir."

Once again the ship descended into the smooth lower atmosphere, the clear layer that seemed so welcoming, yet held the primary threat.

"Make it aggressive," Archer said. "Don't hold back."

"Understood, sir," Mayweather agreed. "I won't."

The ship hummed with power, and soared like a giant albatross on an arctic crest.

"Suliban ships in patrol formation, sir," Reed instantly reported. "They've seen us!"

"Let's give them a closer look, Mr. Mayweather."

"Aye, sir!"

"Mr. Reed, open fire."

"Oh, thank you, sir, so much."

"Ready that grappling system."

"It shall indeed be ready, sir."

The ship took a compressive dive into the clear,

burst out, and trumpeted her presence in the sky. Rapid-blast torpedoes of compressed energy made a luminous announcement.

The artillery shells spoke out across the giant's sky-bound seas and scattered through the Suliban patrol. Were there hits? Archer couldn't tell. The Suliban returned fire, but also broke formation.

*Enterprise* absorbed a tremendous hit.

"The ventral plating's down!" Reed called over the noise. "I'm having trouble getting a weapons lock! These scanners weren't designed for a liquid atmosphere!" Again the ship was hit, driving him to comment, "Though apparently theirs were . . ."

A hard shake caused the console next to Hoshi to blow a plume of sparks. She shrieked and leapt back.

"Hold your position, Travis," Archer said calmly.

"The lead ship's closing," Reed reported. "Seven thousand meters . . . six thousand . . ."

"We should ascend!" T'Pol called.

"Hold your position!" Archer repeated. He didn't like repeating.

Reed glanced at him. "One thousand meters. Forward plating's off-line!"

"Now, Mr. Reed!"

One of the cell ships veered almost directly to the starship's bow. Reed struck his controls. Two grappling devices shot from ports on the launch bay arm, trailing thin cables that Archer could see partly on the forward screen.

The grapplers struck the Suliban ship and magnetically adhered to its hull. Archer gripped his chair, glad that metal was metal on any side of the galaxy.

"He's ejecting!" Hoshi called, and pointed.

A cockpit hatch sprang open on the Suliban cell. The pilot was gone in a blast of vapor and disappeared through the layer below.

To land where? Archer winced. No surface . . .

He hoped the Suliban had that covered, but there was no way to tell.

"Back up, Travis," he ordered.

"Rising, sir."

The ship moved back up toward the turbulent layers, now trailing its prey on a silken cord, drawing it closer and closer to the hangar bay.

Reed eyed his station and uttered, "Hello . . . their ship is in the launch bay, sir."

Archer nodded. Reed smiled. A new toy.

Fifteen minutes later, he and Mayweather and Tucker crowded around a table graphic in the situation room off the bridge. The table showed graphics of the cell ship, all different angles of the exterior, engine schematics, flight controls . . . they tried to study these while the starship trembled and shook around them, battling the turbulence, but she was built to do that, like ships immemorial before her.

"All right, what's this?" Mayweather was pointing at something.

"The pitch control," Tucker said. He sounded confident about that one.

"No," Mayweather argued. "*That's* the pitch control. This is the guidance system."

"Pitch control . . . guidance system . . . I got it."

"The docking interface," Mayweather went on. "How do you deploy it?"

Archer hunched over the graphics. "Looks like you release the inertial clamps here, here, and here, then initialize the coaxial ports."

"Good. Where's the auxiliary throttle?"

"Mmmm—" Tucker squinted. "It's not this one . . ."

Mayweather straightened up then. "With all due respect to Commander Tucker, I'm pretty sure I could fly this thing, sir."

"I don't doubt it," Archer agreed. "But I need you here."

"Captain?" T'Pol's voice thrummed under a low-frequency *boooom* that suddenly grew louder and erupted in a hard *bam*.

They turned.

"That charge contained a proximity sweep," she said from her post. "If we remain here, they're going to locate us."

Archer nodded and turned to Mayweather. "You're gonna have to speed this up a little, Travis."

"How complicated can it be?" Tucker howled. "Up, down, forward, reverse! We'll figure it out."

*Booooom! Boooooom!*

"Inverted depth charges, Captain!" T'Pol called.

She didn't have to report the damage. Archer could feel it. He stepped out to her, and she met him in the middle of the bridge. "We'll be back before you know it. Have Mayweather plot a course for Qo'noS."

"There's a Vulcan ship less than two days away," T'Pol offered. "It's illogical to attempt this alone."

"I was beginning to think you understood *why* we have to do this alone."

She paused. "You could both be killed."

He looked up, rather sharply. "Am I sensing concern? Last time I checked, that was considered an emotion."

For an instant—no more—he thought he sensed a flicker of emotion in her eyes, too swift for him to identify it as either anger or regret.

T'Pol's expression turned blank again. "If anything happens to either of you, the Vulcan High Council will hold me responsible."

Archer smiled at her, offering a little understanding. Then Reed approached with two silver equipment cases, and Archer's attention went there. "You're finished?"

Reed flipped the lid on one case to reveal a rectangular device. "It should reverse the polarity of any maglock within a hundred meters. Once you've set the sequence, you'll have five seconds."

Archer looked down at the device with appreciation.

"One more thing," Reed added. He flipped open the second case and pulled out two Starfleet-colored hand weapons with pistol grips and handed them both to Archer.

"Ah—our new weapons?"

"They're called 'phase pistols,'" Reed introduced. "They have two settings. Stun and kill. It would be best not to confuse them."

Another low *boom* shook the vessel under them, followed by a startling jolt that rocked them back to the moment.

To T'Pol he said, almost with delight, "The ship is yours! Trip, let's go!"

# Chapter 14

CRAMPED, TREMBLING, COLD, AND ADMITTEDLY OUT OF their element, Jonathan Archer and Trip Tucker hunkered elbow to elbow inside the little Suliban cell ship as it blew free of the *Enterprise* and shot out into the swirling atmospheric sea. Visibility was almost nil—just a wall of blue gas.

Tucker gripped the controls with passionate terror and forced himself to concentrate almost yard by yard as the ship raced forward, fighting its own power and the turbulence at the same time.

Archer flinched when a light came on. "What's that?"

"Travis said not to worry about that panel."

"That's reassuring . . ."

They were thrown against each other when the

cell hit an atmospheric pocket. Tucker held the steering mechanism with both hands and battled to compensate. He was dripping sweat despite the cold.

Queasy and bloodless, Archer fought to keep steady himself. "They sure didn't build these things for comfort."

"Wait till we get the Klingon in here with us. If I'm reading this right, we should be about twenty kilometers from *Enterprise*."

"Drop the pitch thirty degrees."

"Look! The *Enterprise!*"

For just an instant, the visibility cleared, just enough to show a portion of the starship above them taking a hard whack from a luminous weapon stream.

"They're taking a lot of bad fire," Archer mentioned. "I should've given her permission for evasive maneuvers. If they change position, the Suliban'll have to look for them all over again."

"If they move, *we* might never find them again," Tucker reminded. "She'll probably just ride it out."

Archer gazed at the vision of the ship just as it disappeared again in a curtain of blue muck. He saw T'Pol's face, determined to hold position and give them their best shot, and he silently apologized to her for his snotty remarks. "That's what I'm counting on."

Tucker shouldered into a maneuver, his lips

tight and his eyes squinting. "You've changed your tune about her. . . ."

"I think it's changing some," Archer agreed. "After a whole lifetime of watching Vulcans generalize about humans, seems I was doing the same thing about them. I just took it out on her." He found a sheepish little grin and bounced it off Tucker. "I think I'll stop now."

Tucker's expression was dubious, but accepting of the redesigned attitude. Even hopeful?

"Look at this," he said then, pointing at the adjusting screens. "I think we're there."

"Bring the docking interface on-line."

Tucker went for a button—then stopped. He chose a completely different button. The interface hummed to life. The cell ship rattled around them.

"Coaxial ports," Archer ordered.

Another control twanged. A quick, hissing sound blew some kind of ballast or docking mechanisms somewhere on the skin of the cell ship. Tucker embraced the steering mechanism and began to ease the ship downward. Through the ports, they could see blue phosphorous clouds begin to thin out. A moment later, they broke into clear space.

"Where is it?" Tucker gulped. "It was right there!"

Squinting through a sheet of sweat, Archer studied the graphic. "Bank starboard ninety degrees."

Tucker heaved the controller over. The ship banked sharply, taking their stomachs with it.

A dizzying view of the Suliban complex rose directly below them.

"There you are!" Tucker howled.

"That's the upper support radius," Archer said, proud that he could recognize anything in that mass. "Drop down right below it. Start a counter-clockwise sweep."

The cell ship descended further, down past numerous levels of the aggregate. Other cell ships, most larger, engaged and disengaged from the huge structure for reasons of their own. Tucker slowed their descent just in time. He was getting the hang of maneuvering this contraption. Archer didn't make any distracting comments, but did help judge distances.

"A little more . . . little more . . . almost there . . ."

*Scrrrape.*

Again they were thrown against each other. Archer shot him a look as they both got a touch of nostalgia about their inspection tour—how many days ago now?

"Right here," Archer said. "All stop."

The cell bonked to a halt. Through the port, they could see a circular airlock protruding from the Suliban complex. Tucker looked at him. Archer nodded. Why not?

They both began manipulating the controls.

The ship began moving horizontally now, through the airlock.

*Chhhh-UNK.*

Contact. The cell jolted slightly. A series of whirring mechanical sounds signaled that the docking ports were locking into place. They knew those sounds. Everybody who flew knew those sounds.

Abruptly, the hatch opened—on its own!

Archer flinched and put his hand on Tucker's arm. Before them was a long, dimly lit corridor, completely unoccupied. Their own private entrance.

Tucker looked at him. "Well?"

Archer pulled out his phase pistol. "Why not?"

With their weapons drawn, they moved quickly through the corridor. Tucker carried the silver case with the magnetic disruption device inside. Archer kept eyeing the sensor scanner he held in his other hand. They rounded a corner, and came face to face with a—a face!

Caught by surprise, the Suliban soldier clutched for his own sidearm, but Archer fired first.

The soldier dropped like a bag of sand.

For a moment, Archer and Tucker stood over him and looked at the weapon in Archer's hand. Nice little unit.

"Stun seems to work . . ." he commented.

And they kept moving.

**Enterprise**

"Anything?"

T'Pol's question provided mostly irritation to the crew around her.

Lieutenant Reed had nothing to report, but simply gripped his console as they rode out the nasty bit of weather and artillery fire. Beside him, Hoshi Sato had her earpiece tightly wedged in.

"The phosphorous is distorting all the EM bands," she said dubiously—then she yanked her earpiece out and called, "Grab onto something!"

Two rapid *booms* throbbed through the skin of the ship, followed immediately by two sharp jolts powerful enough to send the whole ship on a dive. Reed flinched as the console before him blew out, lathering his face with sparks. Streams of gas and showers of debris doused the bridge.

Reed pulled himself back to the console as the sparking reduced itself automatically. Was anyone hurt? He glanced around—no, Mayweather seemed all right. So did Hoshi, though shaken. T'Pol still held the command chair, and gave no orders to break off their course or altitude.

"This is ridiculous!" Reed complained. "If we don't move the ship, Captain Archer won't have anything to look for when he gets back!"

T'Pol had a stubborn streak, but she wasn't foolish. After a moment of consideration, she turned to Hoshi. "We're going to need that ear of yours."

Hoshi pulled herself back to her position and pressed the listening device to her ear again.

"Mr. Mayweather," T'Pol addressed, "move us away, five kilometers."

"In what direction?"

"Any direction."

The ship trembled with effort, and began to rise. Malcolm Reed held his breath, knew this was his suggestion, and although he also knew everyone else was thinking the same thing, he began now a whole new worry.

With Trip at his side, Archer moved as silently as possible through the eerily blue-lit, narrow Suliban corridors. Attuned to Klingon biosigns, the sensor in his left hand served as guide, while the phase pistol in his right served as reassurance.

At last, the two men stood before the closed door, beyond which Klaang most certainly rested.

Archer went through the door first, with Tucker right behind him, weapons drawn. And there was their big buddy, restrained in an elaborate chair-like thing, with tubes and devices attached to his body. He was alive, but semiconscious. Through a window, steel-blue light flowed from the phosphorous layer, lending a weird cast to the Klingon's skin, and Archer's and Tucker's, too.

Archer gestured. Tucker immediately went to

the Klingon and started unstrapping him. The Klingon stared, but didn't fight or make any noise.

"This is gonna be easier than I thought," Tucker said winningly. "It's okay," he added to Klaang. "We're getting you off this thing."

The third and final restraint slapped to the floor. Klaang, now free, suddenly erupted. He raised his arm, clubbed Tucker in the chest, and very easily blew the engineer across the room. Tucker landed in a heap, shocked. Klaang stood to his full height and ripped the tubes and wires from his limbs.

Locking his stance, Archer raised his weapon—the interstellar common language.

"I really don't want to have to carry you out of here," he warned.

Klaang grew much more passive in the face of the unfriendly weapon. He wisely hesitated.

"I think he gets the idea," Archer said. "Give him a hand."

Tucker hesitated, too, not wanting to get close to the enormity again, but he steeled himself and gave Klaang a supporting hand as they followed Archer out the door.

Bearing the weight of the huge Klingon, Tucker rapidly became a gasping lump following Archer through the corridor.

"*Qu'taw boh!*" the Klingon roared, half dazed.

"Be quiet," Archer snapped.

"*Muh tok!*"

A blast tore a chunk out of the wall. Suliban soldiers!

Archer dove to the left, Tucker and Klaang to the right, for cover.

*"Dajvo Tagh! Borat!"*

"You tell him, big guy." Tucker hid behind the Klingon—or was he pinned back there?

"Give me the box," Archer called.

Trip slid the silver case's strap off his shoulder and handed it to him. Just then, a Suliban attacker rushed into view from an adjoining corridor and caught them by surprise. As the Suliban took aim at Archer and Tucker, the Klingon suddenly rose like a grizzly bear.

The Suliban was caught under its chin and went flying into a bulkhead. Klaang followed him, caught him, and joyously pounded him unconscious.

A moment later he simply turned and came back to Archer and Tucker, rumbling with satisfaction.

"Thanks," Tucker said—more of that interstellar language.

But their moment of unity was ruined by another Suliban, and another after him, and more weapons blasting at them.

"Get to the ship!" Archer ordered. "I'll be right behind you!"

Tucker shot him a horrified look, but he had agreed not to argue. Getting the Klingon off was the important thing. Tucker grabbed the mountainous stranger and hauled him down the corridor.

Archer crouched, alone now, with the silver case. He removed the rectangular device and attached it with its own magnetics to the nearest wall, then activated it with the encoded authorization.

Then he dropped to his knees and covered his head, and hoped to live.

# Chapter 15

A LOW-PITCHED WHINE DEAFENED ARCHER AS HE HUD-
dled too near the magnetic damper. Only two seconds passed before the device emitted a blinding
pulse of energy that radiated in all directions.

Archer was blown over onto his side. As the
light receded, he struggled to his feet and found
all his arms and legs still with him. The corridor
was trembling, shuddering! Thousands of magnetic docking ports unlocking—

The floor began to separate under his feet—the
entire corridor was splitting in two! Force fields
flashed on as the interlocking elements making
up this section of the aggregate lost their cohe-
sion. He was cut off.

He had no choice but to turn and run in the
other direction, and hope Tucker and Klaang got
through.

The entire upper section of the Suliban aggregate was dismantling over Archer's head. He imagined the huge sections, comprised of dozens of cell ships, disengaging from the central mass, tumbling away into the blue atmosphere, powerless and pilotless.

"Captain? Captain!" Tucker's voice called at him under the *boom* and *clack* of disengagement.

Archer found a corner to duck behind and clawed for his communicator. "It worked," he said without formality.

"Where are you?"

"I'm still in the central core. Get Klaang back to *Enterprise*."

"What about you, sir?"

"Get him back to the ship! You can come back for me."

Lies, all lies.

"It's going to be hard to isolate your biosigns," Tucker protested. "So stay as far away from the Suliban as you can."

Archer breathed a gush of relief that Tucker intended to follow the very hard order to leave someone behind. Nobody liked that one. Nobody ever wanted to do it the first time out.

"Believe me," he vowed, "I'll try."

Inside the Suliban cell ship, Trip Tucker gritted his teeth against leaving John Archer on that floating junkheap. Beside him, crammed in like a sausage in its skin, the Klingon spat and coughed protests about the accommodations.

"*RaQpo jadICH!*"

"I don't particularly like the way you smell, either," Tucker opined.

"*MajQa!*"

Tucker ignored the comment and kept sweeping for the *Enterprise*.

"I don't get it . . . this is right where they're supposed to be."

He adjusted his scanners, hoping the alien contraption was just plain wrong.

It wasn't. There was no one out there. Nothing.

"The charges are getting closer again."

Malcolm Reed tugged at the collar of his uniform tunic as the fifth low-frequency *boom* in as many seconds rolled over the starship.

"Another five kilometers, Ensign," T'Pol ordered.

Mayweather worked the controls on the helm. "At this rate, the captain'll never find us."

"Wait a minute!" Hoshi interrupted. "I think I've got something!"

"Amplify it!" T'Pol ordered with endearing passion.

Hoshi tapped her controls. A cacophony of noises, radio signals, background noise, and distortion blasted through the bridge.

"It's Commander Tucker!"

How had she deciphered that from these crackles?

"All I hear is noise," Reed pointed out.

"Sshhh! Listen . . . it's just a narrow notch in the midrange . . . he says he's about to ignite his thruster exhaust!"

T'Pol moved quickly to her viewing hood and peered inside. "Coordinates—one fifty-eight mark . . . one three."

"Laid in!" Mayweather confirmed.

"Ahead, fifty kph." She turned to Hoshi, and for the first time regarded the other woman with respect. "*Shaya tonat.*"

Hoshi offered a small smile. "You're welcome."

They all watched the sensors, though they could see very little on any screen that wasn't the shifting of atmospheric chaos.

"Two kilometers, dead ahead," Mayweather said, carefully maneuvering the ship to avoid a deadly collision—deadly for the Suliban pod that held their shipmates.

"Initiate docking procedures." T'Pol authorized.

Hoshi turned to them, her face gray. "I'm only picking up two biosigns . . . one Klingon . . . one human."

Somehow, a hunted animal knows, senses, that it's being hunted. Jonathan Archer felt like a rabbit in a fox's den. He clung to the help of his little scanning device, which showed two Suliban moving away from a central indicator. They'd lost him.

But he was far from out of trouble. He squatted behind a metal beam more than eight feet off the deck. When he was sure he could jump down safely, without being heard, he did.

He landed near a wall and steadied himself for a few seconds, and used those seconds to tap the scanner and give himself a wider view of the vicinity. Other blips showed still more Suliban, but there was a large area to one side with no life-signs at all.

Sanctuary. If he could get there, he might be able to hide for . . . long enough.

He made sure he wasn't going to collapse on that leg and hurried down the corridor.

When he found the pass to the empty area, the narrow passage looked completely different from anything he'd seen here before. It ended at a single door. Archer hesitated. Was he being herded? Funneled? He got that feeling. This area was too empty. Had he been lured here with a sense of safety?

Suddenly he felt vulnerable and somewhat foolish. On the other hand, he had nowhere else to go. Maybe there were still answers to be found here. He owed himself those answers, and he was beginning to realize that he owed them to T'Pol, to Admiral Forrest, and even to Soval and the Vulcans. He owed them a good, solid representation that humans and Vulcans *could* work together—yes, they could.

*We can.*

His vulnerability went away. If there was someone here who knew what was going on, Archer very much wanted a confrontation. As he closed in on the single door, his fears for himself dissolved. Escape went away as his primary objective.

The scanner's information was now heavily distorted. Why would it be?

As he approached the door, it opened for him. That alone confirmed his suspicion that someone was inviting him here.

He cautiously stepped through, expecting for a moment to be assaulted, but that didn't make sense. He could easily have been a sitting duck in the closed corridor.

Inside was some kind of vestibule—a passage without an exit.

He raised his arm—it stayed up after he put it down. . . . Lights distorted his vision . . . time began to slow . . . to slow . . .

Was he underwater? His movements slowed further. Time effect!

This was some kind of temporal alteration chamber. And Archer had walked right into it. His arms and legs blurred as he moved. Gradually, deliberately, he learned to make forward progress, to ignore the echoes he saw, movement echoes that unnerved him and confused his eyes. He moved his arms, and a second set made the same movement seconds later—or seconds before?

He looked down. The sound of his footsteps preceded the actual steps. He stopped walking. Soon he had only two feet again. When he had a little control—although his heartbeat had other ideas—he clapped his hands.

The sound came before his hands met.

Now what?

Definitely time distortion, contained somehow. Could he trust his own thoughts?

Moving with great deliberation, he began to explore the room, the alien architecture, the technology on undecipherable panels. After all, someone wanted him to see all this. He would oblige them.

A podium rose before him. As it did, as he was able to focus on it, the temporal distortions began to fade. Had someone been giving him a taste of what they could do, and now they were finished showing off? Had it been a test? A mistake?

There was the podium, clear now before him, and a large weird-looking archway—metallic, huge, obviously purposeful in design and whatever its function was. Certainly not just interior decor.

He drew his pistol and turned sharply when a reverberation rang through the chamber—the door was opening. Beyond it, the dark vestibule appeared empty. The door closed and sealed again, as if a ghost had entered . . . or left.

Archer backed away, silent, listening. His senses chimed with intuition.

"You're wasting your time. Klaang knows nothing."

A voice! Real words. What a relief—more or less.

The sound of footsteps in the preecho chamber rumbled with strange sounds and repeats. Archer tried to track the sound with his pistol, ready to shoot. The voice preechoed, too. He heard two, three, four of each word.

"It would be unwise to discharge that weapon in this room," the voice said.

"What is this room?" Archer asked. "What goes on here?"

"You're very curious, Jonathan. May I call you Jonathan?"

"Am I supposed to be impressed that you know my name?" he asked reasonably.

"I've learned a great deal about you. Even more than you know."

"Well, I guess you have me at a disadvantage," Archer said, leading this person on. He knew by now that whoever was talking desperately wanted to tell him many things, or he/it wouldn't be talking at all. "So why don't you drop the invisible man routine and let me see who I'm talking to?"

*Because you know you're going to show me eventually.*

"You wouldn't have come looking for Klaang," the voice said, "if Sarin had told you what she knew. That means you're no threat to me, Jonathan. But I do need you to leave this room."

The time-door hissed again, and opened invitingly.

"Now, please."

The footsteps echoed again, but this time Archer saw something, a slight distortion against the far wall.

Instead of leaving, he fired his phase pistol. A blurred preshot flowed in before the blast itself, and the sound had no attachment to what he saw. The beam struck the far wall. A jagged wave of energy blew from the point of impact and swept the room. Archer was blown back, slamming his head against a wall. Pain drummed in his skull— he held his head and waited for the wave to pass. It passed four times.

"I warned you not to fire the weapon," the voice said.

Again the distortion moved across the room.

Archer gasped, tried to steady his breathing, then spoke. "This chameleon thing . . . pretty fancy. Was it payment for pitting the Klingons against each other? A trophy from your temporal cold war?"

An embittered action blew across the room, ultrafast, and slammed Archer again against the wall. But this was different from the weapon shot. This one had pure anger in it. He'd made the intruder angry.

His pistol! His hand was empty! He grabbed around, but the weapon was gone.

Before him was a Suliban, now normalized against the background, its dappled face and skull still looking vaguely unreal. It held his pistol on him. As he stood with his eyes locked on those alien eyes, he recognized this as the leader of the attackers back at the spaceport on Rigel Ten. Not exactly a big surprise, and in a way, its own kind of win. Now he knew who he was up against, if not why.

"I was going to let you go," the Suliban said.

"Really?" Archer backed away slowly, trying to remember the timing of those echoes. "Then you obviously don't know as much about me as you thought you did."

"On the contrary," the Suliban said, "I could've told you the day you were going to die. But I suppose that's about to change."

The Suliban opened fire on him with his own phase pistol.

The preecho struck Archer in the chest and drove him back. He brought up every muscle he could control and darted sideways before the actual bolt could strike him. Instead, it missed by an inch and burrowed into the wall. Archer spun behind a bank of alien consoles as the shock wave swept the room, knocking the Suliban down completely.

Archer was ready for that shock and braced against it. "What's the matter?" he chided. "No genetic tricks to keep you from getting knocked on your butt?"

"What you call tricks, we call progress!" the Suliban declared. "Are you aware that your genome is almost identical to that of an ape? The Suliban don't share humanity's patience with natural selection!"

"So, to speed things up a little, you struck a deal with the devil."

Archer was careful to hide. Assault might work against him. The Suliban's confusion in this echo chamber could be a weapon in itself, for, as advanced as the Suliban thought he was, Archer was able to adjust to this place. He was getting used to it. As he spoke, he positioned himself between the Suliban leader and the open time-lock. Moving behind the consoles, he slowly removed the communicator from his belt. Carefully, he calculated the next trajectory of the temporal wave, then threw the communicator against a monitor on the far wall.

The monitor sparked. The preecho effect made a dozen communicators sail through the air, drawing the Suliban's attention. The Suliban, disoriented, aimed clumsily and fired at the sparking monitor.

The shock wave thundered outward from the strike zone. The Suliban tried to brace himself against it this time, and managed to stay on his feet. But Archer had situated himself in the perfect spot to be thrown into the open time-lock vestibule.

He tumbled like a snowball through the door. The door began to close.

At the last moment, the intelligent and obviously strong-willed Suliban plunged toward the door and slipped through. The temporal compression began as the door locked and sealed itself.

Archer was locked in this small place, a place where time was in convulsions, with a Suliban whose plans he had wrecked. Each of them battled to be the first to gain control of his body.

The Suliban was raising the weapon again. . . .

Summoning every ounce of muscle control and sheer will, Archer shoved himself off the wall behind him and smashed into the Suliban in this eerie slow-motion chamber. The pistol jarred against his shoulder, dislodged from the Suliban's hand, and tumbled toward the floor. It struck the deck just as time returned to something like normal, and the fight was on.

Archer realized quickly he was no match for combat with an enhanced alien. He had to get the pistol!

Twisting viciously, he managed to pin the Suliban to the floor and lean on his opponent's wrists. It seemed to work, until the Suliban dislocated his own shoulder and wrist in a grotesque rotation and found a way to reach for the pistol, and got it. Archer acted on instinct: he balled up his fist, focused all his strength there, and swung squarely at the center of the Suliban's face.

He half expected the alien to metamorphose, to melt away, but the right cross connected with a solid *thunk*. The Suliban writhed and went momentarily limp. Archer shoved off him and bolted to the door.

The Suliban had the weapon.

Archer ran for his life. He hadn't intended for ass-n-elbows to be his plan, or the great final moments he ever had in mind for himself, but there was method in his madness—if he could keep the stubborn Suliban chasing him, then the *Enterprise* would have a chance to get away. A few minutes here, a few there . . . if Trip Tucker or Reed were in command, this would never work. He had left T'Pol in charge.

A Vulcan—the bane of his life—was going to make sure his plan was fulfilled. T'Pol would stick to her line of demarcation and do the logical thing. She would know there was no way for him to be found in this maze, no way for them to infiltrate, to risk a half dozen lives on a rescue mission into the guts of this aggregate, which was breaking up. She would make all the right arguments, shout Trip down, over-British Reed, deal with Hoshi's shrieks of protest, and she would finally seize the command Archer himself had confirmed. She would take the ship out of this mess, and Klaang, and she would succeed.

*Not a bad legacy, Dad, for you or for me*.

So he ran harder, taking the ache in his leg as validation of his personal honor. Behind him, the Suliban was coming out of the time-lock, aiming, firing—

# Chapter 16

"OUR MISSION IS TO RETURN THE KLINGON TO HIS home-world. Another rescue attempt could jeopardize that mission—"

"The captain specifically told us to come back for him!"

"As commanding officer, it's *my* job to interpret the captain's orders."

Trip Tucker's anger flushed right up into his face and out the top of his head. "I just told you his orders! What's there to 'interpret'!"

Everyone on the bridge watched tensely as Tucker confronted T'Pol with his report and watched it pulled apart, brick by brick, and the captain with it.

T'Pol contained herself with damnable reserve. "Captain Archer may very well have told you to return for him later because he knew how stubborn you can **be**."

"What's that supposed to mean?"

"You might've risked Klaang's life in a foolish attempt to swing back and rescue the captain."

Tucker grimaced. "I can't believe this!"

A jolt from outside rocked the ship and punctuated his fury as the tension rose for them all. Reed was standing behind him, but said nothing. Hoshi looked positively destroyed at T'Pol's refusal. Mayweather's hands on the helm were stiff and flushed.

"The situation must be analyzed logically," T'Pol said, but this time it sounded like she was trying to convince herself as much as them.

"I don't remember the captain analyzing anything when he went back for you on that roof!" Tucker roared.

"That's a specious analogy."

"Is it?"

"We have work to do. We must stabilize our flight condition before we can move out of the atmosphere. Take your posts, please. That was not a request."

Well, she might not be Starfleet, but she had the style down. Everyone responded, though with a bitter silence. Tucker ground his teeth and went to the engineering master control station. What could he do? Was there a way to neutralize her command status?

"Hull plating's been repolarized," Reed reported. His voice was hardly more than a rasp. Behind it was the question in everyone's mind. *Leave the captain? Would he leave us?*

"Stand by the impulse engines. Mr. Tucker, status?"

Tucker felt a vicious tone rise from his throat. He thought about lying, stalling. But, ultimately, he couldn't do it. "The autosequencer's on-line, but annular confinement's still off by two microns."

"That should suffice," T'Pol said.

"Easy for you to say."

"If the Suliban have reestablished their defense, we'll have no other option."

The ship roared through the gas giant's atmosphere directly below the roiling blue layer. Several cell ships appeared on the scanners and began an attack pattern, strafing the underside of the huge dove-gray vessel. Reed, still under his fire-at-will order, took out his frustration with T'Pol on the incoming assault vessels.

"We have four more coming up off starboard!" he called.

T'Pol paused. "Can we dock, Ensign?"

Mayweather blinked. "These aren't ideal conditions—"

"Mr. Tucker, we're going to plan B."

Tucker swung around. What had changed her mind? Why would a person who claimed to be ruled by logic suddenly whip around to a completely crazy plan of action?

Who cared!

"I'm on my way!" he declared, and rushed off the bridge.

It was crazy, and he embraced it with everything he had. In less than two minutes he was in the newly installed transport-materializing chamber, summoning power from deep in the bowels of the ship's impulse drive system. Yes, crazy—he might find himself standing over the shredded, gurgling remains—

No, don't think that way. The control station fell under his trembling hands. Just work the controls . . . make the numbers line up . . . focus the beams . . .

"I'll do it," he murmured. "I'll do it, I can do it—"

He only had seconds. He felt the presence of T'Pol and Reed and all the others, even though they were decks away from him. This was it. T'Pol would never give him another chance. There was no plan C.

The chamber began to whine a god-awful noise. He focused and focused, adjusted and hoped. If only Porthos were here, he could cross his paws.

A column of light appeared inside the chamber, between the two pie plates on floor and ceiling that would act as a receiver. Human readings . . . he was sure those were human readings. There was only one human on that big Suliban knot out there!

A humanoid shape appeared, forming between

the lights. But the Suliban were humanoid. Tucker held his breath.

There was nothing more he could do with the controls. They would either do what they were designed to do, or there would be a disaster here.

The captain's build—the captain's hair and hands—a crouched position. Running?

Long seconds finally pulled Jonathan Archer together out of a puzzle of lights and whines. He stumbled forward on sheer momentum, then skidded and stopped himself, and looked around in shock at his new surroundings. He wavered, disoriented, then patted himself to see if he was all there.

"Bridge!" Trip called. "We've got him!" He rushed to the pad platform and reached for Archer. "Sorry, Captain! We had no other choice!"

He finally caught hold of Archer's arm, and was relieved to feel normal skin and muscle and bone beneath a normal-looking uniform. He scanned his friend's face: eyes, nose, mouth . . . everything seemed to be there, in the right place.

Archer stumbled down with Tucker's help.

"Are you hurt? Are you all here?"

"Well, I think so, most of me, anyway." Archer offered him a tremulous smile and a grip on the arm to prove to them both that they were together again.

"T'Pol wanted to leave you behind!"

Archer steadied himself with a hand on Tucker's shoulder. "She *wanted* to. Notice she didn't act on what she wanted. She acted on what she *could* do." He drew a breath of life and actually laughed. "Trip, old man, I believe I can work with that!"

# Chapter 17

*The Planet Qo'noS*

THE GNARLED TOWERS OF THE KLINGON HIGH COUN-
cil chamber rose above a smoggy yellow haze in
the capital city. Inside the chambers, an ancient
room of stone and wooden beams was hung with
ceremonial banners and echoes of conquests
stemming back through the pages of alien time.
Guards stood everywhere, more for show than
function, dressed in regalia and armed with ar-
chaic weapons. The Council members, seated at a
serpentine table, pounded and shouted in their
idea of debate.

There was great strife here today.

Jonathan Archer presented a calm demeanor,
hoping his colleagues would take his cue in this

shockingly alien environment. Alien, yes, but there was something hauntingly medieval about this place and these people, not really so far out of the human realm of imagination. Perhaps that was the disturbing part—the fact that they could empathize with being Klingon.

In a noble queue, Archer, T'Pol, and Hoshi moved into the enormous chamber, led by Klaang, who was so calm now as to be arguably majestic. Klaang was clearly working at both strength and dignity, despite what he had suffered physically.

He stopped before the Chancellor. *"Wo'migh Qagh! Q'apla!"*

Hoshi leaned toward Archer and whispered, "Something about disgracing the Empire . . . he says he's ready to die."

Archer murmured, "That's all we get out of this?"

The Chancellor was on his feet now, glaring in open curiosity at the humans. The wide-shouldered leader walked down the great stone steps, and as he did this, he drew a jagged dagger from its sheath.

Klaang tensed but never flinched as the Chancellor stopped in front of him.

Archer tensed also. If this thing were carried out, he would be helpless to stop it. At least he would show them that humans weren't squeamish and would stand up beside Klaang to the

last. They hadn't brought him here just to be arbi-
trarily killed. The Chancellor would be forced to
think about what he was doing, rather than just
act by rote.

The Chancellor snatched Klaang's wrist and
drew the blade across the palm, drawing blood.
Archer winced and put his hand out slightly to his
side to keep Hoshi steady. T'Pol remained unfazed.

*"Poq!"* the Chancellor called.

An aide approached with a vial, held it up, and
caught several drops of Klaang's blood, while
Klaang stood there, completely dumbfounded by
all this.

The aide hurried to a large apparatus that remained undefined until he opened it and inserted
the vial into a sensor padd. A large screen came to
life suddenly, displaying a highly magnified cluster of lavender blood cells.

The Council members grumbled with sounds
that might have been approval.

The image continued to enlarge, and became
spirals of DNA. The spirals became larger and
larger, until a distinctive pattern showed itself
even to the untrained eye. The aide kept working
the controls until individual molecules rose before the audience.

Hoshi drew a breath to speak, but Archer motioned her silent.

The molecular pattern began to rotate, revealing . . . what were those? Maps!

Maps, and text! Alien script written on a molecular level!

"Phlox should see this," Archer murmured. "He'd have a kitten."

Text, schedules, coordinates . . .

The entire chamber erupted in a rumble of approval. Then the Chancellor, purple-faced with excitement, stalked over to Archer.

He lifted the dagger to Archer's throat. Archer remained steady, but it took some doing.

*"ChugDah hegh . . . volcha vay."*

Just like that, the Chancellor lowered the weapon and stalked away.

Archer let himself breathe again. "I'll take that as a thank you. . . ."

Beside him, Hoshi offered, "I don't think they have a word for thank you."

"Then what'd he say?"

"You don't want to know."

The Klingon chamber began to shuffle with activity as the meeting broke up and the Council adored its DNA treasure. Now they could move on with whatever internal conflicts they had with their neighbors, the Suliban, or they could use the contraband information to get the Suliban to leave them alone. At least they knew now that their internal structure was being tampered with. They wouldn't turn against each other now. At least, not for a while.

Archer was willing to wait it out. Able to

breathe normally for the first time in days, he turned and motioned his crew toward the door. "Ladies? Allow me to escort you to a much better place. We've done all we can here. Anybody got a silver bullet?"

# Chapter 18

Jonathan Archer stood up as the door chime on his ready room jingled. "Come in."

T'Pol and Tucker came in, oddly side by side and not even spitting. What had gone on here while he was incommunicado?

"I've just gotten a response to the message I sent to Admiral Forrest," he told them. "He enjoyed telling the Vulcan High Command about the Suliban we ran into. It's not every day *he* gets to be the one dispensing information."

T'Pol looked quizzical, but she got the inference. Archer grinned and decided he owed Forrest an apology. The admiral had proven more canny than Archer had given him credit for. They now had a formally logged record of humans and Vulcans working together under duress, with two completely different methods of command—and doing all right together. Starfleet could do worse. It gave them all a platform from which to spring.

"I wanted you both to hear Starfleet's new orders before I inform the crew."

"Orders?" Tucker asked.

Archer nodded and looked at T'Pol. "Your people are sending a transport to pick you up."

She seemed hesitant, but buried it. "I was under the impression that *Enterprise* would be taking me back to Earth."

"It would be a little out of our way. Admiral Forrest sees no reason why we shouldn't keep going."

Tucker went up on his toes. "Son of a bitch!"

Archer smiled and agreed, "I have a feeling Dr. Phlox won't mind staying around for a while. He's developing a fondness for the human endocrine system."

"I'll get double watches on the repair work!"

"I think the outer hull's going to need a little patching up," Archer said. "Let's hope that's the last time somebody takes a shot at us."

"Let's hope!"

Oh, well, famous last words. *We'll see*.

Tucker, now very happy, spun on a heel and headed for the door. T'Pol started to follow him, but Archer stopped her.

"Would you stick around for a minute?" he asked.

She glanced at Tucker as the door shut between them, but turned again to the captain.

"Ever since I can remember," he began, "I've seen Vulcans as an obstacle, always keeping us from standing on our own two feet."

"I understand," she said quietly.

"No, I don't think you do. If I'm going to pull this off, there are a few things I have to leave behind. Things like preconceptions . . . holding grudges . . ." He paused, and tilted his head to soften his meaning. "This mission would've failed without your help."

"I won't dispute that," she said.

A retort popped up behind Archer's tongue, but he bit it off. Maybe she was joking. "I was thinking a Vulcan science officer could come in handy . . . but if I ask you to stay, it might look like I wasn't ready to do this on my own."

She raised her chin in that way she had. "Perhaps you should add pride to your list."

"Perhaps I should."

She considered his honesty, then said, "It might be best if I were to contact my superiors and make the request myself. With your permission," she added decorously.

Finally they understood each other. It felt good to be on the same page.

Archer smiled again. "Permission granted."

They stood together in companionable unity

for a few moments as the ship streaked along at its new high-warp cruising speed.

"Will you join me on the bridge, Sub-Commander?" he asked, and gestured toward the door. "We have some good news for the crew, don't we?"

"Captain," she said with a lilt, "I will be honored to assist."

The other crew members were at their stations as he and T'Pol came out of the ready room. They might have suspected something was going on, but they seemed to be assuming the worst. Reed was straight as a stick. Mayweather was leaning forward on his helm controls, almost sagging. Hoshi's eyebrows were both up in anticipation. Tucker's absence bothered Archer a little, but he knew the engineer was larking about belowdecks, doing what he liked to do.

Archer came to a place on the bridge where he could see them all, and they could all see him. T'Pol politely moved a little off to one side and let him have the stage.

"I hope nobody's in a big hurry to get home," he began. "Starfleet seems to think we're ready to begin our mission. Mr. Reed, I understand there is an inhabited planet a few light-years from here?"

"We've detected it, sir," Reed confirmed, exhilaration in his tone. "Sensors show a nitrogen-sulfide atmosphere."

"Probably not humanoids," Hoshi clarified.

"That's what we're here to find out," Archer reminded. "Travis, prepare to break orbit and lay in a course."

Mayweather looked up at him, beaming. "I'm reading an ion storm on that trajectory, sir . . . should I go around it?"

Archer smiled at him, at all of them, and turned to look at the swirl of open space, all the oxtails and elephant trunks, nebulae and anomalies out there to be gone through, and he brushed his toe on the deck of the ship that would take them there.

"We can't be afraid of the wind, Ensign," he said. "Take us to warp four."

# BEHIND THE SCENES OF *ENTERPRISE*

## Paul Ruditis

# Concept

*"Take her out . . . straight and steady."*

"SOMEBODY ONCE SAID THAT THE TWO THINGS THAT first started the Internet," explains Rick Berman, co-creator and executive producer of *Enterprise*, "were pornography and *Star Trek*."

Rick Berman isn't making a joke.

After working for two and a half years developing the idea for the fifth television installment of the entertainment monolith known as *Star Trek*, he has heard any number of rumors detailing exactly what the series is going to be. From a Starfleet Academy show, to a series about a futuristic special-missions force, to a look at the future from the Klingon point of view, all sorts of ideas have been bandied about the Internet detailing what the fans *know* the production team is working on.

"Fans discussing the past, present, and future of *Star Trek* is something that has gone on forever," Berman admits. "We are conscious of it. We are respectful of it. We have people who are in touch with it and who keep us abreast of what the feelings of the fans are. But we have to eventually do what we think is best. That's not to say that some of the things that we hear don't influence us to some degree, but we can't let the fans create the show."

No matter what the rumors flying around fandom were, they all seemed to share a basic feeling of which Berman already was well aware.

It was time for a change.

Rick Berman began working on the basic framework of the fifth series long before the *U.S.S. Voyager* made its way home. "About two and a half years ago, the studio came to me and said they were interested in having me create a new series either to overlap with the last half-year of [*Star Trek:*] *Voyager* or to start after *Voyager* ended. I knew that I was not interested in just doing another twenty-fourth-century series. I felt that after [*Star Trek:*] *The Next Generation* and [*Star Trek:*] *Deep Space Nine* and *Voyager*, to just slap another seven characters into a new ship and send it out in the same time period with the same technology and the same attitudes—for me, for the writers, and I think also for the fans, we had done enough.

"My interest in developing another *Star Trek* series was really contingent upon doing something dramatically different. To me, the most logical thing to do was to take the show back a couple of centuries. We had done a wonderful movie in *Star Trek: First Contact*. In the movie we met Zefram Cochrane in the twenty-first century and we saw Earth in a very distraught state. We knew when we made contact with the Vulcans and we had our first warp flight. We also knew that two hundred years later would be Kirk and Spock and *Star Trek*. But what happened during those two hundred years? What happened between those years of despair and renewal and the era of near perfection that existed when the original *Star Trek* series began? So came the thought of placing a show somewhere in between."

With the time period chosen, a whole new vista for storytelling emerged—one that would allow for ideas that Berman and his team had not been able to explore with the more recent incarnations of *Star Trek*. "I felt that with *Deep Space Nine* and *Voyager* we had captains and crews who were not filled with the charm and fun of doing what they wanted to do. They were, in fact, people who were in uncomfortable positions in places where they really didn't want to be. Benjamin Sisko was not crazy about being on Deep Space 9. He was a recent widower who was filled with despair, which he got rid of to a large degree, but this was not a man who was an adventurer in the sense of where the series took him. Kathryn Janeway also was a rather severe character who felt responsible for having nearly two hundred people lost in space for seven years.

"I felt it was really important that we got back to the basics and we got back to where we had a crew that were doing exactly what they wanted to do—who were explorers, who had a captain who was an adventurer and who was lighthearted. A little bit of Captain Kirk and a little bit of Chuck Yeager. And to have a group going off where no man has gone before. And also a group that—because they were more accessible, because they were more contemporary—we could relate to in a lot of ways. If you or I were on a spaceship and suddenly we came upon an inhabited planet, it would scare the shit out of us. I'm not saying we wouldn't be excited. I'm not saying we wouldn't be filled with awe and amazement. But we'd also be terrified, we'd be nervous. We'd have a whole lot of feelings that people like Jean-Luc Picard never had because this was day-to-day work for him. He took a lot of this stuff for granted. This was all fodder for the creation of what I thought was going to be a wonderful new direction to take the series.

"To see the first humans to truly go out where

no one has gone before—this seemed very exciting to me. It seemed exciting to me for the reasons I've just said, but also because it would let the fans see all the things that they had come to know as part of *Star Trek* in their infancy. To see them being developed. To see them not working all that right. Which would mean a lot of fun. It would also make our characters seem closer to the present, which would enable them to be a little bit more contemporary, a little bit more human, a little bit more fun."

With the time period chosen and the basic outline formed, Berman took the idea to Paramount, hoping for the green light that would allow him to start assembling his team. "The studio was a little resistant at first," he admits. "There was a question of 'Why not go further into the future?' But we have found that further into the future tends to mean suits that are a little bit tighter and consoles that are a little bit sleeker. And basically, we'd done that. We've done many episodes where we've had to sneak into the future a little bit. It doesn't bring us that much. By going back, it brought us a great deal. Eventually, when the studio embraced the idea, and Brannon was brought into the process, we began developing the characters and eventually the story and the script."

Brannon Braga, co-creator and executive producer, recalls the morning Berman called him from his cell phone while heading to the studio and asked him to help develop the new show. At the time, Braga was co-executive producer on *Voyager*, and he found the concept of going back to the beginning an exciting proposition. Together, the pair started laying out the universe of the twenty-second century.

"What I can tell you is there's no Federation," Braga explains. "Starfleet is very young. It's only been around for a decade or more. There are some vessels flying around, some low-warp ships like cargo vessels. We've got a colony on the moon. We've got a space station around Mars. We've been exploring, but in a very limited way, because we just didn't have the warp capacity to go very far. We've met some other aliens, courtesy of the Vulcans, but we've never bolted out on our own. We've always been under the Vulcans' close watch. We haven't gone that far. So we're itching to go.

"In terms of how close this Earth is to Roddenberry's vision, I think it falls somewhere between now and Kirk's time. Not everything is perfect. I think humanity has gotten its act together to a large degree. I think that war and disease and poverty are pretty much wiped out. But what's important is that the people aren't quite there yet. I don't think these people have fully evolved into the Captain Picards and Rikers."

The direction of the new series was a dramatic departure from previous series, and the producers knew that the difference had to be reflected in the show's name. The question became how to keep it linked to the proud *Star Trek* history while at the same time making it unique. "Since *The Next Generation*, we've had so many *Star Trek* entities that were called *Star Trek* 'colon' something." Berman rattles off the list: *"Star Trek: The Next Generation, Star Trek: Deep Space Nine, Star Trek: Voyager, Star Trek Generations, Star Trek: First Contact, Star Trek: Insurrection*—just one after another. Our feeling was to try and make this show dramatically different—which we are trying to do—and that it might be fun not to have a divided title like that. I think if there's any one word that says *Star Trek* without actually saying *Star Trek* it's the word *Enterprise*." And with that, the title was born.

With a concept, theme, and title, the show needed to find its crew. As always, the most integral role is that of the captain. In this case, they created Captain Jonathan Archer (Scott Bakula), a man in his mid-forties; as the script for "Broken Bow" says, "unlike the captains in centuries to come, he exhibits a sense of wonder and excitement" over his new ship and the chance to explore the stars.

With the captain in place, the senior staff fills in down the line. Chief Engineer Commander Charlie "Trip" Tucker (Connor Trinneer), a Southerner who "enjoys using his 'country' persona to disarm people." Tactical Officer Lieutenant Malcolm Reed (Dominic Keating), a "buttoned-up Englishman" with a flair for weaponry. Helmsman Ensign Travis Mayweather (Anthony Montgomery), an African-American "space-boomer" who grew up on a cargo vessel. And Com Officer Ensign Hoshi Sato (Linda Park), an exolinguist described as "a spirited young Japanese woman" with a fear of space travel.

Though the crew complement is set at around eighty humans, the pre-Federation ship does have characters from alien races thrown into the mix, as is the custom for all *Star Trek* series. T'Pol (Jolene Blalock), a "severe yet sensual" Vulcan observer, accompanies the crew on their first mission and later joins on as science officer. And Dr. Phlox (John Billingsly), an "exotic-looking alien with a benevolent smile," just happens to be the most convenient doctor around when Archer is charged with the task of preparing his crew for departure in three days.

As the audience realized long ago, *Star Trek*, though set in a science-fiction universe, is first and foremost a show about characters. These seven characters will now be added to the *Star Trek* family, and the producers can begin to craft their adventures.

"It's always an ensemble on these shows," Braga explains. "But we're not going to concern ourselves, necessarily, with divvying up episodes between characters. The star of this show is the captain and he really will drive the stories, but everyone will be involved. Trip is a major character, and T'Pol is certainly a major character. And the others—it's hard to predict. For instance, the first episode after the pilot, to our surprise, is a big Hoshi episode. It just so happens that that's the show we came up with.

"You can't always predict how it's going to develop over the course of the season. You're also not sure which characters are going to pop out. For instance, I think now we're finding, at least early on, that Trip is really a character that's popping out and with whom we're really having a lot of fun. But, by the end of the season, we could discover that Reed is really jumping off the page. It's hard to say."

Typically, the role of the captain has been the most difficult to fill. The right blend of leadership and compassion are essential if the audience is to connect with the person in the big chair. In this case, according to Berman, the choice was easy from the start. Though the actors cast to play the previous captains of the *Star Trek* series did have followings before being asked on board, Scott Bakula is the most widely known actor to be hired to helm a *Star Trek* series.

Rick Berman explains the benefits of having Bakula sign on. "As a recognized actor he brings a little validity to the show. It doesn't hurt to have someone who is recognizable. I've yet to find people who don't find Scott tremendously talented and likable. When his name was brought up to us by the studio, we jumped for it. We were looking for a little Han Solo quality. We were looking for a little boyishness. We were looking for somebody who had a sense of excitement and awe and was his own man, someone who was young and fit, someone who embodied those heroic qualities that haven't really existed since Captain Kirk. We had a meeting with Scott and just sort of fell in love with him. I cannot think of a single soul I would rather have playing that role."

Once the producers gauged Bakula's interest, casting the rest of the crew became the task at hand. As with any new series, some of the job proved difficult, while some of it was surprisingly easy. "Interestingly, Dominic was someone who read for a role on an episodic show a year before," Berman says. "And I was so impressed with him that—even though it was a year away—I didn't hire him because I thought he'd be great to save for this show. Also, ironically, he was the first actor who came in on the first day of casting."

"The other characters took some time," Braga adds. "But we eventually found the right people. The hardest role to cast was T'Pol. Anytime you're trying to cast a complex character who's an intelligent, mysterious, complicated alien and also who happens to be a *babe*, it is not an easy task.

The last time we really had to do this was with Seven of Nine, and it took a lot of time. So the last role we cast was T'Pol. It took a lot of searching to find that actress who was at once striking and yet had an intelligence about her, who also is a good actress. It is a hard combo, for whatever reason."

Though the search may have been difficult at times, Berman is sure that they have found the perfect crew for *Enterprise*. "I cannot go on more about this cast," he says. "They are extraordinary. I've never been as pleased with putting together a cast of characters as I have with them. Now that we have shot the two-hour pilot and the first episode and are halfway through the second episode, I'm seeing it in every sense."

And as filming progresses through the first season, Berman is excited to see how things develop. "We spent a year and a half creating these characters," he continues. "Then you hire actors to play them. And then, together, these characters are brought to life with both the writing on one side and the actors doing what they do on the other. The characters always—as one season leads to the next—become richer and richer, because there's more and more backstory to them and the actors begin to feel comfortable and they bring unique things to the characters that we as writers and producers would never dream of that are unique to those specific actors."

With the universe and cast firmly in place, the

next detail was to lay out the basic themes for the storytelling. Braga notes that, while the series is deeply entrenched in the excitement of exploration, it will still have its roots closer to home. "We are going to do stories that have ramifications back on Earth," he says. "This is the first ship going out there and they represent humanity. So there are going to be more references to Earth. We are going to deal with certain situations that are closer to Earth and have ramifications closer to home.

"In terms of actually flying the ship back to Earth, that remains to be seen. We haven't decided. I will say that it will not be a frequent thing we'll do, simply because when you're traveling at warp five you get pretty far from Earth pretty fast. To turn all the way around, you're going to have to have a damn good reason. A lot of the pilot takes place on Earth and it's really a fun place to be, strangely enough, because it's kind of a fresh setting for us."

Although the concept for the show took a step back in time, the producers decided to include a bit of a futuristic element as well, adding a shadowed man out of temporal sync with the twenty-second century and a faction of an alien race, known as the Suliban, involved in some mysterious war. Their activities form an intentionally unresolved plotline in the series pilot—part of a story arc the producers hope will continue throughout the life of the series.

"Certain elements came out of discussions that we had with the studio," Berman explains. "We were very impressed with the idea of creating what I like to call a temporal cold war. There are some people from the distant future—maybe as far as the thirtieth century—who have developed time travel. For reasons that we do not understand, there are some people back in the twenty-second century who are doing the bidding of the people from the future.

"Our new breed of bad guys, the Suliban, we learn from the pilot, have been given a great degree of information regarding genetic engineering in exchange for doing the bidding. Why have they come back to the twenty-second century? What is their purpose? Is there one faction from the future? Are there many? We don't know and, in an *X-Files* kind of way, we may not know for years.

"We thought it would be fun," Braga adds, "since this show is a prequel, if we just made it a little bit of a sequel, too. So you have the temporal cold war going on, where factions in the distant future are waging secret battles on various fronts and in various centuries. And the twenty-second century is one of these fronts. We thought it would be interesting to slowly play out a mystery regarding all of this that somehow involves Archer. We're going to be doing that, hopefully, over the course of many, many episodes, possibly seasons. We haven't figured it all out ourselves yet, but we thought that would be a cool idea to layer in."

As for the mysterious man pulling the strings? The script only describes him as "a humanoid figure . . . of indeterminate age." Braga himself is just as cryptic when asked about the man behind the war. "We have several possibilities," he admits. "But we have not settled on any of them and we may come up with yet another one. I think we're going to see how it plays out. . . . We have some ideas, but honestly we don't know for sure. We'll find out along with Archer."

# Design

*"THIS NEW SHOW CANNOT BE JUST ANOTHER* STAR TREK *series. That's really item number one. It will be a ship show, but with an entirely new, entirely different* Enterprise—*one which is both retro and cool at the same time, gritty and utilitarian with space-efficient interior and hands-on equipment. A ship which shows the audience a lot more nuts and bolts than other* Star Trek *series while still having an incredibly futuristic look. In a subtle, very recognizable way, the ship must foreshadow the design of* Enterprises *to come.*

*"Chronologically, the drama takes place one hundred years beyond* First Contact *and one hundred years before Captain Kirk. Warring factions on Earth have made peace, Starfleet exists, and hundreds of spacecraft of various design*

*have been in use for some time, exploring nearby planets.*

*"This* Enterprise *is the first spaceship to be filled with the best, to date, Cochrane warp drive—an engine capable of speeds up to warp five. It's a ship with the power to go faster and farther into space than any previous ship and to be able to explore planets far outside our solar system."*

With those marching orders from Rick Berman, Production Designer Herman Zimmerman began work on what was to become the fifth *Star Trek* series, *Enterprise*—and, more specifically, the *S.S. Enterprise* NX-01. Zimmerman, who served as production designer for two of the *Star Trek* television incarnations—*Star Trek: The Next Generation*, and *Star Trek: Deep Space Nine*—as well as for the more recent films, was excited to have a chance to take a fresh look at the franchise.

"In designing something," Zimmerman says, "you need to have someplace to hang your hat, some philosophy to go on. The first thing that I have to do is, certainly, read the script and be cognizant of the demands of that series on scenes and characters. But also to look further down the line without any actual concrete information as to what might be necessary to flesh out more of the ship than what we're going to see in the first two hours. That's part of the consideration when I start thinking about it."

The production design team must anticipate

how each room may be used by this new crew in this new time period. Although, chronologically, this may be the first time a Starfleet crew has manned such a ship, Zimmerman explains, "In the case of *Star Trek*, it's a special kind of vehicle—no pun intended—for storytelling because it has such a rich history."

With his script as a blueprint, Zimmerman began his research. "I do a lot of looking at other science-fiction films," he admits. "While also looking at, particularly in this case, what's current at NASA. What's on the drawing boards for new space shuttles and, again in this case, what's happening in the U.S. military—particularly the Navy, because, as you know, *Star Trek* originated from Roddenberry's interest in the C. S. Forester series of *Horatio Hornblower* novels. The new series has similar models for defining the characters in relationship to each other. That's kind of a *Star Trek* given by this time."

With the series taking place only 150 years from today, Zimmerman made the most logical possible extrapolations of the directions in which he believed the technology will evolve. Then he was able to bridge the gap between spacecraft in current reality and the previously developed *Star Trek* starships of the future. Because, as Zimmerman himself says, "One of our main concerns . . . is to remain true to our position, historically, in the *Star Trek* family."

Paul Ruditis

## EXT. SPACE—*ENTERPRISE*

Our first full view of the majestic ship as it clears the dock and moves into open space. More rocketship than starship, *Enterprise* is lean and masculine—yet its deflector dish and twin warp nacelles suggest the shape of Starfleet vessels to come.

With those lines, the *Enterprise* makes its first full appearance in the script for "Broken Bow." The words on the page, however, fail to convey the full dramatic impact of the ship on the screen. Likewise, they fail to reflect the amount of work it takes to get from the drawing board to the reality. "The design was originally a different concept entirely than the one with which we ended up," Zimmerman admits. "Which is often the case. You sometimes spend days, weeks, or whatever period of time it takes before the reality sets in, thinking about what you think is the right design for the exterior of the ship, and then someday somebody along the line says, 'Well, that doesn't look very good.' Or in this case, 'Gee, it looks like the old *Enterprise*.' And you realize that you have to go in a totally different direction."

Braga expands on the idea behind the original concept. "I had just gotten back from the LA car show, and I had seen the new 2002 Thunderbird. What I really liked about it was that it was the classic Thunderbird design, but modernized. So it was kind of the best of both worlds. It was at once tantalizingly modern and yet very, very familiar at the same time. So we discussed it and we thought, Well, let's take Kirk's ship, the original *Enterprise*, and let's soup it up and make it more futuristic and bring it into the twenty-first century. And we worked on that for a while, but it ultimately looked just too much like the other ships. It was too familiar. It wasn't new enough. So we ended up completely abandoning that approach and starting from scratch."

"In this case," Zimmerman adds, "we had about a month of sketches and computer-generated images roughly showing shapes of different ships that eventually evolved into a ship that was really cool, but it looked very much like the classic *Star Trek Enterprise*. Now, that was a really cool ship and the series would have been well served by it. But, I don't think it represented what Rick and Brannon see as the vision of this new *Enterprise*. So we went to work again."

Though the producers wanted the look to be different, they did not want it to be so dramatically different that it seemed out of place. This was still to be a *Star Trek* series, which naturally required a *Star Trek* vessel. Zimmerman describes the path that led them to the new design: "We found a ship that was in our archives—a minor vessel that had been used in a battle in one of the features that had been created by ILM. We did not use that ship, but we took ideas from it and from those ideas eventually—and this process took about four months, all week and weekend CGI work by a very talented Lightwave artist, Doug Drexler—we finally came up with a shape that everybody loves. I trust the fans will love it as well as the producers and the cast do."

"We ended up with a design that is definitely a *Star Trek* vessel in that it has a saucer section and warp nacelles, but it doesn't have an engineering section at the bottom," Braga explains. "It's more shiny and chromelike on its exterior—more metallic and less kind of a flat gray. . . . It's a little bit more like a cross between a stealth plane, a nuclear sub, and a Starfleet vessel."

With the design in hand, the next step in the ship's evolution was to determine the physical aspects of the ship for filming. "The ship as seen on the screen will probably be entirely CGI," Zimmerman says. "There will be models made, but they won't be the principal photography models. We have found, since 1987, that the state of the art has changed dramatically. One of the things that model photography does is give you a very realistic bounce of light. One of the drawbacks of model photography is that you have to build a model for everything. If you have to articulate a torpedo launch mechanism on the exterior of the ship, you have to build it. You have to make it work. And you have to do it in a scale that can be photographed. . . . With the computer-generated images you can be infinitely more flexible. Everything takes time, but once it's built you can look at it in twelve different ways and they'll all be perfect. They'll all be correctly lit. The moves will all be correct for timing and correct for size and shape. All of that is very useful when you're doing a new one-hour episode every seven days—which is what an hour TV show schedule ends up being. So the CGI modeling has come, since 1987, to a state of the art that is not only as good as but better than model photography."

## INT. *ENTERPRISE*—BRIDGE

Far more basic than future starships, this command center lacks the "airport terminal" feel of *Enterprises* A through E. A central captain's chair is surrounded by various stations, the floors and walls are mostly steel, with source light coming from myriad glowing panels. No carpets on the floors, no wood paneling on the walls, high-tech gauges, dials.

Zimmerman recalls his basic direction for the most familiar interior set of all Starfleet vessels. "Rick and Brannon particularly liked two pieces of equipment from the classic *Star Trek* series bridge: Spock's viewer and Uhura's communications earpiece. They thought some earlier versions of these objects might be found to be useful. Well, we did indeed do that, but we did not go so far as to use Uhura's earpiece. It was proven to be an unnecessary device. We did, however, use a modernized, but retro, version of Spock's viewer, and I think the fans will both identify with it and enjoy the connection."

"As far as the interior goes," Berman adds, "we visited a submarine and got the idea of what confined space was like. We tried to make it a little bit more confined but at the same time a hospitable place that the audience would want to come visit every week."

The rest of the set grew out of that directive. Deeper and slimmer than the familiar bridges of *Star Treks* past, the design appears more functional than comfortable, but still warm and inviting. Though the ever-present captain's chair may be the cozy refurbished seat from a Porsche, most of the surrounding chairs are metal mesh and, as Hoshi notes during a particularly rough patch of turbulence, they do not have seat belts to keep the crew strapped in. There are, however, strong metal guardrails encircling the bridge, similar to the one seen in The Original Series, for the crew to clutch on to as they are tossed about.

"It's more hands-on for the crew," Zimmerman says. "There are knobs and buttons and switches and levers and things that actually move and do something. In previous series, since the original—because the original did have buttons to push—we put things behind black plastic. We're now in possession of all LCD screens and plasma screens, which are out. We see the frames. There's very little that's built in that's not accessible."

A new addition to the bridge is the set that, in previous series, has proven to be one of the largest challenges to the various *Star Trek* directors. Formerly known as the briefing room, the *Enterprise*'s situation room is set off in an alcove behind the captain's chair but still very much a part of the set. In the past, directors have noted the difficulty in creating interesting scenes within a room that is little more than a large table surrounded by chairs. This new design for the situation room places it in the action rather than away from it and opens up the staging possibilities. Though the space is tight, the room does have removable walls to allow for cameras and lighting, as do all the standing sets.

Another feature in all the sets is the addition of what the production crew refers to as "busy boxes," which Zimmerman describes as "things that can be opened up and worked on during an emergency or even during the routine of getting the ship ready for leaving Spacedock. Leaving so much more for the actors to do."

One familiar set for *Enterprise* is the transporter room. However, the transporters of this earlier time have a bit of a twist. "This transporter is not really recommended for biological organisms," Zimmerman explains. "It's basically a cargo transporter. So while we are occasionally forced to use the transporter for a live specimen, it's not recommended. Mostly we use the shuttles to leave the ship."

This design, too, mixes a little of the familiar with the new. Zimmerman explains, "Again, it's an homage to the Original Series transporter and it's a precursor of all the transporters you've seen since. It's got a single pad, but it does have ribs around it that have the same structural pattern that were on the ribs of the transporter on The Original Series. That was one of the things we did as a nod to Matt Jefferies' designs."

## INT. *ENTERPRISE*—MAIN ENGINEERING

Unlike the spacious, brightly lit engine rooms of future starships, this is more like the cramped, redlit nerve center of a nuclear submarine . . .

A more dramatic change in the design of the interior can be found in the heart of the ship, engineering. Zimmerman's directive for the room was that it be a busy place with lots of moving parts. The concept behind the design is that the room is heat-generating and pulsing. The area is more cramped and the core itself is horizontal, rather than vertical, as were warp cores past.

Zimmerman goes on, "We talked of a honeycomb design with multiple push and pull rods, accessible through openable doors. Machine walls cover the bulk of the engine. In other words, you're not going to see a big roiling mass of energy, you're going to see the result of that through small windows. You're going to see a very powerful engine that looks like a very powerful engine." And the audience will also see the process by which the energy is distributed, through tubes leading out of the core directly to the warp nacelles.

In short, the design for the engine reflects a more simple time. As Zimmerman explains, "It doesn't look like you can't understand it or that it wouldn't break down if all the components weren't working perfectly. So, it's a more realistic propulsion system than the fantastic propulsion system."

Other sets include the armory, loaded with missiles instead of the futuristic photon torpedoes, and the sickbay, which also has a new look.

"I think my favorite set is sickbay," Braga admits. "Obviously the bridge is very cool, but sickbay, to me, really captures a nice flavor of *Enterprise* because it's so different. It looks so believable. It's kind of white, gleaming, with lots of chrome, and it kind of looks like a real hospital, a real futuristic hospital. I think people will be surprised at the departure we've taken there. But it's well worth it."

Knowing the look of the main vehicle, the production team could then move on to its shuttlecraft. The *Enterprise* shuttles will play a more integral role in this series than in series past, because transporter technology is so new. As Zimmerman previously noted, the *Enterprise* transporter platform is technically *approved* for biotransport, but shuttlecraft are still the preferred method of getting the crew from one place to another.

"The shuttle design is almost a direct steal from the shuttles that are being built right now," Zimmerman admits. "The X-33 [Reusable Launch Vehicle] is probably the closest model to the actual shuttlecraft that we are using on *Enterprise*. We feel that reentry vehicles, right now, are as close to state-of-the-art as they're going to be in the next hundred years, mainly because we lack the propulsion system that *Star Trek* has so blithely invented without explaining quite how we acquired all that power. Also, I think that will be a delight to the science-oriented viewer, because it's familiar."

The conflicts of designing a series being filmed over thirty years after The Original Series yet taking place almost one hundred years previous to its setting presented a number of problems in the course of the design. At some point in the planning for each set, prop, costume, and even makeup application, a decision needed to be made on where to bridge the gap—whether to make extrapolations based on current technology or on the vision of the future circa 1967. In the end, a combination of periods was achieved, with the emphasis being on a future based on the technology of today.

The most difficult challenge for maintaining design continuity was the props, since some concessions needed to be made along the lines of the more portable equipment. Considering how far technology has come in the last decade alone, what may have appeared futuristic in the sixties does not hold up to today's technological advancements. According to Berman, the decision on how true to remain to the original needed to be made on a case-by-case basis; as an example, he points out that the computer on his desk is less bulky than the one that sat on Captain Janeway's desk on *Voyager*.

One of the most recognized props from The Original Series was the communicator. The wireless handheld device, so ahead of its time for the original audience of Kirk and Spock, is old hat for today's audience, many of whom have similar devices in their homes, cars, and jacket pockets. Again, Zimmerman was required to bridge the gap between the technology of yesterday's future with today's. "They're quite along the lines of the communicators that we saw in the classic series and the early movies, but, because they are being designed now, they are much cooler and much more interesting pieces of equipment. Their function is pretty much the same. We're not doing badges—we're doing flip-open communicators, tricorders, and other diagnostic equipment that is small. It is microminiaturized, but it is not vastly different in its design from the great things that are being done now."

This quickly became the defining element for all props, Zimmerman admits. "The truth is our props are more capable but less slim and compact than what you can buy today. That's part of the dramatic necessity, so the actor has something that the audience recognizes instantly and that works. Having said that, they are really interesting props and they will make interesting devices for the telling of a story."

And it is those stories that the designs will best serve. "There's a lot of wonder and awe and sense of the first time in all of the concepts for the stories," Zimmerman explains. "This is no 'Ho hum, we're out in space again, we know how to do this. Just sit back and watch us.' It's like we're discovering it for the first time and it's really very exciting. It's reinventing the franchise in many, many ways."

And the designer is just as excited about this

new opportunity. "Personally, it's a kick in the right place to get an opportunity to reinvent a *Star Trek* venue like this, because one gets set in one's ways always doing it the same," he continues. "This is so fresh, such a new approach, such an opportunity to go back to the roots of something that you've already done and say, 'Well, how was it that it came to this point? How would it look if it was two hundred or three hundred years before but still in our future and maintained the continuity that eventually leads into Captain Picard and the *Enterprise-E?*' Well, that's a fun job. Why wouldn't you like that?"

Costume designer Robert Blackman started working on *Star Trek* in the third season of *The Next Generation*, and was asked back for the latest installment, ready for his own challenge of reinventing the franchise. To do so, he looked at the series as a whole, focusing first on the evolution of the Starfleet uniform.

"We talked about the *Star Trek* timeline and where [the series] fit," says Blackman. "We've got original *Star Trek*, we've got the movies, we've got *The Next Generation*, *DS9*, and *Voyager*. They all travel in a linear direction. We know where we started, originally, with classic *Star Trek*, and we know where we ended, at this point, which is *DS9*. Where those changes for the garments happened were pretty clear. It was then taking that knowledge of how it progressed and working backward."

The first question naturally became just how far to back up. Blackman's challenge was to determine where the uniform design would have been one hundred years before The Original Series. To do this he chose an approach quite like Zimmerman's approach to the designs for sets and props. Blackman looked to current apparel as his basis for extrapolating a look for the future. "What I chose to do was to back up to now and to do a lot of investigation on, essentially, supersonic jet pilot testing suits, NASA suits, that sort of look, and then play around with those and kind of move forward on them."

Blackman likens his work to the evolution of clothing in general. "It's sort of like the tie, which has been around for a hundred and thirty years and I don't think that people are going to necessarily be tie-less in the next hundred and thirty years. There are aspects that are very familiar to us today that are recognizable aspects. I keep pressing those to really land it closer. We're all well versed in what we imagine life in the universe will be in four or five hundred years, but what it's going to be in a hundred years is another thing. So, my gut response to that is to tie it more to now than to then."

In the case of *Star Trek*, the Starfleet uniforms have become integral to the look of the series.

Blackman explains that the new look is a radical departure from the past. "All of the Starfleet stuff is natural fibers. For the first time ever, there are zippers and pockets. We've never had them. From The Original Series on, they were eliminated. Pockets, because the idea was there was no currency. There was nothing. You didn't need house keys. It was all done electronically. No zippers or buttons because the clothes were imagined to be put on in some sort of way, by forcefield, or whatever the hell you wanted it to be." In fact, the uniforms have taken on a more casual look beyond the addition of pockets and zippers with accessories of utility caps and away jackets.

"They wear black mock turtlenecks underneath," Blackman continues. "The uniforms are a darkish blue, brushed twill that is stonewashed. So they look a little bit worn. There is a whole kind of casualness to it. They're wrinkly. They're just something that is not as formalized as we have done previously. They still are sort of formfit and sleek in the body. All of our people look heroic in them, which is always the goal. So there's always those kinds of things that remain constant."

Among the familiar, however, is the designation of department insignias. "One of the things that we're resonating from the future are the color bars," Blackman adds. "The colors are the same, but they had switched after original *Star Trek* to the movies and then from the movies to *The Next Generation*." For this new series, Blackman reverted to the original. "What command was, and what security was, and what science was made a change that we have honored. Command positions are gold now, not red. Science is still blue. Security and engineering are red." Then he changed the design, making it an accent to the uniform instead of the focal point. In this case, the insignia is simply a thin stripe that goes around the yoke of the uniform.

Environment is also a consideration for the costumes on the series. Since the characters spend most of their time on the ship, the uniforms must contrast with those sets to some degree. While the overall design is an important consideration, Blackman does not allow it to entirely determine his concepts. "I look to see what the designs are, but the colors of the set don't really influence me in this particular world," he explains. "My notion is that if you have that much activity in the background then you need to make the thing in the foreground, which is usually the actor, as simple as possible. Hence, these sort of blue matte fabric uniforms. Yeah, they've got zippers and so on and so forth, but that does all blend eventually and you're really just looking at the surface. There are a couple of scenes I saw being shot where they're standing in front of a lot of moving graphics and you never lose them.

You're never distracted by the graphics. The graphics are brilliant, but they don't talk."

Though the *Enterprise* is an Earth ship with a crew made up almost entirely of humans, two alien characters have been added to the mix in the form of T'Pol, of Vulcan, and Dr. Phlox, of an alien race new to *Star Trek*. These characters represented two distinctly different challenges for Blackman. In T'Pol he has a character of a race the audience is quite familiar with. The task in this case was to maintain the familiar while reinventing the look more for today's audience.

Blackman describes his approach to this new character: "Some of it is about broad-based marketing and other parts of it are about getting a character going. That uniform has a sort of form fit. It's a very beautiful woman. But it has certain things that, over the years, I have distilled out of the original Vulcans. When I say the original Vulcans, I'm talking the return of Spock—the movies' version rather than anything that happened in The Original Series. Those things are very much based on a kind of Chinese silhouette. They were very metallic and very brocadey and flat at the same time. . . . Over the years, I developed a kind of eye that gave you an echo of that. It's a serpentine thing that starts slightly extended from the shoulder point and then curves in and back out so you get the notion that you're creating a very wide shoulder as some of those mandarin clothes do, but without actually doing it. So, that is the basis to her.

"The Vulcan civilization is also X amount of years earlier. She's definitely in earth tones. It's kind of a gray/brown, very sort of striated piece of fabric. The Vulcans tend to be more coolish in color. I've chosen not to do that. I've chosen to warm her up. She plays against it. She's very Vulcan in the script and she's very Vulcan—and will be, I think—throughout. There's a hint of Vulcan in the design and it's got to be a uniform. We've never seen the Vulcans in uniform before. So I just went with this other look."

On the other hand, there is Dr. Phlox, a character from a distinctly new race of what the script refers to only as "an exotic alien species." As there was no *Star Trek* history to look to for his specific character, Blackman started with a basis in familiar Earth design and evolved from there. He describes the look as similar to shirts of East Indian design that tend to be longer and hang down over the pants. Blackman goes on, "I've taken that design—using that as a kind of gentle shape—to pull him away from the rest of the people. These sort of shirt/smock things. And then just added a few odd details to them so that they are very alien to all of the Starfleet stuff that you see, but they're not so alien that you don't forget about it soon, and he just becomes a guy with a really benevolent face."

Another aspect of the design for the series is the more casual tone of an earlier time in Starfleet. To set this tone, Berman has said, the audience will see the crew out of uniform from time to time. Where the concept of the uniform is important, however, Blackman admits that it is the civilian clothes that can prove the larger challenge. "In any of the timeframes, those have always been the more difficult clothing to do. It's just hard to figure out what it is. You get to a uniform or something that is really extreme, then it's easy. You can just make it really extreme. I always sort of hark back to *The Fifth Element*. You look at that and you go, Okay, there are backless T-shirts with straps across them. But we can't go that far. It's not our world. So you'll see Captain Archer in the first two episodes in essentially T-shirts and jean-cut pants with odd shoes. It is a gentle nod to the future with a fairly strong stance in the present."

Also making an appearance in the pilot episode is one of the favorite *Star Trek* races, the Klingons. And with the new setting, an earlier version of this race needed to be defined as well. Of course, makeup applications have come a long way since the sixties. These Klingons will appear more as they do in the later versions of *Star Trek*—a look that had its inception in the film *Star Trek: The Motion Picture* and grew into the Klingons of modern *Star Trek*. Though the appearance may be modern, however, the concept of the race will be entirely fresh.

"The Klingons are to a degree 'proto-Klingons,'" Braga explains. "They're Klingons that come long before the Klingons of Picard's time. Therefore they can be gnarlier, nastier, more warlike Klingons than ever. They'll eat the hearts of their victims and sharpen their teeth and so forth."

This description led Blackman to a very specific look. "It's very rough furs and leathers and chain-maily," he explains. "They still have the kind of boots that we're used to, though nothing is black and gray anymore. It's all kind of earth tone. They're pretty dirty. They look pretty ratty, really. But that was the deal, so it's more primitive than we have seen before."

Another key element to the show will be the ongoing temporal cold war. The foot soldiers of that war in the twenty-second century are the new race of *Star Trek* aliens known as the Suliban. "There are two different groups in the same time period," Blackman explains. "Kind of the good Suliban and the bad Suliban. The bad ones are like chameleons. They are genetically mimetic. They can mimic or become anything they need to. It is not the same as a shapeshifter. Their skin will turn into whatever it needs to turn into. Consequently the bad ones have developed that technique to the point where they can manufacture it. So they have manufactured this as part of their clothing and are then able to change themselves, physically, and their clothing, physically. The good ones haven't done that, or if they have that capability, they don't use it. So they appear in things that are definitely futuristic, but don't relate to their skin."

With these aliens, Blackman worked closely with makeup designer Michael Westmore, as much of the look of the aliens is mirrored in their clothing. "The characters have a very specific, kind of peculiar, skin, which we were able to copy in a pretty good way," Blackman explains. "It's a different color, but when you see them, the skin texture and the texture of the clothing are very reminiscent of one another. They are pretty much very simple jumpsuits with built-in feet. They're just colored this amazing color and they're very slight of stature."

Blackman looks forward to the challenges of the new series, especially because they are *new*. "I think it would have been more daunting and more difficult if the spin that I had to do was to take what I had done over twelve years and split that hair one more time," he explains. "That would have been a really difficult thing. The difficulty here was not really coming up with the ultimate look—the appearance of the uniform—it was the process of evolving that. It required quite a few completely rendered prototypes to get us to say, 'No, no, we don't want it to be a weird synthetic fabric. No, we want it to have a more now, today, this moment, look.' So that was the process that was hard. And that's the process that's hard every day as regards this series right now. We don't have much of a frame of reference for it. So, we're continually reinventing that or inventing that. That becomes the difficulty. But the difficulties kind of get your head in the right place to be able to do it."

**Look for STAR TREK fiction from Pocket Books**

**Star Trek®**

**Star Trek: Voyager®**

## Star Trek®: Gateways

#1 • *One Small Step* • Susan Wright
#2 • *Chainmail* • Diane Carey
#3 • *Doors Into Chaos* • Robert Greenberger
#4 • *Demons of Air and Darkness* • Keith R.A. DeCandido
#5 • *No Man's Land* • Christie Golden
#6 • *Cold Wars* • Peter David
#7 • *What Lay Beyond* • various
*Epilogue: Here There Be Monsters* • Keith R.A. DeCandido

## Star Trek®: The Badlands

#1 • Susan Wright
#2 • Susan Wright

## Star Trek®: Dark Passions

#1 • Susan Wright
#2 • Susan Wright

## Star Trek®: The Brave and the Bold

#1 • Keith R.A. DeCandido
#2 • Keith R.A. DeCandido

## Star Trek® Omnibus Editions

*Invasion! Omnibus* • various
*Day of Honor Omnibus* • various
*The Captain's Table Omnibus* • various
*Star Trek: Odyssey* • William Shatner with Judith and Garfield Reeves-Stevens
*Millennium Omnibus* • Judith and Garfield Reeves-Stevens
*Starfleet: Year One* • Michael Jan Friedman

## Other Star Trek® Fiction

*Legends of the Ferengi* • Ira Steven Behr & Robert Hewitt Wolfe
*Strange New Worlds*, vol. I, II, III, IV, and V • Dean Wesley Smith, ed.
*Adventures in Time and Space* • Mary P. Taylor, ed.
*Captain Proton: Defender of the Earth* • D.W. "Prof" Smith
*New Worlds, New Civilizations* • Michael Jan Friedman
*The Lives of Dax* • Marco Palmieri, ed.
*The Klingon Hamlet* • Wil'yam Shex'pir
*Enterprise Logs* • Carol Greenburg, ed.
*Amazing Stories* • various